FORGET ME NOT

**Center Point
Large Print**

**This Large Print Book carries the
Seal of Approval of N.A.V.H.**

CROSSROADS CRISIS CENTER
BOOK ONE

FORGET ME NOT

VICKI HINZE

CENTER POINT PUBLISHING
THORNDIKE, MAINE

This Center Point Large Print edition is published in
the year 2010 by arrangement with Multnomah Books,
an imprint of The Crown Publishing Group,
a division of Random House, Inc.

The characters and events in this book are fictional, and any
resemblance to actual persons or events is coincidental.

The text of this Large Print edition is unabridged.
In other aspects, this book may vary
from the original edition.
Printed in the United States of America
on permanent paper.
Set in 16-point Times New Roman type.

ISBN: 978-1-60285-723-0

Library of Congress Cataloging-in-Publication Data

Hinze, Vicki.
  Forget me not / Vicki Hinze.
      p. cm.
  ISBN 978-1-60285-723-0 (library binding : alk. paper)
  1. Large type books. I. Title.
  PS3558.I574F67 2010b
  813'.54--dc22
  2009047729

To Kathy Carmichael.
A good friend is a treasure.
Thank you for being a good friend, Kathy.
With blessings and love,
Vicki

Acknowledgments

As always, there are many to thank for taking a work from concept to novel, and only me to blame for flaws or faults found with it. I am particularly grateful for the contributions of:

Kathy Carmichael and Debra Webb, for sharing their experiences and expertise.

James Rollins and Allison Brennan, for their steadfast support in my International Thriller Writers board duties during deadline mania.

Sandie Scarpa, my most magnificent assistant and research whiz, who, among other things, prepares the Readers Guides. I don't pause often enough to express my gratitude, but I do always feel it.

Julee Schwarzburg, who approached, encouraged, and devoted herself above and beyond the call to help me in all ways by asking the right questions at the right times about the right things. Your analytical vision is awesome.

Steve Laube, whose skills and foresight are admirable and appreciated.

The team at WaterBrook Multnomah, who made this adventure a fabulous experience.

My family. Lloyd, Kristen and Brian, Ray and Erin, and all my grands: Thank you for knowing my every flaw and loving me anyway.

To all of you: I am humbled by your generosity and so blessed to have you in my life.

Come unto me, all ye that labour and are heavy laden, and I will give you rest.
MATTHEW 11:28 (KJV)

Prologue

You know what I want."

Hearing him behind her, she jerked and dropped her paintbrush. It slid across the canvas, streaking the emerald gulf water with a bold, jagged slash of white.

"Gregory," she said, her voice half croak, half whisper, her eyes seeing far beyond the easel and canvas in front of her.

She had made this confrontation inevitable, but she hoped to finish one last painting before—

"Well? Are you going to give it to me?"

Shaking, she turned. He stood closer than she expected, towering above her and blocking both studio doors. The one to the deck overlooking the gulf was closer, but with his stride and reach—she didn't stand a chance.

Inevitable.

Putting down her palette, she squared her shoulders and stiffened, unable to see past the bloodlust in his eyes. Would her response push him over the edge?

Regardless, she had only one choice. Her mouth as dry as the sand between her and the surf, she hiked her chin and looked him right in the eye. "No."

"Reconsider—and think carefully." His hands curled into fists at his sides, his face darkened to red, and the blood vessels in his thick neck protruded. "Is that your final answer?"

How could anyone that angry sound that controlled? She darted her gaze from door to door, still seeking a way out. But there wasn't one. No one would interrupt, would hear her scream. There would be no escape.

She glanced to a painting of a young girl hanging on the wall. What more could she have done? The man was rich, powerful, and more manipulative than anyone she'd ever known. She had gone all the way to the mayor looking for help. Well, to his wife, Darla, but even she had to admit how outrageous her claims had sounded. Gregory Chessman *did* seem incapable of anything that wasn't wonderful.

Yet she knew better. She studied the painting, the innocence and promise in that beloved face. If he found her—and sooner or later, he would—then she, too, would die. That left but one option. One. And who knew if it would work?

"I know the truth about you." She injected her tone with confidence and a warning of her own. "If anything happens to me, others will know it too."

"You tried that and failed." He grunted. "You're a crazy woman. No one believes a crazy woman, not even an airhead." He followed her gaze to the painting.

Something inside him snapped. His face contorted and he closed the gap between them in a flash, clamping his fingers around her throat. Fury pounded off him in waves, rivaling the six-foot surf. With a throaty growl, he jerked, lifting her off the ground.

She fought hard, kicking and swinging her frail arms, trying to break his hold, but she couldn't make contact beyond his forearms.

Her vision blurred, her starved lungs burned, craving air. Her limbs turned leaden.

Then the brilliant light flooding the studio faded to black, and she knew no more.

Gregory watched the life leave her eyes, taking pleasure in the fact that his would be the last face she would see. How dare she refuse him? Threaten him? *The crazy fool.*

When the last spark of hope for revival passed and she hung limp and lifeless a foot off the floor, he dropped her.

Her body crumpled in a heap.

He didn't look down, just walked over her, knocked the aged painting off the wall, and then crushed it with the heel of his shoe. Three years, and the subject in it still taunted him. Still made him vulnerable to Alik Demyan. Gregory shuddered.

Now she would suffer for both, for trespassing on his peace.

The portrait lay tattered and torn, its brittle

frame cracked. He went at it again, and kept at it until the painting was utterly destroyed.

Though he despised dirtying his own hands, NINA would be pleased. No one had messed up this one . . .

1

Friday, October 9

It's a bad business decision."

Behind the wheel of the red Jaguar, she checked her rearview mirror, uneasy at being where she shouldn't be after dark. "Maybe"—she braked for a traffic light—"but it's a good heart decision."

The man on the phone grunted his true feelings; his words proved far more diplomatic. "I understand that position on some of your ventures, like your work building the children's center, but I don't understand it on this. We're talking about a run-down beach house three states away, with exorbitant taxes and insurance, that you never visit. Retaining it isn't logical."

Her aunt Beth had loved that run-down beach house, and they'd spent almost twenty wonderful summers together there. But maybe you had to grow up orphaned and denied the privilege of living with your last blood relative to understand the value of that.

"It's in hurricane country and eighty feet from the gulf," she told her financial advisor. "Of course the taxes and insurance premiums are outrageous."

Two blocks ahead, a jazz funeral ambled down St. Charles Avenue. Bluesy music floated on the night. Not wanting to intrude, she flicked her little finger, tapping on the blinker, then turned at the corner and headed out of the French Quarter.

Her uneasiness grew. There had been some police presence in the Quarter. Where she was headed, there wasn't apt to be any.

"That's why you should sell it." His sigh crackled static through the phone. "Look, it's a good offer. Market value plus twenty percent is rare."

She looked down the deserted street. A group of teenage boys were hanging out in front of a half-gutted building. Yet another remnant of Hurricane Katrina; the kids had no place safe to go. She hoped to soon change that. In this neighborhood, being on the street at night wasn't just unsafe, it was dangerous. "Now you're upset."

"I am not upset."

If his tone got any stiffer, it'd make the trek from Atlanta to New Orleans without benefit of the phone. He was definitely upset. "Good." She needed to get past this call and focus on returning to the hotel.

Trash littered the sidewalk and clumped in a pile

near a storm drain carved into the corner's concrete. Smelly garbage, rain-soaked and muddy from that afternoon's thunderstorm, assaulted her.

Finger to her nose, she looked from the grungy walk back to the street. "Why are these 'blind' buyers offering more than fair market value anyway?"

"You've refused their previous offers and they want the property."

"Yes, but why?" That just didn't make sense. "Dozens of homes are on the market. Why not buy one of those? Why Aunt Beth's place?"

"Who cares? Just take the money and run."

She didn't live her life that way. "See, that bothers me. When people hide who they are and push this hard, there's a reason." This property was in Seagrove Village. She couldn't afford to forget that or not to be suspicious.

"Their reason doesn't matter. This is the perfect time to unload it."

"I don't want to unload it." Without the beach house, she wouldn't have any personal family memories after age seven—a fact he well knew since he'd handled her estate from the time of her parents' passing. How could he not understand?

"If you're going to ignore my advice, then why pay me for it?"

She paid handsomely for it, but it was still a bargain. "You're a very good analyst, and I value your opinion, but I make my own decisions. Since

16

I'm accountable for them, that's as it should be." He should understand that; he'd taught it to her.

She pulled up beside a car parked near a stop sign. Sitting stopped on dangerous streets gave her the willies. She wasted no time scanning for oncoming traffic, and then drove on.

"Why are you so eager for me to sell?" Even before she'd reached legal age and he had gone from trustee and replacement guardian to financial advisor, he never pushed her this hard on anything.

"It's in your best interests."

"In your opinion, but not in mine."

"I know you make the final calls—and how you make them." He sighed deeper, heavier. "You've prayed about this and it doesn't feel right, so you're not doing it."

Well, at least he understood that much. "Yes, prayer is my bottom line." Saying the offer didn't feel right would do, but it was an understatement. Down to the marrow of her bones, she felt certain she was supposed to keep the beach house.

As certain as she was that she must never return to it.

God's reasons on both went far deeper than her own, and if and when He was ready to reveal them to her, she'd be eager to know them. Until then, she would act in trust. Follow His will.

"There is another reason you should consider and aren't."

"Oh?" His brittle tone had her stiffening. This wouldn't be good news.

"A man purporting to be an investigator showed up at your neighbor's house this afternoon looking for you."

No. Not again. Please, not again. Fear streaked through her chest, squeezed. No sound came out of her mouth, so she waited on tenterhooks for him to continue.

"You're going to have to run again. NINA's found you."

NINA? She had been running from men, not a woman. "Who is she?"

"Not who, but what. NINA is the name of the group looking for you."

The men were a group? They had been scary; this was terrifying. "What kind of group?"

"Nihilists in Anarchy."

She swallowed hard. "So the biological terrorist threat is still out there, and it's bigger than I thought." A group. An organized *group.* The taste in her mouth turned bitter. "I'd hoped if I disappeared . . ."

"It didn't help. These are not fly-by-night thugs. I wish they were. NINA is a multinational organization—far too substantial to let one woman interfere with their plans."

Her muscles went tight, knotted, and the urge to cry swelled inside her. She blinked fast, fighting it. "I have to disappear again."

"If you want to live, yes."

Her nightmares were starting all over again, and growing worse. "Are they connected? The beach house buyers and these people?"

"What interest would a major terrorist group have in a shack of a beach house?"

"That was my question to you," she reminded him.

"None known to the FBI. I contacted my friend there and made a few inquiries—citing a hypothetical situation again, of course."

"And his advice remained the same," she guessed. "That I should come in and get into Witness Protection."

"Actually, no. With this new development, he doubts he can protect you. His hypothetical advice is to get lost and stay lost somewhere far, far away."

"So he was already familiar with this NINA?"

"Oh yes," her advisor said. "They're on multiple international watch lists."

Boy, had she fallen into it. "I told you the men after me were bioterrorists." She'd overheard that much from that conversation that had kept her looking over her shoulder these past three years.

"Bioterrorism is but one of the threats NINA poses."

"There's more?" The news just kept getting better and better.

"Much more, I'm afraid. NINA embraces the

destruction of all political, social, and religious order. They reject morals and ethics as mere products of pressure. Life, to them, has no meaning. Good and evil are based on perspective, nebulous things. They even reject the significance of family."

Alien philosophies. Spooky ones. And wasn't that just great? Having a duo of cutthroats after her hadn't been bad enough. She had to run into an entire army of them. "Charming. How did you find out NINA was involved?"

He hesitated and then sighed. "It's safer that you don't know."

Not from the FBI apparently. Two trucks blew past her. One had a back end full of wooden crates that wobbled. She tapped the brakes to put more distance between them, not trusting the ropes securing them to hold.

"Did you tell your FBI friend that the men could be members?"

"Of course not. You'd be pulled in for questioning and be at even greater risk. NINA would know the moment you entered the building—even my friend couldn't deny it."

That was her take on the matter too, but it comforted her to know he had hypothetically discussed the situation with a professional, and he was in agreement. Clearly, he considered the men and the anonymous buyers two separate events—and they well might be. At this point, she had no way of knowing. "How did they find me?"

"No idea. You've avoided the press, public gatherings . . . Has the media caught wind of your reasons for being in New Orleans?"

"No." She'd had a close call with a reporter from the *Times-Picayune,* but no direct hits. She'd grown adept at avoiding television cameras and reporters long ago.

"No public records filed?"

"Only the beach house deed."

"That leads to me, not you, and it's in another state." He sighed. "I have no idea how they located your current home. But don't delay down there. They're one step away. Vanish."

In ordinary circumstances, it would be unfortunate to be skilled at vanishing, but in this case, her having a great deal of experience at it was a blessing. "I'll wrap up here in a few hours and then go."

"A few hours? That's risky."

"Yes, but necessary." If NINA knew she was here, they wouldn't have been at her home this afternoon talking to her neighbors. And since she didn't know her neighbors and they didn't know her, she should be safe for a few more hours. That would be long enough. The kids here needed the center. She couldn't raise their hopes and then dash them by leaving without doing anything.

"Invoke your power of attorney. I'll contact you again in six months—sooner, if I can—and when I do, I want to hear that this center is up and running."

"I'll take care of it," he said. "Our usual financial arrangement?"

Her life, the dire straits of the kids here, and the man was concerned about money? He had plenty and was still fixated on amassing more. "Our usual arrangement is fine."

"Very well. I'll decline the offer for the beach house," he said, caving on that issue. "And I'll pay the taxes and insurance."

"Tell the buyers we won't entertain future offers too." This was their third attempt in the three months since Aunt Beth passed away, and she did not need the fear of a fourth offer dangling like a dark cloud on the horizon.

Not knowing their motivations sparked worry. Every time these mysterious people made an offer, it triggered more, and she stayed knotted up like a pretzel for days. Now she discovered her pursuers, who might or might not be connected, had an entire organization behind them, and it was hunting her down. That made these anonymous buyers a lot less intimidating.

"I'll tell them. Though it's never wise to close the door on future opportunities."

"If I'm wrong, it won't be the first time or the last. I'll live with it."

"Very well." He clipped his tone. "I'll handle the matter first thing in the morning."

"On this NINA group," she said, determined to try one last time to learn more. "I know it's safer for me not to know how you found out about them, but have you placed yourself in jeopardy? I need to know that much."

"No, I haven't."

"You're sure?"

"Positive."

That didn't give her much leeway to insist on disclosure. "Just in case, you'd better tell me all you can."

"No. I won't take deliberate action that pushes you further into the fire."

"But—"

"No," he insisted, then softened enough to add, "Let's just say that sometimes people are the exact opposite of who they appear to be."

Which told her nothing. Who was the exact opposite of who they appeared to be? "That's it?"

"That's it."

"Fine." No sense arguing. He wouldn't budge. "Thank you for everything." His warning could take her out of the line of fire. At least she knew they had found her home and were closing in on her. "Take care. I'll call when I can."

"Be smart about it, and do stay alive. You know how I detest having to rearrange my schedule."

Boy, did he. And for him, this comment was intensely personal. So much so that a lump formed in her throat. "I'll do my best not to cause you any inconvenience."

She would; she always had. But would her best be good enough to keep her alive?

"I found her." A gravel-voiced man reported in via phone. "Interception is complete."

"Excellent." He stepped outside and permitted the long-held tension to drain from his body. He'd been expecting this call for weeks. "Where is she now?"

"Don't worry. She hasn't checked out of her hotel. She's scouting sites for the new center."

More good news. He glanced at his watch— 7:15. "So you've enacted the plan? With the red Jag?" That car was crucial for two reasons. One, to signal their men, and the other to signal a key player who didn't yet realize he was a key player. The car would serve notice he couldn't miss.

"Yes sir. The plan is active, the Jag is in place, and our men are in position. All I need is your authorization, and I'll cut them loose." He paused and then added, "It should all be over before you catch the nine o'clock news."

He'd seen this moment in his mind's eye a million times, and he'd studied at least that many possibilities, seeking a different final solution. But all the seeking and sifting had changed nothing. In the end, the same simple truth remained. Pit anything—money, power, or blood—against survival and survival won.

"Two twenty-two," he said, relaying the code.

"Code master?"

His mouth went dry and his tongue stuck to his teeth. He sipped from a crystal glass that cost more than most made in a week and then whispered on a hushed breath the word he had yearned and dreaded to speak. The word that opened craters of fear in those unfortunate enough to understand its meaning: "NINA."

2

Glad to have the conversation with her financial advisor behind her, even if it had carried devastating news, she tipped her phone against her chin to flip it closed and snagged her nail on the steering wheel. The phone flew from her hand, tumbled across the passenger's seat, and then crashed on the floorboard with a sickening thud. "Perfect."

She started to bend to retrieve it, but the light flashed yellow and went straight to red. She hit the brakes hard, stopped not a second too soon—the nose of her car was in the intersection—and then looked around. *Isolated.* For once grateful for that, she shifted into reverse, backed up, and then put the car in first gear.

A blue tarp flapped in the breeze on a nearby

roof. The desolation and weariness of the city, still ravaged from the hurricane, was just heart-breaking. She let herself lose focus, lifted her gaze upward and left. *Lord, bless them.*

She checked the dashboard clock—8:20, less an hour. This was central, not eastern time. It was 7:20, muggy, and still gloomy. Hotel security's safety tip sheet warned her not to venture out alone in this area during the day, much less at night. But how else could she be certain where the new children's center would best serve the community's greatest needs?

Tires squealed. A warning sounded in her mind, and she darted a look back toward the sound. Nothing moved, but she had a bad feeling. She tried but couldn't shake it. Maybe she should have paid attention to security and at least waited until morning to ride through, but she'd wanted to finish up. If she got on the road by 6:00, she could make it home—no. No, she couldn't make it home before dark. Home was gone now. She had to vanish again.

It was so unfair. She'd just gotten settled. She'd done nothing wrong, and yet she was paying a harsh penalty—one that left her with an enormous problem. If NINA was this multinational terrorist group, then where on earth could she hide to get out of its reach?

Tires squealed again and screeched. Someone shouted in the distance.

Lifting her gaze to her rearview, she searched for the source, but only parked cars lined the dark street. An uneasy shiver crept up her back. Nothing was out there, but something was wrong.

Danger. Danger. Danger!

Her pulse rate quickened and urgency flooded her. "That's it. You're going back to the hotel right now." She half-considered running the red light, but even pushed by her instincts, she didn't do it.

Stretching, she snagged her phone from the passenger's side floorboard. Just grasping it helped her to calm down. If she needed help, she could get it. Scanning the street, she breathed easier. All was still. Silent. Nothing to worry about. Everything was just fine.

NINA and nerves—that's what had her hyper-alert and jumpy. For the past week, she had seen too many people hurting, too many struggling to make do. She'd talked to too many moms praying for someone—anyone—to provide what they couldn't: a safe place for their kids to play. The father who had lost his six-year-old son less than a week ago crossed her mind.

Killed in crossfire.

Her eyes stung, and a lump rose from her chest and stuck in her throat.

She wanted to help them all.

She would do all she could.

Empathizing with them had depleted her reserves. She was physically, mentally, and emotionally exhausted. Every nerve in her body had been stretched tight for a week and, bone raw, her body was rebelling. It needed a break it wasn't going to get.

So did the people here, and they wouldn't get one either, unless she provided them with one. She'd suffered a week. They'd suffered the years since Hurricane Katrina flooded the city, and still no real, permanent relief was in sight.

She swiped at her eyes. Once this project got going, parents would be less worried, the kids would be playing safe, and then she—

Her windshield shattered.

She covered her head, protected her eyes. What was happening? She couldn't see anything beyond the spider-web cracks.

A dozen masked men dressed in black with something neon blue on their wrists swarmed her car. They circled it, hurled guttural comments at her. *Gang slang.* Kicked the fenders, the doors. Then they began to chant, *"Get out . . . Get out . . . Get out . . ."*

She had to do something, but what? If she moved the car, she'd run over someone, and she certainly wasn't getting out of it.

"Take her down, man," one of them shouted near the rear fender. "He wants her dead."

A new chant began. *"Kill her . . . Kill her . . . Kill her . . ."*

She couldn't move, couldn't think.

A dark sedan whipped around the corner, its headlights sweeping twin beams across the street, across her car. It paused half a block behind her as if taking stock, then sped up as if determined to mow down her attackers.

The gang members scattered like rats.

She should thank the person in the sedan, yet she didn't dare to not put distance between herself and the gang. They could return as fast as they'd left, and there was no mistake—their attack on her hadn't been random.

Someone had ordered them to murder her.

She stomped the gas.

The Jag shot off and ate up the pavement. A good mile away, she could hold on to the wheel without the shaking of her hands tearing them loose from it. Ahead, a traffic light turned red.

It's okay. You can deal with this. You've dealt with worse.

She braked to a stop, double-checked her door locks, and prayed she'd get back to the hotel before her courage or her nerves gave out. Her chances were at best iffy.

Something sailed through her battered windshield. The wind whistled as it flew past her. A large rock thudded against the passenger's seat.

Outside, a man shouted to someone unseen. "Did it hit her?"

The gang? No, they were on foot. She craned her neck. It was the dark sedan that had rescued her from the gang. Now its driver was after her?

He deliberately busted her windshield. Two groups? Primary and backup attacks? One intentional attack and one random? Or maybe the sedan driver had been on his own and after her all along . . .

"She ain't hurt," he shouted from just outside her driver's window, then flattened his hand and beat on the glass. "Open the door."

Danger!

She stomped the accelerator. Missed and hit the brakes, tried again. The car bolted. She jerked. Her foot slipped.

A white truck slid into the intersection in front of her, then skidded to a stop. She was going to hit him. No way to avoid it. Bracing for impact, she slammed on the brakes. Her tires squealed, the car fishtailed and screeched to a stop, just inches from the truck. She'd almost T-boned him.

He glared at her from the truck. Deliberate. Deliberate. No accident; this was all deliberate.

God, please. Please, help me.

The man who'd beaten on her window appeared beside her again. "Open the door. There's nowhere for you to go."

No way was she opening that door. No way. She opened her phone instead, dialed 911. No bars. How could there be *no bars*? There had to be service here. She shook the phone, punched in the numbers again.

Nothing.

Nothing!

Do something. Help yourself. You're on your own.

She looked out her rear window. The dark sedan blocked her. She slammed the car into reverse anyway, punched the gas, hoping to shove it aside and somehow escape.

Metal crunched against metal, grated and scraped, but the car didn't move. She tried again. Thick smoke obscured her vision of the rear, the car filled with the stench of burning tires, but she couldn't break free.

The driver scrambled out of his truck, left his door open. He stormed toward her, pouring something from a small brown bottle onto a white cloth in his hand. "What are you waiting for? Kick out her window."

The truth settled in. The two men were working together. This wasn't a crime of opportunity. Like the gang, these two had targeted her . . .

NINA. The incident three years ago raced through her mind. She had run out of town in the middle of the night, not even pausing to pack her things. But these events couldn't be connected. These men were strangers. Three years and she'd had to run and start over four times, but she had avoided the men she knew. And she hadn't been back there—not once.

"NINA's found you."

But there was nothing to lead them here. Even her advisor only knew the city she was in and her cell number, and it changed every few weeks.

So why is this happening? If not for NINA, then why did these strangers choose you?

The Jag? Maybe they just wanted the car. What else could it be?

The first man kept pounding on her window. She couldn't see his face, hidden beneath a hooded sweatshirt. It was mid-October but far too hot and humid a night for a sweatshirt. He had to be sweltering.

Deliberate. Dangerous. Targeted.

"I said kick in the window," the truck driver said.

"Gimme a crowbar and I will." The glass didn't muffle his voice, and his accent sounded more like Mississippi than New Orleans, thick with a twang she had often found endearing. But it didn't strike her as endearing now.

Turning, he stared at her through the glass. "We can do this easy or rough." He was a huge man, big and brawny with broad shoulders and a deep, booming voice. "But we are gonna do it, K—"

The second man shouted, cutting him off. "It's Susan."

"But—"

"No buts," the truck driver insisted. "Mistakes carry costs. You want to risk forgetting that again?"

"It ain't likely I will, but I get your point." His twang more pronounced, he jerked at her door's handle. "Unlock it, Susan." It clicked and clicked. *"Now!"*

Susan?

Glass shattered, sprayed over her shoulder, pricked her skin. Guarding her eyes, she looked back at a gaping hole in the rear passenger's window. A beefy arm reached inside. Her heart thudded against her ribs and then seemed to stop.

Shaking, she grappled with her phone, finally got it open, then dialed 911. It still didn't work. *Damaged.*

No. Not now. *Please, not now.* She shoved his hand away from the lock, then dialed again.

Nothing.

He reached again. She went for his sleeve. Missed. The lock *click* magnified inside her head. The passenger door flew open, rocked back on its hinges, and the truck driver charged into the car, choked her, then crammed the white cloth over her nose and mouth.

She fumbled the phone and fought him.

The stench of chemicals filled her nose. She fought harder and harder, trying every defensive measure she knew and then anything at all. But nothing worked; she couldn't break free.

The second man came at her from the backseat and knocked her in the head. Seeing stars, she felt pain shoot through her skull, down her spine. She held her breath, gouged at his eyes, but failed to make contact.

Fighting for her life, she sank her nails into his flesh, clawed deep ruts into his arms. He howled and cursed, but he didn't turn her loose.

Her lungs threatened to explode. The truck driver landed a solid punch to her stomach. She gasped and her arms seemed like lead. Her mouth turned dust-dry, cottony, and her clear thoughts slid behind a misty veil.

She struggled to grasp them, determined to stay conscious and untangle the crackled snippets firing through her mind. But even as she fought, she lost ground. Her strength ebbed and slipped away.

I'm going to die. Right here on this street, I'm going to die.

Her head swam, spots flashed before her eyes. And the truth sank like a stone into her bones. They'd won.

The chemicals took control. She couldn't move, struggle, or fight. But there was one thing she could do, and she gave herself over to it fully.

She prayed.

3

Crickets chirped.

The sound split the silence with a bold, high-pitched hum. Something buzzed near her ear. A mosquito. She reached up to swat it, and intense pain shafted through her arm, her neck, and exploded in her head.

And then she remembered.

The carjackers. The sweatshirt man beating at her window, the truck driver choking her, forcing her to breathe in chemicals. Her chest seized, setting off a series of deep-muscle spasms that stole her breath.

She wasn't dead. She wasn't . . . dead.

Thank You, God. Thank You.

Where was she?

Where were they?

Aching everywhere at once, she fought through the fog clouding her mind. Something pushed against her face and side—dirt. She cranked open one eye.

Outside. Still dark. Thick trunks of twisted trees silhouetted against the night and wooded ground. Were the carjackers still here? She didn't dare move and alert them that she was awake. Instead she focused hard, listened. No sounds signaled anyone close by.

Sprawled in sandy dirt, she lay surrounded by trees and short, spiny bushes she'd seen many times but couldn't name. Twigs and leaves, acorns and broken branches littered the ground, and gritty dirt clung to her face. She swiped at it and braced her arms on the ground, forcing herself to sit up and look closer at her surroundings. Still, normal night sounds. Rustling leaves, an owl's calm call—nothing that indicated anyone else's presence or raised any alarm.

In the strong moonlight, her eyes began to adjust. Rigid shoeprints led away from where she sat, leaving crevices in the sand. They were two different sizes, one larger than the other. The man in the hooded sweatshirt was huge; the truck driver smaller, about five foot ten or maybe five nine—just a few inches taller than she was.

The car. They'd just wanted the car. They jacked it and dumped her here.

Why take me at all? Why not just leave me on the street?

Doubt crept through her. Their bringing her here didn't make sense—even if they had left her for dead. But maybe they were twisted souls who got their kicks out of killing.

She patted herself, checking for wounds. With all the aches and pain, she wasn't sure if she'd been shot, but she definitely had been beaten. Her feet and legs were tender and throbbing, no doubt bruised, but nothing felt broken. Her torso looked muddy even in the moonlight, battered and sore but free of open wounds. Her head—she pulled back her hand.

It was covered in blood.

The beam of a flashlight blinded her.

"Land sakes, girl," a man she couldn't see said from the darkness behind the light. "What in the world are you doing out here?"

She screamed.

"Hold on now." He lifted his hands. The beam of light shifted, slanted through the trees. "Just hold on and calm down. I'm not going to hurt you."

She blinked hard, tried to get up, but fell back to the ground. Her heart beat fast, adrenaline shoving through her veins. "Don't come near me."

She grabbed a rock. Matted blood and bits of her hair clung to its rough surface. She'd either fallen on it or been hit with it. Regardless, the rock probably caused her head injury.

She cranked her arm back, threatening to throw it at him. The pain of stretching throbbed through her, setting off another round of deep-muscle spasms that left her clammy and in a cold sweat. "Stay back. I-I mean it."

"I'm not moving." He held his hands higher, and the strong moonlight slanted across his face.

Early sixties, gray hair, and stubbly jaw—not the sweatshirt man or the truck driver—and this man was wearing . . . *pajamas and slippers?*

She blinked hard again, certain she couldn't be seeing what she thought she was, but nothing changed. He was definitely wearing pajamas. The first thing that crossed her mind tumbled out of her mouth. "You—you're not dressed."

"I'm up at dawn and I hit the rack at eight o'clock every night except Wednesday—choir practice. It's late for me." He softened his voice. "I see blood on your face. Are you hurt?"

"I'm alive." She couldn't be anything but grateful, yet said aloud that would sound too odd. "Who are you?"

"Clyde Parker. I live just over there." He pointed left through the trees.

She needed to get up. The carjackers—they could come back. "Do you often walk in the woods in your pajamas?" Her head swam; she couldn't lift herself and slid back to the ground.

"Only when I get up for a drink of water and see headlights out here through my kitchen window. I didn't see anything else, so I went back to bed. But I couldn't get to sleep. Something just nagged at me to come take a look."

"They're gone then?" Hope sparked to life inside her.

His forehead furrowed and the lines near his mouth settled into grooves. "Who?"

"The men who left me here."

"I've been tromping around out here the better part of an hour, and I haven't seen anyone but you, so I guess they're gone." Clyde winced. "Do you mind if I lower my arms? I've got arthritis pretty bad in my shoulder, and holding my arms up like this hurts."

She nodded and let relief sink in. The carjackers were gone. She was alive. And other than being sore from top to bottom and sporting a wicked headache, she seemed all right. The urge to cry hit her. She fought it and swallowed down a threatening sob.

"Did you come here with them by choice?" Clyde asked.

"No."

"Didn't think so." Pity flashed through his eyes.

Feeling helpless and vulnerable, she stiffened. Something jabbed her thigh from inside her pocket. She reached in and pulled out a card she couldn't read in the dark and a cross on a delicate chain. Seeing it brought comfort. Needing it, she hooked it around her neck. "Can you please get me out of here?"

"I can and will, if you'll tell me who you are and how come you're out in the woods at night with strange men."

She opened her mouth to tell him her name. Her mind went blank. Totally blank. Her insides curled and tightened, triggering earthquakes inside her. Pain radiated through her entire abdomen and chest. "I can't."

"Why not? You doing drugs or something you shouldn't be doing?"

"No." Her voice thick, she cleared her throat and admitted the truth chilling her to the bone. "I was at a red light. They took my car and made me breathe something on a cloth. I-I don't know what was on it. Chemicals." Her stomach roiled. "The next thing I remember is waking up here." An inhalant that induced short-term amnesia? Chloroform? What had those chemicals been? Would there be residual effects?

"I see." His shoulders slumped, pity again burning in his eyes. "Well, you survived. That's the important thing. And your name?"

Meeting his gaze was difficult. "I-I don't know who I am."

He gentled his voice even more. "Did you know when you came into the woods?"

The fear in her swelled and overflowed. "I honestly don't know."

"Do you know where you live? Someone I can call?"

Nothing came to her. Not a thing. Her shaking doubled. Why couldn't she remember these things? "It's like swiss cheese. I remember some things, but . . ." She recalled the card in her pocket and fished it out. "Maybe this will tell us."

He flashed the light on the card. "Crossroads." He looked from her to it. "It's a local crisis center."

It didn't sound familiar. "Maybe I belong there."

He flipped the card. "What's this on the back?"

"I can't read it from here."

He looked over at her. "It says, 'Susan.'"

A vague memory flashed through her mind. *"Unlock this door, Susan . . ."*

"That must be me." She touched a fingertip to her chest. "He called me that."

"The man who brought you here?"

"I don't know who brought me here, but two men pulled me out of my car. The big one called me Susan."

Clyde studied her a long moment, then stared at her neck.

She reached up to the heavy cross. Rubbing it soothed her. Calm flowed through her body, head to heel, gentle and welcoming and reassuring. Her rapid breathing slowed.

"Are you a woman of faith?"

"I am." How she knew that when she didn't know who she was defied explanation, but she had no doubt it was true.

"I guess that's why I couldn't get back to sleep, then," he said, seemingly content with that deduction. "We better get someone to take a look at that gash in your head. I'm going to check and see how bad it is."

Clyde inched toward her, careful not to make any unexpected moves, then examined her head with a gentle, gnarled hand. "Well, the bleeding's always rough on head wounds, but the cut's not too bad. You'll need a stitch or two. Best put some pressure on it."

She pressed her fingers to her head.

"I'm going to help you up now. We'll get my car and I'll take you to the hospital." He reached down, offering her his arm. "It'll be faster to drive in than to wait for an ambulance."

She clasped his arm, then pulled up. Breath-stealing pain wracked her body. She rocked on her feet. *Don't pass out. Don't pass out!* Grappling to steady herself, she leaned against him, needing support to stay upright. "Is it far?"

"No. Just six miles or so—in the village proper."

"I'm sorry. I know this must hurt, with your arthritis." Biting back a groan, she took more of her own weight.

"I'm fine," he said, dry leaves crunching under his feet. "You just hold on all you like."

"Thank you, Mr. Parker."

"Clyde."

"Clyde." She swayed.

"Whoa, there." He wrapped his free arm around her shoulder. "Come on now. Let's get you out of here."

She sniffed his clean and soapy scent. He couldn't be dangerous, and she'd never get out of the woods on her own. Daring to trust him, she said, "I'm glad you were thirsty."

He led her through the woods. "Excuse me?"

"If you hadn't gotten up for a drink of water, I'd be lost out here." The woods were dense and thick, and one direction looked much like the other.

"I'm glad I couldn't go back to sleep and came to look. You could've wandered around here for days."

Glad to have avoided that, she looked up at him. "Thank you, Clyde."

"No need." He patted her hand. "I'm just glad you're all right." Worry raced across his face. "They didn't . . . hurt you, did they?"

She knew what he meant, and an anxious rush gushed through her. "I don't know."

"Well, don't you worry on it." His pats moved to her arm and sped up. "They'll take good care of you at the hospital. It's not big, but the folks there are really good. Guess when you're small you have to be. They get a little bit of everything." He dared a smile meant to reassure her.

"Where are we?"

"Walton County, but the hospital's over in Seagrove."

She stopped cold. "Seagrove Village—that's the village proper you mentioned?"

"Yep."

"I'm in *Florida*?" Shock pumped through her. It couldn't be. *Oh no. Oh, please, no. Anywhere but there. Anywhere else on the planet. Just not there.*

"Yeah," he said, confirming her worst fears. "You know the place?"

She searched her mind, but nothing came. "I can't remember."

"Well, for someone who can't recall, you sure sound surprised and not at all happy about being here."

"I am surprised—and I'm definitely not happy," she confessed, not quite sure what to make of it. "I just don't know why."

A limb encroached onto the path. He held it back and waited for her to walk past, then turned it loose. It swooshed back into place, dropping leaves onto the ground. He didn't doubt her; she saw no skepticism in his eyes.

"Think on it a second. Maybe that knock to your noggin has you a little slow at putting things together. That happens sometimes."

They walked on through the snapping twigs, and she tried but still came up empty. With nowhere left to go, she gave up. "I don't have a clue."

She didn't, but one thing came through loud and clear. Whatever the reason, she didn't just dislike Seagrove Village. She feared it. Yet feeling that fear in every atom of every cell in her body and not knowing its source—that ripped right past fear and plunged into stark terror.

"No, no hospital, Clyde." She pulled the card from her pocket and double-checked the address.

He'd said it was local, and it was at the corner of Gramercy and Seville. "Crossroads Crisis Center."

"All right. Now, it ain't a hospital, but it's got limited medical facilities with docs and everything. Like I said, your head's gonna need some stitches."

"Can they handle that?"

He glanced at her. "Sorry to say it, but they stitch people up all the time."

"Take me there, then." Someone had put that card and necklace in her pocket. She could almost remember being flipped over, a hand shoving them into her pocket. It was fuzzy, but the pressure of that hand was clear. And the necklace was a cross. A cross and the card together offered more protection than the hospital with all its notification rules and regulations.

But would it offer enough? Would she be safe there?

She had no idea. And why was she worried about notification rules and regulations? Her mind raced, and a question popped in that had her shaking like a wind-battered leaf. "Clyde? What day is it today?"

"Saturday."

She licked at her dry lips. "Is it before dawn on Saturday or after dark?"

He stopped and stared at her. "It's after dark."

In the Jag, it'd been Friday night. She vividly remembered that.

"What's wrong, girl? You look white as a sheet."

"You're sure it's Saturday?"

"Sure as sunshine. Saturday, October tenth."

She swallowed hard. "Clyde, I've lost a whole day."

"Sir, we have a problem."

Seated at the head of an exquisitely set table, Gregory Chessman buried his irritation at the interruption of the dinner party he was hosting for thirty of his most influential friends. Those seated closest to him overheard his assistant Paul Johnson's stage whisper, including Mayor John Green's wife, Darla.

"Anything I can do to help?" She eyed Gregory inquisitively.

Airhead. Not eager to be the subject of speculation for the next few days, he patted her hand. "No, my dear, don't trouble your pretty head with this. Just a little man talk."

A piercing look flashed in her eyes. She brushed her napkin onto the floor between her and her husband and clasped his arm, digging in her nails hard enough that John flinched.

"Is something wrong, darling?"

"No." Her clasp on his forearm changed to a stroke. "What could be wrong? Everything is lovely."

Paul rushed to pick up the napkin and return it to her.

Darla pressed the fine linen back to her lap, cupping her hand over its creases.

So, Gregory surmised, she resented his comment about her worrying her pretty head. Odd. She perpetuated her image and routinely fished for compliments. Women did that with monotonous regularity. Perhaps she was just in a mood.

Gregory cast her an indulgent smile, dabbed at his mouth, and forced his tone light. "No rest for the wicked, eh?"

His guests laughed, and because they did, he was genuinely amused. He slid back his chair, then stood. "If you'll excuse me . . ."

"Gregory Chessman, wicked?" Darla let out a dainty laugh, free from any hint of moodiness. "Now doesn't that take a vivid imagination?"

Her remark elicited another round of laughter, one more heartfelt. It would indeed take a vivid imagination for anyone at the table to consider him wicked, with one exception: his secret partner. But for reasons of greed, self-preservation, and a fervent distaste for prison, there was no danger of his exposing Gregory—he couldn't, not without exposing himself and his own duplicity.

Gregory gave his partner no reason to regret their strategic business alliance. He had worked for a decade to build his man-above-reproach image, and he succeeded. Even if presented with irrefutable opposing evidence, none of the other locals would believe him capable of wickedness. That had already been tested and proven. He resisted the urge to puff up with pride. To them, he was ethical and moral—a model citizen—and he would do whatever he had to do to keep it that way.

He had revealed few personal specifics to anyone and fully disclosed them to no one. Self-made, he'd come a long way from the slums to what others viewed as his charmed life of privilege.

Nothing and no one was going to steal even a pinch of it.

"Perhaps I can help." The respected attorney from Atlanta started to stand.

"No, my friend," Gregory told him. No trouble was worth risking the man revealing anything he learned. He had worldwide connections. "Keep your seat." He waved a hand. "Everyone, eat. This is a minor irritant and will be resolved in a moment."

The attorney settled in his seat and returned to his conversation with Benjamin Brandt, the owner of Crossroads Crisis Center.

"Ben," Darla said. "It's good to see you socializing again. We've missed you."

"Thank you." He shifted to look at his host. "It's been three years since I've been to one of your enjoyable parties, Gregory."

"Glad you're back," he said.

Darla set down her water glass. "As I recall, you were alone at the last one."

Pain flashed through Brandt's eyes. "Yes, my son was ill, so my wife stayed home."

"I'm sorry." She lowered her gaze. "I shouldn't have brought that up."

"It's all right," Ben said. "Seagrove is a small village. Few have secrets." He leaned forward and laced his fingers. "I'm sure where I've been is common knowledge."

"It is," Hank Green, the mayor's younger brother, said. "You've been down in the islands, visiting friends."

"Ah." The corner of Ben's mouth lifted. "Nora's been busy, I see."

"No, not your housekeeper," Hank said. "Peggy Crane told me."

"She was my next guess."

"Ben?" the lawyer asked. "Are you at all interested in local landmarks . . . ?"

Gregory's relief was short-lived. Hank leaned over to Darla and whispered just loud enough for Gregory to hear. "You know he's been in isolation with counselors for two months. This is the first social he's attended since his family died. Back off and leave him be."

She fired Hank a frosty glare, then quickly masked it. "I wasn't starting trouble; I was just being friendly."

"Well, don't." Hank's gaze sparkled. "It's bad

enough every tongue in the village is wagging about him. You don't have to flaunt it in his face."

Darla started to object, but John clasped her hand. "Hank's right, honey. I know you meant well, but Ben has really struggled with his loss. He's finally coming around. We wouldn't want to do anything to cause him to regress, would we?"

Her eyes glittered, but her voice sounded soft. "Not for the world, darling."

Gregory nearly puked. But no real damage had been done. Ben hadn't overheard their exchange, thanks to a deep discussion about preserving local landmarks—the stated reason for the lawyer being in the village. Still, the urge to rip out Darla's idiotic tongue had Gregory rushing to leave his opulent dining room.

Darla sat stiff and silent until Gregory disappeared beyond the dining room door and John engaged Hank on the subtleties of being diplomatic. Tuning them out and lowering her lashes, she scanned the table to be sure she had again become invisible and ignored by all.

Convinced she had, she lifted the lumped corner of her napkin and unveiled a small square of white paper. She read it and then tucked it into her beaded bag, its words echoing in her mind: OFFER REFUSED.

· · ·

Gregory strode down the hallway without glancing at Paul Johnson. Mentioning a problem in the presence of guests? What was he thinking?

That faux pas would be dealt with shortly.

Gregory keyed in the code to unlock the door, then entered his private den. It was soundproof and swept for listening devices after anyone other than himself or Paul entered it, just to be safe. One didn't accomplish all Gregory had accomplished the way he had accomplished it without careful planning *and* diligent execution of essential precautions.

His footfall soft on the plush carpet, Paul entered behind him. Gregory shut the double doors, then turned. Slight and stooped, Paul wasn't a man's man. He'd never in his life cast a fishing rod, thrown a football, or played any sport, and his idiosyncrasies made the odd habits of notorious eccentrics pale by comparison. That caused many to underestimate Paul and make the erroneous assumption that Gregory had hired him *faute de mieux*.

But there was no absence of someone better, and Gregory hadn't underestimated anyone. Paul was a decade younger—just shy of twenty-five—but from their first meeting his skills, abilities, and assets had been evident and useful. The man was brilliant, resourceful, meticulous, deviously clever, ridiculously loyal, and he could make anything happen and never leave a trace. More important, he would, could, and had made unpleasant situations disappear for Gregory, *and* he kept his mouth shut. So Paul's social skills were lacking. That was a minor annoyance and required only that Gregory exercise areas of restraint.

Gregory was a master at restraint—and well equipped at controlling all in his domain, including Paul Johnson.

He raised a warning hand. "Don't ever do that again."

Paul shifted his weight from foot to foot, swiped at his left temple. "I know I'm not supposed to interrupt when strangers—"

"Guests. They're my guests, not strangers. I invited them to my home for dinner. Normal people do that."

"Oh." Paul didn't seem to grasp the concept or to take offense at not being considered normal. "Guests."

"Yes." Now the man was twitching. The entire left side of his face went into a series of spasms that almost knocked his black-framed glasses off his nose. Before he went into a full spasmodic meltdown, Gregory diverted Paul's attention with a question. "What is the problem?"

No answer.

Gregory swallowed hard, seeking patience. Upset, Paul would literally blank out. Under certain circumstances that trait could be an asset, but now wasn't the time. "You came into the dining room and said we have a problem. What kind of problem is it?"

Comprehension dawned and Paul's expression darkened, knitting his thick brows and bunching the skin between them into creases. "A big one, sir. You said if anything came up on this matter to inform you right away. Something has come up, so I'm informing you."

No doubt Gregory had issued that directive, but he had issued similar instructions on various potential hazards. Without details, he couldn't pinpoint this specific one. For the sake of efficiency and his growling stomach, he asked, "What exactly is the problem?"

"An anonymous phone call came in. No way to trace it—throwaway cell." Paul walked over to the desk phone. "You need to hear it."

The only anonymous calls he received were from Alik Demyan and related to NINA. True, some of those were enough to turn his hair gray, but anything else doing it was doubtful. Gregory reached for the speaker button.

"No!" Paul shifted his weight on his feet. "Pick it up, sir."

"The room is soundproof, Paul."

"Yes sir. But we always minimize risks. Especially when the house is full of strangers." He caught himself. Squinted. Winced. "I meant, *guests*. The house is full of *guests*."

Gregory lifted the receiver but paused to listen to Paul mutter, "The minute her aunt died, I knew there would be trouble. She just had to record that deed on the beach house."

That deed had been instrumental in locating her. Gregory put two and two together. "So the subject rejected our purchase offer."

"Yes sir." Paul rubbed his neck. "If you'll recall, I projected less than five percent odds of success."

"Her advisor?"

"Ineffectual." Paul adjusted the frame of his glasses at the bridge of his scrunched nose. "He hasn't had much influence with her since she took over her own affairs."

Couldn't dispute that. Even he had been unable to locate her. Gregory stilled, considered his options.

"She won't stay away now," Paul projected. "The temptation will be too strong to resist."

"Why? She hasn't been back here even once."

"But she knew her aunt was here. Now she's not, and all the subject has left of her childhood is in that beach house."

Gregory shrugged. "But it's just a shack."

"Not to her." Paul peered over the tops of his glasses.

The subject was well off. She wasn't homeless. Why would the shack mean anything to her?

"It's all she has left of her family."

"Ah, memories." The light dawned. *Foolish, sentimental dead weight.*

Paul's expression turned uncharacteristically tender. "I suspected she'd hidden to protect herself, but her refusing the purchase offer disputes that. She was protecting her aunt."

"Now it all makes sense." Gregory rubbed his lower lip. "She knows everything we feared she might know."

"Maybe not all of it." Paul seated his glasses at the bridge of his nose. "But more than we hoped."

"And now, with her aunt gone, there's less fear of reprisal." A knot formed in Gregory's chest. He paced from chair to desk. The subject wasn't a fool. She had to know that tangling with him put her in lethal jeopardy. "Are you telling me she called here—herself?"

"No sir. That would be bad. This, I'm sorry to say, is worse."

"Worse?" Gregory pressed in the code to recall the message from his service.

Tapping his fingers on the credenza, Paul grumbled, "I should have handled it, Mr. Chessman. Everything was a mess, and Edward and Harry just disappeared."

Gregory should have allowed Paul to handle it. Unfortunately, three years ago Paul hadn't yet proven himself, and Gregory elected to stick with the tried and true. The subject was a lightweight— or so he'd thought at the time. Everyone had underestimated her—him, his secret partner, Edward and Harry—everyone *except* Paul. And they all had done so on such a grand scale that Edward and Harry had botched things badly.

For weeks, Gregory had sweat bullets—until it became clear that the subject wasn't going to make waves. Still, he found merit in avoiding loose ends. But the subject had evaded his associates and vanished. Worse, she had managed to keep vanishing. He'd spent three years living in fear that she would resurface and, now, it appeared she had.

And Paul claimed this message carried even worse news? There was no worse news.

"Go on, sir." Paul motioned to the phone. "Listen to it. You'll see what I mean."

Gregory played the message. The voice had been modified—man or woman, he couldn't tell—and what was said took two seconds to replay, but the danger in it for him was timeless.

It was worse. It rocked Gregory's entire world.

"Susan's alive."

4

"Do you know me?" Still holding pressure on her head wound, she stood at the receptionist's desk inside Crossroads Crisis Center. "I-I think my name is Susan."

The young woman with spiky dark hair and

chocolate brown eyes was caught off guard by the question. Her jaw dropped open and her gaze slid over to a painting on the wall. It hung above a long, narrow table that was home to two slim lamps and a burst of lilies.

The girl was out of her depth.

"Maybe you'd better get your boss." Clyde stepped forward. "I tried to take her"—he motioned toward Susan—"to the hospital, but—"

"Thank you, but I can speak for myself, Mr. Parker." Susan reached into her pocket, then pulled out a card, smudged with mud and dirt, and tried to wipe it clean. The dirt sprinkled on the countertop between her and the receptionist.

"Sorry." She released the pressure on her head wound long enough to sweep the droppings into her hand. "My car was jacked and I was abducted and beaten."

Blood gathered on her scalp, and Susan put the pressure back on her wound, then wiggled her elbow midair. "That's how I got this gash in my head . . . I think. I'm not sure because I can't remember much of anything, but—"

"Give her the short version," Clyde suggested in a whisper close to Susan's ear. "The girl's confused, and she looks a little scared too."

She did. A brass nameplate identified her. "Melanie, this card was in my pocket." Susan flipped it over and frowned at more dirt smears. "See? Someone wrote 'Susan' on the back of it."

She tried to smile, but her lip was swollen and raw and her jaw was numb. It had to look more like a grimace. "When I saw the name written there, I remembered one of my abductors calling me Susan." She shrugged. A hot arrow of pain shot through her shoulder, across her back.

"Just a moment, please." Melanie bit her lips, lifted the phone receiver, and punched two buttons, her gaze darting back to the wall. "Mrs. Crane, Code One, front desk."

Susan stiffened. "Code One?"

"Uh-oh." Clyde leaned close again. "Codes are always bad news. I told you, you were scaring her."

Susan turned to look at him and her gaze lighted on a painting hanging on the wall above the table. She gasped. "Look, Clyde. It's me!" Transfixed, she walked over to the painting.

A short, sturdy woman rounded the corner at a good clip. Worry lined her face. Clyde intercepted her. "Glad you're here, Peg."

"We're fully staffed every Saturday night," she told Clyde. "Heavy traffic on Saturdays and holidays."

"There's no emergency." He went on to explain the circumstances.

They knew each other, Susan realized. It couldn't hurt to let him talk, and it could help her credibility.

A small gilded mirror hung in a grouping on the

far wall. She rushed to it and examined her face. Swollen, bruised and distorted, dirty, but the resemblance was plain. She moved back to the painting and checked again. Reasonably pretty; chin-length blond hair—clean and coiffed, not strung with bits of leaves and grass; blue eyes— same shape and color; same chin and nose and neck. She gasped again. The cross. She was wearing the same cross!

Susan spun toward Clyde. "It really is me. I'm Susan." She riveted her gaze back to the small brass placket mounted to its frame. "Susan Brandt."

Clyde frowned. So did the woman beside him.

Susan's skin crawled. "I know I'm a mess, but you can't miss it. She's me." A nervous laugh escaped, then she glanced skyward. "God, thank You."

She smoothed her pale hair back from her face. "I can't tell you how unnerving it is not to remember . . ." Susan noticed something else written on the painting's brass placket. *Two dates.*

Two.

Birth and . . .

She gasped and stared at the sober-faced woman beside Clyde. "I'm *dead*?"

"Mel," the woman said, not looking away from Susan. "Get Doctors Talbot and Harper."

Susan couldn't move. She wanted to, tried to, but her feet seemed rooted to the tile floor. "I-I can't be dead. How can that say I died three years ago?" She flipped up a hand, then thumped her chest with a fist. "I'm standing right here."

"It's going to be okay," the woman said.

"Easy for you to say. No one is claiming you're dead."

"No one is claiming you are either," the woman told her.

Susan grunted. "I'd have to disagree. Haven't you seen that?" She pointed to the painting's placket.

"You aren't dead . . ."

"Susan. My name is Susan."

"Susan." The woman stumbled over it. "You're not dead."

Susan stilled, not so sure. Too much was too weird. "Who are you?"

"Peggy Crane. Director here at Crossroads Crisis Center." She started to step toward Susan but then stepped back next to Clyde. "Just stay calm, okay? From what Clyde says, you've been through a lot in a short period of time, but you are safe here. You're safe, and we're going to help you sort out everything."

Tears burned the backs of Susan's eyes and, having trouble catching her breath, she dragged in deep gulps. "But it says I'm dead—and I'm not dead." She blinked hard. "I'm not."

Peggy walked toward her. "Of course you aren't." Her calm seemed forced, but it still helped.

"So you know I'm Susan?"

Melanie passed Peggy a plastic container of wet wipes. She didn't offer one to Susan. Was the receptionist worried about destroying evidence?

"At the moment," Peggy said, "I'm not sure who you are, but we will find out. What I can tell you right now is that you're not the woman in the painting."

How could she say that? Even think that? "But—"

Peggy stopped in front of Susan and searched her face. "You look a lot like her. But you aren't Susan Brandt. I know that for fact."

Unable to believe it—her eyes weren't lying to her—Susan glanced back at the painting, then again at Peggy Crane. "With all due respect, you are mistaken. I'm looking at myself."

"No, you aren't, and I'm not mistaken," Peggy said. "Susan Brandt was my dear friend and she was shot dead." Pain filled Peggy's voice and leaked into her face. "I saw her body at the crime scene, in her casket, and I watched them lower her into the ground."

A tear trailed down Susan's cheek. "I'm so sorry." That must have been horrible for Peggy. Maybe *so* horrible that she'd been wrong. That she'd seen what she expected to see and not what was actually there, before her eyes.

"Me too." Peggy spoke with sincerity, seeing or sensing Susan's doubt. "But truth is truth, and you are not that Susan."

"How can you be certain?" She motioned

between herself and the painting. "Look at us."

"The resemblance is striking—I admit it. But there are differences and, remember, I stood at her husband's side in the cemetery and watched him bury them both." Peggy nodded. "No husband is apt to be mistaken about burying his wife *and* his son."

While that served as sufficient proof for Peggy Crane, it didn't for Susan. Mistaken identity happened all the time. To mothers and their own children even. If it could happen between a mother and child, it could happen between a husband and wife. It was possible.

"The abductors knew me. They called me Susan. I-I am Susan. And I am—" A hitch in her chest made her stutter. "I was a mother? A wife too?" Before she'd *died,* she had a family. *A family.* A deep yearning she didn't understand yawned inside her like physical starvation. It weakened her knees and had her entire body trembling.

Peggy hedged. "Susan Brandt was a wife and mother."

Her head went light. Filled with wonder, Susan glanced at Clyde. "I-I had a family. A husband and a son . . ." As the words left her mouth, the room began to spin; white spots formed before her eyes, and the air evaporated from the room. "And they think I'm . . . dead."

She crumpled to the floor in a dead faint.

• • •

Sunday, October 11

Sunrise broke on the horizon.

Edward breathed in the brisk air and let the rush of wind over his face relax him. It had been a long two days.

"This is not cool." Harry leaned against the fender of the red Jag and poured peroxide on the deep scratches Susan had clawed into his arm. He hissed in air through his teeth. "Yow!" He shot Edward a frown. "I shoulda smacked her harder."

"Get over it, Harry. The woman scratched you. She didn't put out your eye."

"It hurts, man."

"Yeah, well, right now she's feeling a lot worse."

"She should be feeling dead." Harry tossed the empty brown bottle toward the trash drum, then opened a tube of ointment with his teeth and squirted it on the red lines streaking the back of his forearm. He squinted over at Edward. "They're gonna come after us."

"We expected that." Edward looked through his dark sunglasses out on to the sun-streaked Gulf of Mexico. The water was emerald green and clear, and the air fresh, tangy with salt. He loved the view from the shore. "We'll be okay if we stick with the plan."

"Stick with the plan? She was supposed to be dead. She ain't dead, Edward." Harry lit a cigarette and exhaled a puff of smoke. "You think Chessman is going to let us live when his *subject* ain't dead?" Harry grunted. "No way."

"We're not the threat to him that she is."

"Are you snorting dope again? We're breathing. We can tie him to the first murder. We're a huge threat."

"She's worse."

"That don't mean he'll let us live, man." Harry rocked his head back on his shoulders and closed his eyes, lifting his face to the sun. "You think he will, you're making a big mistake. We'll be running forever—at least until Chessman's pit bull, Johnson, runs us down. Then we'll be dead."

"You're panicking, not thinking."

"Oh, I'm thinking plenty." Harry paced between the trash drum at the base of the pier and the front end of the Jag. "I'm thinking I signed on for murder the first time, and we did it." He stopped and stared. "I'm thinking I still ain't been paid. Why should I do anyone else for free?" He screwed the cap back on the tube of ointment and dumped it into his shirt pocket. "But mostly I'm thinking I ain't taking no needle." He kicked the drum. "So don't tell me I ain't thinking."

"Fine, but you're omitting a couple important things." Edward shot his partner a level look. "We messed up."

"Chessman messed up. He tagged her and we did his tag. We didn't do anything wrong."

"Yes, we did," Edward countered. "Chessman blew it for us, that's true. But we didn't verify it ourselves. And, like you said, we can link him to that murder. We put ourselves in this position, and unless we want to keep running from him, we need to give him a reason to keep us alive."

Harry shook his head. "He'll come after us anyway. Her disappearing made us low priority, that's all. As soon as they found her, we were right back on top of his priority list and you know it."

Edward agreed. His finding her had been simple. Her hotshot financial advisor recorded the beach house deed—stupid mistake for a man supposed to be a brainiac. It led Edward straight to him. He intercepted the guy's phone calls for a while, and sure enough, she called in. And if Edward hadn't had to strain to find her, he'd bet Harry's hide Chessman and that Johnson jerk hadn't had to strain either. "Our only hope was to neutralize her before he could. That would move us off Chessman's list. No priority."

"Neutralize her? Then why didn't we do it?"

Tempted, Edward didn't answer.

"Leaving her alive ain't neutralizing her, Edward."

"It will be. She'll disappear again."

"What if she doesn't?"

"She will."

"But what if she doesn't?" Harry insisted.

Anger rose in Edward like the water rose on the shore. "I said, *she will*."

"All right then," Harry said in a way that proved it wasn't all right at all. "But why are we risking it?"

"Because I said so." He slung down a raised hand. "Now drop it."

Harry frowned but didn't ask again.

Good. Because Edward stood dangerously close to pushing back. Hard. He stared out on the water, drank in the steady pitch of the waves hitting the shore.

Harry paced. "No. Not this time. I can't do it. My neck's on the chopping block too." He stopped just outside of striking distance. "We need to kill her, man. Not for Chessman, for us."

"For the last time, Harry, she will disappear again. She's smart and she doesn't want to wake up dead, okay?"

"You still ain't hearing me. She can identify us. That makes this not just about her. It's about Chessman and Johnson too. They'll know it and get us tossed in jail and executed for it. No, no way. Not for her or for Chessman or Johnson."

"Which is why we brought her to Florida and planted the cross and Crossroads card on her. Benjamin Brandt would have to be comatose not to put the two cases together. We got her here for that, remember?"

"Yeah. His castle in Scotland and all that."

"Which is good for her—if she's sent there, Chessman will keep her first priority. But we don't have a castle or anywhere else to hide, and no one is going to help us."

"I get that, but—"

Edward sighed. "Unless we stick to the plan to protect ourselves, we've got two choices. The needle or a bullet." Edward paused for impact. "That's it, Harry. There aren't any more. So which one do you want?"

Harry stiffened, staring at Edward a long moment. "Put that way, I guess I'll stick with the plan."

"Yeah." Edward parked his hands low on his hips. "I guess you will."

5

Ben, it's Peggy."

Benjamin Brandt rolled over and checked the bedside clock. "Didn't your mother teach you not to call people before seven, especially on Sunday morning?"

"I didn't notice the time. We had a long night."

So had he. He hadn't gotten home from Gregory's dinner party until after two o'clock. "What's up?"

"We've got a situation at the crisis center—"

Ben rolled flat on his back and stared at the

fleur-de-lis design in his recessed bedroom ceiling. Peggy knew only too well he didn't get involved at the center. Ever. "Peg—"

"You don't understand," she said before he could reprimand her on the subject for the millionth time.

She hung on to this crazy idea that if she could get him back involved at the center, he'd get right with God.

It wasn't happening.

He'd been right with God. His wife had been right with God. They had been raising their son to be right with God. And she and their son had been murdered, and their killer had gotten away—scot-free.

How did a man—*why* would a man in his position—want to get right with God? What kind of God let that happen to Susan and Christopher? Did the God Ben once fervently believed in even exist?

"I know you don't counsel or get involved in any way anymore, Ben. But this time, you are involved. It's different."

Every time Peggy pulled this "you are involved," it was always different—a different sick, twisted extortion scheme. People would do anything for money, including pretend to have important information on a dead woman and child.

"I'm not going through this again." He swiped

at his sleep-ridden eyes. Bitterness roiled in his throat, tasted as sour as brine on his tongue. Once he had believed—had *known*—had felt connected and protected. Once he had felt loved. Now, he just felt . . . forgotten.

"It is different, Ben."

"I'm hanging up now." He moved the receiver away from his ear.

"It's about Susan!" Peggy shouted, her voice carrying.

Ben stilled, his arm in midair. Chills rippled through his body, knotted his muscles, and tightened his chest. "What are you talking about?"

"Clyde Parker brought a woman into the center. She'd been carjacked and beaten and left for dead. Obviously, she wasn't. She can't remember who she is, but the two men who abducted her called her Susan. And she found a card for the center in her pocket—"

The grip on his chest cinched tighter. A few similarities to Susan's case, but . . . "All of which means—*what*? Nothing," he added before Peggy could answer. "It's a common name and people take those cards by the handfuls."

"They don't handwrite 'Susan' on the back of them and stuff them into the pocket of a woman who looks remarkably like her."

She looks like Susan?

That got Ben's attention, though it too had happened before, just over a year ago. The woman—

the fourth trying to extort money from him by pretending to have information on Susan's case—turned out to be well intentioned but crazy as a loon. She thought she had special powers and could save Ben.

He grunted. What was left to save? He'd failed as a husband, not protecting his wife; as a father, not protecting his son; as a man, not finding the killers he failed to protect them from. Who wanted to be saved? Saved for what? For whom? He could do nothing to bring them back, and without them, he had nothing. He was nothing . . .

"Ben, are you still there?"

His eyes burned. *Survivor's guilt.* That's what Harvey Talbot had called it. The good doctor said Ben needed to forgive himself; what happened wasn't his fault.

But Ben was responsible. He hadn't pulled the trigger or fired the shots that killed his family, but he'd promised to love, honor, and protect. He made vows, and unlike Harvey, who set aside his vows in a divorce, Ben had been determined to keep his forever.

Being married to Susan had been a privilege, keeping those vows, his joy in life. Then he failed her and his son and he lost them both. Lost everything that most mattered to him. He wasn't worthy of forgiveness.

If he found their killers, then maybe he could bear to go on living. That alone kept him going, made it possible to drag himself out of bed every morning and into bed every night without wishing for the permanent escape of oblivion.

He'd been forgotten, but he hadn't forgotten Susan and Christopher. He owed it to them never to forget, so he kept getting up and going to bed and spending all his time in between trying to catch their killers.

Yet he had to admit, in the dead of night when he was staring at his bedroom ceiling in the darkness, that the three years without success had driven him to the breaking point. How much longer could he bear living with his failures?

One minute at a time.

He repeated the litany in his mind. When the nightmare started, he'd worked to get through one day, but as time dragged on and despair grew, he'd gone down to an hour. More time passed, more despair led to hopelessness, and all he could stand was a minute. Without so much as a single solid lead, how much longer would it take to reduce him to fighting to keep going one second at a time?

"Ben?" Peggy sounded uncertain if he was still on the line.

"I'm here." He swallowed around a lump. "Where's the woman now?" No way could he make himself call her Susan.

"Here. She wasn't sexually violated, but she was battered and has a head injury. Lisa Harper ran some tests to be safe. So far everything's come back okay."

"Except she can't remember who she is. And she just so happens to look like my dead wife, and she just so happens to call herself by my dead wife's name." Ben sighed, soul weary.

She was another one out for money. *Thanks, Uncle Rudard.*

When Christopher was three, Ben had inherited more money than he could spend in several lifetimes from his uncle Rudard, an Englishman he'd never met who had amassed a fortune but was spiritually bankrupt. He'd charged Ben, because of his faith, to spend the money to do good things.

Those good things took form in Crossroads Crisis Center, Susan's dream.

Yet with money's perks came its liabilities and, according to police, these types of scams happened all the time to people of means.

"This is nothing new, Peggy."

"No, this has never happened. Trust me, Ben. This woman is different. You haven't seen her or talked to her, or you'd know it. Her injuries are consistent with her claims, and Lisa is convinced the woman is legitimate—and not at all like the one last year. She's sane."

Dr. Lisa Harper was an intern. Gifted, but on this, considering the situation, Ben wanted the most expertise and experience available. "What does Harvey say?" Dr. Harvey Talbot was the senior psychologist at the center. A former military officer, devoted to his job, and uncannily shrewd at detecting impostors.

"He did the first psych interview with Lisa right after they determined Susan was physically okay. Preliminary finding is Dissociative Fugue, but he wants to run more tests."

Ben glanced from the ceiling to the wall, plucked at the edge of the covers. "Temporary amnesia due to head injury or stress."

Peggy's lip smack carried through the phone like static. "Lord knows the poor woman's suffered both."

Ben's heart suffered a tug. He shunned it, refused to allow this stranger's situation to tap into his compassion. He would not, could not, be touched. He had nothing left to touch. "And you know this, of course, because she says so."

"Yes, and because between the hospital and the center I've been at this for nearly a decade, and I can read liars at fifty paces. Granted, Harvey is better at it—and when you were crisis counseling, you were good too—but I'm not a rookie and I'm no slouch. This woman isn't a liar and she's not crazy," Peggy insisted. "I also took a statement from Clyde. He found her in the woods, beaten and bloody. She couldn't even stand up on her own."

"Who did you say found her?"

"Clyde Parker."

A fuzzy image formed in Ben's mind. He could have grasped it but sensed Susan associated with it so he buried it instead. "Don't know him."

"Oh, please." Peggy had no association reservations.

Heat rushed to Ben's face. "Sorry, I can't quite place him."

"Well, you could if you'd get yourself back to church. He sat in the pew in front of you and Susan for a couple years, Ben."

The mental image snapped into sharp focus. "The older guy." The widower he and Susan had visited after his wife passed. A slow, torturous death from cancer. *Heartless disease.*

"Yes. The one who wouldn't lie if his life depended on it."

Ben remembered Clyde Parker only too well, and Peggy knew it. "Of course." Ben gave in, hoping she'd be graceful about it. "So why are you calling me?"

"Because she looks like Susan. They called her Susan. The card, and—"

"All right. All right." He caved, though not graciously. Grace was beyond him. "Where was she abducted?" She remembered she'd been carjacked, so obviously she wasn't suffering a total memory loss.

"She doesn't remember."

"Convenient." *Another scam.*

"Not really."

"Excuse me?"

"Have you ever not known who you were or had your life be a mystery to you?" Peggy asked. "It's many things, arouses a riot of emotions, Ben, but nothing about it is convenient."

Shame burned through him. He had no right to be cold and callous. No matter what he'd been through or lost, this woman could be the real thing. Her experience and injuries could be real too. It was possible. Not probable, but possible. And until he knew otherwise, he should at least be civil. Well, as close to civil as a cynical man could get.

"You're right, of course. But she's claiming to be Susan."

"Not exactly. According to Mel, when the woman arrived, she wasn't claiming to be anyone. She was asking if anyone knew her—because of the card. Then she saw Susan's painting and things changed."

His heart twisted. "Do they resemble each other that much?"

"Honestly, with all the bruises and swelling it's hard to tell. But she must think so. Even with my telling her I saw Susan at the crime scene and in her—um, after she passed, the woman still doubted she wasn't Susan." Peggy paused, then added, "I understand it, Ben. She believes what she's seeing with her own eyes, and what she sees is that she's Susan."

"Susan is dead, and we both know it." The truth hollowed his chest, and its bleak emptiness stretched and filled every crevice, smothering everything good.

"Yes, but this isn't about what we know. It's about this woman and what she knows. And I have to say, there's too much odd in so many similarities. We can't just blow this off. We know that too."

Peggy had one of her funny feelings. She didn't have to say it; she'd hinted, and after three years of experience with her, that hint was enough. Maybe the woman wasn't crazy or a con artist. Maybe she could provide the one piece of evidence or information that would lead him to Susan and Christopher's killers.

Don't dare to hope it, Ben. Don't dare.

He couldn't, wouldn't. But neither could he close that door without looking through it. "When Harvey's finished, conference this." Ben made a judgment call he could tolerate. "I want to see her myself."

"Okay. Good. It'll be probably another half hour. I've given Detective Jeff Meyers the report, but he's waiting for the docs to finish to see her himself."

"She's agreed to talk with him?"

"The docs haven't agreed to it yet. Right now, he's just asking for an eyes-on look."

"Fine, I'll wait for that. I want Harvey and Lisa to sit in."

"You're coming in to the center?" Surprise riddled her tone.

"No. Computer conference."

"You could come down. Frankly, I could use the help. There's been a terrorist attack at a mall in Mobile. We nearly had a catastrophe that would rival 9/11. Fortunately, someone at Homeland Security put the pieces together, and they nearly got the mall evacuated in time. Minimal casualties but a lot of shaken-up people."

"Terrorist attack?"

"It's all over the news. Some group called NINA is taking responsibility," Peggy said. "Emergency Management is asking us for help. They're short on counselors."

"Don't even ask." He didn't counsel anymore. He didn't go to the center anymore. Not since Susan and Christopher . . .

"Computer conference it is, then." Peggy sighed. "I'll set it up."

Somewhere deep inside, the hope that this would lead to something that revealed the truth flickered to life.

Ben snuffed it out.

He'd follow through. He'd always follow through. But his days of being suckered into hoping he wouldn't just hit another dead end were over.

He cradled the phone and pressed his hands over his eyes. A man could only survive that hard a fall so many times.

• • •

By nine thirty Sunday morning, the adrenaline surge that kept Susan's pain minimal subsided. Every conceivable part of her body ached. But at least she had the comfort of knowing she suffered no permanent physical damage—and, while being attacked had been a violation, she was spared that type of violation women most fear.

She felt safe at the crisis center; at least, she had until Dr. Harper and Dr. Talbot and Peggy Crane brought her into this sterile conference room and some guy no one bothered to introduce appeared on a computer screen placed at the far end of the long table. He came out glaring at her, and he still hadn't stopped.

He appeared to be in his early thirties, and he was indisputably a handsome man with black hair, gray eyes, and a strong, angular face that was far more interesting than perfect. The only thing that wrecked his appeal was the bitterness etched into its every line.

The glare and that bitterness warned this wasn't going to be pleasant, and right now she just didn't need the added stress of being subjected to another hostile man. As it was, she felt half a beat from jumping out of her skin.

Be patient with him.

She stilled. Digested. *Yes, Lord.* She whispered that response in her mind. When what she'd done dawned on her, she inwardly gasped. *God?*

No response. And yet she knew it had been. Here, now, God was with her.

Her heart beat fast, hard in her chest. *Be patient with him,* He'd said. Determined to try, she rubbed her gold cross necklace for comfort.

Dressed in olive green Dockers and a golf shirt, Dr. Talbot leaned forward and folded his hands on the conference table. His gold watch glinted in the strong overhead light and reflected in the table's sheen. "Ben, thank you for joining us. Shall I brief you?"

So Mystery Man's name was Ben. She sat up a little straighter. Did he work here too?

"No, thanks, Harvey." On the screen Ben kept his gaze fixated on Susan. "You brief me."

Definitely not pleasant. *Why?* "Excuse me?" She hiked her chin. "Not to be rude, but I don't even know you."

"Oh, I'm sorry," Peggy said. "Totally my fault, Susan. Benjamin Brandt owns Crossroads Crisis Center. He used to be a counselor here."

Susan Brandt's relative? He didn't look at her like a husband or a brother, and she wasn't sure what to make of that.

Peggy swiped her bobbed hair back from her face, tucking it behind her ear, and looked from Susan to her boss. "Ben, Dr. Talbot—"

"Can relax a moment." Ben tipped his chin toward Susan. "Go ahead."

His arrogance wasn't at all becoming. "I'm the

victim, Mr. Brandt. I don't believe I work for you, and from my lack of familiarity with your processes, I'm guessing I'm not a psychiatrist either. So I have no idea what you want to know."

Unless he was chiseled from stone, the man had to know her nerves were ready to snap, and aggression wouldn't help. She didn't deserve it any more than she'd deserved to be carjacked. "I don't know how to brief you."

Dr. Talbot seemed disturbed by her response. He cleared his throat. "Perhaps it would be better—"

Ben lifted a hand and Dr. Talbot fell silent.

Ben looked straight at her. "Since you arrived, everyone at my table has been trying to help you. I'm not asking for a medical briefing. I just want to hear what you have to say." His voice went tight. "I'd appreciate your answering me because I asked."

Be patient with him.

Help from his staff didn't absolve him from offering others common courtesy and respect. The urge to tell him so burned in her throat, but he had eased up a bit, so he was making an attempt not to be obnoxious. Still, she didn't want to be patient; she wanted to blister his ears.

But she couldn't do it. She trusted God more than herself. He had His reasons . . . and so must the people at the table. Not one of them had challenged Ben Brandt. Odd, because they all had been protective of her. When she'd talked to that police detective, Peggy insisted on being in the room, and both Dr. Talbot and Dr. Harper asked if she was sure she was up to talking with him.

So if God was telling her to be patient with Ben and these people weren't challenging the man, more had to be going on here than met the eye. She didn't understand it, and she didn't much like it. Reading Ben the riot act would alleviate a lot of her stress, but rolling it all together left her with a choice to make.

Whom did she follow? Her will or His?

Swallowing a groan of dissent, she made her call. She'd walk in faith. God understood all of this, and He'd make His reasons clear to her in His own time.

Shifting on her seat, she hoped that clarity would come sooner rather than later, though she'd rather not relive last night's events for the fourth time this morning.

Without the massive doses of adrenaline surging through her now as they had been then, this retelling proved the most difficult. Someone wanted her dead. *Dead.* And seeing skepticism written all over Benjamin Brandt's face didn't help a thing. Oh, he tried to hide it, but it was there, and it took its toll. Why did he have to fight himself not to be confrontational with her? She'd done nothing to him.

The back of her nose burned, her eyes stung, and her voice repeatedly cracked, grating and ragged and as raw as she felt inside. The effort was draining, but she kept pushing, relaying everything she remembered from before arriving at his center.

She finished, rubbed her arms, and willed herself to calm down. "I assume you know what's happened since I've been here and I don't have to repeat that too."

"Thank you, I do. I've been briefed on all that."

His expression had grown more sober as she'd spoken, yet something subtle she couldn't pinpoint shifted in him. Maybe he realized his attitude was unfair, or that he'd come across hard, though she doubted it. And, gauging by his grim expression, it would take reaching for the stars to think she'd touched his compassion and his anger was directed at her attackers. So what was that shift in him? What did it mean?

No sense in speculating on it. Yet she couldn't seem to help herself. Whatever it was, it chiseled away her resentment until it nearly disappeared. That made no sense whatsoever—at least, not to her.

"You've been very open, and I appreciate it," Ben said. "I have only one question—curiosity, really." His tone sounded as stiff as his broad shoulders looked. "Why didn't you go to the police?"

Oh, she'd really rather not answer that. How could she make him understand something she didn't understand herself? "I was afraid to go to the police." She slid her gaze down to the table and focused on its sheen.

"Why? Are they looking for you for something? What did you do?"

She worried her lip with her teeth, wrung her hands in her lap. "That's an absurd question to ask someone who has swiss cheese for memory."

Be patient with him.

I'm trying. Could You make him a little less suspicious of me?

No answer.

She squeezed her eyes closed and sighed. "I'm sorry. That was rude, Mr. Brandt, and I shouldn't have said it." She wished she could have said she shouldn't have even thought it, but she was a mere mortal, and that would be asking too much.

"I don't want an apology." He frowned. "I want an answer to my question."

Her resentment returned with a vengeance. She worked to leash it before she said or did something else she would have to apologize for—in her current state, she doubted she could do it twice. The words hung up in her throat. She had to force them out.

"I would if I could, but I can't tell you why I didn't go to the police because I don't know why. That's the truth. When Clyde Parker told me where I was, it scared me. It-it shook me down to my shoes." That worried her more than she let him or anyone else see.

"Then I found that business card for Crossroads in my pants pocket and saw 'Susan' written on it. That's when I remembered the abductor calling me 'Susan.' I thought maybe someone here would know me."

"You're sure you have no idea why being in Seagrove Village frightens you?"

"Swiss cheese, remember?" She tapped her temple. "I don't know a better way to describe it. Some memories are there, and some just are not. Why I'm afraid of this place is not. So, no," she said, feeling foolish, "I don't know why."

"He's not trying to be a jerk," Peggy whispered from behind her hand. "He was married to Susan."

Well, that handy bit of information explained a lot. He hadn't looked at her like a husband or brother because he wasn't her husband or brother. Yet with her looking so much like his dead wife, this interview had to be tough on him too.

When she'd come into the conference room, she believed she was *this* Susan—the one who belonged here. But after meeting Ben, she knew for fact she didn't belong, and she certainly wasn't the Susan who had been married to him. She might not know who she was, but she could never be married to a man who had practiced being hard and bitter and angry long enough to perfect it.

I don't belong here.

Where did she belong? Did she have a family? Was she married?

Am I married? Instinctively she looked to her left hand. No ring. No telltale white band of skin. But that wasn't proof of anything—there were a thousand reasons people didn't wear wedding bands anymore—but disappointment pressed down on her. Seeing a ring or even a thin strip of white skin would have made her feel less isolated and alone. Not knowing herself felt awful. No one else knowing her felt even worse. What kind of woman was she? Wasn't she worth *somebody* at least knowing?

She had to stop this. Right now. Looking at herself through such a jaundiced eye was self-defeating and destructive. Of course she was worth knowing. She was a child of God. He knew her and she knew Him. She couldn't be so awful that the entire human race had shunned her.

She wasn't Benjamin Brandt's Susan, but she could still be *a* Susan.

She could be *someone's* wife or mother or sister. Or not.

But she was definitely someone's daughter.

But whose?

Not a hint. She shivered. *Who wants me dead? Why?* She shifted on her seat. *What is my life? Where do I belong? What's my place in the world?* Lost and lacking answers, she rubbed her cross.

Dr. Harper covered her free hand on the tabletop. "Are you all right, Susan?"

She was anything but all right. "I'm fine, thank you." Swallowing hard, she looked back to Ben's computer image. "Mr. Brandt." She freed her hand and placed it in her lap. "I'm sure, being involved here, you see strange things all the time. From the way my insides are shaking, I'd be surprised if I've ever experienced anything strange." She tingled all over, tense and prickly. "I think I must live a pretty dull life. And I think I must like it that way."

"I know this is difficult," Ben said, "but I do have another question, if you don't mind."

It was a rhetorical permission request, and everyone at the conference table knew it. Steeling for another barrage, she said, "Go ahead."

"You have a head injury, and yet you didn't go to the hospital. I don't understand why not. When injured, even someone who believes they live a dull life would go to the hospital." Ben hiked a broad shoulder. "It's the logical thing to do."

So now she was illogical too? Acid churned inside her and her resentment burned deeper. She had enough to worry about without him being deliberately antagonistic. His doctors had vouched for her—and, frankly, she was frazzled. Who wouldn't be? "Excuse me?"

"Why didn't you go to the hospital? Your head

was bleeding—it had to have been to warrant the bandage on it now."

Resisting the urge to touch the white bandage above her temple, she frowned. The tape stuck to her forehead tugged at her skin, and her patience shrank, razor-thin. "I agree. When injured, going to the hospital is logical. But when you've been dragged out of your car and into the woods and beaten to a pulp, you don't always react logically." In her own defense, she couldn't resist a little jab. "Not if you're human, anyway."

Dr. Talbot cleared his throat. "Immense amounts of adrenaline can mask symptoms like pain, Ben. Susan probably didn't feel the head injury— though she needed four stitches, and I expect she's feeling it now."

The anesthetic had worn off; the wound burned and, thanks to this conversation, now her temples throbbed too. But his was a reminder to Ben to take it easy on her, and grateful for that, she slid Dr. Talbot a silent thank-you.

"I suppose." That subtle shift's hiatus ended, and the hard lines alongside Ben's mouth softened. He swiveled his gaze to the director. "Peggy, what do we have in the way of a background check on our mystery woman?"

"We're a bit hampered, Ben, considering she doesn't know who she is."

Ben. Susan studied him. It didn't suit him. It just

wasn't hard enough for someone so distant. So . . . removed.

"What about a fingerprint check?"

"Nothing yet." Peggy shot Susan an apologetic look that was mirrored on Dr. Talbot and Dr. Harper's faces.

Being discussed as though she weren't in the room irked Susan. She shifted on her chair, feeling a lot like a goldfish stuck in a bowl. The man was definitely on the warpath, looking for any reason to dispute or debunk her.

Still, she had an unshakable sense that his motive, while insulting, was more like a self-preservation tactic than meanness. And in fairness, she was probably a little hypersensitive right now. Still, he should know that. He was a former counselor who owns a crisis center. Maybe he did know . . .

How could she know that the root of his attitude was in self-preservation? How could she feel so sure of it? He'd been nothing but unreceptive, intentionally attempting to intimidate her, but— Wait a minute. That couldn't have anything to do with her. The man didn't know her any more than she knew him.

Susan.

Of course. It had to be about his Susan. She shifted positions mentally, put herself in his place, and looked at her showing up here and the surrounding circumstances. The picture looked very different from his side of the table—or from his side of the computer screen.

This was an awful ordeal for her, but it might even be a worse one for Ben. He'd lost his son and wife—a wife who looked like her and used the same name. Naturally he was rattled. He looked at her and saw someone trying to portray herself as his wife—or, considering the visual similarities, worse. He saw his wife returned from the dead . . .

Susan stroked the little gold cross.

"Peggy?" Ben's gaze riveted to the cross, and his expression turned to granite. "What is that jewelry at her neck?"

Susan stilled her fingers. The sharp edge in his tone terrified her.

Peggy glanced over. "Susan, may I see your necklace?"

"Of course." She lowered her hand to her lap.

"It's a cross." Peggy shrugged and looked from the necklace to the computer screen. "A gold cross."

Ben's face paled, as if every drop of blood instantly drained out of his head. He paused a long moment. Peggy shot Harvey a curious glance. He shrugged. Lisa Harper mimicked him, though the pen she wiggled between her fingertips stilled.

"Ben, is something wrong?" Harvey asked.

"The cross." He blinked, then blinked again. "Check the back of it. See if there's an inscription engraved on it."

Peggy turned to Susan, silently begging her indulgence. "Do you mind?"

"No, not at all." Any insight into her life would be welcome. Susan leaned toward Peggy to ease her reach.

"There is one!" Peggy's gaze danced with excitement. But as she began to read, her smile faded, then quickly morphed to horror. Without a single utterance, she fell silent.

"What does it say?" Susan and Ben asked at the same time. Did the inscription reveal her identity?

Peggy winced, darted a worried glance at Harvey and Lisa, and then finally looked back at Ben. "It says, 'Susan, Love forever, Ben.' "

Shock rippled over his face and his jaw tightened. He glared at Susan, clearly struggling not to erupt. "Lady, I don't know who you are or why you're doing this, but you'd better have a good reason for wearing my wife's cross."

She opened her mouth, but nothing came out. She couldn't think of a single reassuring thing to say.

He swerved his gaze to Peggy. "No one leaves. No one moves." He shoved back away from the computer and then stood. "I'll be right there."

Peggy's jaw dropped. Clearly she was beyond shocked.

"What's going on?" Susan asked. "I don't understand."

Peggy stammered and stuttered half-formed

thoughts Susan couldn't decipher. She touched Peggy's arm. "Slow down and just tell me why you're upset."

"I'm stunned." Her wide eyes echoed her words. "Since Susan died, Ben hasn't once stepped inside Crossroads. We've tried and tried to get him down here and involved, but he wouldn't have any part of it."

"So what does his coming here now mean?" Whatever it was, it couldn't be good for Susan. Not as angry as he'd been on hearing that inscription.

Peggy looked to Dr. Talbot, who shrugged. To Dr. Harper, who didn't move but whose face went pink.

Peggy grunted and looked back at Susan. "I'm not sure what to make of it."

"It's a good sign." Dr. Talbot nodded, lending weight to his deduction. "For three years, I've believed nothing short of a miracle could ever get Ben back through these doors." He cast a speculative glance at the cross necklace around her neck, then back into Susan's eyes. "Maybe nothing has . . ."

Susan didn't feel like a miracle. She felt afraid. An icy chill settled deep in her bones. How had she gotten his dead wife's necklace?

Gregory Chessman sat at his desk in his home office, debating whether or not to phone his secret partner and inform him that their problem had resurfaced. He hated to do it. His partner was invaluable at paving the way and keeping law enforcement out of his way during crucial times. And his connections provided the transport needed to get the right people to their right positions to perform their designated duties. Those connections alone were critical and not apt to be found elsewhere in such a protected position. But beyond all that, Gregory never wanted to relive what he'd experienced three years ago. That text message still haunted him.

YOU KILLED THE WRONG WOMAN. DISCUSSION OVERHEARD, BUT THE VICTIM WAS NOT AT THE PARTY. CORRECT SUBJECT IS BETHANY'S NIECE.

He'd stared at the text message in utter horror. Remembering it now, he broke into a cold sweat. Their sensitive bioterrorism discussion had been overheard, but not by the woman he had identified as hearing it.

No. No, he could not—*would not*—bear the humiliation of admitting such a mistake again. But if his partner discovered the truth, this time Gregory could be putting far more than discovery of this incident in jeopardy. He could end up on the wrong side of NINA.

"Sir?" Paul Johnson walked in. His expression warned of more bad news.

Gregory blanked out his computer screen and braced to receive it. He had worked so hard for so long. Everything couldn't unravel now. Not now. "Tell me something good."

"I wish I could." Paul held a small box in his hand. "Unfortunately, the news is bad."

The bottom dropped out of Gregory's stomach. "How bad?"

"We've lost the subject, sir." Paul cringed. "She was in New Orleans, selecting a location for a new center."

"Is it significant?"

"Just another of her do-gooder projects for kids, Mr. Chessman. Nothing at all unusual about it."

"I see." Gregory respected that, being of a charitable nature and especially eager to assist efforts that enabled kids to forge a better life for themselves. He knew the value of that, having received aid early on. Otherwise, he wouldn't have survived long enough to earn scholarships, much less his current, admittedly opulent, life.

Paul adjusted his glasses. "Security warned her not to leave the hotel at night—bad neighborhood."

"Why is she staying in a hotel in a bad neighborhood?"

"To get a firsthand view of what's going on. That's typical of her."

"It's foolish." Gregory coughed. "She knows that, I'm sure, but does it anyway."

"Yes sir." A hint of admiration actually resonated in Paul's tone. "Then she just disappeared."

"What about an APB?" he asked, though Paul would have seen to it that an all-points bulletin had been issued immediately.

"Done within fifteen minutes. Our recruit, Richard—"

Gregory cut him off. "I don't want to know his name."

"Of course not, sir. Our recruit is looking for her or her car, but nothing's turned up yet on either. Our man on the security staff notified us before she left the hotel, but our recruit was too far away to manage a successful intercept. He mapped the grid but failed to find her."

"Why was he out of range?"

"He'd picked up a lead on Edward and Harry and was tracking it." Paul's gaze slid to the floor for a brief second. "It's my fault, Mr. Chessman. I instructed him not to involve himself. The gang was to handle her. I wanted him to have an iron-clad alibi. My first priority was to limit the exposure of anyone remotely close to us."

Gregory couldn't fault that reasoning, and he'd bet neither the recruit nor the hotel staff knew who was paying them to monitor the subject or why. That was even better.

Paul plucked a staple from the floor and tossed it into the trash. "Our recruit is still searching, and he's hiring trusted help to assist him. I've run a preliminary check on the ones he's taken on so far. They're reasonable risks, and they know nothing of us, of course. So far, though, it's as if she vanished into thin air."

Gregory digested that, pinching his lower lip between his fingertip and thumb. "You're sure the subject wasn't aware she was being watched?"

"Positive."

He leaned forward at his desk and folded his hands atop the blotter. "Then she didn't just vanish or disappear. She had help."

"That's my deduction, sir." Standing beside the leather visitor's chair, Paul thumbed the top of a small box he'd been carrying when he came in.

What was in it? "The question is, did she want help, or was it forced on her?"

Paul hedged. "I can't yet answer that with any degree of certainty."

Gregory put his odds on force. Edward had to know she'd surfaced. And he had to know that her surfacing not only made her a liability, but made him and Harry greater liabilities too.

Harry wouldn't connect those dots.

Edward wouldn't miss them.

Gregory sighed. "Find her, Paul. Now. And shut her up before Edward and Harry make a mess of this too." Gregory narrowed his gaze. "I'm confident one of our NINA allies made the anonymous call here to warn us, but we'd better cover ourselves now." He only hoped that caller didn't prove to be Alik Demyan. "We can't afford additional complications, particularly not with them.

The subject or Edward and Harry could land us in FSCF doing ten to twenty. But NINA doesn't use prisons. It uses death."

"Prison is bad enough." Paul shuddered. "Do you know what they do to men like me in there?" He rocked back and forth on his feet. "I can't do time. Not even for you."

Mentioning the Florida State Correctional Facility and NINA had the intended impact. "Then I suggest you remove the obstacles—the sooner the better—because, frankly, Paul, I won't do time without you."

Paul's Adam's apple bobbed in his bony throat. "Just so we're clear, sir. You want them all taken out? The subject, Edward, and Harry?"

No way was Gregory walking into that admission. "I want them neutralized."

Paul pushed, too clever for his own good. "By neutralized you mean dead, right?"

"I'd never order anyone killed, Paul. I'm a philanthropist. My mission in life is to help people." Gregory covered himself—things like this tended to end up as bargaining chips in trials. "You're a resourceful man. Surely there's another way to neutralize them."

"None as expeditious—or as fail-safe—as elimination." Paul turned to leave the office.

"Paul." Gregory called out as Paul's hand curled around the doorknob. When he looked back, Gregory issued his real instructions. "Do permanently resolve this situation. As a rule, I detest complications. On this matter, I won't tolerate them." They were a luxury he couldn't afford—and one NINA wouldn't forgive or forget. "Deal with the subject first. She can do us the most damage."

"Yes sir."

Paul's cell phone chimed. He checked caller ID and his expression brightened. "Our recruit, sir." Holding up a wait-a-second finger, he took the call. "Talk to me."

A second later, he mumbled something Gregory couldn't hear, then hung up and looked over, his eyes glinting. "Sir, we've found her."

"Excellent." Soon this matter would be firmly in hand. He took a sip of steaming tea and then set the fragile cup back on its saucer. "What is in the box?"

"Oh. I forgot, sir." Paul walked back and passed the box to Gregory. "Something to atone for the gaff of losing our subject."

Gregory opened it. Inside lay a bloody finger. He glanced up at Paul and waited.

"Our recruit assures me he won't be making any further errors."

"Excellent." Gregory tossed the finger and box into the shredder, then reached over and lifted his teacup, pausing to admire the fine bone china and its delicate pattern. *Eclectic. Expensive. Exquisite.* All his favorite things. "About the subject, Paul. What will you do?"

He straightened the knot in his tie, his glasses, and then looked Gregory right in the eye. "The only thing I can do to assure she doesn't put us in prison."

"What exactly is that?"

Grudgingly respectful and unapologetic, Paul stared at him, not in the least repentant. The strong light glinting on his glasses dulled in comparison to the white-hot fire burning in his eyes.

"I'm going to kill her."

6

Ben let his gaze drift across Crossroads Crisis Center's facade.

It looked innocent enough. Just a beige and brown mottled-brick building sitting in the village proper with a wide door set beneath a white-trimmed alcove and welcoming glass windows that stretched in broad arcs nearly all the way across its front. A discreet brass plate with its name hung to the right of the door, and day-and-night electric candles with simulated flames burned in the upper arch of each window.

Susan had paid a small fortune for those candles. She'd been militant, intricately planning everything even tangentially connected to the center and demanding that down to its most minute detail it be welcoming and in no way intimidating.

Her devotion had been a source of enormous

pride, but he would be disingenuous if he didn't admit, at least to himself, that his pride was tainted by regret at knowing what few others knew: the force that drove Susan to militancy.

She hadn't been abused, just deprived of peace. In some ways, that could be equally difficult. The center was her world. She'd worked for years to get everything just right. Then just three weeks before seeing her dream become a reality, she'd been murdered.

Three lousy, heart-wrenching weeks. The worst three weeks of Ben's life.

Again feeling the loss of everything that mattered to him, he fisted his hands in his slacks pockets and stared at the building's gently sloping roof, shaking inside. He couldn't do this. His gaze slid down to the entry. He couldn't make himself walk through that door . . . and remember.

His personal Camelot was no more. And never would be again.

Standing on the sidewalk, he glared at the candle flame in the arch above the door. Why did this have to happen now? Just last night, he'd *finally* accepted a social invitation that didn't offer the promise of some information on Susan's case. It'd taken him three years to be able to do it. Three years . . . and the very next day, this woman shows up.

Wearing Susan's necklace.

Calling herself Susan.

Hating all of the conflicting emotions assaulting him, wishing for numbness again, he briefly closed his eyes. *Don't feel. Just don't feel. If you don't feel, the pain won't rip you apart. You can keep looking for answers.*

Once he'd lived for Susan and Christopher. Now he lived to search for answers. Numb, he could keep going. He could do this. He could go inside and demand answers. The necklace was real, not a sham. Susan had always worn it. It had disappeared at the accident and only reappeared now—on this woman's neck. And where it had been in the interim could hold answers.

Susan and Christopher deserved answers.

Stay focused. Just stay focused. Ignore the woman. She's going to look like Susan, but she's not. He swallowed a knot in his throat. *She's . . . not Susan.*

Taking in a steadying breath, he pulled his fisted hands from his pockets, jerked open the glass door, and then strode inside.

The entrance had been designed to resemble a family room rather than a reception area, and Susan had been right about the warm blue and cream—the colors, textures, and printed fabrics were soothing.

Melanie Ross, the youngest Crossroads staff member at twenty, sat behind her chunky desk. "Mr. Brandt?"

He glanced over at her. Framed by her spiky

black hair, Melanie's face looked stark, and her shock at seeing him was evident. "What are you doing here?"

Avoiding the portrait of Susan, Ben kept his gaze fixed on the girl. "Are they in the conference room, Mel?"

"Y-yes sir." She pulled herself to her feet. "But you can't go back—I mean, you shouldn't. They're with a patient."

He cut across the tiled floor, skirted a plush floral-printed settee, and clipped a stack of magazines on the edge of the table. They splayed across the table but didn't spill onto the rug or the tiled floor.

"Mr. Brandt . . ." Melanie's voice faded.

When he got to the hallway leading to the conference room and private offices, Mel intercepted him. "Mr. Brandt," she said in hushed tones. "You really can't go in there right now. Mrs. Crane and the docs are interviewing a patient who came in last night. She's had a bad, bad experience, and her morning's been rough."

Thanks to that patient, Ben's morning hadn't been a whole lot better. "It's okay, Mel." He moved on down the hallway. His heart thudded erratically against his ribs. Susan's presence here was overwhelming. Somehow she had infiltrated every wall, and though he logically knew it was impossible, he half-expected her to step through one of the office doors.

Stop it. Susan is dead and buried. She's not here. Not anymore.

Outside the conference room, he hesitated and his gaze automatically slid farther down the hall to the etched-glass chapel doors. Prayer was common here, an integral part of the center's work. But prayer hadn't saved his family, and it hadn't spared Ben from loss or grieving.

Bitterness burned his throat. He looked away. The woman on the other side of the door looked like Susan. He had to be prepared for that, and not let it affect him.

How had she gotten Susan's necklace?

"But, Mr. Brandt," Mel persisted.

The phone rang.

Mel didn't move.

Ben looked over at her and saw her defiance. She intended to stop him from entering the conference room, regardless of whether or not he signed her paychecks. He nearly smiled. "Relax, Mel. They're waiting for me. Go on now and get the phone. It could be someone in trouble."

Relief swept over her face. She turned on her heel and began moving. "Knock first. Surprises aren't good for Susan right now, and if Mrs. Crane gets upset with you, don't blame me."

Though it had nothing to do with Mel, Mrs. Crane was already upset—likely nearly as upset as Ben. Peggy had been Susan's dearest friend for most of her life. What a shock it must have been for her when that woman walked in—

No. *No.* He couldn't afford to think of that now. He couldn't afford to think about her. He had to focus on one thing: Susan's cross.

Digging deep for will and sheer grit, Ben steeled himself and prepared to battle the demons of hell to determine the truth about that. Then he opened the door and walked into the conference room.

Susan gripped the arms of her chair, not knowing what to expect. In the flesh, Ben Brandt was larger, more determined, and even more grim-faced than he'd been on the computer screen—and on it, he'd scared her. Now, he had her shaking again.

Without a word to anyone in the room, he walked over and stopped beside her chair, then hiked an eyebrow.

Not sure why, she nodded. He lifted the cross hanging at her neck in his large hand, flipped it over, and then read the inscription.

Pain flashed through his eyes. He clamped his jaw and jerked his hand. The delicate chain broke.

"Ouch!" Her neck burned. She rubbed it with her fingertips.

Peggy Crane and Lisa Harper gasped.

Dr. Talbot stood up. "Ben!"

"Sit down, Harvey," Ben said without sparing him a glance. Crushing the cross that had given her comfort in his clenched fist, Ben glared down at her. "Where did you get this?"

Susan resisted the urge to slide out of her chair and put something substantial between them. "I-I don't know. I told you the cross and card were in my pocket when I came to in the woods. I put the cross on because it made me feel better."

"Save the nonsense." His voice thundered through the room. "I want the truth."

"I told you the truth."

"Ben, you don't understand." Dr. Talbot scooted back his chair, stood, and started around the edge of the table. "Don't do this."

"I understand perfectly." A muscle in his jaw ticked. "This woman walks into Susan's center, wearing Susan's jewelry, pretending to be Susan, and you tell *me* 'don't do this'?" He guffawed. "What's wrong with *you*?"

"You don't . . ." Dr. Talbot stopped. "She doesn't know—"

"She does." Shoving the cross into his slacks pocket, Ben turned back to her. "I don't know why you're doing this to me, but I'm not buying into your game. If it's money you're after, forget it. You're not getting a dime from me."

He thought she was faking all this for money. How dare he? How ridiculous—and insulting. Surely she would never do anything like that. What believer would ever do anything remotely close to that?

Digging her nails into her palms stung and left marks, but it was all that enabled her not to scream at him, to keep her tone soft. "I didn't ask you for money."

"You haven't yet," he shot back. "Consider it a timesaver."

Her back went ramrod stiff and her voice constricted just as tight. "You'd be prudent to wait until an offense against you has been committed before expressing outrage, Mr. Brandt. That is, unless you're fond of humbling yourself with apologies for infractions that exist only in your mind. Or maybe you like being considered arrogant and rude and as cold-hearted as a stone."

"Your offense is right here." He pulled out the cross and then dangled it between them. "At best, you're a thief. At worst . . ."

That was more than enough. She narrowed her eyes. "Be careful, Mr. Brandt."

He stopped suddenly, his face contorted, and his voice dropped low, menacing. "I don't take well to threats."

"Neither do I."

He held her glare. Finally, it seemed to hit him that he had been threatening her, and he stilled, as if torn between civility and outrage. "Be warned," he said, opting for outrage. "I'm going to ask you once—only once—then I'm going to call the police."

"You're doing it again, Mr. Brandt."

"Doing what?"

"Assuming I won't answer before you ask the question." She folded her arms across her chest. "Do you always react to your assumptions before the events occur, or am I a special case because I survived an abduction and beating and made the sorry mistake of coming to your center for help?"

That set him back on his heels. He recovered quickly and clenched his teeth. "Where did you get Susan's cross?"

Susan stood and faced him toe-to-toe. The urge to scream at him coursed through her with a force so strong it nearly knocked her to her knees. She fought to hold back.

God, if You want me to be patient with this man, then You've got to help me, because what I most want at the moment is to slap him, and I'm not sure I'm strong enough to resist the temptation.

Ben didn't budge. He stood feet spread, arms crossed, waiting for her response.

"I've already answered that question. But because you're clearly out of control, I'll do so again." She paused to let that blunt remark sink in. Maybe he'd turn himself around, though she wasn't banking on it. "I don't know where I got the cross. I was unconscious. I had it and the card when I woke up. I put it on. That's it. The whole truth as I know it."

"So you're sticking with your disgusting memory-loss story."

"I don't have a lot of choice." Her hands shook. She clenched them into fists at her sides, lifted her chin, and looked up into his eyes. "It's the truth."

"I don't believe you!"

More afraid than she'd been when the abductor had shattered her car window, she stilled. Everything in her warned her to back out of his reach, but she was too afraid to move.

"Ben!" Peggy Crane stepped between them. "That's more than enough. Back off."

He turned his glare on Peggy. "This isn't your concern."

"This is very much my concern. I'm the director of Crossroads Crisis Center, and that makes everything that goes on in it my business. You will not come in here and browbeat a victim. Now, calm down or I'll call Detective Meyers in and have you removed."

His jaw dropped. "Don't be ridiculous."

"That's my exact advice to you." She turned her back on him and looked at Susan. "Are you all right?"

"I'm fine." Her knees wobbled. If they folded and she fell flat on her face, she'd never forgive herself.

Peggy gave her arm a gentle squeeze. "Lisa, why don't you walk Susan down to the ladies' room so she can freshen up a bit and get rid of some of the mud? I'm sure it itches."

It did. "I'll be fine on my own," she said,

knowing somehow it was true. Had she been on her own a lot? Or had she wished she was but wasn't? *Blank slate.*

"It's no trouble." Lisa rose.

Susan waved her back to her seat. "Stay. I need a few minutes to myself." She looked at Ben, hoping she wasn't taking her life in her hands by speaking to him. "I'm sorry for my part in whatever is happening here, but I am more mystified by it than you." Her mouth stone dry, she licked her lips and removed all emotion from her voice. "That said, I'm going to say something to you— only once—and I suggest you remember it."

She paused to make sure she had his full attention. "I understand that you're under duress and that stress makes people do things they wouldn't ordinarily do. I'm under duress too. But I have suffered the indignities you've shoved on me with the most dignity and grace I could manage. I agree that I fall really short of perfect. But at least I've made the effort. You haven't."

"This is what I need to remember? A lecture?"

"No, Mr. Brandt. This is what you need to remember." She dipped her chin. "Don't scream at me again. Not now, not ever. You may not respect me enough to restrain yourself, but I respect myself too much not to restrain you."

His jaw clamped shut; his eyelids snapped to slits.

She gave him a moment to get a grip and then

went on. "I do see the same multiple connections you see. I intend to find out who I am, and I hope that includes gaining some insight on your wife's cross and why it was in my pocket. If you want me to share what I learn, then you need to adjust your attitude toward me, because I've tolerated all the indignity and disrespect from you I'm going to."

Forestalling any response, she turned to Peggy. "I saw a chapel down the hall. If and when you want me, after I freshen up, I'll be there"—she spared Ben a glance—"praying for patience."

Glass shattered.

From the reception area, Mel screamed.

"Stay here." Ben shot past Susan, then rushed out the door.

Something exploded.

"Mr. Johnson?"

His New Orleans recruit. "Yes?" His cell phone at his ear, Paul stepped out onto the terrace and checked to make sure none of the staff was lurking. He wasn't happy about the recruit knowing his name, but when you cut off a man's finger, you get close.

"Something disturbing has come to light here this morning." He paused, then added, "One of my men found a tap on my line."

Very disturbing news. "How long has it been there?"

"Long enough that some of our conversations might have been intercepted."

"I'm not going to ask how this happened—I don't care. I want to know *who* made it happen and that you've neutralized any threat."

"Yes sir. I'll let you know as soon as the problem's resolved."

Paul flipped his phone shut and flattened his mouth to a slash that had his jaw aching. Losing a finger hadn't made the man more cautious, but he had to be worried now about losing his head. He should be—and he'd have good reason to worry *after* he corrected the problem.

Paul went back inside. Maybe Chessman had been smart about using throwaway cells and text messages. No voiceprints. No indisputable proof of who had sent them.

That he had could be helpful . . .

7

"Mel!" Ben got to the front of the building first, scanned frantically through flame and smoke, and spotted her near a group of sofas. "Are you hurt?"

"It won't work!" Mel wrestled with a fire extinguisher nearly as large as she was. She pushed and pushed on the release button. "Nothing's happening!"

Ben took it from her, released the pin, and began

spraying foam on the blaze burning the rug under the table and the flaming magazines atop it.

Billowing acrid smoke stung his nostrils, burned his eyes. Soon, two other streams flanked his, and the hiss of fire fell to the gush of retardant. Minutes more and the smoke settled enough for him to see beyond the end of his nose. Harvey Talbot stood beside Ben. That woman—he refused to call her Susan—was at the far end of the extinguisher line, the canister strap slung across her chest.

She might not know who she was, but she knew how to use an extinguisher. At some time during the process, she'd torn loose the bandage on her head. Her wound had started bleeding again; fresh blood soaked her blond hair and trickled down her face to her jaw.

The last of the flames snuffed out.

"Is everyone okay?" Peggy yelled out, fluttering around, surveying the damage. Once-white foam clung to her shoes, and shattered glass crunched on the tile under her feet. Some of the stinging smoke drafted out through the broken window, but enough remained that her eyes were red rimmed and watering.

By rote, everyone answered: Mel, from her desk, the phone at her ear. Harvey and Lisa, both within sight. Lisa looked flushed and worried, no doubt thinking her crazy stepfather had gone nuts again and done this. Everyone looked uninjured

. . . except that woman. She stood statue-still, staring at the soot-streaked floor, the extinguisher still in her hand.

Lisa stepped toward her. "Susan, are you all right?"

"I'm fine." She frowned at the damage, clearly anything but fine.

"You're bleeding." Lisa coughed, then coughed again. "I need to check your wound and put on a fresh bandage. Let's get to the exam room."

"No." Ben set his extinguisher down near Mel's desk. "Stay with the group."

"Ben's right. This could have been a diversion." Peggy moved toward the exam room. "I'll get the supplies you need."

"Go with her, Harvey," Ben said. "Run a perimeter check."

"You've got it." Harvey fell into step with Peggy.

"You handled that extinguisher like a pro, Susan." Lisa caught the woman by the arm and led her to a chair in a sitting area away from the damage. "Let's get you seated for a second."

She sat down, seemingly unaware she'd been swaying on her feet. Ben studied her. Shock, maybe?

Harvey returned from the back offices. "No other breach to the building."

That was a relief. Peggy's comment about diversions had crossed his mind too. *Let go of it, Ben.*

It wasn't a diversion. Everyone's fine. He skimmed the damage—more mess than structural damage—and his gaze automatically pivoted back to the woman.

Now that the immediate danger had passed, he saw things a little more objectively. Pale, slumped from exhaustion, and he couldn't mistake the horror haunting her eyes. It was all reflected on her face—a face, sans the bruises and cuts and smudges of blood and soot, remarkably like Susan's. She was shaking too. Good thing Lisa had her sitting. There was no way her knees wouldn't buckle.

Lisa spoke softly to her; he couldn't make out the words, but the woman didn't appear to be making them out either. She gave no outward sign she heard a word. Her lips didn't move, though her jaw quivered and tears brimmed in her eyes, then spilled in jagged trails down her cheeks.

Smoke? Or delayed reaction to being involved in another attack? He rested a hip on a table against the wall. Depended on whether or not there'd been a first attack. The beating had been real enough; her injuries proved that. But had her carjacking and abduction been real or manufactured?

She'd convinced Lisa, Harvey, and Peggy. They sided with her against him. He had always trusted their judgment implicitly, but this was an atypical situation. He didn't dare to even trust his own.

"Hot line call," Mel said.

"I'll take it," Harvey told her, then took off down the hall.

Ben watched him go, then looked back at the woman. *No change. Silent tears.*

If she had been working with someone else to pull a scam, then obviously that person had turned on her. Frankly, though, that didn't fit. She'd acted to protect his property and her shock now wasn't faked. No one was that good an actress.

She could be the real thing.

And he'd treated her . . . He didn't even want to think about how he'd treated her. He didn't want to think at all. Sweating profusely, he swiped at his brow and then turned to Mel. "Did you get through to the fire department and sheriff's office?" They'd need both for the insurance reports.

"On their way." She swiped her nose.

He was tempted to do the same. The stench of burned fabric and paper permeated everything. "Thanks." Ben gave Mel a pat on the shoulder. She was young and unorthodox and she dressed a little funky, but she was one of the center's best success stories. On her own and trying to make something good of her life, she had earned everyone's respect and admiration. "Good initiative."

She responded with a wobbly smile.

"Here you go." Peggy passed Lisa the supplies, then joined Mel and him.

"You okay?" Peggy asked while conducting her own visual inspection.

Since Mel had shown up at the center nearly two years ago, they'd all pseudoadopted her. The kid didn't have anyone else. Even before she had run away from her drug-addict mother and stepfather, she'd been on her own. For all intents and purposes, she'd had to be self-reliant since she was eight years old and her real father died.

Mel stood with her hand soothing her abdomen. "Yeah, I'm okay, Mrs. Crane."

"Everything in order back there?" Ben asked Peggy, motioning toward the exam rooms.

"Yes. Damage is restricted to just the reception area. It appears from the glass shatter that they tossed something burning through it. A little fire and smoke damage right in here and up through the attic, but otherwise it's just the glass and foam mess to clean up. Harvey ran a perimeter check, but he's taking a look outside as a precautionary measure."

Ben surveyed the damage. If someone wanted to cause damage, this was a poor effort. "Better alert the cleaning crew. They can get started right after the sheriff and fire chief are done." He motioned to the plate-glass window, half of which now lay in soot-stained shards on the floor. "Better get Clyde Parker to come in and board up that window. I'm assuming he still does handyman repairs."

Peggy tilted her head. "Would that be the Clyde Parker you couldn't place a couple hours ago?"

Caught red-handed, Ben confessed. "Yes, that would be the one."

"Ah. Good." Peggy smacked her lips. "Your memory is returning."

His memory hadn't left. It just hurt too much to recall things once normal in his life with Susan and Christopher—a fact Peggy knew well, and she still attempted to shove Ben through the past into a future. What she failed to understand was that he had no incentive. The past was rich and full, the future bleak and empty. Why stretch for a bleak and empty future?

He slammed the door shut on his thoughts. "Mel, did you see anything?"

"The car stopped right out front." Hand at her jutted hip, she pointed through the window near the center of the reception area. "The guy in the front seat on the passenger's side was straining his neck to see in here. He glanced left, like he was talking to the driver. A second later, he sticks this thing out the window, lights it on fire, and then hurls it at the window. *Boom,* it explodes, and glass and stuff flies everywhere."

Mel sucked in a shuddery breath. "Then the fire and smoke—I didn't see where he went. I just had to try to put out the fire." She pursed her lips, looking spitting mad and remorseful. "I should have yelled sooner or checked for his tag number or something, but it never dawned on me he'd actually throw a bomb into the building."

"He?" Ben asked for verification. "So, the passenger who threw the bomb was a man?"

"Definitely."

"What about the driver?"

"I don't know." She paused to watch Clyde Parker come through the door, carrying two bags of burgers, then added, "I didn't see the driver."

"I saw him."

Ben turned to Clyde. "Where were you?"

"On the sidewalk, walking back from Burger Barn. The car passed right by me." Clyde lifted the fragrant bags of burgers that smelled a whole lot better than the burn and chemicals from the extinguisher. "I figured Susan had to be starving. She hasn't eaten a thing today and it's nearly noon."

"What did the driver look like?"

"Not too big, dressed kind of like Harvey does in those golf shirts. Late twenties, maybe a little older." Clyde shrugged. "When you get to be my age, it's harder to tell. Most everybody looks like kids. The driver had dark hair too. Did I mention that? I'd guess he's fussy about his appearance. Clean-cut and everything."

"The guy I saw—the passenger—was older." Mel sniffed. "About like you, Mr. Brandt."

No offense was intended, and Ben tried not to take any. A decade and a half made a lot of difference to someone barely twenty.

Oblivious, Mel went on, swiping an ash smudge from her black slacks. "Red hair. More redneck. Kind of cute, but in a goofy way."

Vague but apparently close enough, gauging by Peggy's expression. "The descriptions match the woman's?" Ben asked, referencing her alleged abductors.

Peggy nodded and then relayed the descriptions that the woman had given her and she'd reported to the police.

Mel confirmed them, and then Clyde added his opinion. "Sounds like the same guys to me, Ben."

He frowned. So the men who allegedly abducted her knew she was alive and here—and they had come back to finish the job? It made sense, particularly if they'd left her for dead in the woods. They wouldn't want her to identify them. "What kind of car was it, Mel?"

"I'm not into cars." She shot him an apologetic look. "About all I can tell you is that it was red and looked expensive."

Expensive to Mel could be anything with a windshield and without rust to a Lamborghini.

"Very cool, though." She dipped her chin. "That's why I noticed the redneck in the first place. He didn't fit, you know? In a pickup truck? Yeah. But in a sweet thing like that sporty dream machine? No way. Yet," she slid her gaze to Clyde, "from what you say, the driver fit. It must have been his car."

"I suppose you could say he fit. He drove it like demons were on his heels—nearly sideswiped your SUV, Ben—but he didn't strike me as out of place in the car." Clyde scratched the back of his neck. "If it's his, though, I'd guess it's new."

"Why is that?"

"The guy shifts like a novice."

Sporty. Dream machine. "Mel, you said it was red." When she nodded, a sinking feeling punched him. "You're sure about that?"

"Definitely."

Ben looked to Clyde for confirmation.

"I'm sure. It was red."

Red. Sleek. A sporty, cool dream machine. Tense, Ben walked over to the woman. The color was back in her face, and she'd taken off the strap. The extinguisher was on the floor near her feet. "You okay?"

"I'm fine." She sounded fragile and frail but determined to put on a strong front.

"Good." Ben glanced at Lisa, who signaled that the woman really was okay, which freed Ben to ask the question nagging at him. "When you were abducted, what kind of car were you driving?"

"My Jeep," she said, then paused. "No, wait. That's wrong. It wouldn't start." She hesitated a second, flinching as if recalling her abduction. "It was a Jag."

Ben planted his feet to keep from staggering back a step. "You were driving a Jag?"

119

"It wasn't mine." Frustration lined her face. "In my mind, I see this man handing me the keys, but I don't know him." She squeezed her eyes shut, then reopened them. "I don't know. There's nothing familiar about him, and I don't feel anything when I see his face. He must have been a stranger."

"A rental, maybe?" Lisa suggested.

The woman shrugged. "No idea."

Ben prodded. "But you're sure it was a Jag?"

She paused; uncertainty flitted across her face and then faded. "That's what I recall, Mr. Brandt." Her gaze darted back and forth, as if she was searching her mind. It stopped suddenly. "Yes, I'm positive it was a Jag."

His skin crawled and he broke into a cold sweat. "Um, what color was it? Do you remember that?"

"It was red."

Red. A red Jag.

Just like Susan's . . .

"Tell me again why we're crazy enough to be driving this Jag to pipe bomb a crisis center in broad daylight." Harry looked over at Edward from the passenger's seat of the car. "The only person in there was that kid at the front desk."

"She isn't the only one in there. She's the only one you could see. The whole staff is in." Edward slammed the gearshift into first, then stomped the gas pedal. The tires screeched, a burning smell

120

filled the car, and finally the tires grabbed on to pavement. Fishtailing, he swerved to avoid hitting Ben Brandt's SUV, then wrangled control of the high-performance vehicle and took off down Gramercy headed toward Gulf Drive.

"We want them to see this Jag because it's our proof we tried to save her." Edward sent his slow-witted partner a frown. "I'll explain later, when I have more time."

"Well, that's the first time I've bombed a place to save somebody." Harry harrumphed. "You're losing it, man."

"I'm saving your sorry behind."

"Right. Fine. But slow down now, will you?" Harry strapped on his seat belt, clicked the buckle into place. "You drive like a maniac."

"I am a maniac." Harry, fool that he was, had no idea that the woman was inside. Maybe it was better that way. "I'm also alive, and I'd like to stay alive. In case you've forgotten, Chessman and his henchmen are opposed to that."

"They'll let us live if we kill her."

Edward made a right at the light, then headed east. He could keep driving, right out of town, but Chessman would just send his attack dog, Johnson, after them. "Harry, once in a while I wish you would engage your brain." Edward tightened his grip on the steering wheel. "She's going to die. Chessman will see to that. Which leaves us with two choices. One, we stay out of

121

the way and let him. Or, two, we let her know someone else is coming."

"Why would we want to let her know he's coming? She can identify us, Edward." Harry rubbed at his head. "Sometimes you don't make a lick of sense."

"Sometimes you act as if you don't have a lick of sense. If she dies, we're the first people they're going to suspect. We abducted her, knocked her around, and they'll have our descriptions. We want her taken out of play but not dead. And if Chessman gets her, we don't want to go down for her murder."

The light dawned on Harry's face. "Okay, you want her to know someone else is after her—someone besides us so we don't get blamed. I get it. When Chessman tries to make the hit, she's ready. He—or his goons—get tagged or reported."

Finally. "Yes, and *them* is officially not *us.*"

"That makes sense. But if she reports them after reporting us, Chessman won't dare go after her himself. He'll need us to take her out"—Harry grinned—"and that gets us off his priority list." He went quiet. "But what I don't get is why we don't want her dead."

"You pick up on things at the most inopportune times, Harry."

"You're not answering my question."

"I have my reasons. Let's leave it at that."

Harry frowned. "Let's don't."

"It's personal." Edward checked his rearview mirror, changed lanes. "That's all I'm saying." Hopefully, it wasn't too much.

"Personal?" Harry grunted and waved a hand. "Like what? Did you fall for her or something?"

"No, it's not like that." Edward refused to look at his partner. "Personal means personal."

"It ain't when you're talking about my backside kissing the electric chair, man."

Edward didn't like it, but Harry had a point. "Okay, that's fair. If we can let her live, fine. If not, we kill her. How's that?"

"She's gotten to you." Harry's jaw fell open. "I can't believe it."

"Don't be stupid. She hasn't gotten to me. The situation's gotten to me. Chessman stiffing us on our money—that's gotten to me. But she hasn't gotten to me."

"Whatever." Harry thought a minute, chomping on a wooden toothpick. "Okay, we let her live for now. But the first time it looks dicey, she's going down."

"Agreed."

"And if she goes down, we make sure Chessman's blamed for her murder. That'll teach him to stiff us." Harry clapped a hand to this thigh. "Yeah, I'm liking this. He gets smacked and we walk, free and clear."

"Not exactly."

"Ah, the carjacking." Harry shrugged. "That's easy enough for us to beat in court."

Easier than a murder rap. That was true enough. "You're getting it now." It'd taken his partner a while to catch up, but when he did, he appreciated the genius in Edward's plan. Of course, Harry had stopped short of Edward, who had gone a couple steps further, but no sense in passing it on now and confusing Harry.

Harry chuckled. "You're smarter than you look."

"You're not." Edward let out a deep sigh. "But you are my partner." Harry wasn't long on brains, but he was predictable, loyal, and as strong as an ox.

"We've only got one problem." Worry rippled over Harry's face. "Chessman's lost her. How can he attempt a hit if he can't find her?"

"Ordinarily, that would be problematic." His wiretap had paid off. Huge. "But I've already taken care of it."

Harry's crooked smile returned. "How?"

"Paul Johnson recruited a private investigator down in New Orleans to shadow her. When we abducted her, Johnson's recruit lost her. He put out word he needed help to find her."

"Who put out word? Johnson or the recruit?"

"The recruit."

"I see."

"Not yet, you don't." Edward bit his lower lip. "I got hired."

Harry shifted in his seat. "Oh no, Edward. I ain't believing you did that." He reared back and dragged his hands over his skull. "Are you nuts? Johnson letting his recruiter hire somebody he ain't personally checked out? Come on, man. He'd run a line on his own mother."

"Probably." Edward cast Harry a sidelong look. He was back to worrying, so Edward decided to cheer him up. "There's more good news."

"I hadn't heard *any* yet."

"We get paid." Edward enjoyed Harry's reaction to that. "Not as much as we were supposed to get the first time, but—"

"If you'd stop supporting my ex, we wouldn't need the cash. But—"

"I shouldn't have to do it." Edward glared at him. "Feeding your son is your responsibility. Your ex shouldn't have to beg you to support him." Harry had no idea how strongly Edward felt about this, or why, or how dangerously close he was to getting himself shot.

"I need things too."

"Forget you. You had the boy. You support him. It's that simple."

"If we're dead, he won't get a dime." Harry's eyes glittered. "You thought about that?"

"It's my motivation for staying alive." Edward braked for a traffic light. The van beside them had its radio cranked up. Its thump reverberated through Edward's entire body.

"More motivated than Johnson? Because he's loaded for bear."

"Equally motivated with Johnson." It was in the genes and undeniable.

"Yeah, well, here's hoping you're smarter, because he won't go down easy."

That, too, was in the genes. "I'm smarter. Bank on it."

"I am, man." Harry raked his lip with his teeth. "But that jerk totally creeps me out."

Johnson was creepy, but the real danger was Chessman. He was ruthless with serious connections. *NINA*. It creeped Edward out. Bombing a shopping mall full of kids? And not for money but a stupid cause—and it didn't change a thing. Nut jobs. A man couldn't predict what nut jobs would do. NINA hated family, but they acted a lot like grandparents. Mess with a grandkid and a grandparent would go to the ends of the earth and do anything to make sure you regretted it the rest of your life.

Harry tapped a fist on the door panel. "Johnson always knows everything."

"Not everything." On that, Edward had to disagree. On several fronts, in fact, Edward knew more, and it wasn't for Johnson's lack of trying to find out. Edward had just been better and faster at it.

Satisfied with his own cunning, maybe even a dash proud at messing with Chessman's and

Johnson's heads, Edward popped the clutch, pumped the gas to take off, then shifted into second. They thought they were so smart, so much better than he was. But he'd show them smart. They'd hear about this and not know what was going on.

"If Johnson knew everything," Edward told Harry, "he wouldn't have permitted his New Orleans recruiter to hire Benjamin Brandt."

Benjamin Brandt?

His cell phone at his ear, Paul rushed into the house through the kitchen entrance and breezed by the chef, standing at the center island slicing a tomato. "Where is he?"

"Office," the chef responded, not missing a beat in his work. Light glinted on the blade of the razor-sharp knife.

Paul walked on, out of earshot, clipping his shoulder on the door frame. Pain shot down his arm. Stifling a curse, he muttered into his cell phone. "You're sure it's him?"

"No idea," his recruiter said. "I didn't check him out."

Surprise rippled through Paul. "Why not?"

"He said you sent him. Since you're keeping this under wraps, I figured you had to have sent him or he wouldn't know about me."

"Take no action." Paul needed to think. "I'll get back to you." He hung up the phone, then stuffed it into his pocket, rushing through the house to Mr. Chessman's office.

It was empty.

Returning to the hallway, he spotted Lucille, the head housekeeper. If it were physically possible, the woman looked as if she'd lost even more weight. *Anorexia?* "Mr. Chessman?"

"South lawn veranda, Mr. Johnson."

Paul mumbled his thanks and made his way through the house to the veranda. Before stepping outside, he straightened his tie and observed the area to be sure Mr. Chessman was alone.

He sat in the shade at a table, a tall, chilled glass of something clear and bubbly in front of him. A lemon wedge floated in it. Kicked back and comfortable, Gregory stared out beyond the manicured lawn and into the hedge maze, as if he lacked a care in the world. It was a serene, innocent image he'd perfected. One that he paid Paul well to make sure he could project.

Unfortunately, it was also one that signaled diabolical events were being spun in the man's mind.

Paul had dealt with the scum of the earth most of his life. He'd even been raised by one. But he wanted better—more than mean drunks and greed and nut jobs. Then he'd heard about Chessman. What a good man he was, and he had the thing Paul most wanted: respect.

Paul had turned over a new leaf as an average American, and soon thereafter, he'd heard

Chessman was looking for an assistant. For the first time in his life, fate stepped in to help him. He'd gotten the job with Chessman. Finally, Paul would have the life he'd always wanted.

And he had—until the business with Susan Brandt and her boy had come up. After that, Chessman walked a straight line, at least so far as Paul officially knew, and he dared to hope that maybe there was still a chance. But even wearing blinders hadn't been enough.

Then Chessman went nuts and choked that crazy woman to death in her studio. Paul had made that go away. Even the coroner hadn't figured out the truth. But that was the final blow on the death of a dream. The good life was gone forever. Paul had even blamed himself. Chessman had been such a good man. Paul had contaminated him. Not intentionally. He just couldn't outrun it. Bad to the bone was in his genes, and it infected everyone around him.

And then his boss had taken him deeper into his confidence, and Paul learned that even the worst scum he had dealt with had been rank amateurs compared to Gregory Chessman.

Paul shoved a hand into his pocket, curled it into a fist. *Too little, too late.* Dying was his only way out, being indispensable his only hope for life. Some people just weren't worthy of a normal life, and he was one of them. But at least he'd learned young what to do to feel better.

Take control.

Resigned to that being the best he could hope for, he walked outside. "Sir?"

Chessman turned to look at him. "Well?"

"I had to abort the mission, sir." Paul permitted a small amount of irritation to show in his voice. "When I arrived, someone else had already struck." Cops and firemen had flooded Crossroads Crisis Center.

Chessman wasn't pleased—his jaw tightened and his expression sobered—but he wasn't jumping to conclusions.

Encouraged by his restraint, Paul added, "Apparently the problem has a new wrinkle."

His boss straightened in his seat, folded his hands atop the table, then rolled his gaze up at Paul and waited for an explanation.

"Two men in a red Jag bombed the Crossroads Crisis Center."

"Is she dead?"

"No sir. She was there, but it's statistically impossible that killing her was the bomber's intent—minimal explosives, minor damage restricted to a small area, no injuries. But according to my source, she has memory challenges."

"Real or manufactured ones to protect her?"

"Purportedly very real."

Chessman delved into thought and his gaze lost focus. "Brought here from New Orleans, beaten, drugged, and now an intentional near-miss attack?" He looked at Paul. "Someone fired a warning shot over her bow."

Paul nodded. "Yes."

Disgust filled Chessman's face. "Edward and Harry?"

"Probable, sir, but I can't yet verify it."

"Well." Gregory paused. "As wrinkles go, this one isn't too bad. If it is them, let them kill her—or be blamed for it."

Vintage Chessman response. "I'm afraid that isn't the wrinkle, sir. It's in the extra help brought in for the search."

He sipped from his chilled glass. The lemon wedge bobbed behind moisture droplets clinging to the outside of the glass. "The people your recruiter hired in New Orleans?"

"Yes sir." Paul's chest went tight. "One of the hirelings claims he's Benjamin Brandt."

"Benjamin Brandt?" Mr. Chessman slapped a hand onto the table. "Impossible."

"It is possible, sir."

"It's not Brandt. Edward posing as Brandt, maybe, but not Brandt." Chessman's eyes twinkled with delight. "Edward's launched a preemptive strike."

The left side of Paul's face twitched. He resisted the urge to stroke it into stopping. "You'd be pleased if he's undermined us?"

"Very." Gregory laughed. "You slide in behind

them, kill her, Edward and Harry get arrested for it, and they go to jail."

Where they could claim being hired to kill the subject? What was he thinking? Sacrificing Paul? Or did he have bigger fish to fry? Maybe both. "What about Benjamin Brandt? What if he really is—?"

"Brandt is not your recruit's hireling."

Paul frowned and made no pretense of hiding it. "Brandt has doggedly searched for his family's murderers."

"And he's failed to find a thing." Chessman waved off the possibility.

"I don't think he's above infiltrating to get information, sir. In fact, I believe strongly he would do anything—"

"He's a Christian, Paul."

"He was a Christian, sir. He's not anymore."

"Interesting." Chessman seemed to process that new information. "But say he has hired on. I'm sure your recruiter only told him he needed help to locate a missing woman and that he feared foul play was involved. Where's the link between Susan's case and the subject's? There's nothing there for Brandt to follow."

"There is, sir. Odds are against Brandt making that connection, but it isn't statistically impossible. Edward could have planted clues."

"Edward isn't that stupid." Chessman grunted. "And without him, nothing connects the two cases that would lead Brandt to your recruiter to find the subject."

Typically, Chessman was quick. But this time, he was being blockheaded or naive. "Unfortunately, we don't know that for a fact either."

"We know we've revealed nothing that connects the subject to Brandt's wife, don't we?"

"Our concern is in what Edward's revealed." Brandt becoming part of the equation at this close range was a bad sign of something being dangerously wrong. "Edward is out to save Edward. He could have revealed anything, or done anything, including drawing Brandt a map to your front door."

"He wouldn't dare." Mr. Chessman stood, though he looked less sure of himself now than he had before. "No. No, it's Edward passing himself off as Brandt. Alone, he might risk doing more, but saddled with Harry, there's no way."

"He could disassociate from Harry."

"Never happen." Chessman rubbed his lower lip.

"Are you willing to bet your life on that, sir? Because, sensible or not, I'm not willing to bet mine."

Chessman slid his hands off the table and studied Paul. "If Edward and Harry act against the subject, that's good news for us."

"A fact of which Edward is well aware. We

wouldn't be wise to underestimate him. It didn't work out well for us last time."

That reminder knocked the self-assurance right off Chessman's face. He sighed. "So what do you think Edward is doing?"

"I don't know that he's done anything yet, or that he plans any action. But neither do I know that Brandt hasn't infiltrated. He could have caught wind of something and acted on it."

"From where?"

"Edward." Paul sent Gregory a level look. He could be annoyed at his raising that possibility again, but Chessman needed to give it due consideration. Paul understood how the man's mind worked—his own worked in the same way, only wiser and better. But in Edward's convoluted way, tapping Brandt on the shoulder made sense. "Maybe Edward knows you'll sacrifice him to save yourself."

"Of course he knows that."

"Then statistically speaking, Edward is going to do what any man in that position would do."

"What's that?"

"Kiss loyalty good-bye." Paul put a warning bite in his tone he wanted Chessman to hear. "And sacrifice you first."

Gregory dismissed Paul's warning—he had squashed others just like Edward—and thought through the possibility. Would Edward be so stupid as to get Benjamin Brandt involved? Would Brandt so stupidly get involved?

Either or both might, especially with their knowing nothing about NINA. Edward, to save his neck. Ben, to find the truth. He'd been obsessed with finding his family's killers from the start, following all leads—even those deemed impossible—and there was that two-month stint in seclusion with his docs. Very little was known about that, but the village grapevine had been hot with speculation.

Peggy Crane had denied the rumors, no doubt out of loyalty to Ben and to Susan. Yet Melanie Ross, being young and guileless, had been far less discreet. Ben apparently had spent two months in total seclusion with an army of psychiatrists and crisis counselors—Dr. Harvey Talbot among them. Supposedly they were doing extensive research on incidental shootings. With Talbot gone, Lisa Harper had been hired to fill in at the crisis center.

Maybe Edward wasn't involved at all. He could still be in hiding with Harry. Maybe Brandt had discovered something and had hired on with the recruiter.

Not nearly so certain as he had been, Gregory looked at Paul.

"You see now." Paul pulled out a handkerchief and sneezed into it. "It is possible."

"Okay, it's possible. But if it isn't Brandt and it is Edward, what is he doing?"

"Posturing, sir." Paul frowned. "I'm just not yet sure why."

Paul unsure? The same Paul who stayed at least three steps ahead of everyone else? The same Paul who routinely examined multiple scenarios, formed multiple strategies, and never had been more than two percentage points off anything in his adult life? Paul, who made murder disappear and delivered a recruit's bloody finger to assure Gregory the man wouldn't make future errors? Now, when most desperately needed, that Paul stood unsure?

That worried Gregory most of all.

8

Susan swallowed a bite of burger. The flavor burst in her mouth, wiping out the pain of chewing, and her stomach grumbled, protesting its long absence of food.

"You've got to chew and swallow it for the food to do your gut any good."

Sitting in Crossroads' kitchen, she glanced over the tabletop to Clyde. "Thanks."

"You feeling bad?" He dabbed at his mouth with a scrunched-up paper napkin.

"Define *bad*." She grunted and sipped from her paper cup of soda. Her jaw was so sore that her teeth hurt. Using the straw had been impossible. "I ache from head to toe, but that's nothing com-pared to how—"

No. She stopped herself suddenly. She couldn't think about that. Fear was insulting to God. She had survived and she would be fine. Her memory would come back . . . sometime.

Dr. Talbot came in. "I have some good news."

"You know who I am?"

"Not yet." He slid onto a seat beside Clyde. "May I speak about your condition here, or would you prefer privacy?"

"Here's fine." Clyde knew everything she knew already.

"We've gone through all your test results, and you don't have Dissociative Fugue."

She took a sip from her cup. "What is it, then?"

"We think it's the result of your head injury and/or an effect of the drug used to subdue you. Probably a combination of the two, though we can't be sure. If we'd gotten blood right away, maybe. But—"

"This is the good news, right?"

"Far less complicated to treat, yes."

"And my memory?"

"We're not sure, Susan. It could return at any time, all at once, or in pieces. It could take a while. The important thing to remember is that forcing it won't work and could exacerbate the problem. Anxiety and stress won't do you any good either." He smiled. "So you're under direct orders not to worry."

This sounded better, but in her position, how

could she avoid worry, anxiety, and stress? "I'll try."

"Try hard," Talbot said. "It's important."

"So is remembering." She dusted salt from a fry off her fingertips. "This has wiped out my past—I remember nothing from before the attack—and it's punched in huge holes of what happened during it. I see flashes, little snips and snatches. They're not always connected and they don't always make sense."

"I understand. Just try to let it come as it will." Harvey got up and grabbed a bottle of tea from the fridge. "Still nothing on your lost day?"

"Not a thing," Susan said, "which sure sounds like chloroform or some combination of it and short-term amnesia drugs."

"They use them in surgery all the time," Clyde chimed in. "I had an arteriogram last spring. Don't recall a thing about it."

"They are common," Dr. Talbot said, "in some diagnostic procedures."

She asked the question she wasn't sure she wanted answered. "Do you think there'll be long-term effects?" That worried her with the first diagnosis. It worried her with this new one.

"We'll know more in a few days. You're doing well now. That's encouraging." His beeper went off. "Sorry. I've got to run."

Susan watched him go.

"You're worrying," Clyde said, assuming his

self-defined protector role. "Harvey's encouraged. He said to avoid worry."

"Wouldn't you worry, Clyde?" She automatically reached for the cross that had hung at her neck. Not finding it, she felt empty. "Someone wants me dead, and I have no idea why."

"Yeah, I reckon I would be a mess. But I hope I'd remember what we both know too. God's in control. He'll set things to right."

She believed that. It was just beyond unsettling to have all these things happening and not to know what was behind them. That she was in danger was apparent. But from whom, and for what reason? And what kind of person was she to warrant all this criminal activity? It couldn't be good. Actually, it had to be pretty bad. And knowing it had her nerves raw, tight, and threatening to fray.

Hearing voices, Susan looked at the kitchen door just as Peggy and Ben walked in. Seeing her, Peggy smiled. "Glad to see you eating."

Susan nodded. "I need the fuel to figure out what to do."

"What do you have in mind?" Ben asked.

"I don't know. I have no memory so there's no one to call, no money, no—" A catch stuck in her throat. To cover it, she paused and took a sip of her drink. "I don't have many options."

"We're going to help you." Peggy sat beside her. "You have no reason to panic and every reason not to worry."

Everyone telling you not to worry made you worry. Didn't they realize that? Susan paused, refocused. "I appreciate it, really. But I don't think you can afford much more of me being here. I've already gotten you bombed."

"You'll come home with me." Clyde polished off a french fry. "I've got plenty of room."

"Absolutely not." He'd taken on a fatherly role with her, but she couldn't do this to him. "I do thank you. It means the world to me that you'd offer, but—"

"Then why not accept?" He frowned.

She clasped his hand on the table. "Clyde, you've been in danger twice for me. I can't put you in danger again, and I don't dare risk anything happening to you. You're all I've got."

"Which is why you should let me help you."

Peggy stepped in. "Susan, we're a crisis center. This is what we do."

"I can't." She stiffened. "It's too dangerous for all of you."

"It's common for us," Peggy countered. "We don't dump victims in the street. You're the reason we exist."

Susan looked down, afraid she'd cry.

"We own a lovely hotel called The Towers," Peggy said. "You can stay there while we sort things out."

Unable to talk past the lump in her throat, she blinked hard.

"No." Ben crossed his arms over his chest.

"No?" Peggy looked stunned, her round, affable face reddening.

"It's okay, Peggy." What Susan would do, she had no idea, but if Ben didn't want her at his hotel, well, under the circumstances, she couldn't blame him. This all had to be really tough on him. "Ben's right. It's not a good idea to put the others at The Towers at risk."

"No, no. I didn't mean we wouldn't help you." Ben turned his gaze to a skeptical-looking Peggy. "I meant that, considering the attacks, I don't think The Towers is a good idea."

"Oh." Peggy looked decidedly relieved. "You do recall what Harvey and Lisa said. Feeling safe is essential to Susan's memory returning."

"Yes, I recall." Ben sat beside Clyde, across the table from her. "She's right about The Towers. We have twenty-seven people there right now."

"Twenty-six." Peggy grimaced. "One left this morning."

That she wasn't happy about that was clear. Susan knew why; she'd overheard Lisa telling Peggy about the abused wife who had returned home that morning.

"Twenty-six." Ben acknowledged the change. "The security there is good, but at Three Gables it's better, and there aren't other victims at risk."

"Three Gables." Susan cocked her head. "Like Sir Arthur Conan Doyle's story?"

"Very interesting." Ben's eyes shone. "Most who make the connection go right to Sherlock Holmes."

"Never mind that," Peggy said. "There's no connection to either of them, Susan." She turned a frown on Ben. "She can't stay at Three Gables. It's not proper."

"It is proper. I'm talking about the cottage, not the house." He swung his gaze to Susan. "Three Gables is my home. There are two guest cottages on the grounds. Both are empty. You'll be safe, and you're welcome to stay there as long as you like."

All this and he'd also open his home to her? Overwhelmed, she couldn't speak.

"The security is first-rate, Susan," Peggy said. "Mark Taylor, Ben's security chief, is excellent. You'll like him. And until we find out who's attacking you, we need to keep you isolated and out of pocket."

Clyde reached over, patted her hand. "I'd enjoy the company, but Ben's right. Three Gables is best for you."

"Thank you. All of you." Susan finally found her voice. "Hopefully, someone will file a missing person's report with the police soon, and I won't have to impose on you long."

"It's no imposition." Peggy snitched a fry. "Like I said, it's why we exist."

Susan flipped the bag of fries around to share them. Her hand trembled, and she quickly drew it back, then tucked it into her lap. "What if they come back?"

"It's easy to say don't worry about that, but anyone would." Ben reached over and took a fry. "Instead, I'll say that until they hit the center, we didn't know they were there. Now we do." Ben snapped down his teeth, nipping a bite. "If they come back, we'll be ready for them."

"We?" Surprise rippled through her body. "As in, you and me?"

"You and me and Mark Taylor and the security staff at Three Gables, Peggy and our staff here, the police—everyone who needs to be prepared." Ben motioned to her food. "You're not eating. Should this discussion wait until you're done?"

He sounded a bit irked about having a security staff and contrite about her not eating. The second surprised her more than the first, though why he'd be irked at having protection she couldn't imagine. It sounded great to her—at least, at the moment. Would it normally? Not knowing, the tart bite of pickle in her mouth seemed to swell. When she finally could swallow, she did and then said, "I'm fine. Just slow."

Clyde cleared his throat. "Her jaw's sore and her teeth ache. She can hardly chew."

Her face burned. "I'm fine. Really."

"When you're done here, we'll get going then." Ben glanced at his watch. "It's after six o'clock. Where'd the afternoon go?"

"Tied up getting counselors for Mobile, dealing with the police chief, the mayor and his wife, the fire department, the insurance—"

"Enough, Peg. Don't make me relive it." Ben looked at the burger, at Susan. "That was supposed to be your lunch."

"She couldn't eat. Nervous stomach," Clyde said. "So we waited a spell."

Susan frowned at him. "Do you tell everyone everything?"

" 'Course not," Clyde said, not at all ruffled. "Just those who need to understand you're a mite fragile right now and they need to mind their manners."

He'd heard about Ben being hard on her and he was not happy.

Ben had the grace to look away.

Susan wanted to relieve the tension, but anything she said would make matters worse.

Peggy, being Peggy, stepped in and paved the way. "We'll get you some fresh clothes in the morning, Susan. Shopping in the village is limited, and the stores open on Sunday shut down at six. A couple sets of scrubs is the best we can do right now."

"That would be great. Thank you." At war with herself, Susan glanced down at the table. On the one hand, Ben opening his home—well, his cottage—to her, and on the other, humbled and grateful for the assistance the center offered her. Yet never in her life had she felt more alone.

Or more frightened.

They would come back.

Imagining the two men who'd abducted her, she shivered. Her every instinct blared an alarm that they wouldn't stop coming back. Not until they felt they had nothing to fear.

Not until she was dead.

Paul Johnson parked his black Lexus and caught up with Chessman on the well-lit driving range, a new addition to Seagrove Village Country Club's world-class golf course added by its nongolfing owner, Mrs. Mayor, Darla Green. Paul waited, admiring Chessman's flawless swing.

When Chessman spotted Paul, he stuffed his club into his bag, then grabbed a bottle of water from his cart. Twisting off its cap, he walked over. "Smile, Paul. You look like the Grim Reaper."

"Soon enough, sir." Tonight, the subject would be at The Towers, and so would he. When she was no longer a threat, then Paul would have reason to smile.

Chessman took a long drink of water. "Have you located Edward or Harry?"

"Not yet, sir. Last sighting was at Crossroads. Harry bombed it while Edward drove the subject's Jag." The fool had no sense. Totally unprofessional. That alone was reason enough to kill him.

"What about her?"

"Still playing princess in the ivory tower." He cleared his throat, pausing while two men walked by, heading toward the club. "There is an interesting development on that front. Benjamin Brandt was in the center when it was bombed. Could mean he was hired by our New Orleans recruit, and Edward and Harry were trying to take care of that problem for us."

"Edward would see the benefit in doing that."

"Yes, he would." Paul had. And Harry would do whatever he was told.

"So which is it? Are they working for or against us?"

"The investigation continues."

"Where's Brandt?"

"Still at the center, sir."

Worry dragged at the lines in Chessman's face, proving he clearly understood the danger of Brandt and the woman being in close proximity. "I thought he never went to the center."

"This is the first time he's been there since his wife's death." Paul tucked his chin to his chest. "Today."

"Hmm." Chessman paused. "I don't like it. It's too convenient to be coincidental. Maybe he did hire on with your recruit."

"The jury is still out on that, sir, and I fear it will be for a time." Paul resented having to admit that. It was an unfortunate reflection on his competence that he'd pay for in due time.

"Why? What's the delay with the recruit?" Gregory took another long drink.

It was warm, even for October, and sticky from the high humidity. Paul squinted against the dying sun and looked into his boss's face. "I faxed over a photo of Brandt, but to no avail."

"To no avail." That infuriated Gregory; it showed in the tension in his body, the set of his shoulders, the fire in his eyes. "Exactly what do you mean, Paul?"

His boss was going to hate this, almost as much as Paul hated it. "Our recruit never saw the hireling, so he can't tell from a photo if he hired Brandt or Edward or someone else."

A couple set up near them with a bucket of balls. Chessman turned his back on them, deepened his frown, and dropped his voice so only Paul would hear. "What are you going to do about it?" Before Paul could answer, Chessman added, "I need that information, Paul. And I need it now."

"Yes sir." He rushed to reassure his boss. When Gregory Chessman succumbed to rage, bad, bad things happened. Even crazy women died. "I have a plan to get it and settle the question conclusively, sir."

"Conclusively?"

"Relative to Brandt, yes. A hundred percent conclusive."

"How?"

"Voiceprint."

Chessman nodded. "Very well."

Paul dabbed at his damp brow with a spotless white hanky. "But to get it, I'll need your help."

9

Susan sat in the front seat of Ben's SUV, not quite sure what to make of the man. Why had he opened his crisis center and his cottage to her?

It was a question that had plundered her mind while at the center and did now on the ride down Seville Avenue to St. Charles Place, where he hung a left into an affluent neighborhood.

At the end of the broad street on the right stood a gated estate. Beyond it, stretching upward three stories, was a gray stone house with three turrets, a long stretch of welcoming windows, and a gabled roof that managed to look like a home and not a museum or the off-limits property of some rich eccentric.

"This is Three Gables," Ben said, then drove through the gate with a friendly wave to the security guard who appeared from a small building surrounded with thick evergreen shrubs nestled behind a broad brick fence post.

"It's beautiful." Susan looked from the house to the grounds. Swatches of lush green grass dotted with tree-studded islands stretched out to the distant woods. A circular driveway led to the front landing. It branched off and went to the back of the property, where she assumed the guest cottages were. "Did your wife design it too?"

"We designed the house together." He blinked hard. "How did you know she was involved?"

"I see her touch. Just like at the center. She liked soft edges and natural stone. Lots of greenery, and the islands are a dead giveaway." She smiled. "Little pockets of refuge scattered everywhere."

Her insight clearly surprised him. "So that's why she insisted on benches in every island." He let out a little moan. "I can't believe I missed that."

"She needed peaceful places," Susan said, focusing on one of the cast-iron benches. "It was important for her to know she always had a protected place to go. A haven, so to speak."

Ben hit the brakes. The SUV jerked to a halt. "How do you know that?"

Surprised by the venom in his voice, Susan drew back, half-afraid of him. "I-I don't know. It just seems . . . well, obvious."

"Did you know my wife?" His grip on the wheel had his knuckles bulging and white.

"I don't know, Ben." Susan deliberately dropped her voice, hoping to calm him down. "Three Gables doesn't seem at all familiar to me, so I don't think I've been here. But who knows? I wouldn't want to say I didn't know her and then when my memory returns, discover that I did."

Susan met his gaze and held it. It was hard, very hard, but she sensed it was critically important too—as important as being patient with him. "I wish I could say one way or the other, but I honestly don't know."

The reminder of her memory challenge seemed to work, gauging by his rapidly changing expressions: fury falling to uncertainty, hinting at regret, and then wooden. He diverted his gaze, stared through the windshield, and drove alongside the house. Behind it, he stopped the SUV outside an oversized garage.

From the edge of the concrete pad, two paths led through natural greenbelts of old oaks and fat bushes that had lost most of their buds. In the distance, two rooftops peeked through the fall foliage. "Is there a specific reason you have two guest cottages?"

He cleared his throat. "No." He opened his door and got out, walked around, and then opened her door.

She grabbed the scrubs Peggy had given her and scooted out of the SUV, her muscles in knots. *So much for no stress or tension.*

The air was warm but thankfully not stagnant. A stiff breeze crackled through the trees, tugged at her eyelids.

Ben closed the door and it clicked shut. "I talked with Mark."

"Mark?"

"Mark Taylor, the head of my security staff. He recommends you stay in the cottage on the right." Ben started down the stone path. "It's most interior on the property and easier to defend."

No doubt Ben intended that comment to make her feel safe. Instead, it tightened the knots in her muscles. Yet walking beside Ben, she took in the tranquil sounds of chirping birds. Something scuttled in the undergrowth to her left—a squirrel. It scampered up the trunk of a moss-laden oak and leapt to a distant branch.

Leaves rustled and crunched underfoot, and she felt her tension draining away. Ben might have every reason to resent her and wish her out of his life, but he would defend her, even if it meant putting himself at risk—which he was by having her stay here. She liked that about him. A lot. It spoke volumes about his character, and about his views on being a man. "Ben?"

"Yes, Su—" He stopped cold, swallowed hard, and then started again. "Yes?"

He couldn't do it, Susan realized. He couldn't call her by his wife's name. She understood that, especially considering their physical resemblance. And since she didn't know that the name actually belonged to her, she could at least make that hurdle easier for him. "I expect I've been quite a shock for you."

Something between a grunt and a moan escaped him.

"No, it's okay. Of course I would be a shock. Roles reversed, I'd be stunned." She stared at the ground and walked on down the path. Her throat went thick. "I'm sorry about your wife and son," she said softly. "Peggy told me what happened—mostly to dissuade me from believing I was Susan—because of our strong physical resemblance."

He shoved his hands into his pockets. "It's been hard for both of us."

Ah, a truce was in sight—or at least on the horizon. "I've accepted that I'm not Susan."

"I'm glad."

"But it leaves me in a lurch." She shrugged. "Since I don't know who I am, I don't have any idea what to use for a name." Letting him see how much that troubled her, she added, "It's disconcerting, having your identity stripped from you."

"I'm sure it is." He dragged out a hand and swept it across his forehead.

"But I know who I am inside, where it matters. A name is just a name."

He respected that. It shone in his eyes.

"I thought maybe until I remember my own, we could pick a name for me that you can say without . . . well, without pain." She looked up and met his gaze. "You've been good to me and I don't want to hurt you."

Every line in his face tightened. "How can you do this?"

"Do what?"

"How can you stand there and be so reasonable and rational and thoughtful? You should be terrified. Furious. Outraged. *Something.* Instead you seem to take in stride everything that's happened to you. How can you expect me to believe you?"

She stopped on the walk and squeezed the scrubs to her chest. "I *am* terrified." Admitting it was easier than she thought it would be. She feared if she said it aloud, she'd crumble. She didn't. "I'm angry too. No one likes being a victim. Why you wouldn't get that without me becoming a drama queen to prove it is beyond me. But I made allowances because if a man who looked like my dead husband showed up at my crisis center, I'd be a freaked-out basket case."

"So it's an act, then? Is that what you're saying?"

"No, that's not what I'm saying." She glared up at him. "To act, I'd have to know what is normal, now wouldn't I? I don't. I'm just doing the best I can. That's all, Ben. Just the best I can."

He rolled his gaze heavenward. "But how are you holding it all together?" He lifted a hand. "You don't even know your name. Why aren't you frantic and coming apart at the seams?" He frowned. "Don't tell me that you are, because it's clear that you're not."

"I can explain, but you won't understand."

"Try me. Because from where I'm standing, it

makes you look disingenuous. Are you—disingenuous, I mean?"

"I don't believe I am, but I don't know. When I can have faith in my response, I'll answer you." She gave him a frown intended to buckle knees. "I have to say the question offends me at gut level." She walked on. "I know that beyond any doubt."

Moments later, he caught up and fell into step at her side without a word.

The moment of indulgence was over. She couldn't stay wrapped in righteous indignation. *Be patient with him.*

"I feel, Ben. All those things you mentioned and more." She paused at a low-slung limb and plucked off a leaf. It was dry and crunchy. "But I'm not facing this alone. If I were, well, I doubt I could face it at all."

A hard glint lit in his eyes. "So you've remembered a partner?"

Don't take offense. Don't do it. Don't . . . "Actually, I remember a Father," she said with a gentle smile. "It's an amazing thing. Through all of this, I've never forgotten Him, only me."

"So your father is involved." Ben hiked his chin. "Then what is this all about? Is it a scam? And don't lie to me, okay? You've gotten my crisis center bombed. Mel could have been seriously injured. And I have helped you." He cocked his head. "Did you have plastic surgery to look like Susan?"

Her smile faded. "My Father is God, Ben. And the reason I'm not falling apart is because I'm resting under the shadow of His wing. He's carrying me right now." Her eyes burned. She would not cry. She would *not* cry. "You know, this isn't going to work. Thank you for everything. Seriously. But I can make my way from here."

She turned and went back down the path toward the driveway, eager to leave Three Gables. Where she'd go, she wasn't sure. The only option she had was to call Clyde.

"Wait," Ben called out. "Please."

She steeled herself, paused, then looked back at him over the slope of her shoulder.

"Are you telling me you don't remember you but you remember your faith?"

A smile threatened, tugging at the corner of her mouth. It annoyed her, but she couldn't bite it away. She was insulted. Why did she feel like smiling? *Senseless.* "Yes, that's what I'm telling you. Amazing, isn't it?"

"The cottage is open and ready for you. Dinner is in an hour. Tomorrow we'll get some groceries and you can do what you like at the cottage. For tonight, you're stuck having dinner with me—provided you're up to it."

That was as close to an apology as she was going to get, and she'd give him the gracious exit and accept it. "I'm up to it."

A man built like a wrestler came barreling

toward them through the woods. Susan slid between the two men. "Run, Ben! Run!"

"No, it's okay." He stepped around to her side. "It's Mark—my security chief."

Mark Taylor stopped next to her and looked at Ben. "Get inside now. We've had a perimeter breach."

"Oh no. No. They're here, Ben." Susan swallowed a shriek. "They're here!"

Edward scanned the woods. Two lanky teens ran full out across Three Gables' sweeping lawn, heading for the cover of the reservation woods that backed up to it.

From the passenger's seat, Harry pointed through the trees. "Who's that guy?"

"Mark Taylor," Edward said, looking out through the windshield, parked curbside. "Brandt's security chief."

"He's going to catch them."

The teens wore baseball caps with something strapped just above the bills, and they were less than thirty seconds ahead of Taylor. "Harry, move."

Harry grabbed the wire cutter from the floorboard, tumbled out, and scrambled through the greenbelt brush to Three Gables' perimeter fence, then cut through the chain-link.

An alarm blared. Taylor stopped dead in his tracks, then touched his ear—as if listening to someone on his staff give him the location of the breach, then he doubled back, heading for the fence.

Harry dove into the car and tossed the cutter onto the backseat. "Go! Go! Go!"

Edward laid on the horn, stomped the gas. The Jag shot down the street.

In the rearview, he saw Taylor reach the fence and round the corner.

"There they are." Harry pointed.

The teens ran out of the woods and down the sidewalk to a black Lexus. Recognizing it, Edward hit the brakes hard and tucked in behind a white van.

Harry lurched forward and grabbed the dash. "What are you doing, man?"

"Look, the Lexus."

Harry craned to see. "Van's blocking me. What's he doing?"

Had to be cameras or sensors on the caps. "My guess is he just used those kids to check out Brandt's perimeter security, which tells us—"

"He's going to make the hit here."

Edward spared Harry a glance, keeping the two teens in his peripheral vision. "Apparently Three Gables is going to be ground zero."

"Oh, man." Harry whacked a closed fist against the side door panel. "You knew this was gonna happen. That's why you had me trip the alarm."

"Actually, it's not. Taylor knew the minute the

perimeter was breached. I didn't have to tell him."

"Yeah, he was already chasing the kids." Harry frowned, furrowing the skin between his brows. "Then why did I trip the alarm?"

"Because Taylor didn't know this was going to be ground zero," Edward said. "And he doesn't stand a chance against the forces coming against them."

"Come on, man. He's supposed to be good."

"I never said he wasn't good. The man has a background in Special Operations." He was better than good. "I said he didn't stand a chance against those coming."

"Why not?"

Edward cocked his head. "He's flawed in a way they're not."

"Flawed?" Harry guffawed. "If he's Special Ops, the man's got a chest full of medals."

"Which proves my point." Edward stiffened, seeing Paul Johnson pull out into traffic and drive away. "Unfortunately, his is a problem that can't be fixed."

"I wish you'd just say what you have to say." Harry glared over at Edward. "What's Taylor's flaw?"

Cranking the engine, Edward swiveled his gaze to Harry. "He's honest."

That dropped Harry's jaw. He thought a second, then said, "That could get in the way, but it doesn't mean Taylor won't one-up them."

Edward took the break in traffic to pull out onto the road. "Oh, but it does, my friend. It really does."

"There you go again. Just say it."

"He's honest," Edward repeated. "They're not." Harry stilled. "They'll do anything. He won't."

"Exactly."

"So we're helping Taylor now too?" Surprise rippled through Harry's voice.

Edward hiked a shoulder. "If we don't, would you rather take a needle or a bullet?"

"Got it." Resignation slid down over Harry's face. "I'll stick to your plan." He motioned to the two teens on the sidewalk, walking past. One's T-shirt showed a distinct imprint. "They're packing, Edward."

"They sure are." The sorry jerk had hired two kids to do the hit. "Let's go."

"Oh, man, Edward. I don't want to take out two kids."

"Don't be ridiculous." Harry knew Edward. He should know he'd never deliberately hit a kid. Christopher had been an unfortunate accident—one that still haunted Edward.

"Ah, we're going to beat the—"

Edward didn't want to hear it. "We're going to discourage them from their current paths of activity and give Brandt and the woman a gift."

"That helps Taylor. Got it."

He pulled to the curb, left the engine running. "Ready?"

"Let's go."

The teens didn't know what hit them.

But they felt it—and then they fought hard. Being no match for grown men, their resistance was short-lived. Soon both boys were out cold in Edward's backseat. He drove back around the corner straddling Three Gables and hugged the curb where he had been parked earlier. "Let's get them out there."

Rushing, he and Harry dumped the teens onto Brandt's property just inside the cut fence.

Harry dropped a kid on the ground. He was still out. "I've got to cut back on my smoking, man." Huffing, he swiped grit from his hands.

"Worry about that later." Edward hustled back to the car, grabbed the binoculars from the center console. As soon as he settled in his seat, he shoved them at Harry, then pulled away from the curb.

"The kids saw who they were fighting, Edward. They'll describe us to Brandt."

"They'd better. Otherwise Brandt and the woman won't know we stopped something going on against them."

Harry parked an elbow on the window. "The cops will know somebody's scoping out security—"

"Stretch your mind, Harry." Edward hung a left onto Highway 98 and headed toward Panama City. "They'll know someone else is trying to kill her and we alerted them."

"Yeah." Harry grunted. "Yeah, and even if we get popped for jacking her—"

"That would be kidnapping her. We jacked the car."

"Whatever. We can say we were trying to protect her."

"Yes." Edward allowed himself the hint of a smile. "And it'll be the truth."

"Man, you are something," Harry said, then sobered. "Remind me never to cross you."

Edward's humor faded. "Cross me and I won't need to remind you."

Fear flashed in Harry's eyes. "You threatening to kill me, man?"

"Absolutely not. You're my partner."

"Sounded like a threat to me."

"Harry, are you planning on crossing me?" Edward pulled into a coffee shop drive-through.

"No." Harry sounded as flustered as he looked. "No way, man."

"Then neither of us has anything to worry about, do we?"

Harry squinted, slid Edward a wary look. "No, we don't have anything to worry about."

Edward relaxed, satisfied. They both had plenty to worry about, but he hoped those issues could be postponed until after they'd dealt with Chessman and his legion of henchmen. Johnson wasn't the worst of them, but he was bad enough.

So was the woman who could bury them all.

10

Tires squealed at the west boundary of Three Gables, on the street paralleling the property. Without thinking, Susan ran toward the sound.

Ben followed her. "Stop! Stop!"

She should stop, but every instinct warned her to run, warned her that running would give her a much-needed answer.

Twilight flirted with deep shadows in the green-belt woods beyond the landscaped lawn. Branches and spiny bushes scraped her legs and slapped her arms. A twig caught her right across the neck. She swatted it aside and ran on—and nearly tripped over a teenage boy sprawled on the ground. She dropped down and checked. He had a pulse, but he was out cold. Another boy lay a short distance away.

"Ben! Hurry!" She scanned the street and caught a glimpse of a red Jag. Inside, she saw one of her abductors, the hooded-sweatshirt guy Mel had described as the crisis center bomber. "Ben!"

He caught up to her, breathing hard. "Why did you take off like that? You heard Mark. You could have been hurt or even killed."

"They're gone, and I'm fine." She stepped aside. "Check that boy. This one is breathing."

Ben went to the second teen, bent down, and checked him. "He's alive." Using his cell, he hit speed dial. Seconds later, he said, "Mark, where are you?" He paused, then said, "Forget the reservation. The intruders are here. Two teenage boys. They've been beaten unconscious." Another pause, then, "Where the fence was cut." He grimaced. "Better get an ambulance."

"It was my abductor, Ben. At least, the passenger was, and they were in the Jag." She wished Ben had seen it too.

Sweat beaded on his brow. "Why would your abductors beat up two kids and dump them here?"

"I don't know. But maybe the teens do."

Ben looked at the kids, then back at her. "Why did you run here? Mark told us there'd been a breach."

"I had a feeling that if I followed the screeching tires, I'd find answers."

"A divine push kind of feeling?"

"Yes." She shrugged. "You might not want to hear it. I know you've sworn off God—don't look shocked. Peggy inadvertently told me, explaining your behavior toward me."

"I haven't sworn off God. I no longer believe He exists."

"I'm so sorry," she said and meant it. "That's a hard way to live."

"Frankly, it is. But reality is what reality is. It's honest. You live with it."

Angry and betrayed. If she'd lost her family, she might feel the same way—short-term. But she hoped she'd realize that was a misguided and lonely way to live. Three years was pushing the bounds on short-term—at least in her view. Maybe that's why God had brought her into Ben's life and told her to be patient with him: to help him find his way back—to life and to God.

Having a better grip on her instructions, she didn't push. "You'll work through it your way in your own time, I'm sure." Pushed, his shield would become a brick wall. Ben didn't need to hear about faith; he needed to see it in action. "Me, I know this was a divine push—and the proof is right at your feet."

To Ben's credit, he didn't argue.

A twig snapped.

Susan spun toward the sound and saw a flash-light beam sweeping the woods. Memories of Clyde Parker and the crippling fear she'd felt on seeing his flashlight's beam flooded her. Every muscle in her body tensed. She stood rigid, still. *Give me strength. Please, give me strength.*

Mark stepped over a downed branch and dropped to examine the boys. One groaned. The other was still out.

"Someone worked them over pretty good. Wake up." Mark roused one, then the other with gentle shakes and a loud voice. "Who are you?"

Neither spoke.

Mark's tone turned gruff. "Look, you're going to jail for destroying the fence and trespassing. If you want any chance of avoiding the worst you can get, you'd better start talking right now."

"Jason Marsh," the one closest to Susan said.

"Shut up!" the other kid shouted.

Mark turned to Ben. "Why don't you take Jason over to the fence and have a little chat with him."

Ben looked down at the boy. "Can you walk, Jason?"

"Yeah." He pulled himself to his feet. "I can take a punch."

"What about you?" Mark asked the reluctant one with blond hair and wide eyes. "You okay?"

"Ticked off. Only a coward hits you from behind."

Susan muttered, "It doesn't hurt less when they hit you head-on. Trust me on that one."

The boy blinked up at her. "They do that to your face?"

"Yeah, they did. Only after they beat me up, they cracked me in the head with a rock and left me for dead." She gave him a steady look. "You got off a little better."

The boy sucked in a shuddered breath. "Whoa."

"So who are you?" she asked. "And why did you cut the fence?"

"Lance Green. My dad's the mayor. But I didn't cut any fence." He lifted an arm, swiped at his nose. "Me and Jason were taking the shortcut to Snapper's. We hang there."

Mark nodded, letting her know that wasn't uncommon.

"So why were you on the property? You knew it'd trigger the alarm, right?" She shrugged. "I mean, if you take the shortcut all the time, you know if you cross the fence, the alarm's going to go off."

Lance rocked his head on his shoulders. "Yeah, everybody knows it. But we wanted the twenty bucks."

"What twenty bucks?" she asked.

"The twenty the guy paid us."

"For beating you up?"

"No, for running across the property. That's it. We just ran across the property, cut through the woods, and met him on the other side."

So they wanted to sound the alarm. "Did he ask you any questions about the property or what you saw?"

"No." Lance shook his head. "He took the hats, gave us our money, and then left."

Something was wrong here. "Wait a second. What hats?"

"The ones he wanted us to wear while we were running across the property."

"Why the hats?"

"They were rigged with some electronics. I don't know what kind. Never seen anything like them before."

"You're lucky they weren't bombs."

"Yeah, I guess so." He shuddered. "He said it was a joke on Mr. Brandt. We didn't think much about it. He's a good guy—Mr. Brandt, I mean."

166

So the man and the boys knew Ben, or knew of him. "So you were paid the twenty and then the men beat you up."

"That's right." Lance grunted, frustrated. "Like I said, we never saw them coming."

"But you took the money from them. How could you not have seen them coming?"

"No." He looked up at her, confused. "The guys who beat us up didn't give us any money. I don't know who they were. But the big one packed a wicked punch."

A chill swept up Susan's back, and her worry reflected in Mark's eyes. "The man with the money and the hats wasn't the same man who beat you up?"

"No ma'am. The guy with the hats—I don't know him. He was by himself. He took the hats, paid us, and left. These other two guys beat us up and brought us here. I don't know where they came from. Me and Jason were just walking down 98 minding our own business. The next thing I know, we're creamed from behind and fighting them. I took a bad lick, and that's all I remember until I woke up here."

Susan clenched her hands and dug deep not to panic. "There are two sets of them."

"Looks that way," Mark said.

Why would they dump the kids here? Susan couldn't see the logic in it. She puzzled through it while Mark continued talking to Lance.

Then the obvious became clear.

She went over to Ben, tugged at his sleeve. "I need to talk to you."

He stepped away from Jason. "What is it?"

She filled him in on what she'd learned from Lance. "Ben, there's only one reason my abductors would dump those kids here. They wanted us to find them."

"It's deeper than that." Ben looked into her eyes. "They wanted us to know that they weren't trying to kill you."

"I don't know if I agree with that." Susan needed more time to think before making that one-eighty. "They jack my car, kidnap and drug me, beat me to a pulp, and leave me for dead. That's not exactly expressing goodwill."

"If they wanted you dead, you'd be dead. You were drugged and not in a position to stop them, right?"

"True." A leaf clung to the shoulder of his shirt. She reached over and plucked it off, then tossed it to the ground.

Ben jerked back at her touch.

"I'm sorry." Heat flooded her face. "I shouldn't have touched you. I wasn't thinking . . ."

The look in his eyes softened. "It's okay. I-I just wasn't expecting . . ." He paused and let out a self-deprecating grunt. "Sorry. I definitely overreacted."

When he wasn't snarling, he really was an

attractive man. "No problem." She dragged her lip between her teeth. "So either they weren't trying to kill me, or they were and they've changed their minds."

"Seems that way to me."

But why? Her insides quaked. Her knees turned to water, but she followed his line of thinking to its next logical step. "If they're not trying to kill me, then what's this with these kids?"

"A warning?"

That struck her like a heavy hammer blow. "A warning that someone else is . . ."

Detective Jeff Meyers interrogated the boys and got the same stories Ben, Susan, and Mark had gotten. Lance Green pleaded with Jeff until seven thirty not to call his parents. He swore he'd be on restriction until he turned twenty-one.

Jeff had refused and phoned the mayor.

He might have caved, but weapons were involved. That sealed the boys' fates.

Susan returned to the cottage before Mr. and Mrs. Mayor showed up to claim their son, happy to be spared from witnessing the fallout. She'd had all the tension and frustration and upset and everything else she could take. She needed a little serenity and peace.

A shower, the clean scents of shampoo and soap clinging to her skin and filling her nose, and then dressing in fresh, soft blue scrubs helped.

Afterward, she explored the cottage. Susan Brandt's touch was everywhere. Warm sage and cream color palette, overstuffed, cushy sofa and chairs, lots of comforting touches that invited and welcomed. The cottage wasn't large—a single bedroom, living room and kitchen combination, and a bath—but it had a little patio off its back door that was littered with white wicker furniture and lots of greenery. Susan liked it best of all.

She walked outside, closed the french door behind her, then sat in a rocking chair. Its squeak was comforting, soothing her nerves. For long moments, she let her mind just drift, and then her situation intruded. She sought the courage to deal with everything that had happened and what she feared was yet to come.

"Lord"—she folded her hands—"You are my refuge and strength . . ."

Ben heated the dinner his housekeeper, Nora, had prepared and left in the fridge before departing for the day. Then at eight o'clock sharp, he brought Susan from the cottage to the house.

"I usually eat in here," he said, talking about the kitchen. "But if you'd be more comfortable in the dining room—"

"No." Susan looked around. The kitchen was large but very informal. A fireplace with a rocker beside it took up the far wall. A breakfast bar with several stools stood center of the room, across from the sink, and in a nook stood a standard table and four matching chairs. In the corner there was a telltale highchair that must have once belonged to Ben's son.

"It was Christopher's," Ben said, his voice reverent and thick. "He'd be six now, if he'd lived. I just can't make myself put it away."

Unable not to, she reached across the bar and gave his hand a gentle squeeze. "I'd have a difficult time with that too."

He looked at her—really looked at her—as if seeing her the first time. "You're not Susan."

Of all he could have said, that she never expected. "No, I'm not."

"I'm sorry." He stepped back. "I didn't mean it like that. I just meant, you resemble her, but more like a sister might. You're distinctly different."

"I'll take your word for it. It's tough for me to tell with all the bruises." She tried to smile. "Can I help?"

"It's done."

He grabbed a blue oven mitt and removed something that smelled great out of the oven.

"Pot roast?" she asked.

"Yes. And rosemary potatoes and squash casserole. Last of the season, Nora said."

"Nora?" Susan lifted the silverware from the bar and set the table.

"She comes in every day to cook and clean." He filled two glasses with ice and poured tea from a glass pitcher. "And to do a fair share of nagging me."

There was a fondness in his voice Susan loved. Indulgent fondness. "Are you related?"

"Not by blood, but by choice, yes." He motioned to a chair. "Have a seat. Please."

She sat down and waited for him to settle in. "You have a wonderful home."

"Thank you." He cleared his throat. Stiff. Distant.

"You don't love it?"

"I do." He passed her the bowl of potatoes. "It's just too big. I ramble around here lost most of the time."

He didn't admit that often. How she knew it, she couldn't say, but she was sure of it. And she couldn't explain why, but it struck a familiar chord in her. "I think I understand what you mean." She tilted her head and placed her napkin in her lap. "I think I feel lost a lot too."

He gave her a slow blink. "You really don't remember, do you?"

She shook her head, let him see how vulnerable that made her feel. "But when you talked about feeling lost, I knew exactly what you meant. It hurts deep."

Hesitating, he paused to study her. "Yes," he finally said. "It does hurt deep."

She spooned squash casserole onto her plate. "I think I know that feeling well."

Ben reached for her hand, then squeezed it as she had his. "I'm sorry."

Too tender! Tears brimmed in her eyes, blurred her focus. She blinked hard to clear them. "Me too."

The room stilled, the tension between them melted, and an understanding borne in a common bond of loneliness and isolation formed between them.

It was a welcome respite.

They talked about what they'd learned from Lance and Jason, prodded her memory for details on the carjacking and her lost day, and ate their dinner. It was companionable, easy. It was nice.

Relaxed, Susan sipped from her tea, then set the chilled glass down. "What do you think of the name Karen?"

"I don't know." Ben took a bite of roast. "Why?"

"I mentioned shortly after we got here that Susan isn't my name, and I think if it's something else, you might be able to say it. So what about Karen? Can you say Karen?"

"Karen would be great." He rewarded her with a smile.

She smiled back at him. "Karen it is, then."

He took another bite of roast. "I'm curious. Why Karen?"

"No reason, I'm sorry to say." She pushed her potatoes with the tines of her fork. "It just, well, it isn't Susan."

That surprised him. "You're very blunt, aren't you?"

"I suppose I am. At least, that's how I see myself." She paused. "I don't mean to offend; I just don't have anything left for being subtle or playing nice. Right now, I'm struggling to stay upright."

"You've been through a lot in a short period of time. That's scary, but having these men after you and not knowing why . . . Well, I appreciate the difficulty." Admiration shone in his eyes. "You're dealing with it well."

She had no choice. "Nothing is easy, and if I told you how often I've been praying I don't find out I'm some kind of slug who's done terrible things, you'd take back thinking I'm dealing well with anything."

He chewed slowly, took his time before answering. "Before I met you at the center, I'd have worried about that too. In fact, I did worry about it."

"But?" she urged him to go on. He wanted to say more; she could see it. Better to get it out in the open rather than have it hanging between them.

"But I'm not worried anymore. I don't know what all of this is about, Karen, but my gut says you're as much a victim as Susan and Christopher were."

She suddenly felt a lot better. "Thank you, Ben."

"For what?"

"That measure of trust"—she smiled at him—"and for using my adopted name."

"You're welcome." He smiled back.

A genuine smile. Enjoying that small victory, she took another bite.

Ben's house phone rang just as he and Karen finished dinner.

He excused himself and answered it. "Hello."

"Ben, it's Gregory Chessman."

"How are you, Gregory?"

"Fine. Just fine. Is it convenient for me to drop by in about five minutes? I'm out and I wanted to drop off that check for the crisis center I promised you at my dinner party."

"Sure, I'll be here."

"Great. I'll see you in five, then."

Ben hung up the phone, thoughtful.

"Everything okay?"

"Yeah." Ben watched Karen clear the table. "Gregory Chessman's just going to drop off a check for the center."

"Oh." She smiled. "Well, I'll finish up here and then go back to the cottage."

"No," Ben said forcefully enough that she stilled. He didn't want her to leave. Surprise riddled through him, fell hard and fast under an onslaught of guilt. "Stay. I want you to meet Gregory. He's famous around here."

She dried her hands on a dishtowel and then tossed it onto the counter. "For what?"

"His generosity mostly." Ben smiled and guided her to the living room. "If there's a charity in a forty-mile radius of Seagrove Village, he's done something significant to support it."

"Sounds like a good man." She looked around. "This is the first formal room I've seen in the house."

"I don't come in here much."

"I'm not surprised."

"Why not?"

"Honestly?"

He nodded, eager to hear what she would say.

"It's got that perfect, useless look." She glanced over at him. "It doesn't suit you."

"I'll take that as a compliment."

She smiled. "I intended it as one."

He liked her. Blunt to a fault . . . and unabashedly honest.

"I have the perimeter security mapped out, Mr. Chessman."

"I heard." Gregory turned down Brandt's street. "From whom, sir?"

"I got a text message from the mayor." Gregory worked hard to keep his temper under control. "Paul, you do realize one of the boys you hired to run across Three Gables was the mayor's son, Lance, right?"

Silence.

"Do I need to repeat the question?"

"No sir." Paul's voice shook. "No sir, I didn't know."

A lie. Gregory hadn't gotten to where he was by not recognizing a lie when he heard one. "Let me rephrase the question. Why did you recruit Lance Green for this recon job?"

"I didn't know the boy was the mayor's son, sir." Paul paused. "Have I created a complication?"

Now why had Paul lied to him? Only one reason made sense. He suspected that there was an association between Gregory and the mayor. Paul hired Lance to test his theory. But had he tested it to protect Gregory or to obtain a security pass in case Gregory turned on him? Could be either. Time would tell.

"No, no complication. I've taken care of it." Gregory twisted his hand, gripping the steering wheel hard. "Don't put me in this position again."

"No sir. I won't—"

Gregory snapped shut his phone, certain Paul was either twitching like a madman or had blanked out and frozen in place. He'd be humiliated and rattled to the core at making such a boneheaded mistake. And well he should be. If this error had occurred with anyone but the mayor, the consequences would have been devastating.

Fortunately, the mayor had chosen his path

years ago in forming a strategic business alliance involving property useful for purposes never openly discussed but that had made them both wealthy men. Better, that alliance wasn't known to anyone else or ever discussed in person between them.

The mayor liked being a big fish in a small pond as much as his wife liked it. He enjoyed sitting in church on Sunday and being admired and respected in his town. He was a proud man. Gregory fully appreciated the obscure relationship between them. Nothing related in any form or manner other than text messages.

That protection made the mayor the perfect secret partner.

11

Gregory Chessman was a sharp dresser and a very attractive man with sandy brown hair, murky hazel eyes, and Romanesque features, and yet something about him made Karen edgy. She couldn't explain it, but her internal radar had gone on alert the moment he walked through the door.

She stood near the sofa in Ben's living room and waited for the men to enter. They greeted each other warmly, and that unnerved her too. Why?

Nothing. No idea.

Please, help me remember.

Still nothing.

They walked in. "Gregory, this is Karen. Karen, this is Gregory Chessman."

Gregory hesitated, clearly surprised to see her. Was that because Ben didn't typically have female guests over, or was it her bruises? Or maybe he recognized her.

For a flash of a second, she felt sure he knew her. But then a shield slipped so firmly over his face that she wasn't sure if she'd seen that flash because it had been there, or because she had wanted to see it.

Stop it, Karen. Your face looks as if you've been through a war. Of course he's looking at you like you're weird.

Trying to redeem herself, she walked over and extended her hand. "Mr. Chessman, I'm pleased to meet you."

"Hello, Karen." He visibly relaxed. "I'm sorry to interrupt your evening."

"No. If anyone is intruding, it's me." He seemed nice enough, but just looking at him had her upset. "I should go."

"No, no." Gregory held up a hand. "I just wanted to drop this by." He reached into his inside jacket pocket, pulled out an envelope, and passed it to Ben. "There you go."

"Thanks." Ben took it. "We appreciate your support, Gregory. Harvey Talbot will be a very happy man."

"Glad to do it." Gregory dipped his chin in her

direction. "Pleasure meeting you, Karen. Hope to see you again soon."

"Thank you." She returned his nod with a stiff one of her own.

" 'Night, Ben."

"Good night." Ben showed Gregory out and then returned to the living room. "What's wrong, Karen?"

"I have no idea. But that man scares me right out of my skin."

"Gregory?" Surprise rolled over his face in a wave. "Why? He's a philanthropist."

"Boy, do I wish I could answer that." She stood, paced a short path alongside the sofa, and tried to force her mind to work, her memory to kick in. She failed and felt every atom of that frustration. "I don't know why, Ben."

"If you don't know, then why are you afraid?"

Good question. Why am I? She paused directly in front of Ben, stared up into his eyes. "I think he's the reason I was so afraid to be in Seagrove Village."

Ben didn't say anything; clearly he had no idea what to say.

"I don't remember him, so I can't be sure, of course." Karen licked at her lips. "But when I look at him, I have that same terrified feeling I had about being here and going to the police." She pressed her hands over her abdomen. "He puts so many knots in my stomach I can barely breathe."

He searched her face. "I won't pretend to understand. Gregory has a sterling reputation. But I see that you believe what you're saying, and I've developed a deep respect for instincts."

Grateful he'd given her that much, she squeezed his upper arm. "Thank you."

"You could be associating something about him that's totally unconnected. You do realize that."

No way. She knew it as well as she knew where she stood. "Yes, I do understand it."

"But you don't believe you're doing it."

"No." She blinked. "No, I honestly don't."

And that certainty might just scare her most of all.

Gregory walked down the lighted sidewalk from Brandt's front door, heading back to his car. He'd pulled deeper into the driveway to get a look at where this cottage was placed on the property.

It was dark, but through the thicket of trees, he saw a brick path and a light in a window beyond it.

Paul shouldn't have any trouble hitting her there.

He drew in a deep breath, scanned for security cameras, and spotted none that would record him. The recorder in his pocket had Brandt's voice. From it, Paul would have his voiceprint and know whether Brandt had infiltrated or Edward had manufactured a pretense. Would Paul tell

Gregory? That he didn't know, which is why he had taken the matter into his own hands with a backup plan.

In short order, Gregory could put this ordeal behind him, and that time couldn't come soon enough for his peace of mind.

His cell phone rang. Gregory reached down to the clip on his belt and retrieved the phone. "Hello." He opened the car door, slid inside, dropping a second envelope onto the concrete driveway, and then pulled the door shut.

It was time to find out himself if Paul's New Orleans contact—a.k.a. one Richard Massey— had recruited Edward or Benjamin Brandt.

12

Thanks for walking me back, Ben." Karen moved toward the cottage door.

"My pleasure." He gave her a disarming smile. "It's been rougher on you being here than I'd hoped it would be. I'm sorry about that."

"Not your fault." She glanced beyond the light into the dark woods. That Mark Taylor and his security staff were on alert did make her feel safer, though meeting Gregory Chessman still had her trembling inside. Oh, how she wished she knew why.

Ben had talked to her for a solid fifteen minutes, reciting the man's golden qualities. Oddly enough that hadn't reassured her but raised her concerns. No mere mortal could be that altruistic.

"I appreciate everything you've done for me," she said, deliberately lingering and debating on whether to tell him what she most wanted to say. Figuring he couldn't think any less of her than he already did, she went ahead. "Especially for a normal dinner. That was such a pleasant surprise."

He gave her a slow blink that had her heart racing. "For me too." He shifted on his feet. "I didn't expect . . ."

"What?" She glanced up and their gazes locked. A flutter of attraction sparked in her. *Oh no. Not a smart move. Not in his position and certainly not in yours.*

"I didn't expect it to be so . . . easy," he said with a little shrug and looked away. "I thought it would be hard."

"Because I look like Susan?"

"No." He kept his gaze diverted for a long moment, then finally returned it to her. "Because I haven't brought another woman into her house." Stuffing his hands into his pockets, he glanced at the velvety night sky. "I thought I would resent seeing you working in her kitchen, but I didn't." He looked down at his feet.

"Ben, are you feeling guilty because you didn't resent me being there?"

He bit at his lip. "Yeah. I guess I am." He

sighed. "No, I know I am. But it has nothing to do with you personally."

His honesty surprised her, but it really shouldn't have. According to Peggy Crane, he had been a good Christian before Susan and Christopher died. Now he was wealthy, respected, and half the women in the village and many beyond it would love to take him off the marriage market, but he wouldn't have any part of that.

Peggy thought he had gotten used to being alone and liked it, but she was wrong. Karen saw in him what she felt inside and hadn't spoken of aloud. That horrible loneliness, so painful and heavy it can't be acknowledged, because if it is, its weight crushes the spirit. Why or how she knew that feeling remained a mystery to her, but she was certain of it.

Ben had an even harder time of it. He was horribly lonely *and* lost. She had her faith to sustain her, God to rely on and shelter her during life's storms. Ben had turned away from God. He faced those storms on his own. How he could survive that was beyond her. It had to be agonizing.

"Karen? Did I offend you?"

"Oh no." She smiled, waved that possibility off. "Sorry, my mind's a little scattered at the moment, and I lost my thoughts."

"I really didn't mean to offend you."

"You didn't." She gripped his arm and gave it a

reassuring squeeze. "Seriously. I was just thinking that I'd probably feel guilty too."

His eyebrows shot up. "You would?"

"Oh yeah." She plucked a leaf off a bush near the edge of the porch, then dropped down into the swing and patted the seat for him to join her. "It wouldn't be justified, of course, but I'd still feel it."

He sat beside her. "Do you know why?"

She twisted to look into his eyes. "Because I'd survived and they hadn't."

He looked at her. Waited.

"I'd feel like I'd failed them, I think." She tucked her hair behind her ear. "It'd eat at me that I was supposed to protect them and I hadn't. I'd blame myself." She saw in his eyes that she'd knocked a home run. That's exactly what Ben felt. *Bless his heart.*

"I'd be an idiot to think any of that, but you know emotions." She lightened her tone. "They don't care about logic or reason or even common sense. They just hang out and drive you nuts wherever they can find a nook or cranny to rip you apart inside."

Ben let out a sigh that heaved his shoulders. "I was supposed to protect them."

"No one can protect themselves, much less anyone else, all the time, Ben. It's an impossible standard."

"You say that, but admit in my place, you'd feel guilty too."

"Well, sure. When it comes to people you love, you expect more than the possible; you expect perfection—because you love them."

He slid her a sidelong look. "Are you a shrink or something?"

"Mmm." Was she? No subtle innate reaction either way. Yet Doctors Harper and Talbot had used medical terms unfamiliar to her. If she was a shrink, she'd be familiar with the words, wouldn't she? "I don't think I am. But don't I wish I knew?"

"Whatever you are, I think you're a strong woman."

"I'm not." She whispered that confession. "To tell you the truth, I'm scared stiff."

"You hide it well."

"I hide nothing." She looked out to the gently rustling leaves. "I lean hard on God. He holds me up." She swerved her gaze back to Ben. "Frankly, if I just relied on me, I'd be laid out flat on the floor somewhere."

"I don't believe that."

"Believe it. I promise you, it's true."

"You're not going preach to me, are you?"

"Absolutely not." She stared off into the night and relaxed for the first time since she'd been carjacked. "You're a grown man, fully capable of making your own decisions and defining your own path." She leaned back. "I'm having enough trouble making sense of my own life right now. I don't dare take on yours too."

He grunted and looked out at the trees. "I envy you, Karen."

"Me? Whatever for?"

"Because even though you don't know who you are, you know exactly whose you are."

"God's child?"

He nodded.

He had a point. Still . . . "I'll tell you a secret." She let out a little laugh. "I'd be less than honest if I didn't admit it'd be really nice to have someone human to hold my hand right now."

"Even under guard, you're afraid."

"Scared half to death." But not just of these two groups after her. She was afraid of all she didn't know.

Their gazes locked, and he slowly lifted his arm. "I'll hold your hand."

Touched, she swallowed hard. The back of her nose stung and her eyes burned. She clasped his hand and twined their fingers. "Thank you, Ben."

Long minutes passed with only the sounds of the squeaking swing and the deep night between them. It was comfortable. Companionable. And in it, they created a bond forged in having faced trials and challenges alone. And, if only for now, they would face them together.

In that, Karen found solace and an unexpected peace.

Ben broke the silence, talking about his life with Susan and Christopher—something Karen felt he hadn't done often or with many. The conversation was relaxed and easy, and as midnight approached, she realized they had talked about nothing and everything, about all manner of things. Ben was sharp and witty and compassionate, and at some time, he'd probably been a strong debater.

"Well, it's late and you've got to be exhausted." He released her hand, staring at it as if he had forgotten he held it or he was reluctant to let go.

Sharing both those feelings, she stood. "It's been a very long day after a very long night, but I really enjoyed this. A normal dinner and conversation was exactly what I needed. Thank you."

He touched her cheek. "Thank you, Karen. I think I needed this too."

"I expect you did." She felt her smile falter. "I want to say something, but I'm not preaching, okay?"

He stiffened.

"You couldn't have saved them," she said softly. "And Susan would hate you kicking yourself because you felt you could."

"Would she?" Hope tinged his voice.

"Absolutely, she would." Karen touched his sleeve. "You loved her, Ben, but you have to remember that she loved you too."

"She did."

"Actually, she's probably pretty ticked off at you for feeling that guilt."

"You didn't know her, Karen. How can you say that?"

"It's how I would react. I'd be really ticked off at you."

"Three years, and I've never once thought of it that way." He shook his head. "But, you know, you could be right. She likely would be ticked off at me."

"Worse, if we're being totally honest."

"Worse?"

"Much worse." She hiked up her jaw. "Susan had her life stolen. That's one thing. But she'd see what you're doing as you giving yours away as if it's worth nothing."

He looked away. "I don't think I like the way that feels."

"She wouldn't like it either." Karen certainly wouldn't. "Just something to think about."

He mumbled something under his breath, rubbing his neck.

Pleased he was thinking about it, she turned the doorknob and then stepped inside. "Good night."

"If you need anything, call."

"Thanks." He seemed a little dazed. *God, I hope that's a good thing and what You had in mind.*

She took a last look—still dazed—then closed the door, a smile tugging at the corner of her mouth. It was amazing how much her opinion of him had changed.

Understanding can do that, she thought, spotting

a baseball bat and glove near the door. An uneasy feeling shimmered over her skin. *Stop it. Mark and his team, Ben, an elaborate security system— surely you're safe.*

Logical, reasonable, yet the moment she closed the door and was alone, wariness settled back in. She'd been deliberately targeted, set up to believe she was Susan. Guided to the crisis center, to Ben specifically with Susan's cross, and no one went to that much trouble for nothing.

Then there was her reaction to Gregory Chessman. It was instinctive. Overwhelming. Certain. What was that all about?

Having no answers, she needed a diversion to keep from getting worked up. She grabbed the bat and walked down the hall. A hot shower would do her a world of good.

Twenty minutes later, wearing a fresh set of scrubs and too wound up to sleep, she went out onto the little patio and sat in the white wicker rocker, then propped the ball bat against the table beside her. There were exterior lamps, but she didn't turn them on. Soft amber rays from the light on the stove streaked through the window and stretched across the tile floor and furniture. She loved the feel of the little patio. Serene and quiet and comfortable—somehow special: a perfect place for prayer.

Karen bowed her head, expressing her gratitude for her life and safety, for Clyde finding her, and for the kindnesses Doctors Talbot and Harper and Peggy and Mel had shown her. For Ben. Maybe especially for Ben, who had stepped out of his own comfort zone to hold her hand.

Gunfire blasted the silence.

Boom! Boom! Boom!

Three shots in rapid succession fired from inside the cottage!

Startled, Karen grabbed the ball bat, then dropped to a crouch in the deep shadows.

Inside, a man cursed, his muffled voice carried through the door to Karen. Her heart raced. She held the bat in a death grip, poised to strike.

With little warning, a man dressed head-to-toe in black and wearing a ski mask burst through the door in a near run.

Karen swung hard, caught him across the back.

He staggered, glanced back, then ran full out away from the cottage. The dark night swallowed him.

Karen stood scanning the woods, her knees locked to keep them from buckling, her blood pounding in her ears. The crunching sounds of someone approaching from the trees carried to her. He was coming back! He had a gun!

Hide, Karen. Hide!

Her feet didn't want to move. She forced them, dropping again into the deep shadows. *God, help me. Please, help me!*

"Karen!" Ben rushed toward the patio. "Karen, where are you?"

It was Ben. *Ben.* She dropped the bat and ran toward him, slamming against his chest, holding on to him for dear life. "He—he left."

Mark arrived, a menacing black gun in his hand. "How many of them?"

She burrowed against Ben, hugged him hard, shaking like a leaf. "One. He was inside. I-I hit him with the bat."

Ben closed his arms around her. "You weren't injured?"

"No." She spoke into his chest, not yet ready to give up the safety she felt in his arms. "He shot three times inside the cottage. I don't know at what."

"Which way did he go?"

She pointed to the side of the cottage, at the greenbelt between the cottage and the street.

Mark talked on a mike and ordered his men to search the grounds. "I'll check the cottage, Ben," he said, then went inside.

"You're sure you're okay?" Ben rubbed little circles on her back.

"I'm scared." Her voice cracked. "I'm really scared."

He hooked her chin with his thumb and tilted her face up to look into her eyes. "Me too. But we'll get through this, okay?"

"Okay."

Mark came out. "All clear." He listened to something being transmitted, then added, "Fresh prints where the fence was cut."

They'd come back. "So much for my abductors not wanting to kill me."

"It's too soon to tell who it was, Karen." Ben nudged her to move. "Let's get inside. We're easy targets out here."

She didn't want to let go of him. Had to make herself release him. Snagging a steadying breath, she walked into the cottage, feeling violated down to the marrow of her bones. This was to be her haven. Her safe place.

Instead, it warned her that there was no safe place.

Nowhere to run, nowhere to hide.

The familiar feeling settled over her like a well-worn coat. She shivered with resentment, despising the sensation with authority and conviction.

"Stay here while I check the damage." Ben left her at the kitchen bar and walked through the cottage.

She didn't move. Couldn't think.

Long minutes later, Ben returned, frowning. "He came in through the bedroom window. Popped the lock."

"What did he shoot?"

"The bed." His frown deepened and grim lines set alongside his mouth. "Obviously he thought you'd be in it, sleeping."

Considering it was nearly one o'clock in the morning, that was a logical expectation. "So he wasn't in there watching me when I came inside?"

"If he had been, he would have known where you were. He clearly didn't, so I'd say no."

That made her feel a lot better. "He must have come in after I went out onto the patio."

"That's where you were when he fired the shots?"

"Yes."

"Then I'd agree." Ben leaned a hip against the kitchen counter. "But he knew where the bedroom was, and that says he was watching closer than he should have been." His jaw clamped shut. "We'll fix that first thing in the morning."

"I'm so sorry I've brought you all this trouble. I wish I could take it back." She swallowed a hard lump in her throat and lowered her gaze to the glossy, black flat-top stove. His partial reflection shone in it. "You've had so much sorrow, and now I'm bringing it all back to you and adding more."

"Karen, no." Ben stepped toward her, gently clasped her upper arms. "This isn't your fault. You didn't do any of it."

"But I might have done something to provoke it." She risked a glance up, praying she wouldn't see condemnation in his eyes. "I might have done something horrible, Ben."

"Listen to me." His expression softened. "No one has been harder on you than me. You can't dispute it." He paused, but she didn't know what to say, so she remained silent, and he continued. "I was wrong about you. I nailed you as a scam artist after money. But now I know that's not you or your way of living your life."

"How do you know?"

He gave her a little smile. "In many ways. In your concern for causing the crisis center trouble. Crisis centers are breeding grounds for trouble. It's why they exist." He lifted a hand to halt her response. "I know because the more I talk with you, the more I see a gentle woman with great courage." Ben stepped back. "More than all of that, though, I know because I've watched you pray. Not when you thought I was looking, but when you were unaware."

What was he talking about? Had he been watching her in the wicker rocker? "When?"

"During our computer interview. You prayed half a dozen times during that discussion."

She stiffened. "How did you know that?"

He chuckled. "I can't believe you don't realize you do it."

"Do what?"

"When you silently pray, your gaze loses focus, like you're looking off into the distance, and you look upward and left. Every time."

"I do?"

"You do." His tone proved he found that endearing.

She loved knowing that and hated knowing she loved that. She was in no position to be attracted to any man, but especially not this one.

"And that tells me more than everything else combined that you're not under attack because you've done something terrible."

"Then why else would two sets of men be after me?"

The amusement left his eyes and his posture stiffened. "I don't know. Could be any of a thousand reasons. We'll know more when your memory returns."

That sent a chill down her spine. "Ben, Dr. Harper said that could be a month or maybe longer. I can't wait. Not when they're attacking me every time I turn around—and not when everyone around me is in danger." What she needed was a place where she could just disappear long enough to recover.

I am with you. None against you will prosper.

God's voice sounded so clearly in her mind. She couldn't leave without this being resolved. She couldn't disappear; she had to stay and get to the truth.

A flood of warmth and surety washed over her. Resigned if not elated, she rubbed her neck. "I know you said I was welcome here, but if you've changed your mind, I—"

"Absolutely not. The right response isn't to leave, Karen. The right response is to make you safer and find out who's trying to harm you."

The tears she'd battled all day blurred her vision. "Thank you, Ben."

Mark Taylor came into the kitchen through the patio door, carrying a clear plastic bag. Inside it was a white envelope marred by writing and a black tire tread print. "He avoided our scanners. We've combed the property, and he's gone. I've put in a call to Jeff."

So he was still out there. Karen's knees folded, and she dropped onto a stool at the bar. "Who is Jeff?"

"Detective Meyers," Ben said. "You spoke with him at the center."

Mark looked at Karen. "Was this guy one of the carjackers?"

"He wore a mask, so I can't be positive, but I don't think so."

"Why?" Ben asked.

"One abductor was a lot bigger than this man. The other was heavier."

Mark pulled a pen and notepad out of his pocket, then poised the pen above the paper and looked back at her. "So you'd describe him as . . ."

"About five eight or five nine and thin. When I hit him with the bat, I probably cracked his ribs."

"I'll alert the hospitals." He made a notation. "What about his eyes?"

"Too dark and he wore a mask." She shook her head. "I can't say."

"Anything else?"

"He was dressed in all black. And his shoes were good quality." She paused as if that struck her as odd. "I'm not sure how I know that, but . . ." Her voice trailed and she ended with a shrug.

Mark turned to Ben. "One of our guys found this in the driveway." Mark passed him the bag containing an envelope.

Ben took it and read what was written on it. "Richard Massey." He glanced from Mark to Karen. "Know him?"

"Never heard of him." Mark shrugged.

Karen shook her head. "No, not ringing any bells."

"The handwriting looks familiar," Ben said.

A memory from Ben's living room, the quick meeting with Gregory Chessman, flashed through Karen's mind. "Chessman. His envelope looked like that one. He could have dropped this one on the driveway."

"Did the camera pick up anything?" Ben asked.

"Chessman going to his car, yes, but nothing that shows the envelope."

"What's inside it?" Ben asked Mark.

"Nothing." Suspicion filled Mark's eyes and stayed put. "It's empty."

Karen tensed. The muscles in her abdomen twisted and her nerves sizzled. Why did Gregory Chessman make her a nervous wreck? Every inch of her skin crawled.

Ben passed the envelope back to Mark. "Run a check on this Massey guy. Let's see what he's about."

Surprise rippled through Karen. "You're not going to call and ask Chessman if the envelope is his?"

"No." Ben didn't elaborate.

Karen pushed him. "Is there a specific reason why not?"

"There are two. One, your instinctive reaction to him earlier—and now you're in a cold sweat. And, two, the tread mark is on top of the writing, which means he dropped it and ran over it. I would check the envelopes to see if they match, but it's just for confirmation. It belongs to him. The one he gave me had the same clipped corner emblem as this one."

"That's significant?" Her brows lifted.

"A lot of high-level executives use one. It's an expensive, personal watermark used to verify that a postmarked envelope mailed to someone is actually the one the executive mailed and not a substitution or a forgery."

Mark frowned. "Now why would a philanthropist need to worry about things like verification and forgery?"

Ben swiveled a look at Mark. "Those are very good questions. Ones we need to answer."

Tension among them ratcheted up, nearly crackled, and yet Karen's uneasiness on one level toned down. Ben believed her.

"Actually," he said, "I think I was too hasty. An innocent man has nothing to hide."

Did that mean he didn't believe her, then? Karen watched, waiting for a sign.

Ben pulled out his cell phone and dialed.

Karen gestured to Mark, silently asking what Ben was doing.

"Calling Chessman," Mark told her.

Was that a good or a bad thing? She unabashedly listened to find out.

"Gregory, this is Ben." He paused. "I found an envelope in the driveway and wondered if you'd dropped it." Another pause. "Yeah, sorry to wake you. I forgot to check the time before I called." He rolled his gaze heavenward. "We had a little incident out at Three Gables."

Ben glanced over at Karen, and something shifted in his eyes, turned hard. "No, everyone's fine. It wasn't anything personal. Just a crisis center patron."

That hurt. It shouldn't; it was true. But it did. And if that didn't prove she needed to check her emotions on this absurd attraction, nothing would.

Ben ended the call and closed his phone. "Chessman said he knew nothing about the envelope and he's never heard of Richard Massey." Ben let his gaze slide from Mark to Karen and sobered even further. "I never asked him about Massey."

He hadn't, and no doubt Chessman still being half-asleep had been the catalyst for that slip.

Karen gasped. "He lied."

Monday, October 12

"Harry, wake up." Edward roughly shook the sleeping man's shoulder. The room stank of stale smoke and beer. An open can sat on a bedside table full of water rings.

Edward couldn't wait to get out of Harry's dump of a trailer. The man took no pride in his home. Weeds were knee high in the yard, and trash littered what should have been the front lawn. His neighbors had every right to hate him. Their lawns were trimmed and neat, and he'd seen baskets of flowers hanging from more than one front porch.

Edward grabbed the nonrousing slob's shoulder again and shook him even harder. "Get up, you disgrace to the human race."

Harry cranked open an eye. "What is wrong with you, man? It's barely daylight."

"It's after six o'clock. Clear your head." Edward backed up to the wall, not touching anything. An inch of dust covered every surface. How could anyone live in such filth? "We've got work to do."

"What's going on?" Harry tossed back the covers and swung his legs over the side of the bed, then planted his feet on the floor. "You look scared."

"I am scared. I just watched Johnson attempt the hit. He blew it."

Harry's eyes stretched wide. "You saw it?"

"From a distance." He still couldn't believe what he'd seen through his night-vision gear. "The woman clubbed him with a bat."

Harry laughed. "Man, I hope she got him good."

"You're missing the point, Harry. There's nothing funny about this."

"Sorry. Johnson getting whacked is very funny to me." Still, he sobered. "So she's still alive and she knows we didn't make the attempt. No one is gonna mistake Johnson for you or me. That's what we wanted." Harry ruffled a hand through his sleep-tossed hair. "So what's the problem, man?"

Edward shoved a hand into his pocket and paced the short distance to the door. "The problem is Brandt knows about Massey." Edward's wiry tension blanketed the room, but he resisted the urge to share the information he'd intercepted on Massey's wiretap about NINA. No way could Harry handle that. It left Edward reeling. The last thing they needed were those cutthroats coming after them.

"How did he find out?"

"I saw an envelope on Brandt's driveway with Massey's name on it. Brandt's got it, and you know he's going to check him out."

Now Harry looked worried too. "Not if Johnson gets to him first. He'll cut the lines to him and Chessman. Massey's history." Harry's eyes narrowed. "But if Brandt gets to Massey first, he could find out about you setting him up."

"It gets worse."

"Don't it always?" Harry pulled on a pair of jeans, then slung on the same shirt he'd worn the day before and began buttoning it. "Chessman will figure we fronted for Brandt. That'll put us back at the top of his priority list."

"Harry," Edward said from between clenched teeth, "sometimes you make me want to knock some sense into you."

Harry glared at him. "Go for it, man."

Edward considered it, but Harry was twice his size and one punch would likely kill Edward. "Would you just think a little bit? That's all I ask."

Harry sniffed, still ticked. He shoved a package of cigarettes into his pocket, scooped up his change and dumped it into his front pocket, then stretched his arm and crammed in his wallet. "Massey will be dead by noon."

"Unless we intercede, yes, he will."

"Is there anybody we don't have to help?" Harry groused and scratched his head. "Don't say it, I know. Needle or bullet."

Edward was content to leave it there.

Harry squinted over at him. "So are we going to intercede?"

Ah, good. He'd gotten the point. Edward lifted his chin, jutted his jaw. "We're going to do what's in our best interests."

13

"Why don't you take a nap on the sofa while I clear up a few things and run a check on Richard Massey?" Ben sipped coffee from a steaming mug.

Enjoying the deep, rich aroma, Karen set her mug in the stainless sink. "I can go back to the cottage."

"I'd prefer you stay here. For safety. Mark has some work to do before you return to the cottage."

"All right." Something in the way he leaned away made her wonder. Safety for her? Or to keep his mind at ease? Maybe it was a bit of both, and she had to admit, she'd rest easier with someone around.

Nora, Ben's housekeeper, rushed in through the back door, stomping her feet on the rug. In her late sixties, round, and as warm and welcoming as a doting grandmother, she gave Karen a smile, then frowned at Ben. "I hear it's been a busy morn," she said, her Scottish brogue pronounced. She scanned Karen from head to toe and must have been satisfied with her findings because she turned to Ben. "Why didn't you call me?"

"Stop worrying, Nora." Ben clasped Nora's shoulder. "We're fine."

"Some dimwit trespassing and shooting holes in my freshly made cottage bed is far from fine, Benjamin." She ducked into the butler's pantry and returned without her purse, tying a starched white apron around her ample middle. "That was a Stearns & Foster mattress, you know—and six hundred thread count Egyptian cotton sheets." She looked at Karen with fire in her eyes. "Mark says you landed a lick on the viper. I hope it was a good one, dearie."

Karen wanted to laugh but didn't. Behind the complaining about the bed and sheets was a worried woman, venting her way through a justified snit. "He did yelp."

"Glad to hear it." Nora sniffed, walked over, and caught Karen's face between her forefinger and thumb. "You're needing a good sleep, I'm thinking. But we'll settle for forty winks—if Himself can keep looters off his land that long."

Ben sighed. "Mark is making the necessary security adjustments, Nora."

Himself. Karen loved the endearment and gave Nora a smile. "They've been really busy with it," she said, supporting Ben. "I'll just go back to the cottage and give everyone some space—"

"No ma'am, you'll not." Nora glared at Ben. "I

know you're not letting her go over there alone, Benjamin Brandt. The girl won't sleep a wink, and none of us will get a thing done."

"I told her I preferred she rest here. But she's an adult, Nora. I can't order her to stay here. It's her call."

"Sometimes you men have all the wits of a dead stump." Nora rolled her eyes heavenward, then focused on Karen. "You'll be resting here, dearie. Follow me." She took off and promptly walked right into the edge of the bar. "Humph."

Karen looked at Ben, who shook his head, then hiked her shoulders. "I'm following her."

"Wise choice," he said, a twinkle in his eye. "When she makes up her mind, refusing her means war."

Karen bet Nora rarely lost.

"Oh, I forgot." Nora stopped suddenly and lifted a wait-a-second finger. "I'll be just a moment." She snagged the house phone, then stepped back into the pantry. "Mark?" A pause, then Nora's propped hand on her hip appeared in the door opening. "When we spoke, I failed to mention that some soul with a sweet tooth has been tossing wadded-up candy wrappers in my garden. I'm thinking you should mention to the boys that I'm taking exception to it. Because if I catch the rascal at it, I'm going to be blistering his ears and calling you to clean up the mess."

Another pause where she listened and then

turned and looked at the stove clock. Misjudging her distance from the wall, she clipped her shoulder. "Fifteen minutes—and bring me an apology from my garden vandal if you're wanting some hot cinnamon rolls to go with it. Otherwise, you're just getting coffee and a sniff, but not the first bite."

She cleared her throat. "Hold on a second. Ben"—she raised her voice—"preheat the top oven for me—425 degrees, and make sure there's fresh coffee. Decaf."

"Will do."

"Yes, I heard you." Nora returned her attention to Mark. "You can hush your bellyaching; you'll be getting decaf. You've probably guzzled a pot full already this morning." A slight pause, then she added, "I can't believe you let some vagrant shoot up my new sheets."

Ben and Karen stood staring at each other, grinning.

"They were Egyptian cotton—"

"Six hundred thread count," Ben whispered.

Biting back a giggle, Karen tapped his arm. "Stop."

Nora grunted. "You'd better work in some target practice, I'm thinking. We're lucky the varmint couldn't shoot." She hung up the phone.

Karen had no doubt Nora would do exactly what she said—and that Mark and Ben would let her. Totally enchanted, Karen asked Ben, "Is something wrong with her eyes? She just nicked the wall with her elbow." She'd bumped into a lot of things already.

Ben pressed a shushing finger over his mouth, stepped closer, then whispered, "Don't mention it. Her vision isn't what it should be, but there's nothing the docs can do."

"I'm so sorry."

He nodded. "She won't give up or give in," he said, pride tinting his tone. "She's determined to live a normal life for as long as possible."

Karen folded her hands in front of her. "Admirable woman."

"Very. Stubborn too."

Ben adored her. Karen smiled.

Nora came out of the pantry, pulled a pan of rolls out of the fridge, then popped them into the oven. "All rightie, then." Dusting her hands, she glanced over at Ben. "I'll be taking Herself for a wee wink, so keep down the racket—and when Mark comes in, tell him not to be a slacker about wiping his shoes. I don't want no dirt muddying up my kitchen floor."

"Yes ma'am." Ben winked at Karen. "Have a good nap."

"I don't dare not to."

Nora hooked her arm with Karen's and led her toward the living room.

Karen stopped in the hallway just outside it. "Nora, is there anywhere else I can nap?"

"Why?" She looked up at Karen, her eyes huge behind her thick glasses. "Don't you like the living room?"

Karen glanced away. "It's lovely."

"But . . ."

"Never mind. I don't mean to be rude. Anywhere is fine."

"You don't like it either?"

"Honestly?" Karen shouldn't have started this conversation. She should have just kept quiet. But she hadn't.

"What's wrong with it?"

"Nothing. It's perfect," Karen said. "It's just, well, I'm not."

"Perfect?"

"Or formal."

Nora cackled. "I know just what you mean, dearie. You're scared to sit down in there. You might mess up something." She patted Karen's arm and turned toward another wing of the house. "It was Susan's folly. She and her mama saw it in a magazine. Her mama just loved it, so Susan had to have it." She shook her head. "Benjamin hated it from the start, but if Susan wanted it, she would have it, and have it she did." Nora sighed. "Oh, but she was excited that day."

"I'm sure she was." Interesting. It was so not Susan's typical tastes. "Did she spend a lot of time in there?"

"I don't think she ever went into it unless her

mama was here. Benjamin avoids it like it's got the plague."

The respect and love they showed each other was touching, and doubt niggled at Karen. Did someone love and respect her? Did she feel that bond with some special man? If she did, wouldn't her heart know it? "I think Susan must have been a very special woman."

"Special as they come," Nora said with a little smile. "But I have a feeling you're a special woman too."

"Thank you." Karen nearly cried. "I hope I am."

"Ah, don't you be worrying about your little problem, dearie." She led Karen into a den that was cozy and comfortable, burgundy leather and masculine but inviting. "You'll remember all about yourself soon enough." She elbowed Karen gently. "If you're like the rest of us, you probably remember a fair share of things you'll wish you could forget. Enjoy the reprieve."

Stunned by that bald remark, Karen laughed. "Nora, you're a breath of fresh air."

"Don't I know it?" She motioned to the sofa. "Now, crawl your wee self up there and settle in for a nice, long snooze. You look ready to drop."

"I'm exhausted." Karen curled up on the sofa and accepted a throw Nora handed her. "Thank you for everything."

Nora pulled up the cover on Karen's shoulder. "You've been through the mill, but don't you be worrying. Ben and Mark will be sorting all this out, and I'll be watching over you while you sleep. Nobody will be bothering you on my watch. So you just rest easy."

Karen smiled at the kindness even as worry filled her. Nora meant well and her heart was in the right place, but people were out to kill her—and Nora, bless her, was bat blind.

But I am not. I am with you always . . .

Karen let that certainty sink in and began a heartfelt prayer of gratitude.

"Karen?" Ben stood beside the sofa, not wanting to wake her but having little choice. She had her arm flung up over her head and her mouth opened just a touch. Very pretty. Very vulnerable.

Protect her. The desire rammed into him like a sucker punch to the gut. He stiffened against it. He didn't want to care about this woman, or any woman. After Susan, he didn't dare.

But something inside him did want to care, and he resented it. He'd shed too many tears, spent too many sleepless nights reliving every moment of his life with Susan. He carried that burden of guilt at not being able to protect her and their son, and he spent far too many days fighting the demons in his mind that insisted he should have died in their place.

She didn't awaken.

"Karen?"

Her eyes fluttered open and she smiled. Then she started and sat up straight. "What? What's wrong?"

"Everything's okay."

"Oh, good." She rubbed her eyes. "What time is it?"

"Almost noon." He cleared his throat. "I'm sorry to wake you, but I need to talk to you and it shouldn't wait."

"Okay."

"Nora went to the grocery store. While she was there, a man came up to her and told her to check in New Orleans for Richard Massey. To tell me right away."

Karen touched a hand to her chest. "Was he one of the abductors, the one who paid the teens, or the man who shot—?"

"We don't know. Mark's asked, but no one else in the store noticed the guy, and if he was picked up on the security camera, Nora couldn't identify him from the tape."

"Her eyes?"

"I'm afraid so. Mark's picked up lines on several Richard Masseys in the Greater New Orleans area. He's got a couple dozen photos he needs you to look at. Sorry, but it really can't wait. We've got to get to Richard Massey as soon as possible."

"Why?" Karen tossed the throw aside, slid into her shoes, then stood.

"Because the man in the store told Nora that Massey was marked for death."

She gasped. "He must know me or something about me, then. Is that why he's going to be killed?"

Ben couldn't miss the regret and upset in her voice. "We don't know that."

"This is no time for diplomacy, Ben."

"We believe it could be, yes."

Karen squeezed her eyes shut. *God, give me strength.* "We'd better hurry, then."

Ben stepped back, giving her room to rise from the sofa. "Mark's got the photos on the computer screen in my office. It's this way."

Karen followed Ben down the hallway, passing three closed doors, a long table with a sweet-smelling vase of daisies, a painting of Three Gables, and then finally they stepped into his office.

It smelled like him. And like the rest of the house, it was comfortable and free from pretense. Karen loved the feel of it, of his whole house, except that extremely formal living room.

Mark sat at Ben's desk in front of a computer. "Karen. Great." He stood and motioned for her to sit down. "Sorry about interrupting the nap—and I'd appreciate it if you didn't mention it to Nora. I'll be old and gray before I get another cinnamon bun."

"No problem." His hopes were up; she could see it in his eyes. "What do you want me to do?" She settled into the chair.

"See if you recognize anyone."

"I probably won't, Mark." She glanced up at him. "Don't be disappointed, okay?"

"I won't. We know it's unlikely, but it's worth a shot."

"Okay, then." She scooted the chair closer to the desk and looked at the screen. "Where are they?"

He reached over and tapped a button. "Just click here when you're ready to advance to the next slide."

"Got it." The slide show of photos began. She studied the first. Nothing. The second and third. Nothing and still nothing. The fourth through the eighth netted the same. The ninth, again nothing, and Karen's hope began to dwindle, her spirits to sink. This was useless. She didn't know who she was, much less anyone else. She tapped the advance key . . . and stopped cold.

"What is it?" Ben asked from behind her left shoulder.

She studied the man in the photograph a minute longer, then glanced back at Ben. "I know him. He's the guy who handed me the keys to the Jag— after my Jeep broke down."

"Okay." Ben signaled and Mark left the room, dialing his cell phone.

She stared at the familiar face. "Who is he, Ben?"

214

"Richard Massey."

She'd figured that much. "Is he from New Orleans?"

"He's a private investigator there. Has a small firm down in the French Quarter."

"Does he know me?" Excitement bubbled in her. "He could know me." She jumped up and hugged Ben. "He must know me."

He stiffened, hesitated, and then hugged her back. "He must know you."

"I must be from New Orleans, then."

"Maybe." Ben stepped away, then pulled out his cell. "Mark, check with NOPD and see if anyone there's filed a missing person's report on Karen." Seconds later, he hung up the phone, slipped it back into his pocket. "He's faxing over a photo of you to the police department now."

Mark always seemed to stay a step ahead. "Maybe we'll get lucky." She gave him a half smile.

"We'll hope."

Karen stared at Ben a long moment, worked up her courage, and finally spoke her heart. "Would it sound ridiculous if I said I'd miss you?"

Relief and panic warred in Ben's eyes. "No crazier than me saying I'd miss you."

Her heart leapt. "Would you, really?"

He shrugged. "I would."

She smiled and offered him her hand.

Ben clasped it and gave hers a gentle squeeze.

Mark cleared his throat at the door to Ben's office.

Ben stepped away and rubbed his hands together. "Anything?"

Frowning, hesitancy in his step, Mark walked into the office. "Sorry, Karen. No missing person's report has been filed on you in New Orleans."

Disappointment speared through her. She put on a brave face. "So I guess I'm not from there, after all."

"That, or no one is waiting," Mark said.

That hurt. It shouldn't—he simply recited a fact—but it did hurt. She was a good person; she believed that now. But how could she disappear and have no family or friends or work associates or anyone else even notice?

Whoever she was, she had no one. *No one.* The absence weighed her down. Small, insignificant, unimportant, useless . . . *Neither blessed nor a blessing.*

"Are you okay?" Ben asked.

She stiffened her spine, trying hard to bury her emotions. "I'm fine, thank you."

Mark shot a worried look from Karen to Ben, as if he wanted to say something but wasn't sure he should.

"Okay, I'm not fine, but I'm not going to get fine if you keep things from me." Karen searched for her emotional rhino-hide. At the moment, it seemed elusive. "So just say what needs saying."

"There's still no missing person's report."

"So no one cares if I'm dead or alive or missing." She hid behind a sniff. "Well, if I had an overinflated sense of importance, it's gone now, isn't it?"

"Karen, I'm sorry." Ben stepped toward her.

She lifted a hand, silently asking him not to touch her. If he did at this moment, she was going to lose it and wail.

Why didn't anyone care about her? *Why?*

"And so it is with great pleasure that I dedicate the Chessman Wing to Seagrove Village Community Hospital." Gregory stepped forward and clipped the ceremonial ribbon.

To thunderous applause from the small group gathered, he passed the scissors to Hank Green, coroner and the younger brother of the esteemed mayor. Waving to the crowd, Gregory spotted a stiff-backed Paul Johnson standing to the side, waiting for him.

"Go on inside, Hank," Gregory told the coroner. "I'll be right in."

Jovial, Hank hooked up with the manager of the local supermarket, and they entered the building for the celebratory reception. When the door closed behind them, Gregory joined a solemn-faced Paul. "Where have you been?"

"Mobile, sir." Paul grimaced. "I was injured last night and went to have myself checked out."

Mobile, Alabama. The site of the mall bombing.
NINA. "Do I need to know what happened?" The subject wasn't dead. Brandt himself had told Gregory everyone was fine, not that the entire village wasn't talking about the attack. Why wasn't she dead? That was all Gregory wanted to know.

"I've got two cracked ribs and a bruised kidney," Paul said.

NINA in close proximity and he gives Gregory useless personal information? "I meant what happened at the cottage." Gregory glared at him. "I assume from your injuries you levied the attack."

"Yes sir." Paul dropped his gaze, shielding his eyes. "She wasn't inside."

"So you shot up her bed for kicks?" He'd gotten a text message from his secret partner sharing that detail at the crack of dawn. Unpleasant, having your competence questioned, but it was the phone call with Brandt that most troubled Gregory. He couldn't expressly remember Brandt asking if Gregory knew Massey, but he must have. Even awakened from a dead sleep, Gregory wouldn't volunteer that information unless asked. Would he? Why couldn't he recall specifically?

"One in the morning, rumpled covers—statistically speaking, sir, the risk ratio was less than one percent that she wouldn't be in it."

"You couldn't just look and see that the bed was empty?"

Paul grimaced and the muscle in his left cheek

twitched. "Stacked pillows gave the illusion that someone was there. She's staying alone, ergo . . . But that's not why I came to find you. This event wasn't on your schedule."

The flicker of irritation tinting Paul's tone raised Gregory's hackles. Putting it down to him being in pain, Gregory ignored it. "The mayor and his wife went to New Orleans for an Emergency Management summit of the coastal states. Hurricane preparedness. Darla wanted to get there early, so John asked me last minute to fill in here."

"New Orleans?" Paul's eyes narrowed and his chin jutted out.

Uninterested in pursuing further talk about the mayor and his eye candy, Gregory asked, "Why are you looking for me?"

"Our recruiter was shot to death in his office this morning."

A shudder rippled through Gregory. "Do we know why?"

"Not yet, sir. Nor do we know who is responsible."

"Well, I suggest you find out quickly." Gregory checked his watch—2:20. "The sooner, the better."

"I'm working on it, sir."

"Did you at least get his feedback on that voice-print of Brandt's?"

"No sir, I'm afraid not."

Truth or lie? For now, only Paul knew. "Unfortunate."

If true, then Massey had died before Paul could get the information. Maybe a coincidence, but with his secret partner in New Orleans, who knew? Coincidence didn't often coincide with murder.

Gregory straightened his tie. John Green had been a good mayor and the perfect secret partner, but if he'd killed Massey, he better have a good reason for not first discussing it.

Otherwise, he'd soon be joining the recruit.

Yet John making the hit wasn't logical. He had no reason to go after Massey. He didn't know Paul had hired the man, and Paul didn't know Gregory knew Massey's identity. At least, to Gregory's knowledge, that was the case.

But what if John did know about Massey?

A chill swept through him. He could know. Paul had tested Gregory; he had lied to him. Had that been about Massey? Was Paul doubling down on Gregory, playing both sides of the fence with John Green to cover his own assets?

Possible. Knowing Paul, probable. He was fiercely loyal, but his first loyalty was, of course, to himself. So if he believed it best served his interests, he could have told John anything.

Yet it was also possible that something else had misfired or hadn't connected as anticipated. He looked at Paul. "What do you think happened?"

"Our recruit put the subject into the Jag to signal the gang to hit her. Someone interrupted, and the gang scattered. He could've stiffed them on payment, and they took exception to it."

Gregory waved to a couple walking inside. "Or Edward took him out."

Paul's eyes darted around, as if calculating. "High rate of probability on that, sir. If he set up Brandt as a hireling to misdirect us and he interrupted the gang hit, then he'd want to eliminate that connection and any evidence."

Edward. Gregory grimaced. The voiceprint wasn't necessary after all. "It's time for a priority shift."

14

Karen." Mark walked into Ben's kitchen.
The doom-and-gloom expression he wore had Karen fighting panic. "Something else is wrong, isn't it?" A glance across the table to Ben didn't reassure her.

Ben put down his fork. "I'm afraid so." He pivoted his gaze to Mark. "Did you talk to Massey?"

Mark looked as if he'd rather be anywhere than standing in Ben's kitchen facing the two of them, sharing a late lunch. "I tried, but no. Karen, I'm so sorry to have to say this, but Richard Massey is dead."

The force of his words knocked her back in her chair. Her only tie to her past—gone. She cleared her throat, summoned her voice. "What happened to him?"

"He was shot this morning," Mark said. "Somewhere around eleven o'clock."

Nora silently poured Mark a glass of iced tea, set it on the table, then with a hand to his shoulder nudged Mark to take a seat beside Ben. She gave Karen's shoulder a gentle squeeze. "Be strong, girl. God's in control."

Nora went back and fixed Mark a plate, returned to the table with it, then went back, scrubbed the bar, and motioned for Karen to eat.

Mark hadn't taken a bite and Ben wasn't eating either. Doubting she could swallow, Karen picked up her fork. "Do they know who shot him?"

"No suspects." Mark lifted his fork and filled it with sweet corn. "At least, not yet."

Ben reached over and clasped Karen's hand, his warm fingers covering hers like a protective blanket. "I'm sorry."

"Me too. The problem is, what do we do now?"

Mark set down his chilled glass, swallowed. "I got through to his receptionist, Emily, and faxed her your photo. She didn't recognize you, but she'd been out on maternity leave and just returned this morning."

"She picked a bad day to return to work." Karen chewed and swallowed a bite of the best meatloaf she'd ever tasted. "Nora, I love this meatloaf."

"Plenty more over here."

Mark reached for the shaker.

"Don't you dare be adding salt to my food, Mark Taylor. It's got plenty."

He pulled back his hand and sighed. "Emily said she'd talk to the temp who's been filling in for her and look through their files. I checked with the police again. Still no reports showing up on you being missing. We're pretty much stuck on that end until we hear what Emily uncovers."

Ben polished off the last bite of meatloaf. "Nora, is that fresh apple pie?"

"It is. But don't get your mind set on it. It's for the ingathering at church tonight."

"Shoot," Mark grumbled under his breath. "Nora makes good apple pie."

"And everything else," Ben added. "Did you take care of upgrading the security at the cottage?" he asked Mark.

"It was finished about three—a good hour ago. No one can walk within fifty feet of it without being monitored at the security shack. And if they drop from a helicopter onto the roof, we've still got them."

"Good." Ben looked at Karen. "You had a fear of being in Seagrove Village. All things considered, it's a compelling one."

Where was he going with this? Karen's throat felt dry, but she shook too badly to trust herself to pick up her glass and take a drink. She'd end up wearing half her tea. "I still fear it. I just wish I knew why. I've tried to remember, Ben. Really, I have."

"Harvey and Lisa said you shouldn't do that," he told her, his concern evident.

"The center's been bombed, everyone there's at risk, all that's happened here, and now my one link to my life, this Richard Massey, is dead. I can't just sit here and do nothing until they find a way to kill me—and maybe hurt you and Mark and Nora in the process. I've got to try to remember." She put down her fork. "Actually, I should leave so you're not in jeopardy."

"Your leaving won't help." Mark grabbed another biscuit from the basket at the center of the table. "It's clear that Ben's as involved in this as you are. If you did leave, they'd still be after him." He broke the biscuit and slathered it with butter. "It won't help, but it could hurt."

"Mark's right," Nora added her two cents. "All this is about you and Susan, I'm thinking." She snatched the butter off the table and stared down her nose at Mark. "I can feel your arteries hardening from across the room. Moderation, my boy."

Ben hid a snicker behind his hand. "I agree with Nora."

Karen couldn't resist. "About Mark's arteries, or this being about me and Susan?"

"Both," he said. "There are too many connections for it to be anything else."

Shame flooded her. "I'm so sorry, Ben."

"Why?"

"I don't know. I just . . . am."

"Mark, you stay on Massey's receptionist." Ben stood. "Karen, let's take a ride."

She dabbed at her mouth with her napkin. "Where are we going?"

"Something in this village frightens you. Maybe if we ride around, you'll see something that spurs a memory."

She brightened. "That's a great idea." Feeling better at doing something, anything, she stood and gathered their dishes, then moved toward the sink.

"You go on." Nora intercepted her and snagged their plates. "I'll take care of this."

"Thank you, Nora." Looking into the older woman's eyes, Karen let her know she was grateful for this kindness and more.

"My privilege." She gave her a wink. "You be strong. Something will be coming to you. I believe it."

Her certainty seeped into Karen. "It could. It really could."

"Will." Nora nodded. "Have faith, girl."

Karen smiled. "Right. You're right." She took in a breath and squared her shoulders. *God willing.* "Will."

A gloomy sunset threatened.

For the last two hours, Ben and Karen had driven through most of the sleepy seaside village. Would anything ever strike her as familiar?

It won't happen. You're not going to find any-thing.

I will, Karen countered. *Leave me, doubt. I don't believe you. Sooner or later, I will.*

Fifteen minutes later, doubt again crept in.

And again she fought it.

"You okay?" Ben hooked his little finger on the turn signal. "You look a little frazzled."

Karen exaggerated a sigh. "Just what I needed to complement my bruises and bandages and complete my ensemble, eh?"

Ben laughed.

The sound warmed her through to her bones. It was a pleasant laugh, not mocking but genuine. She loved the tone of it, but even more she loved the easiness she felt on hearing it. Ben's laughter helped her fight the demons trying to make her doubt. They were an insidious bunch, subtly chipping away at a person until suddenly one awakened and found faith gone. And it shocked because one had no idea what had happened to it.

That wasn't going to happen to her. *God stands with me. No one against me can prosper.*

"I was getting a little discouraged," she told Ben. "But if you can still laugh—even if it's at me—then so can I." She smiled a little wider, and this time, the cracked skin at the corner of her mouth didn't hurt. She was healing—inside and out.

Ben looked contrite. "I didn't mean anything by

that. I hope I didn't hurt your feelings, because I certainly didn't intend—"

"No, of course not." She covered his hand on the gearshift with hers. "I loved hearing you laugh. It reminded me that things are never as dire as we see them."

"Oh."

Definitely at a loss. She giggled. "Look, what's happening is horrible. That I don't know why it's happening makes it worse. And that it's impacted so many others, well, that's just awful."

"Karen, we've talked about this. It's—"

"Wait." She held up a staying hand. "Let me finish."

He waited.

"But if you can go through all this not knowing who I am or if I deserve all that's happening, then I can get through it too." She swept her hair back from her face. "Whatever comes isn't too big for God, or for you, so it's not too big for me to deal with either."

He stopped at a red light and looked over at her with longing in his eyes. "I want what you've got."

What was he talking about? Curiosity got the better of her. "What do I have?"

"Faith." The light turned green and he drove on.

"It's not being withheld from you."

"It died with Susan and Christopher."

"Actually, it didn't, Ben. You let go of it."

Silently, he crossed the main highway that ran along the water and missed a turn to double back. Taking the next left, he drove through a little neighborhood of small beach houses.

He was going to ignore her. Feeling a nudge, she pushed. "If you don't want faith, that's one thing. God gave us free will. We get to choose. But—and you've learned this the hard way—that's a lonely road."

"I'd agree with you on that."

"So if you want faith back, change your choice. It's that simple."

"And that complex. I don't believe anymore. That's what eats me alive. When I did believe, I knew this was just the tip of the iceberg—life, I mean. Eternity was so much bigger. I miss the serenity in knowing that."

The sun sank and she flipped up her sun visor, no longer needing it. "That, too, is a choice."

"Yes." He turned right and followed the curvy road along the shore. "But it's the only one I can make and keep my integrity."

"You're right."

"What?" His voice elevated, revealing his surprise.

"If you don't believe it and declare it, you're just harming yourself. Feeling you have to forfeit your integrity to have faith, well, who can say that's the right thing to do?" She grunted. "It's just not."

He slid her a sidelong look. "Why do I feel a 'but' coming on?"

"Because you know that faith in what's seen requires nothing. Faith in the absence of view, that's worthy of God." She sighed. "The problem isn't that God ran out on you, Ben. You walked out on Him. And it isn't faith in Him you've lost, or you wouldn't miss it and want it back. It's faith in you."

Anger flushed his cheeks.

Not wanting to see it, she looked out the window and saw a little shack of a beach house. Her skin prickled and warmth flowed through her whole body. "Stop!"

"What?" Ben hit the brakes.

She opened the door, got out, and then crossed the street. The low picket fence had peeling paint now, but in her mind it flashed sparkly white. Weed-ridden flower beds with dead blooms lined the brick walkway, but she saw bountiful marigolds and hanging baskets on the tiny porch's eaves.

A lone rocker sat empty and silent beside the front door. In her mind it wasn't empty. An elderly woman wearing a paint-smeared smock rocked and shelled peas into a large hand-thrown pottery bowl. The rocker. She'd sat in that rocker—as a girl, as a teen, as a woman!

Gasping, she rushed through the gate and knocked on the door.

No answer.

She knocked again. Harder. "Hello. Is anyone here?"

Ben came up behind her. "Karen, what is it?"

Sparing him a glance, she knocked again, banging on the door. "I've been here—often." Her excitement bubbled over into her voice. "Ben, I spent a lot of summers here. I remember this house!"

Halfway down the block, Edward watched the woman bang on the beach house door from the front seat of his new Impala. The Jag was now buried for all time in a marsh a long way from Seagrove Village and even farther from New Orleans.

It would never be found.

"Do you think she remembers?" Harry sounded worried.

"No. If she did, she wouldn't be knocking."

"Guess not." Harry parked an elbow on the center console. "Did you lead her here?"

"No, I didn't." Edward checked through the binoculars. "She looks pretty excited." Had Chessman led her here? NINA operatives tipped her off?

"Maybe when she saw the place, she remembered on her own."

"Maybe." Harry needed to shut up so he could think. Chessman wouldn't do anything to trigger his subject's memory. Her recall was the last thing he wanted. She could put him in jail. Johnson wouldn't do anything either, not with those teenagers able to identify him. Besides, if Chessman went down, they'd all go down, including Johnson. No way would he risk that.

"Chessman's secret partner?" Harry asked. "Maybe he did something to get her here."

"So he could go to jail with Chessman?" Edward guffawed, regretting telling Harry that Chessman had a secret partner. The phone taps had provided that useful information, though Edward hadn't yet identified that partner. Text messages didn't have voices that could be matched, and the phone wasn't a landline or a traceable cell. "I don't think so."

"Well, something got her here."

Edward lowered the binoculars. "None of the usual suspects, including us, want her to remember, Harry. She's got us on this place. We'll all go to prison. What we want is her far away and scared to talk—"

"She's right here, man."

"—or dead," Edward finished.

"So shoot her." Harry pointed to the .45 on the seat at Edward's thigh.

"No, not when she's with Brandt."

"Shoot him too."

"No." Killing Brandt wasn't negotiable.

Harry's frustration manifested in a sigh so deep

it swelled his chest and hunched his shoulders. "Sometimes I don't get you. The guy means nothing. He's just in the way. We're already down for her. What's the difference if he's on the list too?"

Edward glared at Harry. "The difference is we messed up. We killed his son and his wife by mistake, moron. We're not taking him out too."

"But, Edward—"

"No!" Edward elevated his voice, something he rarely permitted himself to do. "Brandt's off-limits. That's final."

Harry shook his head, then glared out the rear window. "Well, I hope Paul Johnson feels the same way you do. Otherwise, we've probably got ourselves a problem."

Edward wiped at a speck on his thigh. "What are you talking about?"

"Behind us." Harry hooked a thumb backward. "Johnson."

Edward looked back. Johnson was there, all right, and he sat in his Lexus with the barrel of a scoped rifle aimed at the woman standing at the beach house's front door.

15

There's no one here, Karen." She had to be disappointed. Ben touched her shoulder to soften that blow. "I'll check the window to be sure."

"I'll look on this side." She stepped off the porch and disappeared around the west side of the house.

Ben rounded the east corner, stepped through the weeds, and cupped his hands at the window. *Empty.* The paint on the walls looked dull and dirty, and trash lay heaped in the corner. Empty long enough that homeless people had been using the place as shelter from the weather. One thing was clear. Ben started toward the front of the beach house. From the amount of trash around, the place hadn't just become empty; no one had lived here for months.

Near the porch, he looked but didn't see Karen. "Where are you?"

No answer.

"Karen?"

Still no answer.

A warning blared in his mind. Ben moved quickly, kicking up a spray of sand. Nothing out front. He kept running, made the western corner, and caught a flash of a man in black running down the beach. Ben scanned the shore and stopped cold.

Down near the water Karen lay sprawled on the sand.

And she wasn't moving.

Gregory paced his office, turning on the box to generate white noise to ensure that his conversation wasn't overheard. There hadn't been time to sweep the office before the call from Johnson had come in, and Gregory was too upset to postpone the conversation to run one.

"What do you mean Harry attacked you and Edward snatched the subject?" he said into the phone.

"I had her in my cross hairs," Johnson said, still sounding groggy. "The next thing I know, I'm taking one in the jaw and fighting for my life. The subject was looking through the window at the beach house and Edward dropped her on a dime."

"He shot her?"

"No, knocked her out."

Fear had Gregory rabid. "What was she doing there?"

"I don't know, sir."

"She's remembered." He stared at the ceiling, hoping for deliverance from the incompetent people who seemed to have permeated his inner circle at the worst possible time in his life. How was he going to explain this to NINA?

"I don't think so," Johnson said. "She'd just have gone inside. She knocked on the door a long time before she gave up and went to the window."

That made sense. "If she hasn't remembered, then how did she find the beach house?"

"I have no idea. I was tailing her and Brandt. When they got to the beach house, he stopped abruptly and she dashed out of the car. He wasn't expecting it. He was across the street, not pulled to the curb."

Gregory digested that, then plopped down in the seat behind his desk. "So you think she just recognized the place?"

"I think that's exactly what happened."

"Then explain Harry and Edward being there."

"They were either tailing her or me."

Gregory leaned forward and tapped an impatient fingertip on his blotter. "Lucille!"

His housekeeper stuck her head in the door. "Yes, Mr. Chessman?"

"Tea. Now."

"Yes sir." She disappeared.

He returned his attention to Johnson, having spent the intervening seconds thinking. "Edward's buying leverage. Which means he didn't take out Massey."

"Then who did, sir?"

"If I knew that, I wouldn't need you, Paul. Why don't you do your job and tell me?"

"I'm working on it, sir."

"Work faster," Gregory said from between clenched teeth. "If she finds out what we're doing at the beach house, we're not just looking at state charges. We'll be lost forever in Leavenworth."

"She has no idea what's going on in her aunt's beach house, sir."

"You'd better be right, Paul." Gregory wished she'd just sold him the place. "Our largest shipment ever is due in tomorrow night, and if anything goes wrong . . ." NINA would nail his hide to a wall in Siberia.

"I'm on it, sir."

"You'd better be, Paul. You're betting your life on getting it right—and mine."

"I'm aware of the risks." His agitation crackled through the line like static.

"Then stop messing up. Find the subject and kill her."

16

Ben fell to his knees in the sand. Karen lay deathly pale. He checked her throat for a pulse. Feeling the rhythmic pressure pound against his fingertip, he let out a sigh. "Karen." He stroked her face. "Karen."

She opened her eyes, blinked as if dazed, and appeared to finally focus. "Ben?" She sat up. "What am I doing out here?"

Waves crashing against the shore nearly drowned out her trembling voice. "I have no idea." He cupped her shoulders, scanning the stretch of sand. "Are you all right?"

"Yes." Swaying, she grasped his arm and pulled herself to her feet. "I was looking in the window. Something hit me in the head and"—she gave her head a shake—"and I don't remember anything after that."

The flash of the man in black returned to Ben. "Did you see anyone?"

"No." The wind swept her hair over her face.

Ben brushed it back and let her see his worry. "You're sure you're not hurt?" He ran his finger-tips over her crown and collided with a lump. "Someone whacked you pretty hard. You've got a goose egg." He steered her back toward the beach house. "We'd better go have one of the docs take a look at you—just to be sure you're okay."

"I'm all right." She cocked her head against the wind. "Actually, I'm not. I'm very confused." She looked up at him. "Once again, they've tried to kill me without killing me."

Ben debated keeping his thoughts to himself, but she really did look all right, and his silence wouldn't benefit either of them. "I think we're dealing with warring parties, Karen."

"What do you mean?"

"It's like you said." Ben elevated his voice to be heard above the gulls. "They had you after the carjacking. If they wanted you dead, you would be."

"True. And at the cottage, if I'd been in bed, where most people are at one in the morning, I would have been."

"Right. Those bullets were real. He wanted to kill you." Ben frowned.

"Now this attacker. If he wanted to kill me, he would have done it." She swiped at her elbows and arms. "So why knock me out? Why attack me just to knock me out? All I was doing was looking through the window."

Valid point. "Let's get back to the car." Ben clasped her arm. "We're a big target out in the open." He nudged her, and she started walking. "I think this someone just wanted you out of the way." Karen's shoes sank into the sand, and Ben held her tighter, helping her keep her balance. "I saw a man in black run down the beach."

"All black, like at the cottage?"

"Yes."

"I see what you mean about the warring. Two groups after me, jockeying for control."

Arriving back at his SUV, Ben opened the door and Karen got in. He walked around the front end, trying not to think about her comment turning his stomach to jelly, got in behind the wheel, and then looked down the street. "Where did all the cars go?"

"What do you mean?" Karen stretched her seat belt and clicked it into place.

"When I parked, there were four or five cars on

the street. Some neighborhoods prohibit street parking. Your car gets towed." He shrugged, a hand on the wheel. "I'm not familiar with this neighborhood, but it's on the beach, so the owners need the protection or they'd be blocked in all season long. If the street had been empty, I wouldn't have parked here. I'd have pulled into the driveway."

"Maybe they just left."

"All at once?" He grunted. "No. No, this doesn't fit."

"So what are you telling me?" She rubbed at her throat like she had rubbed Susan's cross.

Guilt seeped through him, and shame followed on its heels. He had ripped Susan's cross off her neck. The scratch where the chain had scraped her skin was still red. He should never have done that. She was a victim, and he'd made her one again.

"What's wrong, Ben?"

"Excuse me?"

Karen shrugged. "You look so . . . I don't know. Bothered?"

"I'm fine." He cranked the car engine, put the gearshift into drive, and took off. "Actually, I'm not fine; I'm angry. I should have been more alert. We were being watched, and I should have noticed it." He grimaced and turned off the radio. "I should have expected it." He shot her an apologetic look. "I'm so sorry, Karen."

She rubbed his arm. "I didn't notice anyone

either, and I definitely should have been watching." She squinted. "Tell you what, let's forget it and make a pact that we'll both be alert from here on out."

How could she be so gracious . . . and calm? He was a wreck inside. They both could have been killed, and they would have died not knowing why.

"Ben?"

He looked from the road to her. "What?"

"Watch that truck," she said, then went on. "What if it wasn't me? What if it was the beach house someone didn't want us to see?"

"But why?" Ben didn't consider it possible, but he couldn't fathom a reason for it either. "It was empty. Maybe some homeless folks have been using it, but no one is living there."

"Something else was strange." Karen checked the side mirror. "There were stairs in the bedroom. When I looked in the window, I saw them."

"You've lost me." He passed a blue Tahoe. "Why is that significant?"

"The house is built on the beach. Dig down a foot, and you hit water." She stiffened in her seat, gasped. "It's a one-story house."

Ben's heart thumped against his ribs. "There's no need for stairs."

"Red light!" She grabbed the dash.

Ben hit the brakes. "There's no need for stairs."

"I know, but they're there. Why?"

"Good question." He pulled out his cell phone and dialed.

"Taylor."

"Mark, it's Ben." He checked the streetlight. "Any word from Jeff Meyers?"

"Not yet."

Ben shook his head to let her know there was no news. "Keep looking."

"We're all over it, Ben. I've even solicited help from a couple buddies and called in favors from all over the place."

"I appreciate it, and I'm sure she does too. I need a records search run on a beach house." He relayed the address and glanced at Karen, who nodded that he'd gotten it right. "See who owns it, how long it's been empty, and anything else of interest."

"Find out who the neighbors are on either side too," Karen said. "If it's not too much trouble. Maybe they can explain why it's so familiar to me."

Ben relayed that request. "Thanks, Mark." He ended the call.

When he flipped the phone closed, Karen said, "Let's go back and check with the neighbors—oh, Ben. Look at that sky. God's such an amazing artist."

How did she do that? Notice the sky when she was up to her neck in problems? He glanced up.

The last strands of daylight streaked the twilight sky burnished orange. "It is beautiful."

He moved over a lane, positioning to turn around. His cell phone rang. He made the turn and then answered. "Brandt."

"Ben, it's Peg. How's Karen?"

"She's fine." He decided not to mention what had happened at the beach house. Peggy would pitch a fit, especially after the attempted shooting at Three Gables, and she'd be right. She'd probably insist Karen go to The Towers, and, though Ben was a jerk for it, he didn't want her to go.

She was his link to finding out what happened to Susan and Christopher. The first decent lead he'd had in more than a year. And that aside, though he hated to admit it, he wanted her with him. Whether because he didn't want to face this challenge alone anymore, or because—no. No, he didn't care about her personally. He didn't dare. He just needed her help to resolve this situation as much as she needed his help to resolve it. Alone, neither of them would be successful, but together maybe, just maybe, they stood a chance.

"We've been riding around to see if anything triggers a memory."

"The docs said not to force anything, Ben."

"Someone is trying to shoot her, Peg. The sooner we figure out who it is, the better our odds are of stopping him. She's setting the agenda."

"Are you pushing her?"

"Absolutely not."

"I'm going to ask her myself."

"Go ahead," he said, not at all affronted. Peg had learned to be persistent in her work at the center—maybe too well. "Karen, am I pushing you?"

"Not at all," she said loudly enough so Peggy could hear her.

"Satisfied?" Ben asked.

"For the moment. Listen, you two need to get to the center—right away."

It was Peg's worried tone. He hadn't heard it often, and that he did now had his skin creeping. "Why?"

"We got a fax from Emily at Richard Massey's office that you'll want to see," Peggy said. "Susan—I mean, Karen—will want to see it even more."

"Why?"

"Because it's about her."

"So you know who she is, then?"

"Not exactly." Peg sighed. "This is too delicate for the phone, Ben. Just get here as soon as you can."

Ben stopped suddenly. Cut across two lanes of traffic and pushed hard on the gas. "Ten minutes."

Karen swayed in her seat. "What are you doing?"

"We've got some news at the center."

"Well, let's hope we live long enough to get there and see what it is."

He deserved that. "Sorry."

243

"Have they found out who I am?"

"Not exactly."

Her face fell. "What does that mean?"

"I don't know. I asked, and that's what Peggy said to me."

Her hand in her lap was shaking. Ben reached over and laced their fingers. "Hang on, Karen. Things will work out."

She gripped his hand tighter. "I pray they work out well." She sent him an earnest look. "I don't know if I could get through this without you. I really don't."

He wouldn't admit it. But in a very formidable sense, he felt the same way.

"Did I upset you—saying that?"

"No." He swallowed. "Part of me wishes I could say you did, but the truth is, I like it very much."

"Thank you." Karen sniffed. "It's daunting to feel totally alone in the world. I don't mean to weigh you down, but I appreciate your being with me and holding my hand."

"It's the first time I've felt useful in a long time. I should thank you."

She stared out the windshield into the growing darkness. "What if I don't like the person I discover I am?"

"That's easy." He waited for her to look at him. "Change."

She grunted. "Throwing my own words back at me, huh?"

"They were good ones."

"They were."

"Don't worry."

She lifted a fingertip. "Every time someone says that, it makes me worry more."

He supposed that it did. "Look, whatever the truth about you is, it can't be that bad. You're a woman of faith."

She managed a little smile. "Yes, I am." She looked outside, clearly eager to get to the center and see what news awaited.

Edward wound through the neighborhood and stayed on back streets until well away from the beach house. "You're sure Johnson was out?"

"Positive." Harry took a drag from his cigarette. "I cold-cocked him. Jerk never could take a punch." Harry's voice jittered, his hand shook, and he darted his gaze everywhere at once.

"The police aren't going to come screaming after us, Harry. Relax."

He looked over at Edward as if he'd lost his mind. "What did you do back there?"

"Knocked her out and left her where Johnson couldn't get a bead on her and Brandt would find her."

"Knocked her out?" Exasperated, Harry slapped his thigh and rounded on Edward. "Why didn't you kill her?"

Edward buried his disgust behind lowered lids.

"That would have been a significant tactical error." A cop car slid into a gap behind him. Nearing the corner, Edward signaled and watched his rearview. No signal. *Good, so far.*

"What now?" Harry swung around and looked back. "Oh, man."

"Don't panic." Edward took the turn and pulled into a grocery store parking lot.

The cop turned too.

Edward parked and cut the engine.

"I can't believe it." He huffed. "Man, this—"

"Shut up, Harry." Edward stuffed his gun under his seat.

The cop slowed to a crawl behind them.

Watching the rearview, Edward told Harry, "Do not look back."

Finally, the cop drove on, passing them, then left the lot and got back on the highway.

"Whew." Clearing his throat, Harry expelled a smoke-laden breath. "I get what you mean about the tactical error."

"No." Edward restarted the car. "I don't think you do." Amused, Edward backed out of the slot. "Not killing her wasn't about the cops, Harry."

He didn't understand, but to his credit, Harry had finally learned to be patient and wait for answers. Maybe he wasn't hopeless about learning, after all.

"We've been approaching this from the perspective of Chessman and his subject. But it really isn't about her."

Harry frowned. "It's not?"

"Well, it is, but it isn't. It's about the woman, but only because she's tied to something else. So it isn't about her personally."

"Something else?" Harry struggled to keep up. "What?"

Edward looked at him and smiled. "That beach house."

And Edward was betting the bank that it was tied to NINA.

17

"I'm scared, Ben." Karen walked beside him on the wide sidewalk in front of the crisis center. "What if I find out something awful?"

He clasped her hand. "What if you find out something wonderful?"

Her hand trembled in his. Was it a lack of faith, her worrying? "What if I'm not remembering it because I don't want to remember it?"

He stopped and faced her, waited for a giggling couple to walk past, then said, "If we could block out things in our lives because they are terrible, I'd be a permanent amnesiac. It doesn't work that way."

"I know you're right." She lowered her gaze to his chest. "It's really awful that I'm not trusting God more on this. It's just that . . ."

"You're human and the unknown is always scary. Karen, look at me."

She forced her gaze to meet his.

He smiled. "You've been through a lot. So much that most people would be hiding in a closet somewhere, shaking in their shoes."

"I'm shaking plenty."

"Of course you are. You'd have to lack sense not to be." He softened his voice, watched a man walking his dog talk to it as if it were a small child. "How is that not trusting God?"

She thought a minute. "I should trust Him and not be afraid."

"Well, you know I don't believe anymore, but if I did—no, never mind."

"If you did . . . ?"

He stalled out.

"Please, Ben." She let him see her vulnerability. "I need shoring up right now, and I'm not too proud to admit it. I have faith, but . . . I don't know."

"If I did believe, I'd tell you that God created everything, including fear. Fear isn't an enemy. It warns us of danger. It makes us notice things so we protect ourselves. Fear isn't a failing. Sometimes it's a weapon, but sometimes it's a shield too."

"A shield?"

"Like now." He lifted their clasped hands. "I'm letting you into my life. I haven't done that since

Susan, and I don't know why I'm doing it now. I told myself it was just that you were in crisis and needed help, and that's plenty enough reason, but it's not the whole truth. For a crisis, it wouldn't get personal, and I don't know about you, but for me, holding your hand and talking to you about the things we've discussed—private things— that's personal."

Joy burst and spread through her chest, seeped deep into her heart. "It's personal for me too, Ben." She watched a blue van move down the street. "My challenge with that is I don't know what's waiting for me on the other side of that door." She motioned toward the center's entrance. "I could find out I have no right to feel things I'm beginning to feel for you. I could find out that I have a husband and children waiting."

He lowered his gaze. "I've thought of that too."

"Have you?"

Ben nodded. "This makes things even more difficult, doesn't it?"

"It does." She swallowed hard and took a leap of faith. "We could both get hurt, and we've been hurt enough."

"Yes." He looked her straight in the eye.

"So what do we do about it?"

"I wish I could say that it just stops here. But I don't want that. Do you?"

"No, I don't." She paused, gathered her thoughts. "I respect you, Ben. And I trust you. I like you. I think those are rare privileges in my life—they feel rare—and I don't want to turn away from them."

"Then let's just not think too much about it right now. Let's just go inside and find out what's waiting, and we'll go from there."

Be patient with him.

She glanced upward and left. *God, please, be patient with me. I am so much a work in progress. Just please don't let me end up with a broken heart. Or him either.*

"Okay," she told Ben. "One step at a time."

They walked on, and just as Ben reached for the door, she touched his arm. "Wait." When he stopped, she looked up at him. "I'm going to dare to feel for you, Ben, and pray hard that neither of us regrets it. I just wanted you to know that. So if you're not serious about whatever this is between us, I'd appreciate it if you'd be honest and just tell me so now."

"I'm not sure what to say." He wasn't; it was written all over his face. "I feel things for you, but I've got unresolved issues because of what happened with Susan. We both know it."

True. Very true. "And you won't pray about it."

"I . . . can't."

Competing for her own space in his heart and life against Susan was something Karen could do. Susan wouldn't want or expect Ben to live in the past, and his heart was big enough for them both. But to allow herself to fall for a man who wouldn't pray? A man who'd banned God from his life?

That she couldn't do. Or accept. So where did that leave her on this?

She wished she knew.

Seven thirty on a Monday night when it wasn't tourist season, and the crisis center still bustled. Karen shuddered at how busy it must be during the season, and at all the hurting people who came through its doors.

Clyde had replaced the windows, and no sign of any other damage from the bomb remained. The center had healed, and so would Karen. The receptionist sat at her desk. "Hi, Mel."

"Hi, Karen." She smiled broadly, her gaze darting between Karen and Ben. "Mrs. Crane is in her office. She's waiting for you guys."

"Thanks." Karen didn't recall where Peggy's office was located, so she followed Ben.

They passed a closed door, but Lisa Harper's voice was raised and carried out into the hallway. "I have a restraining order, Dutch. Are you going to make me use it?" A pause. "Why won't you leave me alone? I don't call, visit, or bother you. I have nothing to do with you." A quick pause, then, "Look, I'm not asking, I'm telling you. Call me again and you'll be arrested."

A loud thump warned she'd slammed down the phone.

Karen shot Ben a worried look.

"Long story," he whispered. "Her stepfather is a near-miss stalker. He does just enough to drive her nuts but too little to get arrested."

Awful. Everyone had a burden to bear. "How long has this been going on?"

"Since she was a kid and her mother married the jerk." His eyes shone bright. "The laws are still catching up."

"Lawmakers need to move it." Karen frowned. "No one should have to put up with that."

"She takes more than she has to—to keep peace with her mother. Otherwise, he takes it out on her. It drives Mark nuts."

"Why?"

"I think he's got a thing for her, but she's so buried between work and family, she hasn't noticed. He's worried about the stress Dutch causes Lisa."

Or maybe Lisa had all she could handle without another relationship to worry about. Why didn't Lisa's mother leave? God didn't mean for anyone to suffer abuse. Karen kept her thoughts to herself. Was that being respectful or cowardly? If she knew more about herself, maybe she could answer that. But right now, she didn't know who she was and couldn't judge her own choices or life, much less question anyone else's.

God should judge, anyway, not her. And He has rendered judgment against abuse. Put Him first and love one another. All the laws are based there, and abuse isn't sanctioned in either commandment.

Lisa Harper knew this, of course. Working here, she had to know. So why did her mother stay?

Probably money. It's what kept most abused women stuck in those situations. *Tragic.* Karen made a mental note to add Lisa's mother to her prayer list.

"Sorry you had to hear that." Ben tapped on Peggy's door.

Karen glanced his way. "Sorry it's happening."

Ben sighed. "We've tried to get her mother out, Karen. She won't leave. He's got her convinced he'll kill her and Lisa if she leaves, and she won't risk it."

"Can nothing be done?"

"We're working on it." He knocked again. "I've offered to send her to my castle in Scotland, but she says the world isn't big enough to hide her from Dutch."

Karen knew that feeling only too well.

"Enter," Peggy said from inside.

Karen and Ben walked in. *Please, don't let it be anything terrible.*

Peggy looked at her watch. "You made good time." She removed her glasses and looked Karen over. "You look better. Why are you still wearing scrubs?"

Karen shrugged. "No time to shop today. We got busy."

Peggy reached over to the wall behind her desk, grabbed a shopping bag, and then passed it over her cluttered desk to Karen. "I figured that would happen, especially after the trouble last night—Nora's still fussing about her sheets." Peggy grinned and then shot Ben a reprimanding look. "Here are a few things to tide you over."

Karen smiled. "Thank you."

"Don't thank me yet," Peggy said. "Actually, you should probably sit down."

Uh-oh. Bad news. No one sits for good news. Karen slid onto a forest-green leather visitor's chair and set the bag on the floor near her feet.

Ben took the seat beside her. "Is this about the fax?"

"I'm afraid it is." Peggy passed a copy to each of them. "I'll give you a minute to read through the pages. Then I'll brief you on my discussion with Emily. After that, we can decide what to do next."

Karen scanned the papers and saw her own photograph smiling back at her—one free of bruises. Hope flared in her, but as she read, it began to diminish.

"So your name is really Kelly." Ben looked at her. "You look like a Kelly. It fits."

"Kelly." She shrugged. "I like it. But why is there no last name?"

Peggy leaned forward, over her desk. "Emily says it was a quirk of Massey's to protect his clients. None of his records contain last names."

"Harder to subpoena, I expect," Ben said. "He doesn't list clients either. FL0301. What does that mean?"

Kelly floundered. "Florida something."

"Maybe," Ben said.

"We're the third county from the state line, coming from New Orleans." Peggy lifted a hand. "I've been conferring with Mark, and that's the best we could come up with."

"In other words," Kelly said, "it's a key only Massey could decipher."

"That was Emily's position."

"So we know I'm Kelly, that I was in New Orleans, and that Massey had been hired to follow me. We don't know why or who he was working for, but it could be someone from here in Florida."

"That's about it." Peggy looked as disappointed as Kelly felt.

"Don't be down. At least now we know your first name. We'll find the rest."

"Will we, Ben?"

"Mark's working on it right now," Peggy said. "He's checking missing persons nationwide and with DMV to see if they can trace your car or get anything on you going that route." Peggy leaned back. "We're on a system that connects with hospitals and emergency care facilities, and other staff are working those resources. Something will turn up."

Ben clasped Kelly's hand, gave it a reassuring squeeze. "You've been strong. Now isn't the time to let despair get a hold of you."

Peggy stared at their linked hands and failed to bury her shock.

Kelly let go of Ben and stood. "If you don't mind, I'm going to step down to the chapel." It was difficult to talk around the lump in her throat. Her chest was tight, her head throbbed, and disappointment and despair threatened to overtake her. Hopelessness was sinking in, and if she wanted to shirk it, then she needed to fight it. She couldn't do that alone. "I need a few minutes."

Ben shrugged, obviously considering her chapel visit a waste of her time. But that longing look was back in his eyes, and it helped fight her despair.

"Of course." Peggy moved to stand. "I'll walk you down."

"No," Kelly said. "I know the way."

"Mrs. Crane?"

Peggy stopped talking to Ben and said, "Come on in, Mel."

"Sorry to interrupt but this is important." She passed Peggy a single sheet of paper. "It just came in—from that Emily woman. She said she'd stepped away from the fax and just realized it had jammed and not come through."

"Thanks." Peggy took the paper and waited for Mel to leave the office and close the door behind her.

"What does it say?" Ben scooted forward on his seat.

Peggy positioned her glasses on her nose, then scanned the page. The color drained from her face.

"What is it?" Ben insisted, glad Kelly wasn't here to see Peggy's reaction. "Is she an ax murderess or something?"

"It's not about her, Ben." Peggy passed the sheet of paper across the desk to him. "It's about you."

He was late.

Paul Johnson parked in a lot two blocks down Canal Street, paid the attendant in cash, then offered him a generous tip sufficient enough to assure the man got convenient amnesia, should anyone later ask about him. "Not a mark on it." He hooked a thumb toward his car.

"No problem," the eager kid said.

Figuring at best his odds of keeping that promise were fifty-fifty, Paul hustled two blocks south to the hotel hosting the Emergency Management summit. He checked his watch three times—8:18 p.m. He'd be ten minutes late.

He hoped that ten minutes hadn't blown this operation.

Two women came toward him on the sidewalk. He smiled.

They smiled back, not missing a step. They'd never recall him. Paul had learned well from the best, the best way to hide in plain sight. Dress well, but not flashy. Be nondescript, bland, and boring. A recent study determined that eighty-six percent of Americans ignore bland and boring people. He'd take those odds.

Do nothing to snag anyone's interest. After years of experience, he could out-bore anyone, hands down.

That put a spring in his step. He walked through the revolving glass door and into the hotel lobby. It'd take patience to get the desired room number. Ordinarily he could finagle it in no time, but this visit, he didn't want any avoidable interaction.

For this visit, he had to get in and out of New Orleans without notice, and that included Chessman's notice. Paul smiled to himself. The man intended to hang Paul out to dry, but of course Paul had no intention of allowing that to happen.

In this case, stealth was a synonym for freedom. And when he was done, Paul would be free.

18

Kneeling at the altar in the little chapel, Kelly recited the Lord's Prayer and her personal prayer of gratitude to God for keeping His word to never forsake her, for giving her that peace of knowing He was with her no matter what happened.

By the time she rose, she was near tears, though she couldn't say exactly why.

The chapel had three short pews, and she went to the first one and sat down. Calm settled over her, and an ease she hadn't felt before coming to the chapel and praying seeped into her. Her troubles remained. The million questions about herself and her life were still with her. Her fear of her feelings for Ben and not knowing whether or not she had the right to feel anything for him remained. And yet she sensed that, while danger surrounded them both, she would be okay.

She looked up at the cross on the wall between two small stained-glass windows. *Will we be okay?*

Did she have a family? a husband? children? Was she committed to another man? What was her life? Was she content? happy?

She had no idea. *Help me not to dishonor myself or anyone else. Help me not to hurt anyone. Especially Ben. He's been hurt so badly, Lord.*

She closed her eyes and dared to say the thing most on her mind. *You told me to be patient with him, and I've tried. I didn't expect to come to care for him, especially so quickly. But I do care, Lord, and I know these feelings are real. Still, I can't let myself care for a man who shuts You out of his life.*

Tears burned the backs of her eyes. *I can't face all this on my own, Lord. But if I can choose one thing and You'll grant it, then I'll do my best on my own if You'll please help Ben find his way back to You.*

Lacing her fingers in her lap, she stiffened against the tightening in her chest. Forfeiting Ben had been difficult, but she'd done the right thing. Anyone facing life without God . . . well, that had to be the hardest thing in the world to do, even if one lived a charmed life. A charmed life, too, had its challenges. But when one faced the life Ben faced—the loss of his beloved wife and son, the life they'd built serving others . . .

He wanted to believe again, but he was more afraid than lost. More fearful of living without his family than of dying. Ben needed the reprieve and certainty of faith.

Totally exhausted, Kelly yawned and closed her eyes to let them rest. The world was a lonely place when you stood in it alone. Friends were terrific, but they had families, bonds, and connections. And you always stood on the fringes, welcome but not belonging, acutely aware of your isolation. And when all was said and done, you remained an outsider.

Oh yes. Ben needed faith desperately. In God and in himself. Her mind drifted and she relaxed more, flirting with sleep, sliding deeper and deeper. Only God's anchor could save Ben.

His anchor . . . and His grace.

"Lucille, where is Johnson?" In the hallway outside his home office, Gregory paused long enough to ask while checking his watch. Eight thirty. "He isn't answering his cell."

"It's out, sir." She straightened her glasses on the tip of her nose. "He went to get it repaired or get a new one."

That explained that. He never stayed out of touch. "How long ago?"

Lucille checked her watch. "Fifteen minutes. Maybe twenty."

"If he calls in, I want to talk with him." Gregory went into his office, swept it for listening devices, started the white noise to block any communication interceptions, and then sat at his desk.

What was Edward doing? Blocking the hit on Kelly? He knew more than he should; that much was clear. But about what? The subject, his strategic business alliance with the mayor, or— anything but this—NINA?

With Edward, it could be any of those things.

And that meant John Green could be in dire jeopardy. So what did Gregory want to do about that?

He rocked back, propped his feet on his desk, and stared into the pool of light his green banker's lamp cast on his blotter. He could warn John. Gregory folded his arms behind his head. But the wisdom of that was at best dubious, especially not knowing if John, who had access and means and motive, had taken out Massey and how he'd learned of him in the first place.

The truth rammed into Gregory with the force of a sledgehammer. Edward had discovered the alliance between them, and he'd undercut Gregory by cutting a deal with John.

Gregory thought through that possibility from all sides, trying to find a gap in its logic. Just one single flaw.

He failed.

And that left him no choice. No one doublecrossed Gregory Chessman and lived.

A stray thought flickered through his mind. He grabbed it and tested it. *Wait.* He stilled. *Wait.* There was one other possibility. Johnson.

So which of them was it? Edward or Johnson?

Hard to decide; they were a great deal alike. But Gregory was determined to find out. He reached for his throwaway cell, dialed, and then communicated the only way he ever had with his secret partner: by keying in the text: DISCOVERED RM CONNECTION. GOOD WORK.

If John had taken out Richard Massey, soon Gregory would know it. And it should reveal whether John Green had formed a secondary alliance with Edward or with Johnson.

Five minutes passed. Tense, Gregory called the kitchen on the house phone. "Lucille, tea."

"Yes sir."

Another five minutes—8:40. His nerves jangled. He paced at his desk, watching the cell phone, waiting . . . Oh, but he hated waiting.

Lucille brought in a tray, then set it on the edge of his desk.

"Just leave it." He waved her out. "Shut the door."

She departed holding her silence, grasping that now wasn't the time to speak.

He poured a cup of tea and admired the crisp, white china, so sleek and fragile. He vowed at twelve years old he'd never drink out of a jar again, and he hadn't. Not once.

The phone chirped.

Gregory set down his cup and reached for it.

Seated at a vanity, Darla Green clipped on her earring and in the mirror watched her husband come out of the bath, his shirttail hanging out over his pants. "What's wrong?"

He tugged at his sleeve. "I can't get this cuff link to work. Did you pack a spare?"

"Of course, John." She retrieved it from her

jewelry roll, then helped put it on, sliding it through the fabric and twisting it closed to hold. "There you go, darling."

He looked at her with the same adoration as he had on their first date, nearly fifteen years ago. She'd married him for that adoration. And stayed with him because of it.

Darla adored John too, but he wasn't exactly bright or terribly ambitious. Fortunately, she was both.

"Thank you." He pecked a kiss to her cheek. "If they have rubber chicken, let's leave the dinner early and get some real food."

"Absolutely, darling." She clasped his arm, genuinely enthused. "New Orleans has the most marvelous food."

"We could not risk it. Just skip the dinner."

Darla seriously considered it. "No. You owe it to your constituents to listen to the boring speeches."

"So you're making me go but slipping away without me?"

"No." She slipped her arms around his neck and kissed him soundly. "I'm going with you."

"Why?"

"Because I owe it to you to listen to the boring speeches." She backed away. "Now, hurry. It's 8:45. We're going to be late."

"Yes dear." John smiled and headed back toward the bath. "I'm the luckiest man alive."

"You have no idea." Darla smiled.

John closed the door. Seconds later, her cell phone vibrated. *It's about time.*

She checked the number and then answered. "You're late."

"Traffic had Interstate 10 backed up. Get your purse and open your door."

"All right." Snapping her phone shut, she snagged her evening bag, opened it, and then cracked open the suite's outer door and pushed her bag through the gap.

Something plunked down inside it.

She pulled it back, closed the door, and then glanced into the bag. Hypodermic needles filled with clear liquid. *Leave it to him to include a spare.* "Excellent." All systems were a go.

John came out of the bath. "Was that the door I heard?"

"No, darling. Just me rambling around making noise." She snapped her handbag shut and gave him a smile meant to dazzle.

He chuckled. "Are you ready?"

"Almost. Just looking for my heels." She pretended to search. She slid her feet into her heels, and then they left the hotel room.

The elevator was mirrored. Darla checked her lipstick. "John, you haven't said if you like my dress."

He let his gaze wander over it. "It's black."

"Black is chic."

"I prefer red." His eyes glinted mischievously. "You look gorgeous in red."

The door opened, and they stepped into the lobby, their arms linked. "We make a dashing couple, I have to say."

John smiled at her.

She smiled back. "Oh, I forgot to tell you. While you were in the shower, you got a text message on your private business phone." He'd had her monitor that phone for him since he'd been in office.

"Should I check it?"

"No need, darling." She patted his arm. "It wasn't a legitimate call, just some teenager sending a text to a friend. I deleted it."

"I'd be lost without you." He gently pinched her chin.

"Yes, my dear, you would." They walked into the predinner reception and were met by a waiter, offering them drinks from a tray. John took two fluted glasses, then passed one to Darla. "Cheers."

She allowed him to tap their rims. "Cheers."

Across the room, the waiter extended his tray. "Drink, sir?"

Paul Johnson took a fluted glass and paused until the waiter walked on, then lifted it to the backs of Darla and John Green. *Nothing beats a sure thing.*

He watched them drink. Waited until they drained their glasses, then set his untouched glass onto a receiving tray near the wall and left the hotel.

The loose thread would soon be severed.

Playing Gregory Chessman, acting subservient, routinely lying to him and getting away with it had proven less difficult than Paul had anticipated. Gregory never should have threatened him. The Greens had presented the greater difficulty.

But who better than Paul knew that appearances could be deceiving? Or that people and their situations often proved to be the diametric opposite of their facades?

He'd done his research, run the numbers, and taken his risks—and on discovering he'd been right, he formed an alliance that only recently had become a liability, requiring further action—action now taken.

His purpose here was done.

19

"Do you want me to go in with you to tell her?" Peggy asked Ben outside the chapel.

"No, but thanks." Ben gave Peggy a resigned look. "I need to do it myself."

"You like her, don't you?"

Ben swallowed hard. "I shouldn't. Susan—"

"Is gone." Peggy clasped his upper arm. "She'd want you to find someone you could care about and to live your life."

"My head knows that, but my heart still sees it as betrayal." Guilt washed through him. He squeezed his eyes shut. "I feel as if I'm abandoning her."

"No." Peggy sent him a tender look. "You loved well. Susan loved well. You haven't abandoned her any more than she did you. There's a place in your heart she'll always hold."

His throat went thick. "There is," he managed to eke out.

"I've known you a long time, Ben. Your heart is plenty big enough to love them both."

He snapped his neck around to look at her.

"Susan and Kelly, if that's what you choose to do."

"Don't be ridiculous."

"I'm not." Peggy shrugged. "It was obvious to me the moment you saw her."

"I like her. That I'll admit." Ben shared his fear. "But is it because she looks like Susan or because of her?"

"Only you can answer that, but they're nothing alike. Not really. And that only took minutes for me to see, so I'm sure you spotted it sooner."

"I really did." He leaned away from the door, not at all happy about that. "They resemble each other, but there are stark differences. Personality-wise, they're very different. Kelly is far more blunt than Susan."

"You like that?"

"Yeah, I do." He dragged his lower lip between his teeth, not happy about that either.

"Then quit frowning. It's good." The corner of Peggy's mouth curved, hinting at a smile.

"Maybe it would have been." He looked at the paper, then grunted. "But when she hears this . . ."

Worry tightened Peggy's lips and the smile faded. "Yes, I can see where that could be problematic."

"Oh yeah." Ben sucked in a steadying breath, exhaled on a sigh. "Well, might as well get it done."

"Good luck, Ben."

Peggy had been trying for a long time to get him interested in life. He'd believed it would never happen, but he'd been wrong.

If he'd known about this, he might have fought it harder.

Kelly slipped in under his guard. He wasn't sure exactly how. What he did know was that she'd claimed his attention, then his interest, and maybe a corner of his tattered heart. The one he would have sworn could never feel anything good again.

How had she done that? He couldn't figure it out.

Does it really matter?

She'd done it. He'd accepted it. Now he had to go in there, face her, and break his heart all over again.

And worse, his instincts warned him that he would also break hers.

If he still believed in God, he'd definitely be on his knees about this. As it was, he just hated it. She'd been through so much, and now he'd put her through even more.

Resigned, he opened the etched-glass door and walked inside.

She sat slumped in the front-row pew.

Was she hurt? Maybe a head injury from being knocked out at the beach house? He rushed over, went to reach for her, but saw her chest lightly lift and stopped.

Kelly was fine. Just sound asleep.

Should he wake her up?

She was running on sheer adrenaline, and she had been for far too long to be heeding Harvey and Lisa's medical instructions. Wake her for more bad news?

No. He dropped down to sit beside her. This bad news could wait. And if he was lucky, maybe he could figure out a way to tell her about this and actually have her believe him.

He glanced up at the stained-glass window. The odds against that seemed astronomical.

"You're worrying." Kelly's head rested braced on her hand against the back of the pew. "What's wrong, Ben?"

A frown creased the skin between his brows. "Did I wake you?"

"No." She breathed deeply, exhaled slowly. He

seemed tense. Very tense—almost afraid. "I was just dozing, not really sleeping. I heard you come in."

"Your eyes were closed. How did you know it was me?"

"I recognized your footfall."

He flinched. "Seriously?"

She let out a soft moan. "So what has that frown fixed on your face?"

"I have to tell you something." He dropped his voice to just above a whisper. "It's going to sound odd, but I want to tell you that I'm as confused by it as you will be."

Worried, she thought, and from his eye movements and clenched hands, not at all sure of his reception.

"You'll probably hold this against me." He glanced away, then pulled his gaze back to meet hers. "No, that's not true. You will hold it against me. You'll doubt me."

"Are you planning on lying to me, Ben?"

"No, I'm not."

"Then just tell me and give me the chance to hear what you have to say with an open mind. I promise to try."

"It won't be easy to hear."

She sat up, then turned to face him, her leg folded under her on the seat. "Okay, I'm prepared."

He licked his lips and looked her right in the

eyes. "Emily from Richard Massey's office sent another page over. Her fax jammed." He lifted a hand. "It says she found a check from Massey to me, Kelly."

Her heart beat hard and fast. "But you said you didn't know him."

"I'd never heard of him before all this." Ben expelled a deep breath. "But according to his records, he paid me to follow you."

"What?" The shock he'd dreaded pumped hard through her veins, thudded in her temples.

"I don't know why, Kelly," he said in a rush. "I didn't work for him, period. Not following you or doing anything else. I haven't gotten a check from him or ever even spoken to the man." He lifted his shoulders, clamped his jaw. "I promise you I don't know anything about any of this."

Her mind raced. Was he playing her? Had he been all along? She gave herself a mental shake. This was Ben. *Ben.* He wouldn't do that.

"Let's just say that sometimes people are the exact opposite of who they appear to be . . ."

A man's voice, a memory. She squeezed her fingers into her palm. Who had told her that? She could hear him speak so clearly. It had to be a memory. But of whom?

Think, Kelly. Think. She tried to form an image of the owner of the voice. *Who are you?*

Nothing came.

She tried harder.

Still nothing.

"Kelly." Ben claimed her attention. "I'm telling you the truth. I didn't do this, and I never saw that check."

She pursed her lips, studied him. "Was it cashed?"

He tilted his head. "I know this is hardly the time, but if you choose not to believe me, I don't expect I'll have another chance—"

"What do you want to say, Ben?"

"Even now, you're practical and to the point." He snapped the air with a straight hand. "You cut to the chase. I like that about you."

Her heart suffered a little tug. She ignored it. This wasn't a time for emotion. It was a time for logic. "So be practical and to the point back and answer my question. Was the check cashed?"

"No, it wasn't." He stopped short, then started over. "It hasn't been cashed yet, anyway."

"Okay." Kelly stared past his left shoulder a long minute, grappling to wrap her mind around these new events. "What does this mean?"

"I honestly don't know."

Fair enough. He wasn't feeding her some song and dance, and she was grateful for it. "Well, we'd better find out." She tapped her fingertips against her knee. "Obviously, they're marking us both, and our not knowing why puts us in even more danger." Prickly-skinned, she rubbed her arms. "There must be a compelling reason for—" His grave expression stole her thought. "Ben, are you still worried that I don't believe you?"

His face flushed in the diffused light. "Frankly, yes." Ben shrugged as if it didn't much matter, which of course meant it mattered a great deal. "In your position, I'm not sure I'd believe me, and saying we need to find out what it means isn't absolution or belief." He looked away. "It was a lot to ask, much less expect." He swerved his gaze back to her. "But I am telling you the truth."

Worry. Fear. Hope. All of that and more played out on his face, in his body language, for her to see. "Ben." She lifted her hand and cupped his face. "I believe you."

His jaw dropped open and he just sat there.

"You look stunned." She liked it. Was that awful of her? It couldn't be. The desire to kiss him arced through her, settled, and stayed put. *Bad idea. Very bad idea.* She pulled her hand back, sat on it to be sure it stayed in place, and stared deeply into his eyes.

Shadows slanted across his face, making him appear even more torn. "You do believe me?" Before she could answer, he added, "I want you to, but if you don't, I won't blame you. I know how bad this looks."

"It looks awful," she admitted. "But you have no reason to lie, Ben, and you've given me every reason to trust you."

· · ·

She trusts me.

His throat went thick. He closed his eyes, let that trust flow over him and seep deep inside. Where did she get the strength to believe? In the face of such strong evidence, how—why—did she dare to believe?

He glanced at the cross above the altar. Remembered with longing a time when he had the peace that came with faith. The certainty that regardless of what happened, everything would work out. That the crooked places would be made straight. But after Susan and Christopher . . . he hadn't believed in anything but the absence of those things. Its acute sting had been his constant companion. But had his bitterness blinded him? Even when logic and evidence said she shouldn't believe a word that came out of his mouth, she trusted him. He choked up and whispered, "Thank you, Kelly."

"Oh, Ben." Her voice went soft, her eyes softer.

He wanted to kiss her. Anticipated it, but he couldn't do it. Not here. Not in Susan's chapel.

She twined their hands atop his knee, stroked the back of his hand. "Is there more?"

"No—no, that's all of it." *Coward.* It rippled through him. *If you weren't, you'd at least tell her you'd like to kiss her.*

Maybe he would. But it wouldn't be right, would it?

Not if she isn't free. What if she isn't? What would that do to her? To you? You could let this relationship develop and then find out she belongs to another man . . .

The thought alone had him sick inside. With everything else, he couldn't put her through that—and he couldn't go through it himself.

His phone rang. "Sorry." He answered it, thankful for the reprieve. "Brandt."

"Ben, it's Mark."

"Yeah, Mark." His gaze locked with Kelly's. A man could get lost and stay lost in those blue eyes.

"I've got the ownership information you wanted on that beach house."

"Great." He shifted on the pew, putting a little distance between them.

"For forty years, it belonged to a woman named Bethany Bennett."

"Never heard of her."

"I'm surprised," Mark said. "She lived here most of her adult life—a local artist."

"Oh, wow. You mean Beth Bennett." Kelly showed no reaction to hearing the name. Not a flicker. "She did paintings and pottery."

"Yeah, that's her."

"I knew Beth," Ben said. "I haven't seen her in a while. Did she move away?"

"She died three months ago."

Another loss in the village that had gone unnoticed while he'd been distancing himself from everyone and everything. "What happened to her?"

"Natural causes, according to the death certificate. I put a call into Hank Green to see if I could get some specifics out of him."

Hank had been the coroner for as long as Ben could remember. "Wait a second. If she's gone, then who owns it now?"

"Kelly Jean Walker."

Kelly. Ben stiffened. "Um, related?"

"Yeah, her niece and only surviving relative. She inherited it, but someone else paid the taxes. Today, in fact."

"Who?"

"A lawyer from Atlanta. Alexander Denham."

A chill swept up Ben's back. "He was at Chessman's dinner party. I met him. We talked about historical landmarks."

"Yeah, I remembered you mentioning that."

"This smells funny, Mark. I'm not sure why, but—"

"Yes, it does. And thanks to Kelly, I now know why."

"Kelly?"

"She suggested we check the ownership of the beach houses flanking Beth's. Guess who owns them."

"Denham?"

"Think closer to home."

"Gregory Chessman?"

"Exactly."

Ben sifted through everything, taking into account this new information. "So what does that tell us?"

"It tells us that someone is going to a lot of trouble to hook you to Kelly, and they're really nervous about something to do with that beach house."

"You're sure they're one and the same?" he asked, certain Mark would surmise he meant his Kelly and Beth's Kelly.

"Positive," Mark said. "I ran her background twice."

Ben resisted the urge to ask if she was married.

"Her folks died when she was a kid. Samuel Johnson was her guardian. No relation to her—"

"Then why not Beth?" A blood relative would have priority when it came to custody.

"Beth wasn't stable. At least not enough to get custody, though she did try. But Kelly's parents designated Samuel as her guardian and according to the case file, Beth had been committed to a mental hospital twice."

Everyone in the village considered her crazy, but Nora swore she was just an eccentric artist with an active imagination.

Mark went on. "Kelly's dad and Samuel grew up together and stayed close until her dad died."

"What have you got on him?"

"No immediate family, but guess who turned up in his background check?"

"Chessman?"

"No, but close," Mark said. "Paul Johnson."

"You're kidding."

"Afraid not. Samuel is his uncle."

"What?" Kelly whispered from beside him.

Ben tilted the phone. "Give me a minute. It's complicated." He spoke again to Mark. "But Paul didn't recognize her. Clyde, Mel, and Harvey have canvassed all over the village. No one knew her."

"Paul wouldn't know her. Samuel's branch and Paul's branch of the family are estranged and have been for thirty years. I don't know why. But Samuel is the self-made man and the hated rich uncle. No interaction."

How was Kelly going to take this? It was a lot to digest. "I see."

"Not yet," Mark said. "It gets even more bizarre."

It couldn't possibly.

"Something happened early on. I can't tell from the paper trail what exactly, but in short order, this attorney, Denham, took over Kelly's guardianship. I'm still waiting on a lot of the personal stuff, so the reason may turn up. I can tell you she looks good on paper. No arrests, no record, or anything like that. Not even a parking ticket." Mark let out a little chuckle. "She's got as much money as you do. That'll be good news for her to hear."

"She'll need some."

"Yeah, I expect so."

Ben again fought the urge to ask if she was married, had a family. "What does she do?"

"Pretty much what you used to do—philanthropic work."

"What kind?"

"Building centers for at-risk teens mostly, and funding programs for latchkey kids. I spoke to a hotel concierge in New Orleans. He said they had a drive-by shooting and a kid was killed. A few days later she showed up out of the blue saying she was going to build a place they'd be safe. She was there about a week and went to leave to site a center location, but her Jeep wouldn't start. A part-timer working for him got her a rental—the red Jag. She left the hotel that night and never returned."

"I see." Ben let his gaze lose focus a second, processing that.

"You're not going to believe who that part-timer was, Ben."

"Who?"

"Richard Massey."

"You're kidding me."

"No, I'm not," Mark said.

Which tied right back to Chessman. "What about the other guy? Did you personally get in touch with him?"

"Denham?"

"Yeah." Kelly looked eager to know what he was hearing. He held up a wait-a-minute finger, certain seeing it would exasperate her. It did; her sigh could power a windmill.

"He was out," Mark said. "I left a message on his voice mail."

Ben filled him in on the fax from Massey's Emily.

"Ben, the way I see it, someone's playing connect-the-dots between you two. It's transparent." Mark paused. "Well, between Susan and Kelly. Do you have any idea why?"

"Other than the obvious physical similarities, no, I don't." Ben couldn't stand not knowing any longer. "When are you expecting that personal information?"

"Not sure. I've got inquiries out. Waiting to hear."

"Let me know when you do, okay?"

"Sure thing."

"Thanks, Mark." Ben bit back his disappointment at not knowing if she had her own family. That was the one thing Kelly and he most wanted to know, which probably made him the most selfish person in the world right now.

He closed the phone and tucked it into his pocket.

Her eyes gleamed. "So who am I?"

She didn't doubt he knew. Astute woman. "Your name is Kelly Jean Walker."

"Kelly Jean Walker." She let it roll off her tongue, tried it out. Then whispered it again.

"Ring any bells?"

"Not really." She hiked a shoulder. "But I like it. Does that count?"

"It all counts."

Excitement danced in her eyes. "What did Mark learn about the beach house? I definitely remember it, Ben. I see myself sitting on the rocker on the front porch." She swept back her hair. "Who owns it?"

Ben had to force himself not to look away. She was going to be disappointed. Deeply disappointed, and then deeply saddened. He hated to have to tell her about her aunt. Should he?

On top of everything else, it could be too much for her. Maybe he should check with Harvey or Lisa first. Just to be sure he wasn't doing anything to make this harder on her.

"Ben, I asked a question." Her impatience sharpened her tone. "Who owns the cottage?"

Humbled by her faith in him, he was reluctant to damage it or put her to a further test. But one look at the set of her jaw made it apparent there was no way she would give him the luxury of first checking with Harvey or Lisa. It was better to tell her here. At least being at the center, if she freaked out, they were close by and could immediately assist.

He twisted the band on his watch, covering his uncertainty, blinked, then blinked again. "You do."

• • •

Edward took advantage of the night and parked his Impala two blocks down the street and a block over from the beach house. There was a reason Gregory wanted this place, and Edward had pieced together enough from Johnson's and Chessman's actions, which were not exactly working in tandem, to know that something in addition to that nasty guardian business was at play here—and he was betting it had to do with NINA. But whether that connection was with Johnson or Chessman, Edward didn't know.

Massey was NINA connected, and he interacted with Johnson. So it likely was him. But Chessman wanted this beach house, and Johnson might well be just interacting with Massey on his orders. Regardless, why this beach house?

Strangely enough, Harry, big and brawny and slow on the uptake, had first raised that question. In a sense, it stunned Edward, because he truly hadn't considered that there was more involved than the error forcing the woman and Brandt's paths to cross in the first place. But after that phone call intercept between Johnson and Massey, Edward had known plenty. And while he wasn't eager to play in NINA's ballpark, he couldn't just bail and be safe. So his back was against the wall.

Then she'd come to the beach house. With Benjamin Brandt. And Paul Johnson had lain in wait for them there. Johnson had arrived first, which meant he had prior knowledge of the beach house and hadn't followed the woman there. For all the plotting and planning, her arrival had made her a target of opportunity.

So what was significant about this beach house?

Edward walked down the sidewalk, a beach bag slung over his shoulder. He wore jean shorts, a T-shirt with a sailfish emblem on its front, and sneakers: what locals called "Florida formal."

Lights inside the little houses burned, and through filmy curtains, Edward could see people inside. Homes flanking *the* beach house were dark. Empty. That was odd for this area, even considering the downturn in the real-estate market. Properties along the beach brought in healthy rental incomes and rarely sat vacant.

More and more mysterious . . .

Edward double-checked his surroundings, scanning, looking back over his shoulder. The street was quiet. *Dinnertime.* He hopped the short picket fence, cut across the lawn, and headed to the back—the beach side—of the property. Sand stretched to the moonlit gulf. The sound of waves hitting the shore muffled other noises.

Edward pulled down his bag, unzipped it, and pulled out his tools. He popped the lock on the back door, which was old and clearly intended to keep out honest people. He opened the door and went inside, then clicked on his flashlight. If anyone happened to notice the light, they'd ignore it. From the looks of the place—trash and newspapers crumpled and tossed into every corner—it was being used often as a shelter by transients.

He made his way through and nearly tripped down a staircase in one of the bedrooms. He hadn't expected to see it there. One-level home, on the water. Surely the beach house didn't have a basement.

Edward went down the stairs, hyperalert. No sense anyone was around. No sounds or scents. Nothing. He took the bottom step and fanned the opening with light.

The room was about ten by ten, cinder block and concrete, and not a thing was in it. He walked down and looked under the stairs, saw a door, and opened it. A tunnel?

Great. Just great. Someone is running drugs.

The aunt had been an artist, but also a health nut. She wouldn't be running drugs. And it didn't seem to fit her pattern, but assigning patterns to anyone was dangerous business. Chessman? Maybe. But her? Drugs? That would take a significant stretch.

So how did she figure into this? Or did she?

And where exactly did that tunnel lead?

20

W e'll have more information on you and your life soon," Ben promised Kelly at the cottage door. "I know it's hard, but be patient. It won't be long now."

Ben scrawled a phone number on the back of his business card. "This is Alexander Denham's phone number. Call and talk to him. Mark's been trying to get in touch, but the guy's either freezing him out or out of pocket. Either way, Mark hasn't yet gotten him."

She took the card. Her hand trembled. "Thanks."

Ben obviously noticed. "Why don't I stay with you while you make the call?"

Her tummy fluttered. "Would you mind?" Heat crept up her neck, flooded her face. "I'm being a wimp about this, and I've already imposed so much on you that I hate to ask, but it's daunting and—"

"Kelly, no." Ben stepped closer. "You haven't imposed at all. I'm as involved as you are, though in a different way, and I know what it's like to face something unknown on your own. It is daunting . . . and more."

He understood perfectly. She'd so misjudged him initially, and now she saw his admirable qualities. "Thank you, Ben. If you're sure you can spare the time, then please do stay." She gave him a faltering smile. "I'm really nervous." And grateful that she didn't have to explain that she stood at the edge of her comfort zone and had to step out of it.

She might well discover that she didn't like herself very much or that she had spouted but not touted her Christian principles. That worried her most of all. Being a disappointment to God. What believer wouldn't be a total wreck about maybe facing that in herself?

She had no idea what to expect, but not a single living soul had even noticed her missing and notified the authorities anywhere in the United States . . . Well, that didn't bode well for her, and she'd be foolish not to admit it—if only to herself and to God.

Ben walked back over to the kitchen counter and honestly seemed pleased not to be leaving. "No problem. You're worrying about learning bad things, aren't you?"

"Wouldn't you be?" She laced her fingers in front of her, not sure what to do with them. "I'm unclaimed, Ben. There's got to be a reason."

Sympathy etched into the lines of his face, softened the hard angle of his jaw. "Maybe you take trips without notice. Maybe those around you do. Maybe your plans were to be unavailable for a while." He offered her a reassuring look. "There could be a thousand reasons a missing persons report hasn't been filed, Kelly."

Her nerves sizzled and snapped. "And one could be that no one knows or cares." Unable to handle seeing pity in his eyes, she turned and picked up the phone. Her palms were sweaty.

"Coffee or tea?"

"Tea," she said. "Sweet."

He smiled, grabbed the kettle, filled it, and then set it on the stove. Twisted the burner knob. "I don't believe that no one cares."

"You don't know me, Ben."

He chuckled. "I know you far better than you think." He pivoted from the stove, planted his hands on the countertop, and looked across the bar to her. "I fully intended to hate you, Kelly. Because you look like Susan, because you wore her cross and drove a red Jag, because you made me remember things I didn't want to remember but can't forget."

She sat at the table, her knees giving out on her. She was attracted to him, probably more than she should be, maybe more than she had a right to be, and he hated her? *Oh, God, with everything else, I must deal with this too?*

Be patient with him.

"But," Ben said.

"Thank goodness there's a 'but,'" she quipped before she could stop herself.

Ben's expression grew tender. "I couldn't do it."

That she hadn't expected. "You couldn't?"

"No." Ben grunted. "Though I have to admit it took me a couple hours to conclude you weren't running a scam or doing anything else nefarious."

That fell just shy of miraculous. "I'd pretend to be offended at it taking you so long, but considering Susan and the surrounding circumstances, a few hours is really pretty terrific." She dared to hope that he meant what she thought he did. "So you've decided to trust me, then?"

"It wasn't a conscious decision. I'm not even sure exactly when it happened, but when you shared your story at the center, I felt it." He lowered his gaze, unable to meet her eyes. "But I was too fixated on Susan's cross to remember anything you said, so it took a little longer to accept it."

She let out a little groan. "You have no idea how valuable that is to me right now."

"I don't. But I can imagine."

She smiled and studied his eyes. Fascinating eyes. Gray, soft and piercing at once, unusual and captivating. Caught staring, she looked away. It wasn't right. She could be committed, have a family. She had to honor her commitment, even if she had no memory of one.

The teakettle whistled. Ben moved to the stove.

It'd be easier to keep her thoughts in check if he wasn't so attractive. But he was, so she'd just have to work harder at it. Resolved, she took a deep breath and then dialed the number.

Please don't let me find out I'm an awful person. Please . . .

"Hello." A woman answered.

Kelly didn't recognize the voice. "Hello. This is Kelly Walker. May I speak to Mr. Denham?"

"Kelly?" The woman sounded uncertain.

"Yes."

"Is it really you?" Stunned. She was stunned.

Kelly stiffened. "It's really me." She looked at Ben and shrugged. "Who's speaking, please?"

"It's me, Doris Brown." She harrumphed. "This is no time for you to be teasing me, Kelly Jean Walker. I've been half-crazy worried about you."

This Doris cared about her. It rippled through in her crackling voice. "Why have you been worried?"

"Girl, you've called me every Sunday since you moved out of this house. Without fail. And you didn't call me yesterday. I went straight to Mr. Denham first thing this morning, and he's hiring half the world to look for you."

Her former guardian. He was worried too. "Doris, I'm sorry," Kelly said, feeling elated and guilty at once. She had a past. And she'd upset the people in it. "Let me explain."

"Now that's a fine idea, missy, and I'm all ears."

"I was in New Orleans. I'm not sure what for exactly. Supposedly I was looking for a place to build—"

"A new Safe Center," Doris cut in. "I'm aware

290

of all this. What I don't know is where you've been for the last day, leaving me to worry myself sick you were somewhere dead in a ditch."

"I was carjacked and have no memory, Doris."

"You were *what*?"

Kelly wanted to cry at Doris's outrage but didn't. "I was beaten and now I can't remember much. I just found out who I am today—and about Mr. Denham being my former guardian."

"Are you all right? What does the doctor say?"

Kelly related that information and glimpsed three little flashes of memory. Her at a table with Doris bustling around the kitchen. Doris in the audience, Kelly on the stage, dancing at a recital. Doris under an umbrella walking Kelly home from where the school bus had dropped her off. "You took care of me."

"Most of your life, child. Ever since Mr. Denham brought you home from that cretin your parents left in charge of you," Doris said with a click of her tongue. "Where are you?"

"Florida." She swallowed hard. More and more memories flooded through her. Her as a child, a gangly teen, a young woman. Mr. Denham bringing her into his home. Stern and sober, always teaching or instructing—or so it'd seemed until much later. Such a master at manipulation! His weapons? Domination and control—and he'd led her by the nose a lot longer than he should have.

But he hadn't locked her in closets. And he was cold, but he wasn't mean unless his patience wore thin. When it did, he reverted to Alik Demyan and his Russian roots. She didn't like Alik Demyan at all. He terrified her, so for years she hid from him. The first time she bucked his advice and followed her own heart, the tension between them thickened to sludge. It had never thinned again.

Doris . . . she and Doris in church, shopping, praying. "I remember you."

Ben set down a glass of iced sweet tea on the table at her elbow. She flashed a look up at him, and he smiled. "You remember her?"

Kelly nodded.

Ben clasped her hand, gave it a little squeeze. "Terrific." He headed toward the door, looking as if he were no longer needed.

"Wait. Ben, wait. Please." She didn't want him to leave. He stopped, came back toward her. "Doris, where are you located?"

"Oh, honey, you really can't remember?"

"No. I'm remembering little things, like you and me baking cookies."

"We did." Doris sounded elated. "Every time Mr. Denham was gone, we baked."

"Oh, it was our ritual, then?" Kelly smiled into the phone.

"So to speak. He forbade you to be in the kitchen. It wasn't seemly for an heiress. I don't mind saying we disagreed on that, but he is the boss, so I had to do what he said."

Heiress. Kelly stiffened. "Doris, where are you?"

"Marietta, honey."

That told Kelly next to nothing. "Is that in Florida?"

"No, it's Georgia." Doris sounded flustered. "Tell me where you are right now. I'm coming to see about you myself."

"Will Mr. Denham be coming too?" Kelly had gut-level resistance to that. Her own fears? Or just cause? She had no idea.

"Of course he won't be there," Doris said. "You know he always winters in Europe."

Something in her voice set off a warning in Kelly. "Did I go to Europe every winter too, then?"

Doris didn't answer.

"Doris?"

"Um, no. You stayed here with me."

"I see." So her guardian hadn't been a typical guardian, then. "I'm going to put Ben Brandt on the phone. He owns the Crossroads Crisis Center. They're helping me." She bit back further questions, then added, "He'll give you directions. We'll talk more when you arrive."

Kelly passed the phone to a puzzled Ben and then took a long drink of tea. Her hands shook so badly she had to hold the glass with both hands to keep the tea from sloshing over the rim. In the periphery, she heard Ben talking to Doris, but the weight of wondering sidetracked her. Why was she a grown woman on her own with apparently no financial worries who had no friends, no one who cared for her?

What is wrong with me?

She could take being loved or hated. But others' indifference cut deep. She didn't matter, she was insignificant, and that was the most awful testament of a human being. It spoke volumes. *Insignificant. Ignored. Unworthy.*

"Kelly?" Ben said from seemingly far away. "Kelly?" He cupped a hand on her shoulder. "Are you all right?"

"Oh." She jumped. "I'm sorry. I was lost in thought." She reached for the phone.

He shrugged. "Doris hung up. She'll be here by dawn."

"Good." Kelly took another drink.

"What are you thinking?" He sat down, his chair scraping the tile floor. "Are you okay?"

"I'm fine." *Lost again, but fine.* A former guardian who avoided her but had apparently levied heavy restrictions and controls on her. An heiress. That meant she had money, which was good. But it also meant that her family was dead and gone. She was alone. Except for Doris: a woman who seemed kind and concerned but who was paid to care for her. A tear leaked from her eye.

"Hey." Ben squatted beside her chair, swept the tear away with a gentle thumb. "This doesn't look like a happy tear. Is it the stress?"

She shook her head.

"Well, what is it, then?"

He would understand. She hated knowing it even as she took solace in not having to explain. These were depths she had no desire to plumb. Looking into his eyes, she let him see her hurt and disappointment.

"No one loves me, Ben. Not one person in this whole world."

"I'm sorry, Kelly." He pulled her into a hug. Held her head to his shoulder with a big hand cupping her crown. "I know how hard it is to get used to that."

"At least you remember being loved." She sniffed, pulled back to look at him. "I don't remember it. I'm afraid I've never had that."

He pressed a tender kiss to her forehead. "I'm so sorry."

"Me too." In his eyes she saw the bond between them deepen, a new dimension forged in shared pain creating a new layer. "We're a pair, aren't we?" She didn't smile.

Neither did he. "We are."

Be patient.

She wasn't being impatient, but if she were, this would be a bitter pill to swallow.

A glimpse of gleaming eyes filled with mirth

pressed into her memory. A woman. Gray-streaked black hair, eyes shaped like Kelly's. Thin and airy, expansive and expressive, she sat in the rocker at the cottage, smiling down at Kelly, who sat leaning back against a white post.

"Wait. Ben, I think I was loved." Her tone lightened. "This is coming out all wrong." She lifted a hand. "I know God loves me. I have no doubt whatsoever about that. I was talking about a human being."

Ben smiled. "You're one up on me, then."

Kelly cupped his face in her hands. "No, Ben, I'm not. He loves you too, whether or not you recognize or accept it. His love is still there."

Ben frowned, warning her off.

"I'm not going to push, but it's true. He promised, and God doesn't lie."

Ben opened his mouth to say something but stopped.

Before he could complain about the verbal dilemma she'd neatly folded him into, she kissed him. Soundly.

And he kissed her back. Gentle. Tender. Deliberate.

A long minute later, breathless and quaking, Kelly parted their mouths and looked deeply into Ben's eyes. "Should I apologize for that?"

He hesitated. Uncertainty teemed in his eyes and slowly crept across his face. "No. Should I?"

Amazingly happy, Kelly smiled. "I'd be terribly disappointed if you did."

"Good." His return smile spread into his eyes.

She loved that. Respected it. He had issues to resolve about moving on with his life. So did she—not in moving on, but in discovering if she had a life. But she couldn't deny that doing so felt less daunting than it had moments ago. That bond between them was real and growing, and while it had a long way to go, it was there. She wasn't alone in life. And neither was Ben. They could both be grateful for that. And a lot more.

God had been working overtime for her lately, and knowing it, she couldn't deny being concerned. Ben was important to her. He mattered. But God mattered most. And she couldn't see herself long-term in a relationship with a man not dedicated to God. It just wouldn't work.

But for now, they were in the same world, dealing with many of the same issues and facing the same unknown people who clearly meant them harm.

Be patient with him.

For now, that directive carried reassurance. Following it required faith—no woman eagerly rushed to embrace getting a broken heart. But follow it she would, and hopefully her faith would be strong enough for both of them until Ben could again find his own.

Exactly.

• • •

John stumbled into Darla, nearly knocking her off her feet.

"Okay, Mr. Mayor, it's time to put the glass down and change to water." Darla gave him a stern sniff. Nine o'clock. Too early. Had he been drinking earlier?

John leaned closer to her, dropped his voice. "I've only had the one glass. Something's wrong, missy. My head won't clear, and I feel like the top of it is going to blow off."

Darla hooked her arm in his. There was no way she'd allow him to be seen in public like this. The reception was crawling with media, who would be only too thrilled to report nasty snippets filled with innuendos alleging John was drunk. If they only knew what a prude her beloved really was, they would be bored stiff.

John stumbled, having challenges putting one foot in front of the other. Darla struggled to keep him upright, the task more difficult in four-inch heels tricking her own sense of balance.

They finally made it to the door and then to the elevator. Inside it, John held on until the door closed behind them, then he leaned against its mirrored wall, his face pale, sweat beading at his brow.

"John, what is it?" Darla pressed two buttons— one two floors below theirs and then their floor. She snatched his handkerchief from his pocket, dabbed at his face.

"I-I'm not well, honey." He groaned and let his eyes close. "I just need to lie down for a bit."

Darla turned away, pulled the syringe from her bag, and injected herself for protection, urging the elevator to hurry. It stopped. John tried to pull away from the wall.

"No, dear." She hastily wiped the syringe. "This isn't our floor." Under the cover of pushing the button for their floor again, she reached out and dropped the syringe into the trash can just outside the door.

John slumped back against the wall. "Oh, this is awful."

The elevator shot up, then stopped. A bell chimed, and the door crept open.

"Come on." She wrapped her arm around his waist. "Lean on me." Fumbling, she fished the key card from her purse. "It's just a few more steps to the door."

"Oh, this is bad." John groaned.

The hallway was empty. Grateful for that, Darla, aided by John's hand to the wall, got them to the door, fiddled with the key until the little light turned green, then shoved open the door and got them inside.

The door shut behind them. "Come on, honey. A few more steps."

"I . . . can't."

"Sure you can."

John looked at her, his eyes liquid. "Honey, I . . . can't. Call a doctor."

She stilled. "It's an upset stomach. What do you mean, call a doctor?"

"It's not." His eyes clouded. "I'm dying."

A chill shot through her body. He wasn't supposed to know. Her ally had said he wouldn't suffer. He wouldn't know until the very end. "Don't be ridiculous. You can't be dying." She tugged at his sleeve. "I'll get you to bed and then phone a doctor. You'll see. He'll tell you you're going to be fine."

John looked her in the eye and didn't budge. "I love you."

"John, please. You're scaring me." She licked her lips, her mouth bone-dry. The last thing she needed was to have to fight him to keep him away from the phone. He was twice her size. "Please move."

"Nagging me even now." He took a step that had his face drenched with sweat. "That's my girl."

"One more, John. One more."

He fell onto the bed on his back and let out a swooshed breath. "Thank You, God."

From the vanity across the room, a phone beeped. John's special line.

Darla ignored it.

"You'd better get that. It's important."

"It's nothing." She removed John's shoes, loosened his tie.

"Darla." The tone of his voice stopped her cold. She paused and met his gaze.

"I know the truth."

Her heart beat hard, thumping against her ribs. "The truth about what, darling?" But she already knew. It was there in his eyes.

"What you're doing with Chessman."

She stood wooden, waited.

"Did you think I wouldn't notice?"

Silence. She couldn't talk if her life depended on it—and it well might.

John doubled over, gripping his chest. Pain contorted his face. "I forgive you."

Darla hesitated. She could save his life. Give him the injection from the syringe in her purse, make one phone call, and he'd live. But he knew the truth. He couldn't doubt or wonder anymore, which was the only reason he hadn't already addressed this. Plausible deniability. He might have suspected, but until now, until this moment, he didn't know for sure. But that doubt was now gone.

And her husband might be her husband, but he would not cover her sins. He would prosecute her. His morals and ethics would demand it.

"So that's the way of it, then. You'll watch me die." Pity settled into John's gaze. He closed his eyes. "Forgive her, Father . . ."

Darla silently watched John, torn between saving him and saving herself.

The battle, if brief, was fierce. She turned away and lifted John's special business phone from her vanity. A text message waited. She recalled it, then read Gregory's message. It was, of course, from him. Only he and her ally had the number.

ON SPOT FOR TOMORROW NIGHT.

She looked back at John, now writhing on the bed, unable to do anything to help himself. He'd stopped trying to get to the phone. She hadn't even been forced to move it out of reach.

John stilled. Darla went to him. His eyes were rolled back in his head, his mouth slightly open. She pressed her fingertips to his throat. *No pulse.* John had drawn his last breath.

She thought quickly, then decided on the only course of action open to her that would keep the truth buried forever. After keying in a return message, she hit send.

Her course was now firmly charted, and there was no turning back.

It meant spending the night with a corpse, but she'd been married to John far too long for one more night to matter. She was fond of him and she would miss him. He had loved her, and that was rare in most long-term relationships. It was unfortunate that they had become embroiled in a battle of the fittest. But even for love, that was a battle she refused to lose. She had learned young. *Above all, survive.* And to survive, she would do what she must—even to John.

No one other than her ally—particularly not the arrogant Gregory Chessman—could know that John was dead until tomorrow. Otherwise Gregory would surely interrupt the shipment to the beach house, and that would cost them both a fortune.

That stupid woman surely knew her identity by now and that she owned the beach house. Odds were against her being willing to sell it—she'd been adamant thus far, despite Gregory's best efforts to persuade her. So if not tomorrow night, their opportunity for shipping would be lost forever.

She looked down at John, recalled his inane banter in the elevator. He preferred her wearing red.

But black had been appropriate. She looked gorgeous in black. Darla turned to the mirror and studied her expressions, practiced responding to the well-intended if trite expressions of sympathy. Oh, there'd be comments about it being a blessing he went so peacefully in his sleep. About his unexpected death being such a shock. About how tragic his death was for her.

She walked to the door, opened it, hung the Do Not Disturb sign on the knob, then closed and locked the door. The one risk was that John would be discovered too early tomorrow, word would get back to the village, and Gregory would interrupt the beach house shipment. To prevent that, Darla and her ally had developed a simple but highly effective plan. One with very high odds of success.

As she passed the beveled-glass mirror, she smiled at her reflection. "Oh, Darla. You'll make a dazzling widow."

Kicked back at his desk, Gregory drew on a Cuban cigar in his study and waited for a response to his text message. He sipped at an insanely expensive brandy. Frankly, he'd never cared for the taste, but it was the best the world had to offer, and drinking it reminded Gregory he'd acquired the best of everything. He loved the taste of that knowledge.

A soft sound chimed.

Gregory set down his glass and reached for his phone. A return text from John waited. Eager to see it, he reached over and pressed the button necessary to recall it. PERFECT TIMING.

He snapped the phone closed, tossed it onto his desk, then rocked back and took a content sip from his snifter. "Excellent."

21

The smell of coffee teased Kelly's nostrils.

She flipped over in bed and scrunched her pillow, not yet ready to wake up, but the rich scent called to her, tempting her to give up and get out of bed.

She groaned, turned over, and memories flooded her mind, taking her back . . .

Kelly had stood alone at her parents' graves, a child of seven all dressed up in a pristine dress, her black patent leather shoes sparkling in the sunlight. Tears rolled down her cheeks. She didn't wipe at them, just stood twisting, wishing herself back to a time when her mom and dad would be standing beside her.

She was so scared.

A beefy arm draped over her shoulders. "They're not coming home again," her father's friend, Samuel Johnson, said. "You understand that, right?"

"The lady told me." Kelly had come with the policewoman, who had been kind.

The funeral ended and the pastor came over and clasped her hand. "I'm so sorry for your loss." He looked up at Mr. Johnson. "You take good care of her."

"I will." Mr. Johnson nudged her to move.

They left the cemetery and he put her in the backseat of his car. She looked back, watching the coffins for as long as she could see them, tears still blurring her eyes, wetting her cheeks.

"Stop that crying now. Your sniffing is wearing thin."

"I'm sad."

He glared back at her in the rearview mirror. "I said, stop."

Why was he being mean to her? "Yes sir." He'd never before been mean to her. "Where are we going?"

"Atlanta, to my penthouse." He sighed. "I'm not crazy about having a kid underfoot, but if you stay out of my way, we'll do fine."

"I want my aunt." She choked down a sob. "Take me to her." Aunt Beth wouldn't tell Kelly to stay out of her way.

He stopped suddenly and glared back at her. "Do *not* tell me what you want. I don't care what you want. You'll do as I say, and you'll keep your mouth shut."

Too shocked to answer—no one had ever talked to her that way—she didn't dare risk even a nod. And she'd kept her mouth shut the entire way.

The penthouse was white—walls, ceilings, floors, and furniture. She hated it.

"This way." He walked straight through to a hallway and then to the second door on the left. "Your room. Stay in it when I'm home."

There were no toys. Just a bed and an empty box. No dresser for her clothes, no pretty pictures like her mom had hung on her walls at home.

"Come with me."

She followed him back down the hall to the front entryway, where he opened a door. "Get in."

"But it's a closet."

"I know it's a closet." He shoved her back, pushed her inside, and slammed the door shut. "I'll be back in a little while—and you'd better be in there."

Swallowed by darkness, she sank to the floor and cried until she couldn't cry anymore. "Mama, help me. It's so hot," she whispered. "Help me . . ."

The die had been cast that first night.

Whenever Samuel had left home, he locked her in the front entryway closet—until he'd discovered her passed out and drenched in sweat from the heat.

That had scared him. He hadn't gone anywhere or let her leave her room for days. But he'd been itchy to go, and soon he did. This time, he'd come to her room. "Come on, girl."

She dreaded what was to come. He was going to put her in the closet again. She just knew it. *Please, don't let him. Please.*

He led her to the terrace instead. "You can stay out there while I run some errands. Lots of fresh air on the terrace, and it's not too hot."

It was sweltering, and he'd locked the door so she couldn't get back inside—or get down to the ground. Following her pointed finger, she counted the stories to the ground. *Fifteen. And no stairs. No door. Nothing but the railing.* She swatted at another mosquito, then another, and what that firefighter had told her in school on his visit to her classroom haunted her: *"Always have an escape plan in case of fire."*

She had no escape plan.

Tears welled in her eyes, and something flashed in the trees in the distance. Her mom had put a chain ladder in her room. If there was a fire, she was to hook it to the window and crawl down.

But there was no ladder here. There was nothing here.

God, can You help me? My mom and dad are with You in heaven. She swatted at a mosquito, squashing it. It dotted her arm with blood. She smeared it with her hand. *Can You be my escape plan?*

Shaking, she dropped to her knees on the rough concrete. *I'm sorry I'm so bad that he locks me up. I'll try really hard to be good. Just please don't let there be a fire. I don't want to burn.* A sob tore loose from her throat. *Please, don't let me burn . . .*

It was the longest night of her life. Dark and wet—it rained and she couldn't get anywhere to stay dry. Bugs she couldn't see buzzed in the air.

She swatted at them half the night, cried most of it, and prayed all of it. God had made it rain so there wouldn't be a fire—or if there was, the rain would put it out.

He'd helped her. Kept her safe.

Sometime before dawn, she heard noises inside and looked through the slats in the blind on the french door. Samuel Johnson had returned—and he was walking funny. She started to call out to him, to knock on the glass, but something warned her not to make a sound. So she bit her fisted hand and stayed silent.

Dawn finally came, and then the sun rose. She looked at herself in the glass door. She was shocked. Nearly eaten up by mosquitoes, her face and arms were dotted red and swollen. She looked like a monster. A drenched, gross monster.

The door swung open.

She jerked back, gasped.

"Stupid, stupid girl." Samuel's red-rimmed eyes bulged. "Get in here." He snagged her shirt at her shoulders and dragged her in, nearly sweeping her off her feet. "Didn't you hear me come home?"

"Yes." He was still staggering, and he stank like the alcohol her mother had used to dab her ears when she'd had them pierced, only his smelled sour.

"Why didn't you knock?" He turned her loose.

She caught her balance. "I don't know." She'd been scared of him, but she couldn't say that.

Dropping her gaze, she saw just how swollen her arms were. Would they fall off? They might. They were huge and peppered with welts and red spots, dotted with streaks of blood. "I need some medicine."

"No." He swiped at his rumpled hair. "No medicine, no doctors—and don't you tell a soul about this."

He was scared somebody would get mad at him.

"Promise me. Right now."

Her arms might fall off. She blinked to clear the tears blurring her eyes, her chin trembling. "I promise."

"You should have knocked. This is your fault, girl." He huffed and slammed the terrace door. "If you tell anyone—anyone at all—the police will come. You know what will happen then?"

She didn't answer. He sounded too angry and she didn't want him to get worse. What was the right thing to say?

"Do you?" he pushed. Then before she could think of what to say to get him to stop so she could run to her room and hide from him, he answered himself. "They'll lock you away forever." He looked down his nose at her. "That's what they do with stupid girls."

"I won't tell. I'll never tell . . ."

She'd missed school for three days.

When her teacher, Mrs. Williams, asked why she'd been absent, Kelly nearly had told her. But afraid she'd call the police and they would lock her up forever, or that Mr. Johnson would put her on the terrace again, she lied.

He hadn't locked her on the terrace anymore. He moved her back to the entryway closet.

Oh, she hated that closet. Sometimes he'd leave her there so long she felt starved. Her stomach pushed against her backbone, and more than once she had to sneak to look at the television to see whether the time it showed meant it was day or night. He hated her being in his life almost as much as Kelly hated being in his life and being locked up.

When she grew up and moved far away, no one would ever lock her up again. Ever!

Mr. Johnson left home a lot.

She couldn't stop him from shoving her in that closet, but she did get smarter about being there. She stashed a jar with a lid on it for emergency bathroom services, hid packaged crackers and bottles of water deep in the closet inside a camera case. She even folded a thick sheet of paper and made herself a fan, then put it in her secret place too. She could have gotten a candle, but the firefighter that had come to her school said they were dangerous, so she decided against it. The dark wasn't nearly so scary as Mr. Johnson. But she did miss her mom and dad a lot sometimes. When it got real bad, she'd talk to God. He was a good listener, and He made her not so scared.

That went on for what felt like forever.

In truth, it couldn't have been very long. But when you're a kid and scared and miserable and lost, time moves differently than when you have some type of control over your own life.

Then one night Mr. Johnson didn't come back. She waited and waited and waited.

Her crackers were gone.

Her water bottles stood empty, her pee-jar full.

And her tummy hurt something fierce. She prayed and cried and prayed and prayed until she couldn't pray anymore.

Huddled in the back of the closet, she crossed her arms, freezing. Her teeth chattered until her jaw ached.

Then she began to sweat. It poured off her, dripping and splashing on her chest, her knees. She slumped to rest her head on the floor. The carpet scratched her face, but her head felt too heavy to hold up anymore—and again she started shivering. Shivering. Sweating. Shivering. Sweating.

Oh, but she was sick. So sick . . . Her stomach rebelled. A bad taste warned she was going to throw up. She swallowed hard. It would stink so bad . . . Her stomach churned and churned, her head swam, and she felt the bad taste rise in her throat.

The door opened.

She vomited all over some man's shoes.

"Kelly!"

He knew her. Knew her! She cranked open her eye, tilted her head, hoping she didn't get sick again, and looked up at him. Mr. Denham. "Help me."

He pulled his phone from his pocket and told someone to come.

"No! Don't call the police. They'll lock me away forever. Please don't call them. Please!"

"It's all right. A doctor is coming. Just be still until he and his helpers get here."

"Oh no," she cried. "He's going to be so mad. He'll lock me in here until I die."

Alexander Denham's face turned dark and red and she feared him too. "No one will ever lock you in a closet again. I give you my word on it."

He was mad but not at her. "Thank you, Mr. Denham. I-I don't feel good." She threw up again but this time missed his shoes.

The ambulance people tended to her, but she could hear Mr. Denham talking to the policeman. She stayed very quiet, hoping he wouldn't notice her and lock her up.

"I had a meeting with Mr. Johnson to go over some estate matters—her estate matters."

The ambulance lady with the gentle voice asked her, "Kelly, how long have you been in the closet?"

She struggled to remember. "I don't know what day it is." She licked her lips, hoping for more water. They'd given her some, but her mouth was still so dry.

"What day did Mr. Johnson put you in the closet?"

Had she told? No, no, Mr. Denham had. The police wouldn't lock her up for him telling. "Saturday."

"You're sure?" The nice lady gave her a sip of water.

"Uh-huh." Water dribbled down her chin.

"Saturday," the woman repeated, looking at the man helping her.

It was Friday afternoon.

Kelly lay in bed in the cottage, her cheeks wet at the vivid memories of that awful time. She clenched the wadded edge of her pillowcase and rubbed her cheeks dry.

The ambulance had taken her to the hospital, and she'd been so surprised that the nurses and doctors hadn't been mad at her. They'd been kind. Mr. Denham hadn't been angry with her either, even though she'd ruined his shoes.

She'd slept a lot. Sometimes he had been there; sometimes he hadn't. A nurse was always with her, and whoever she was, she always assured Kelly on awakening that Mr. Johnson could not come into her room and Mr. Denham would be back shortly. Amazingly he had been back.

It took her three days to work up the courage to ask when Mr. Johnson would be taking her back to his house. The nurse grimaced and said, "Don't you worry, Kelly. He won't hurt you anymore." She stroked Kelly's forehead, shoving back her hair. "Mr. Denham will explain everything."

She didn't believe the nurse. He wouldn't hurt her while anyone was looking, but he'd lock her in the closet again, and she knew it.

She did not want to go back into that closet—and she'd do what she had to do to stay out of it. She'd hide or run away and disappear. She'd do something—*anything!*

The nurse must have told Mr. Denham that Kelly had asked about Mr. Johnson because as soon as he arrived, he'd told her, "Kelly, you will never return to Mr. Johnson's home."

She felt relief, and joy danced throughout her entire body, set her to tingling, making her giddy.

"Can I go home, then?" she asked.

"I'm afraid not," Mr. Denham said. "You're too young to live alone."

She sat straight up. "Aunt Beth! Oh, please, *please,* can I go to my aunt Beth's?" She loved Aunt Beth and her little house on the beach.

His jaw clamped, and he closed his eyes a second. "I'm afraid not."

"But why?" Kelly grabbed a fistful of sheet. "I have my own room there—and she never puts me in the closet." She crossed her heart. "I promise."

"I'm sorry, but your mother and father forbade it, Kelly. You can't live with your aunt Beth."

She'd tried so hard not to cry. She hadn't

sobbed, but she wanted to, and tears slid down her face. "Then where do I have to go? There isn't anyone else." *God, please don't let him send me back to Mr. Johnson's anyway. Please!*

He stepped closer and looked down at her. "I asked the judge and he said you could come live with me."

Kelly recoiled, sank back against her pillows. "Are you going to lock me in the closet too?"

"No, Kelly," he promised, his eyes burning bright. "I've hired a very nice woman to care for you. Her name is Doris. And we both promise that no one will ever lock you in a closet again." He glanced away, then added, "We can even invite your aunt Beth to visit."

And she did.

Kelly stared at the cottage bedroom ceiling, dabbed at her moist eyes, and let the memories after that time flow through her mind unfettered.

Alexander Denham wasn't home much. When upset, he was a little hard to understand due to an accent she learned from Doris was Russian, and he didn't know what to do with a young girl, but he'd left Doris to it. She was caring and kind, and whenever Mr. Denham returned home from his trips, the first thing he would ask Kelly is if she'd been well treated.

She had been and always felt relieved to say so without lying.

He hadn't been a warm, fuzzy kind of person—

316

he'd never once so much as hugged her—but he hadn't locked her up, and he had come to respect her sharp mind. Kelly worked hard to earn his respect and harder to earn his praise. He was stingy with it but never unkind.

He'd taught her a lot. Doris had too. But even as a child, Kelly had held no illusions. Neither of them had ever loved her.

Alexander was paid well from her estate and her grandmother's trust to care for her, act as trustee and guardian, and she had no doubt that, if she'd been poor, he'd have put her up for adoption immediately—if he'd bothered getting involved with her in the first place. His passion was acquiring money, and she provided a good, steady, long-term source for it.

Aunt Beth, though, had loved her very much. Kelly was first to admit that her mother's "quaint and quirky" baby sister was flaky and considered by kind souls "eccentric," which was why she couldn't take custody of Kelly—her father had flatly refused and insisted her mother go along with him.

Once Mr. Denham had been convinced Kelly would immediately contact him in case of any trouble, he'd permitted her to spend summers with her aunt at her beach house.

Aunt Beth had taught Kelly to paint, the mood of colors, and how to use her potter's wheel. They'd taken midnight swims, eaten ice cream for breakfast, and giggled themselves silly. Kelly had adored her zany aunt. And she had adored Kelly.

Now Aunt Beth was dead.

Her throat thick, Kelly snuggled down deep under the covers and felt her loss afresh. *A heart attack. Unexpected. Unforgiving.* They'd never gotten to say good-bye . . .

Kelly gave in to a good cry. For the little girl, alone and lost, locked in the closet, on the terrace. For the absence of loving parents. For feeling she had no safe haven of her own but lived as a guest in someone else's.

When her tears were spent, she sniffed and wiped her face with her hands.

A scent wafted to her.

What was it? She sniffed, then sniffed again. Bacon.

Bacon?

Fear snipped her thoughts. She was in Ben's cottage. *Alone.* So who was cooking bacon and making coffee?

It's not the carjackers. It's not. They wouldn't come in and cook for—Doris!

Kelly tossed back the covers—and remembered in a flash why she feared Seagrove Village.

Ben!

Edward pulled into Harry's driveway just as dawn was breaking. His truck was parked out front.

With any luck, he wasn't drunk again, but Edward couldn't bank on it.

He got out and looked into Harry's bedroom window. He was flat on his back sprawled out atop sleep-tossed covers, the telltale open can on a ring-marked table beside his bed.

Edward regretted what he had to do, but he had no choice. Wily and slick, where Harry was dumb but dependable, Edward would be forced to live the rest of his life sleeping with one eye open. That was no life at all.

Edward fired his gun through the window. The glass shattered. Harry took the bullet right between his eyes. He never knew what hit him.

His throat thick, Edward whispered, "Sorry, buddy. The plan changed."

He pulled out his tools, but the door wasn't even locked. Edward went inside to collect Harry.

The guy was bigger and heavier; it took Edward longer than he hoped to get him into the car. By the time he'd crunched him into the trunk and gotten in behind the wheel, Edward was soaked with sweat, every muscle in his body ached, and he was completely out of breath.

He'd dump Harry's body on the reservation behind Three Gables. Some kid would find it taking the shortcut through the Brandt land on the way home from school. That way, Harry's body would be found before it decomposed. His son would have something to bury and would know his dad was dead. He wouldn't feel abandoned and wonder if the reason he never came around was his fault. He'd never have to ask himself what he'd done wrong. Or be left not knowing.

Not knowing was never easy.

But in Edward's case, knowing was even worse.

Edward sighed. It wasn't the best solution, but it was the best he could offer the kid. It was a lot better than anyone had offered him. It had taken years for him to learn his father had taken off because of his uncle Samuel Johnson.

Edward had been fourteen. He'd gone to find his father and learned he'd remarried and had a son. Then he and his new family had disappeared. Edward had tried and failed to find any trace of him after that, though he thought of his half brother often and wondered if he'd been left behind by their father too.

Edward had found Uncle Samuel and watched him closely. He'd seen Kelly on that terrace all night. Seen her pack staples into the closet, and he'd figured out what Samuel was doing. Edward bided his time. He finally got the perfect opening and seized it. To this day, no one else knew why Samuel had left one morning and just never came home.

It was nearly a week before Edward discovered Kelly was locked in the apartment. She'd been silent all that time. Edward had been hanging out there, planning his future, and looking for information on his father and half brother but had still found nothing—Samuel was meticulously careful for all his carousing.

While in a spare bedroom, Edward heard something that sounded like a cat. But when he realized the noise was coming from the closet, he'd known it was the girl.

He'd left right then and placed an anonymous call to the lawyer he'd discovered in Samuel's papers. Alexander Denham had come straight over.

Edward waited outside, hidden in a clump of trees, and watched the ambulance leave with Kelly.

He hadn't learned until much later about NINA or that Alexander Denham was an alias for Alik Demyan, a man Kelly's father had met in Russia. He, Samuel, and Alik had become the closest of friends.

That she'd been in the closet so long had been Edward's burden of guilt to carry, and it never left him. That had been one of several reasons Edward was such a stickler about paying Harry's child support. He'd have to do something to help the kid. Maybe say it was a life insurance policy Harry had left for him or something. Yeah, that would work. It might even give the kid a good feeling about his father. Like Harry cared about him. A boy should have at least that much from his father.

Edward cranked the engine and reached for the gearshift.

The car exploded.

22

Kelly scrambled out of bed, washed up, tugged on yet another fresh pair of blue scrubs, then ran for the back door.

"Hey!" Doris yelled out from the stove. "Where are you going? Breakfast is nearly ready."

"Doris." Kelly paused a brief second and clasped Doris's hand. "Thank you for coming. It means the world to me. But I need to talk to Ben. It's critical."

"Ben." Her voice warmed. "Now he's a package."

"Yes, he is." Kelly licked her lips. "I don't mean to be rude, really. But it's urgent I talk to him right away." Kelly grabbed the doorknob. "I'll be back." She glanced at the stove. "Thanks for fixing breakfast."

"He isn't home." Doris lifted fluffy scrambled eggs onto a plate. "He said to tell you he's at the crisis center."

What now? She didn't have a way to get to him. She'd call. "It's barely daylight. They must have had an emergency." According to Peggy, most of them did occur during the night.

"Actually, he's meeting with the insurance adjuster."

The fire. "Oh, Doris. You have a car!"

"Of course." She looked at Kelly over her glasses. "It's a long walk from Marietta."

Kelly grabbed her arm with one hand and Doris's purse with the other. "I need a ride."

"Can't you eat first?"

"No, no, I can't." Kelly accepted her condemning look. "I remember, Doris." Kelly wrung her hands. "He's going to hate me. Seriously. But I have to tell him. I can't not tell him. That would be . . . unforgivable—not that what I have to tell him is forgivable." Hot tears sprang to her eyes. "Oh, this is awful. Worse than awful."

"Well, I'll be." Doris turned off the stove and took possession of her purse. "You're in love with the man."

Was she? Could that be possible? The truth slammed into her. "Oh, Doris. I am!" Kelly covered her mouth with her hand. She really was in love with him. How had that happened? When had it happened? Why hadn't she realized it and stopped it from happening?

"Stupid, stupid girl."

Samuel Johnson's voice rang in her head, and she couldn't dispute it. Not this time. Of all men, she had to fall in love with the one she absolutely should not love—ever. He could never—would never—allow himself to love her back. "Doesn't it figure, Doris?"

"I've always told you that when the time was right you'd find him."

Nothing about this time, or this man, was right. It could never be made right. "You did," she told

Doris, her heart breaking. "But you never told me that when I did, he'd hate me."

"Why will he hate you?" She frowned. "He hasn't known you long enough to hate you."

"Oh, Doris. If I've known him long enough to love him, he's known me long enough to hate me—and he will. He already does; he just doesn't know it yet." Kelly tugged Doris toward the door, the truth she'd spoken hurting her battered heart. She buried the pain under a sniff.

"Then he's not the man I believed he was."

"He's a good man. Maybe a great one," Kelly protested.

"Not if he hates you and doesn't even know it."

"It's not his fault, Doris. It-it—"

"It *what*?"

"Later. We've got to go."

Kelly shuffled Doris out the door, down the walk, and into her green sedan. Then Kelly ran around the front end, got in, slammed the door, and clicked her seat belt in place. He'd have every right to hate her. How could he not hate her? She hated herself for this.

Doris started the car, then sat staring at Kelly.

"What?" Why wouldn't she go?

Doris looked over her glasses and down her nose at Kelly. She wasn't moving. "Why is Ben going to hate you?"

"Doris, please." Kelly shook her head. Honestly, the woman could be mule-stubborn at the worst possible times. "I'll tell you later—I promise. He should hear this first." She gulped and signaled Doris to get going with circular hand motions. "And he should hear it from me."

Paul stopped by a 24/7 Wal-Mart and picked up a new throwaway phone. He paid for it with cash and avoided looking directly into the security cameras both in the store and on his return to the parking lot.

Seated in his Lexus, he pulled out a voice recorder. He'd worked on editing it most of the night, and he'd turned out a fine product. Only the top professionals in the field stood a hope of ever determining the recording had been edited at all.

He'd learned at the hands of a master of deception, and he'd learned well. His father.

"Here we go," he said to himself. He dialed 911.

A woman answered. "Nine-one-one. What's your emergency?"

"Something exploded off Red Bluff Road near Magnolia," the recording told her. "I'm not sure what happened, but I can see the smoke and flames from my terrace. Could be a house, but it's probably a car. Something's fueling it. Flames are above the treetops."

Paul hit pause and waited.

"Who are you, sir?" the emergency operator asked.

Satisfied, Paul pressed the play button. "This is

Gregory Chessman," the recording said, then spilled out his address and phone number.

"I've dispatched the fire department and a police unit, Mr. Chessman. Could you repeat your phone number?"

Paul hadn't prepared for that and didn't dare fake it and insert his own voice, so instead he let the recording play out.

"Thank you. Good-bye."

He hung up to the sound of the woman saying, "Mr. Chessman, wait—"

Paul wiped down the phone with one of Chessman's handkerchiefs, drove down to the gulf, and walked to the edge of the pier. "Cross me, Chessman?" Anger ran deep through his veins, pulsing and pounding in his head. "Big mistake." He tossed the phone into the rough water and watched it sink, knowing it would never again be seen by man.

Satisfied, he stuffed his hand in his pocket, pulled out his cell, then dialed Gregory.

"Yes, Paul, what is it?"

Paul glanced at his watch. "Sorry to disturb your morning swim, sir, but I wanted to let you know that Edward and Harry are no longer on your priority list."

"That's a good way to start an important morning," he said, decidedly cheerful.

"I thought you'd welcome the news." Paul looked at a flock of sea gulls overhead. Their shrieks nearly drowned out Gregory's voice. Paul stuffed his fingertip into his ear to block the racket.

"You're certain?"

"Absolutely positive, sir."

Chessman grunted, judging by the hollow echo, heaving himself out of the lap pool. "What about the woman?"

Kelly Walker. "Not yet, sir." That was the one thing he and his now-deceased half brother had in common. Neither of them relished killing another Samuel Johnson victim. But when push came to shove and survival stood at risk, another truism revealed itself.

Johnsons ate their own.

Edward was the greatest threat to Paul—and if the moron had created problems for him with NINA, Paul would dig him up from his grave and cut him into a million pieces for pure meanness.

Kelly Walker wasn't much better. She had no idea his attempts on her life had failed because Paul had wanted them to fail. But things had changed.

It was crunch time now, and Paul meant to survive. That meant she had to die.

Edward might have died not knowing what had happened to his father and half brother, but Paul knew. He'd paid a high price for the information—Darla demanded an alliance, and given no choice, Paul had accepted. She had obtained a copy of Alexander Denham's court case. The records had been sealed, so only she and God knew how she'd managed, though being the mayor's wife likely had been involved. Agreeing to the alliance had gained Paul access. And the case file included a listing of all Johnson's relatives.

His father had abandoned his new family just as he had his old one. And like Edward, Paul had sought Samuel. Edward had failed. Paul had found him—and had learned what he was doing to Kelly. Locking a kid in a closet . . . just like his brother had done. Until he'd grown large enough to take on his old man, Paul had spent more nights on the closet floor than in a bed. The day Paul had won the fight was the last day he'd seen his father.

His mother had never forgiven him.

She'd moved on to a new man too much like her husband. Paul had left home and never looked back.

He was fifteen.

So Kelly would have lived to fight her battles another day if she'd just not remembered her past or she'd had the good sense to run again. She'd done neither, so she had to die.

And now that Chessman would be tagged for calling in Edward's and Harry's demise, and the police would follow the trail of connections Paul had laid between them, and the probability that they could unearth Gregory's connection to NINA was off the charts high . . . she had to die soon so Paul could be spared.

He would be spared, provided Chessman hadn't somehow discovered Paul's alliance with Darla.

And provided that Paul killed Kelly and then won the one battle left to fight. *Keep your friends close, and your enemies closer.*

It wouldn't be easy to walk this fine line. His opponent was far stronger and smarter and more resourceful and certainly more complex than anyone ever had dreamed.

The battle with or against Darla Green . . .

23

Peggy stood at Mel's desk, and when Kelly ran into the center still wearing scrubs, Peggy clicked her tongue against the roof of her mouth. "The clothes didn't fit?"

"No, I just grabbed the first thing—" Kelly shook her head. "Where's Ben?"

"Kelly, what's wrong?" Peggy moved toward her.

She lifted a hand, her throat going thick, her eyes burning like fire. "I need Ben."

"Come on." Peggy clasped Kelly's elbow. "Are you hurt? Sick?"

Hearing Doris introduce herself to Mel, Kelly blinked hard, rushed her steps, but Peggy's kindness was her undoing. "I remember, Peggy, and it's awful." She swallowed a sob. "He's going to hate me as much as I hate myself."

"Stop that." Peggy jerked Kelly still. "You are a daughter of God, Kelly Walker. He created you exactly as you are, and you're exactly where you're supposed to be. You're a good woman. I've checked. So don't you dare tell me that you're to be hated. Not when the hand of God Himself molded you."

Kelly stiffened, let what Peggy said seep in and take hold. "You're right. My head knows you're right, but my heart . . ."

"Your heart is full of fear." Peggy glanced toward the kitchen. "Ben's at the fridge getting a cold drink. Now, you give him a chance before you fly off with that hate business. You're selling yourself short, but you're selling him short too. And being a child of God too—whether or not Ben wants to be—he deserves better."

"I'll remember." Kelly wrung her hands and couldn't seem to stop except by cramming them into her pockets. She walked into the kitchen. "Ben, hi."

Ducked into the fridge, he straightened, holding a bottle of orange juice. When he saw her, he smiled broadly and he got that twinkle in his eye. "Good morning."

She would likely never see that twinkle again. Pausing to savor it a moment, reluctant to let it go and lose it forever, she said, "Doris drove me over."

"She's terrific. We had a long chat before the crack of dawn." Lifting the bottle, he asked, "Juice?"

She shook her head, forced herself to meet his gaze. "Do you have a minute?"

"Sure."

"We need to talk." Oh, how she wished they didn't. He was everything she'd ever wanted— well, except for the God thing, but she just knew he'd work through that. Yet after this discussion, the odds were astronomical that he'd do it without her in his life.

She couldn't blame him for that.

"You okay?" He shut the door. "Have a seat." He motioned to the table and chairs.

Kelly sat down, her back to the door.

"You're worrying me." His expression mirrored his words. "You don't act like this. Worried, concerned, angry, or touched, you always let me see it. But you're not right now." He sat across from her, folded his hands atop the table. "Why is that?"

Her eyes filled with tears that spilled down her face. "I remember."

"That's wonderful news." Smiling, he reached for her hand.

She refused to take it. "No, Ben." She paused. "I mean, it is wonderful that I have my memory back, but what I remember is awful." Her voice cracked. "Really awful."

He tugged a tissue from a box and passed it to her. "Whatever it is, it can be worked out."

"Not this." She gave up trying not to cry and spilled out what had happened as best she could. "You're going to hate me, Ben. I really, really care about you. It isn't some misplaced fantasy. I know you're the right man for me."

"That's good news. I care a lot about you too, and I've been driving myself nuts, wondering if you're married or—" He stopped, stilled. "You're not married, are you?"

"No. It's nothing like that." She dabbed at her nose with the tissue, but seeing the relief on his face and knowing it'd soon disappear and disgust would replace it had her crying again. "Before I tell you this, listen to me."

"Whatever it is, it can't be that bad. Just tell me."

"It is that bad. I don't expect you to forgive me. I mean, I'd love it if you could, but I know you won't be able to do it. No one could. Not even me." She let out a self-deprecating laugh. "This is going to hurt you, Ben. If I could, I'd take it on myself to spare you, but I can't."

She had his full attention now, and he'd never appeared so solemn and sober. "Kelly, what is it?"

"I know why Susan was killed."

He slammed back in his chair, as if forcefully hit. "What?"

Oh, but she'd stunned him. "Let me start at the

beginning." When he silently signaled, she went on. "The beach house belonged to my aunt Beth. She was my mom's baby sister."

"An artist, yes."

"After my parents died, I spent summers here with her. It was all I had of a home life." And memories of that time were all she had of one now. But that was best left unsaid. "Three years ago, Aunt Beth and I went to a Pirates' Party at Gregory Chessman's house. It was a costume event, but I didn't know it, so I went as myself." She'd taken a few jabs from those behind masks for not being in the spirit enough to dress up. "I went out onto the terrace for some fresh air. Everyone else was inside, but it was so nice out there that I just stayed."

She paused a long second, letting her rioting emotions settle. Ben looked as if he wanted to say something but was totally lost. She knew how he felt. "Two men came outside and talked with a third. They didn't see me, and I didn't want to be seen, so I stepped behind a column."

She pushed her hair back from her face and looked Ben in the eye. "It was Paul Johnson and Gregory Chessman. The third man, I didn't recognize, but Chessman deferred to him, so I expect he was his boss or a higher-up in NINA. They were talking about getting everything and everyone in position for a biological attack, Ben. So it would kill everyone but not damage valuable equipment and materials. I couldn't catch all of it, but I heard more than enough to get me hunted down. I've been running from them ever since."

This was so hard. She let herself absorb it. *Help me get through this. I can't do it alone.* Reassuring warmth spread through her chest. "I wouldn't have listened, but with what they were discussing, I had no choice but to stay hidden and pray they didn't discover me."

"But they did?" Ben took a drink of his untouched juice, and while he sounded steady, his hand shook.

"Yes. They were talking about how the property had been condemned and all that stood in their way was my aunt Beth. They had to have her beach house." Kelly grabbed a staggered breath. "She had told me about being pressured to sell—some of her neighbors had been too, though the buyer was anonymous. She said she had her suspicions on who was behind it, but if she said anything, she'd be driven out of the village on rails."

"Did she say she suspected Johnson or Gregory of something illegal?"

"No. But I heard plenty enough to know that what they were planning with this NINA guy was treason, and if anyone got in their way . . ."

"What?" Ben slid forward on his seat.

"Chessman told Johnson to remove all obstacles. Permanently."

Kelly remembered the sick fear that had assaulted her that night. She'd been terrified. That Gregory talked of killing people was horrific, but the dispassionate tone in his voice chilled her to the bone. "I must have gasped or something because Chessman heard me. He ordered Paul to find me and get rid of me."

Oh, she'd never in her life been so afraid. "I ran, hiding behind bushes in the darkness." Once, Paul had come so close to her she'd smelled his sweat. "He didn't find me. But Chessman and he were close, and Johnson told him not to worry. He'd take care of it. Chessman said, no, he'd have someone else deal with that, he wanted Johnson focused on getting the beach house."

"Good grief."

"I ran, Ben. And I kept on running. I didn't even go back to the beach house for my clothes." Shame burned her face. "I left Aunt Beth a voice mail message that I had to disappear for a while and I'd be in touch when I could."

"Oh, Kelly."

"I know." She parked her elbow on the table and half-covered her face with her hand. "I'm ashamed of myself for running, but I couldn't find another way to keep Aunt Beth safe. If I stayed away—"

"Then she wouldn't be harmed."

"Yes." Kelly cleared her throat. "It worked too. Chessman couldn't find me, and he left Aunt Beth alone because he knew I was out there and could nail him."

Ben dragged a hand across the back of his neck. "Then she had a heart attack and died."

"And I started getting anonymous offers for the beach house—above market-value offers."

"Chessman."

"I would think so, but I can't prove it." She still bristled at Alexander Denham's odd insistence that she sell. Never, not once since he'd transitioned from being her guardian and trustee to her advisor, had he pushed her that hard on anything.

Ben frowned. "I don't understand how this connects—"

Then it hit him; she could see it in his eyes, and though the words were no longer necessary, she gave them to him.

"Johnson and Chessman mistook me for Susan." She licked her lips. "Aunt Beth had hoped Susan and I would meet at the party, but some woman—the mayor's wife, I think—told Aunt Beth that Susan couldn't come. She was home with a sick child."

Ben stared at Kelly, his jaw gaping, his eyes fixed. He looked frozen, as if he couldn't move or even breathe.

"I'm so sorry, Ben." Her tears flowed in earnest. "I didn't know Susan. I had no idea she existed, much less that she'd be mistaken for me."

"My wife and son were killed by mistake?"

He clearly was struggling to wrap his mind around it. Angry and bitter, he raised his voice. *"By mistake?"*

"Oh, Ben. I'm sorry. So sorry." A sob tore loose from deep in her chest. "It's my fault Susan and Christopher are dead . . ."

"Lucille, where is Mr. Chessman?"

"Late breakfast on the terrace, Mr. Johnson."

Paul kept walking. "Thank you."

Lucille looked at him as if he'd lost his mind. Paul supposed it was odd; he didn't typically waste time on chitchat. But he was in a particularly good mood now that he'd covered himself and Gregory was on the hook.

He walked out onto the terrace. Mr. Chessman sat at a glass-topped table, finely set as always, sipping at coffee and reading the paper. "Good morning again, sir."

Chessman lowered the newspaper. It fluttered in the cool breeze. "Paul. What's up?"

He wasn't happy at having his breakfast interrupted, but then Paul didn't recall ever seeing the man happy. Amused, thrilled by a deal, yes. But happy? No. Never.

"I need a little time off. It's a personal matter."

"Today?" Gregory eyed him sharply.

"Just a few hours this morning, sir."

"So it won't interfere with tonight's shipment?"

"Of course not, sir." Paul knew better than to

consider anything that would interfere. The only excuse for upsetting Mr. Chessman's schedule was death. One's own. "It shouldn't take long."

Chessman's eyes glinted like flint. "Anything I can do?"

"No sir." Only a crazy man or a very stupid one would give Gregory Chessman anything on himself.

"Very well."

"Thank you, sir." Paul turned to go.

"Ten o'clock. Don't be late—and let me know when John Green gets back from New Orleans." Gregory chuckled. "He must be having some party."

"Excuse me, sir?"

"He isn't returning my calls."

"If you like, I can phone him to let him know you'd appreciate a more timely response."

"Thank you, Paul, but no. He has need of his fingers, and it's nothing that can't wait."

"Yes sir." Paul left the terrace, smarting from Chessman's snide remark.

Soon enough, the tide would turn. He tamped his temper. Chessman would go down, and because of NINA, he wouldn't be able to say a thing. Not even against Paul. The man was going to need someone loyal on the outside.

And Paul would gladly step into those shoes. He'd be the master of Chessman's universe for the rest of his life.

Everything to make it happen was now in place.

24

Kelly sat at the table across from Ben, staring at him, watching him stare at her, weeping silent tears wrenched from her very soul largely because she knew he had to be weeping inside too.

A rap at the door ended a horrible silence.

"Yes?" Ben swiped at his jaw with his sleeve. "Come in."

Peggy opened the door, took one look at Ben and then at Kelly, and pretended everything was normal. "There's been a development."

"What development?" Ben's voice was soft, disconnected, and distant.

Caught in the past. Her heart twisted even more.

"We got a phone call." She looked at Kelly. "It was about your beach house."

"From whom?" Ben asked.

"We're not sure," Mark said, stepping around Peggy. "It was disguised. We couldn't tell if it was a man or a woman, and the number wasn't traceable." Mark slid a hand through his hair. "We're waiting for Detective Jeff Meyers to report in with the official word, but I suspect it's another throwaway phone."

Kelly found her voice. "What did the caller say about the beach house?"

Peggy leaned against the door frame. "It's critical that you go to the beach house right now and take a hard look around inside."

"I called Jeff," Mark said. "He's going over and will meet you there."

Kelly risked a glance at Ben. Something had died in his eyes. Seeing that, and knowing what it was and that she'd put it there, shattered her fractured heart. She stiffened against the pain. "Doris and I will leave right now."

"No." Ben shoved back his chair and stood. "Doris can stay here. You and I will go right now."

Kelly didn't argue. It would be pointless. But neither would she be foolish enough to think this had anything to do with her. Ben was on a mission for only one woman, and she was his dead wife.

And his son.

Kelly stood, then started walking out.

Peggy stepped into her path, stopping her at the door. "The caller also said for you to expect a special delivery at three o'clock sharp this afternoon."

"Where?" Ben asked.

"Here at the center." Peggy touched Kelly's arm and dropped her voice. "You okay?"

"I'm fine." Kelly forced a shaky smile, doubting she'd ever feel fine again, though she knew better. God has His ways of fixing the unfixable. His wonders often surpassed human understanding, but somehow He'd glue her back together.

Never had she been able to depend on the men

in her life. Not since her father had died—or even
before then. He'd left her with Samuel Johnson,
after all. But she had always trusted God, and
He'd always provided for her. Not always in the
way she wanted or expected, but in hindsight,
always in the perfect way she needed.

Thank You for that.

"You ready?" Ben asked from beside her.

"Ready."

Doris stayed at the center, and Ben drove Kelly
over to the beach house in his SUV.

They made the entire trip in dead silence.

The driveway was empty. Kelly searched the
street, but it was empty. Jeff Meyers hadn't yet
arrived.

"No key." Ben grabbed a crowbar from the
trunk. "I'll break a window."

She spotted a rock in a flower bed just off the
edge of the porch. "No, wait." She lifted the rock,
then pulled the key out of its hollow bottom.

"I should have thought of that." He set down the
crowbar, then took the key from her.

"No problem." Stiff. Uncomfortable.
Unfamiliar between them. That nearly had her
weeping again. She buried her emotions and
waited for him to open the door. He didn't look as
if he hated her, but he looked so sad it cracked her
heart right down the middle. And she couldn't do
anything to help him. She was the reason he was

mourning his wife and son, and patient or not, that was too huge an obstacle to overcome. The relationship building between them couldn't survive this.

Her memory loss had created a bond between them.

Its return had crushed it.

What is, *is*. She had to accept it.

And she would. Her chest squeezed tight. But it was going to take a while. She'd dated, she'd been serious about a guy once, but never had she felt the hand of God in a relationship as she had with Ben. And now it was gone, and for the rest of her life, she'd mourn.

The door creaked open.

Kelly followed Ben inside. The air was dank and stale. Crumpled newspapers curled on the floor in the corner, and someone had put out cigarettes on the hardwood floor. Butts and black smears marred every corner. It felt strange being in Aunt Beth's beach house empty of furniture, her eclectic collections, or her flamboyant art littering the walls.

They searched room by room and found more of the same. "Let's split up, check the bedrooms," Ben said.

Kelly took the first room off the hallway and spotted the staircase. Her heart thumped hard. "Ben! Ben, come here!"

Ben rushed in and Kelly pointed. "This was my

bedroom. When I left three years ago, these stairs were not here."

"I remember. Stay behind me."

"Shouldn't we wait for Jeff?"

"Mark texted me a minute ago. Jeff's tied up. He'll be here as soon as possible."

Kelly raked her teeth over her lower lip. "The caller said to look now. We'd better not wait."

"I agree." Ben headed down the stairs. At the bottom, he made a turn, stepping out of sight. "It's empty."

Kelly rushed down and spotted a door under the staircase. "What's this?"

"Stand back." Ben stood away from the door, opened it, and let it swing wide.

Kelly pulled a miniflashlight from the purse Peg had given her. "Here."

He grabbed it without looking back. A little click, and a beam of light spread down a hollow opening. Nothing was inside. "What is this?"

"A tunnel." Kelly stated the obvious, then frowned. "But where can it go?" Outside, there was sand and beach, and frankly she was shocked the concrete walls weren't damp, being this close to the water.

Ben closed the door and steered Kelly back to the stairs. "We'll find out, but I'd feel better with some backup. No idea what we're walking into—or have you remembered something about this too?"

"Nothing. None of this was here."

"It looks new." Ben pulled out his cell phone and dialed.

Kelly sat on the second to last step. "Aunt Beth was half-crazy, I'll admit, but she'd never do anything illegal, and there'd be no need for a tunnel for anything that wasn't."

"Sure about that?"

She started to respond by rote, then decided against it. "No." That hurt, but truth was truth.

Ben sent her a look too tender to bear. She looked away.

"Mark, Ben. You tied up?" He paused. "I need you over at the beach house. We found something."

Kelly couldn't reason through it, and she hated being suspicious of her aunt. It wasn't fair. Why couldn't life be fair, just once in a while?

"A tunnel." He sighed. "Yeah, on the beach. Actually"—Ben swiveled and walked two steps—"under it." Another pause, and then, "Great. See you in ten." He flipped his phone closed, then put it in its holster at his belt. "He'll be right over."

Kelly propped her hands on her knees. "Good."

Ben studied her a long moment, then sat beside her on the step. Their knees brushed, and though she knew she should move away, she didn't. "Can we talk?"

Fear gripped her hard. He was going to tell her he was sorry, but under the circumstances, he didn't want to see her anymore. He was going to say they had moved too fast; he couldn't feel the same about her. He was going to walk away. And because she couldn't blame him if he felt half the pain she felt on looking at him, she tried to agree, but her voice just wouldn't work. She settled for a nod.

"I care about you, Kelly. A lot." He clasped her hand and pressed their palms together. "I know you think this is about you, but it's not. You didn't do anything to Susan and Christopher, okay? They were victims, just like you."

Gracious, but not true.

"So what I'm about to say, it's not about you, it's about me."

She didn't understand, but she waited, giving him time to say what he had to say in his own time and in his own way.

"You're the first woman I've cared about since Susan." He glanced away, then back at her. "I feel guilty."

"Because I'm the reason she's dead."

"Maybe. In part. But also just because I didn't protect them. I should have protected them."

"Oh, Ben, no." She sighed. "I saw those two that night, and that NINA guy was even worse. No one could protect them. I heard it in their voices. I really did. They would have done anything."

"It doesn't seem right." He lowered his gaze to the stair, between his knees. "My being happy, maybe falling in love again, while she's in the ground." His shoulders heaved. "I-I—"

"You don't have to explain. I understand." So he had been falling in love with her too. Crushed, robbed of this precious treasure, she briefly looked heavenward.

Oh, why? Why must I lose him too? I've lost everyone I've loved my whole life.

"Some obstacles are just too much to overcome, Ben."

"Maybe. Or maybe we just need some time to see how things work out."

Hope sparked to life inside her. She jerked her head up, met his gaze. "God brought us together to resolve this mystery, Ben. I'm crazy about you, but I can't say I know God brought us together for *us,* too. I thought He had. But now I'm not so sure."

"Do we have to be sure right now?"

She blinked, stunned. He didn't hate her. He might not love her, but he didn't hate her.

Be patient with him.

"No, we don't."

"I'm being selfish, Kelly." He squeezed her hand in both of his. "You get me like no one else, and I get you. This bond between us is special and rare. And I don't want to lose it."

"Me neither."

"But I'm not sure I'm ready for it, and I don't want to hurt you."

She summoned her courage and cupped his beloved face in her hand. "Ben, don't you see that I'll hurt anyway? Losing you . . ." She swallowed hard, bent close so their lips brushed. "If we work past this, we'll have something good." A gift straight from God. "If not . . . well, I'll take the risk."

She had money. She had power in her world. It meant nothing. Just once in her life, she wanted to be loved.

"I don't know if I can get back to God. I really don't. And you'd never be content with me if I fail."

Be patient with him.

Kelly might not trust herself, but she trusted God. "It'll work out exactly as it's supposed to work out. I believe that—enough for both of us." She kissed him again.

At noon, Paul parked the Lexus half a block down from the crisis center and walked into the Shipping Store, then on toward the long brown counter.

A young man in uniform greeted him. "Yes sir. May I help you?"

Paul laid a large white envelope on the counter. "I need this delivered promptly at three o'clock today."

The clerk twisted the envelope around and looked at the address. "You can walk this over.

Crossroads Crisis Center is just a few doors down at the end of the block."

Paul dropped a twenty onto the counter. "That's why I'm having you deliver it. You won't be late."

Carl, according to his name badge, shot Paul a suspicious look. "What's in here?"

"Nothing you need to worry about. A legal notice and some photographs. That's all."

"So why won't you take it over yourself?"

"You ever been married, Carl?"

"Divorced."

Paul mentally maneuvered. He could run with that—it could make the man slower to identify him—but another way was better. "My boss is Gregory Chessman. You know him?"

"Who doesn't? He sent my son all the way to Atlanta for eye surgery and paid every bit of it."

Paul smiled. "He's a very good man, and very private." He tapped the envelope. "You know then that he supports a lot of charities around here."

"All of 'em." Carl nodded enthusiastically. "Like you say, a good man. Self-made too. And he isn't one to forget where he came from."

Paul had no idea where Chessman had come from and neither did anyone else, though apparently many thought they knew. "He likes to donate as much as he can anonymously. That's what this is all about."

"No problem. I'll take care of it. You want it dropped to anyone there, or just to this"—he paused to double-check the name—"Kelly Walker?"

"Anyone there is fine." Paul lifted a finger. "Three o'clock."

"I won't be late. You give Mr. Chessman my best."

"I will, Carl." Paul resisted the urge to chuckle. He already had given the best of exactly what Chessman deserved. "Thank you."

"My pleasure, sir."

Sir. Paul liked that. He liked that very much.

25

Ben?"

Ben heard his name called out from the floor above and walked over to the staircase.

"Is that Jeff Meyers?" Kelly asked.

"No." Ben cupped his hands at his mouth, then shouted up, "We're down here, Mark. First bedroom on the right, go down the stairs."

Mark's footfall sounded as if he hit every other step. In short order, he stood before Ben. "This is a one-story beach house. Why are there stairs?" He looked beyond Ben and Kelly to scan the empty room. "What is this?"

"This area isn't significant." Ben walked around the empty cavity to the tunnel door. His voice echoed. "That area"—he pointed—"is probably very significant."

Mark looked through the door into the tunnel. "Been down it yet?" He wiped dust off his hands.

"No," Kelly answered first. "We thought we should wait for Detective Meyers since we have no idea what to expect."

Mark looked from her to Ben. "Good thinking." He reached around his back, then pulled out some kind of handheld meter. "Let's take a peek."

Ben skimmed the wall and found a light switch. "Do I dare turn it on?"

"No heat source on the meter. It should be okay."

Ben flipped the switch. "Kelly, would you go upstairs and keep an eye out? If Jeff shows up, send him down. If you hear an uproar, call 911." He passed her his cell phone.

Their hands brushed, and she lingered a second longer than necessary. "Be careful, okay?" When he clicked his tongue to the roof of his mouth and winked, Kelly turned and went up the stairs.

Ben watched her go, hating the sadness in her eyes, but he had no idea how to remove it.

Mark caught that lingering touch and Ben watching her, but he showed restraint and didn't mention it. Ben was glad about that. "Ready?"

Mark took off, and Ben followed him into the tunnel. Musty and a little damp, but no green mold. Concrete walls and floor. No footprints in the film of dust. "It's been a while since anyone's been down it."

"Maybe," Mark said. "Grainy. More sand than dust. This close to the water, that wouldn't take long."

Ben hadn't thought of that, but sand would penetrate every crack and crevice.

The mouth of the tunnel opened into a large, wide room. In its center stood a shallow swimming pool. Mark motioned Ben to go left. Mark went right so they fanned out in opposing directions and ran a quick check, but no one was around and the two little alcoves weren't outlets but shallow storage rooms.

"This doesn't make sense." Mark looked over at Ben. "The pool's too small for laps, and there are no connecting rooms—no way out."

Diving suits hung on hooks and a metal rack filled with tanks lined the wall. "Oxygen?" Ben guessed.

Mark glanced at his meter while walking over, then checked the tanks. "Appears to be."

Ben squatted at the edge of the pool. The air was heavy and moist and smelled of tangy salt. A darkened spot he hadn't seen through the reflection on the water appeared dead center in the bottom of the pool. "I think there is a way out." He pointed to the spot. "Down there."

Mark stooped down beside Ben. "I see it."

Ben looked from the water to Mark. "You thinking what I'm thinking?"

"I am if you're thinking this goes out into the gulf."

Ben frowned and rubbed at his jaw, his muscles tensing. "They're smuggling something."

"Yeah."

"What? Drugs?"

"I can't see that," Mark said. "It's too easy to get them in straight from the beach, underground tunnels in Mexico and out west." Mark swatted at his neck. "No, this is too elaborate for something as mundane as drugs and too expensive. They're bringing in something less abundant. Something they need to be far more covert about bringing in."

Ben agreed. Bad, bad things ran through his mind on the list of potentials.

"Oh, man." Mark shot Ben a look. "NINA just claimed responsibility for bombing that mall in Mobile."

"That's a big leap, Mark."

"Not so big. I talked to an FBI buddy of mine, and he said they had no idea NINA was functioning in this area. But Meyers mentioned when we talked this morning that the FBI had contacted the sheriff's office on a tip that came through Homeland Security that the mall bombers had flown out of this area."

"Impossible," Ben said. "Our airport uses a military base's runway. Only commercial jets can fly out of here."

"Only commercial jets use our public airport. But we have two small airports private jets can use and a grass strip the banner flyers on the beach use regularly."

"This was a private plane? The one the tip came in on?"

"Yeah, it was." Mark frowned. "I know the manager at Destin Airport, and she'd tag and bag a planeload of terrorists. The woman's been around the military all her adult life."

"What about the others?"

"Just one, Crestburg Airport. But a jet couldn't use the grass strip. Runway's too short."

"Okay," Ben agreed, "that leaves one. What about it?"

"You tell me. Your buddy owns it."

"My buddy?"

"Mayor Green." Mark hiked up his eyebrows.

"Since when does he own it?"

"Since he married Darla."

"She owns the airport?"

"She does."

Ben digested that information. "John would never have ties to NINA, Mark. He's not the kind."

"Maybe not. But maybe he isn't who he appears to be." Mark pulled out his cell, made a call, and put a man on checking out the airport's management.

He also ordered a background check on Darla Green.

While he talked, Ben's mind raced and he

glanced from point to point in the poolroom. They could be smuggling a million different things. But if NINA was involved, then the list of possibilities was so dangerous it had him mentally staggering. Dirty bombs, biocontaminants, weaponry systems, blacklisted technology. Any of those things were likely. His gaze settled on the diving suits. Why were there so many?

When Mark hung up, Ben asked, "How many bombers does the FBI think were here on the Mobile mall bombing?"

"Five."

That information shuddered through him. "There are five suits on that wall, Mark."

He spun, counted. "Yeah, there are, and they could have skin cells, hair—forensic evidence intact that proves who wore them." Mark reached for his phone again.

"Go to the FBI and then contact Jeff. I don't think, under the circumstances, Hank Green should be involved. Not with his sister-in-law owning that airport."

"I couldn't agree more."

"Ben?" Kelly hung close to the door and looked down but saw no signs of Ben or Mark. She called out in a stage whisper, "Ben."

He came toward her, and they met up at the mouth of the tunnel. "It's safe. Has Jeff arrived?"

"Not yet, but I had to tell you." She hooked a thumb, pointing upward. "Something really odd is going on here. I was looking around upstairs and I noticed something."

"What?"

"All those crumpled-up newspapers on the floor—they're foreign. Why would homeless people be reading foreign papers? Where would they get them?"

"They wouldn't," he said. "There's something odd going on down here too." He led her into the poolroom. "See that hole in the bottom?" He pointed. "We suspect it leads out into the gulf."

"Wow." She scanned the room slowly. "What is Chessman sneaking in here?"

"I don't know, but we'd better find out." Ben filled her in on the FBI lead to the mall bombers and NINA's claiming responsibility.

"Oh no." She squeezed her eyes shut. "Ben, NINA is involved. My advisor warned me that it wasn't just Chessman after me, it was a group I hadn't heard of before—NINA." She pulled it from memory. "Nihilists . . . something."

"Nihilists in Anarchy?" Mark asked.

"Yes, that's it."

Ben shot Mark a knowing look. "There's the connection."

"Yeah." Mark slapped at the air. "Chessman. I knew there was something off with that guy."

"You were right," Ben said. "Better call the FBI

355

and update them on Kelly's input. It could help them."

Mark glanced over at her. "You're positive this tunnel and poolroom weren't here when you were?"

"Positive." She adjusted her purse strap on her shoulder. "I wouldn't miss a staircase in my bedroom."

"I doubt you'll know, but I have to ask." Mark faced her.

"Go ahead," she said, scraping the buttons on Ben's cell phone with her thumbnail.

"What would you consider the odds of your aunt being a government agent?"

"Zero or less." Kelly smiled. "I loved her, but she was artsy and eccentric. Not exactly spy material."

"It wasn't an act?"

Kelly's smile faltered. "Aunt Beth also spent time in a mental institution—twice."

"I didn't know that." Ben blinked hard.

"I didn't either until she sued my guardian." Kelly hiked a shoulder. "Aunt Beth heard a different drum and marched to it. That didn't go over well with her father, so he committed her to straighten her out. It didn't. But it did make her lose the lawsuit."

"She was suing your guardian?" Ben asked. "For what?"

"Custody of me. He wanted me for the money.

Don't get me wrong; he was good to me, but Aunt Beth loved me."

"So she lost the suit because of the commitments."

"The judge couldn't in good conscience place me in her care when he knew she'd had stability issues."

"I'm sorry."

"Me too, Ben." She smiled. "So, Mark, to answer your question, no, it wasn't an act. No government agency would touch her."

"That had to be rough, it working out that way for you." Ben squeezed her shoulder.

"I've been fine. My guardian wasn't the warmest man, but he was meticulous about my being treated well."

"That was a blessing."

"Yes, it was." She'd had enough of this conversation. It cut too close to the bone. "Better get that call in to the FBI. My advisor says this NINA group is a bad one. I'm still not sure when they got involved. I thought I had been running from Chessman and Johnson for three years, but apparently NINA's after me too."

"How many times have you been found?" Mark asked.

"They've been close enough that I've had to drop everything and just run four times, and on my heels so many times I've lost count—but I didn't know who they were then. I thought it was just Chessman and Johnson and whoever that guy was they were talking to that night on the terrace. He has to be a NINA connection."

"I'll fill you in later," Ben told Mark. "Make the call."

"Wait." Kelly passed her glance between them. "Remember what Peggy said? There'll be a special delivery to the center this afternoon. Maybe we should see what's in it first before bringing in any outsiders."

"The FBI—"

She cut Mark off. "When my advisor told me about NINA, I asked how he learned they were after me. He said I was safer not knowing—"

"I don't see how that pertains, Kelly."

She pivoted to look only at Ben. "And he told me that people are often the opposite of what they appear. That's why I think we should wait." She shrugged. "We have no idea who we can and cannot trust, and I still haven't identified that NINA man working with them. I just want to be careful. It's how I've stayed alive."

"She's got a point, Mark," Ben said. "Especially considering the local royalty appear to be in up to their necks here."

Mark grimaced. "I hate to agree, but at this point, I have to say anyone's capable of anything."

Ben's cell phone rang. Kelly passed it to him.

He flipped it open. "Hello."

"It's Peg, Ben. That special delivery arrived."

"What is it?"

"A nine-by-twelve white envelope addressed to Kelly. Since it was addressed to her, I didn't open it."

"Any residue or anything like that?"

"Harvey ran it through the new scanner. It's safe."

Relieved, Ben said, "We're on our way."

Ben relayed the information about the envelope's arrival to Kelly and Mark as the three of them went back through the tunnel and then up the stairs. Nearing the top, Mark said, "Maybe I should hang around here until we know what's in that envelope."

"Good idea to have someone here, but you need to come with us to see what's in that delivery."

"I'll be right behind you. Just want to touch base with Jeff Meyers first."

"We'll meet you there, then." Ben headed straight for the front door. "Kelly, let's go."

She turned to Mark. "Do you have everything you need until someone gets here?"

"I'll be fine, Kelly. Jeff's ten minutes away. Thanks."

"Be careful."

Mark gave her a friendly wink, and she headed out to Ben's SUV.

"You okay?" Ben asked, opening her car door.

She waited until he got inside, then reached for

his hand. "Ben, I've got a bad, bad feeling about all this."

"Yeah, so do I."

Kelly entered Crossroads and paused to talk to Doris and Mel. "Everything okay?"

"I've been doing some filing for Mel," Doris said. "We're fine, but you look scared to death."

She was. "No, I'm okay." Okay? Had she really said that? Ben on the proverbial fence; her future, if no longer life, still pretty much a mystery; and that pool at Aunt Beth's. People were out to kill her; Chessman or NINA surely would, if given the chance. Nothing was okay or fine.

But she was upright and fighting to sort it all out, and Ben didn't doubt her anymore about Chessman being dirty. There was solace in that, and knowing the root of that solace stemmed from her faith, she wondered how Ben could handle all this mess with his faith in remission.

On that issue, remission rested much easier on her soul than denial. If the need arose, she'd deal with it later, after they'd resolved some of these other issues. But, oh, it was significant to her, and it just had to be resolved.

Peggy came into the reception area. "Kelly, Harvey and Lisa are in the conference room with the envelope. We're all waiting for you to come open it."

Kelly, Peggy, and Doris went back to the conference room. Ben was already there with Harvey and Lisa, sitting at the long table. The envelope was in front of the chair she'd sat in the last time they'd met. "Should I wear gloves?"

"Oh yes." Peggy sprang from a seat and returned with a pair of gloves. She passed them to Kelly. "I should have thought of that."

"It's okay," Harvey assured her. "I ran it through the paces."

"An equipment gift from Gregory Chessman." Ben groaned. "Double up on the gloves."

"Why? What's wrong with a gift from Gregory?" Harvey asked.

"Later." Ben motioned to Kelly. "Go ahead."

She put on the gloves, then used the letter opener to slice open the envelope and looked inside. Paper and photos. She dumped them out on the table. "No one touch them. If there are fingerprints and they're important, we don't want to mess them up."

Touching only the least bit of the edges, she flipped the photos and lined them up in a row on the tabletop.

Mark Taylor walked in, and Ben came around the table to stand beside Kelly. "Gregory Chessman's dinner party." Ben looked at her. "I was there."

Doris let out an odd noise. "That's Mr. Denham."

"He's a lawyer from Atlanta," Ben said. "We talked." He pointed to the photo. "That's me—well, my sleeve—there beside him."

Kelly looked closely. "It is him."

"Who is he?" Peggy Crane asked.

"My financial advisor," Kelly said. "He was my trustee and then my guardian."

"Your guardian is connected to Chessman?"

"Apparently. He's at Chessman's table." She glanced at Ben. "When was this dinner?"

"A few days ago."

"But that's impossible," Doris said. "Mr. Denham has been in Europe for weeks."

Ben cocked his head. "He might be in Europe now, but he was at Gregory Chessman's dinner party then."

That triggered Kelly's memory. "I talked to him not fifteen minutes before the carjacking."

"Was it a foreign call?" Harvey asked.

"It was his cell number." Kelly shrugged. "I have no idea."

"He could be forwarding from anywhere," Mark said.

"So what is this person trying to tell me with all this?" Kelly couldn't figure it out. She looked to the next photo and gasped. "That's him, Ben." She pointed. "One of the carjackers."

Mark bent over and took a hard look. "His name is Edward Johnson. He and his partner, Harry Donaldson, were killed in a car explosion this morning." He paused. "Well, that might not prove exactly accurate."

Harvey rocked forward in his chair. "How can that not be accurate? They're either dead or they're not."

"Oh, they're dead," Mark said. "Edward was behind the wheel in his car. Someone rigged explosives to the starter. But Harry's body was found in the trunk. Jeff Meyers spotted a bullet hole in Harry's forehead. They're assuming it was Harry, anyway, since the car blew up in his yard and someone bled a lot on his bed. Splatter pattern suggests it was a gunshot, but they're still sorting it all out."

"What does the note say?" Lisa asked.

Kelly opened the folded page and read. " 'If you are reading this, it means I am dead.' "

Ben turned to Peggy. "How did this get here?"

"The Shipping Store messenger brought it. Carl."

"I've already quizzed him," Harvey told the group. "He couldn't really describe the man who'd brought it in, but my money's on Paul Johnson."

"Why?" Mark asked.

"Two reasons," Harvey said. "Edward was already dead, so he couldn't have brought it in. And because Carl said the man told him it wouldn't be appropriate for him to walk it down because it was an anonymous gift from Mr.

Chessman. Who else but Paul Johnson would handle something like that for Gregory?"

Kelly looked at Ben. "A lot of roads are taking us right to him."

"Yes, they are." Ben looked back at the note.

"But why would Paul Johnson say that unless he wanted this connected to Chessman?"

"He wouldn't." Ben frowned. "What else does the note say? Anything?"

"No, that's it," Kelly said. "Wait. There's a second page. It was stuck." She peeled the clinging pages apart and read what was written on it out loud. "Beach house. Tonight. Ten o'clock. Heavily armed. Call in FBI. You must stop them. Severe national consequences."

"Ouch." Lisa grimaced. "That sounds really bad." Her cell phone chimed. She looked at the number and grumbled. "Excuse me." Shoulders bent, she left the room.

From the looks around the table watching her departure, the caller had to be either her harassing stepfather or her conflicted mother. *Bless Lisa's heart.*

Mark asked Peggy, "Is Dutch still harassing her? Even with the restraining order?"

"Not as much. Just when he gets tanked up or Annie is slow to do something he wants her to do." Peggy glanced at Kelly. "Annie is Lisa's mother."

Kelly nodded, noting Mark's special interest in Lisa. It seemed Peggy was fostering it too.

Mark's frown was fierce. "We have to do something about that man."

"We will. But one problem at a time, okay?" Peggy fanned a hand down the table. "So what does all this mean?"

"Whatever this is, it's out of our league." Bent doubled over the photos, Kelly slid a worried look to Ben. "It's time to call in the FBI."

Mumbles of agreement sounded from everyone at the table.

"If you don't want to ruffle feathers, Ben," Mark said, "better call the locals and let them call in reinforcements. They get touchy about anyone invading their turf uninvited."

Ben agreed, and then made the call.

Paul had watched Carl the messenger walk down the block to deliver the envelope promptly at three. He could be trusted, and Paul made a mental note of that.

Then he'd waited until he'd seen Kelly and Ben return to Crossroads. Minutes later, Mark Taylor arrived. Where they'd been, Paul didn't know. He hadn't been able to trail them all day. When they all came to the center, however, he knew all was well. They'd get the message in time to coordinate the bust.

Paul flipped open his phone and called Chessman. He was either at or watching a ball game. "Hello, sir."

"Get your business done?"

"Absolutely." More than the man could ever imagine. He'd be in prison at least forty years. Maybe longer. Of course, he'd be dead before then, but regardless, his days of a life of luxury were nearly at an end.

"Are you calling for a reason? I'm a bit busy."

"Sorry to intrude, sir. You asked me to let you know when the mayor returned. He isn't yet officially back, but Mrs. Green is out and about, so unless they traveled separately, I'd say the mayor is back in the village."

"Thank you, Paul. Anything else?"

"No sir."

"See you at ten sharp."

"Yes sir."

He shouldn't have betrayed Paul Johnson. No one set him up to take the fall.

Soon, Gregory Chessman would learn the penalty for that, and he would pay it.

Gregory hung up the phone, dialed John's personal business number, then texted him yet another message: THIRD CONTACT ATTEMPT. ON SCHEDULE. TRANSPORT POSITIONED. FINAL COUNT TWELVE. ACKNOWLEDGE RECEIPT OF THIS MESSAGE.

Extremely irritating thing for a secret partner to do, ignoring messages—particularly at this critical time. If his cooperation wasn't crucial—his trophy wife, the airhead, who owned the Crestburg Airport—then Gregory would drop John Green so fast his head would spin. He'd been a solid partner, at times perfect. But mayor or not, his lack of professionalism on this shipment was dangerous and annoying.

Gregory didn't like being annoyed. Especially on shipment nights . . .

26

Detective Meyers stashed Ben, Kelly, and Mark across the street from the beach house. "Watch that water hose," Meyers told Kelly. "Don't trip."

Kelly stepped over the hose snaking across the lawn and followed Ben and Mark onto the porch. "Won't these people mind us being here?"

"They're seasonal," Jeff said. "No one's here this time of year."

"Jeff," Mark said from behind her, "I still don't like the idea of Kelly being out here. We have no idea—"

"I'm fine."

"You can't know that." Ben stepped closer, protectively clasping her hand.

Jeff swiped at his pug nose. "I had no choice, Mark. The mayor isn't back from New Orleans yet—still out of reach—which is an advantage, considering we're keeping him out of the loop on this. But Kelly summoning us here is all that's saving us and the FBI from issues with authorization. We could do it without her, but the timing could be problematic."

At least that had worked out for them. From the corner of her eye, she watched Ben scan the beach house and the neighboring properties. Unless his eyes were far better than hers, he couldn't see much of anything through the darkness and fog, and no one else seemed to be in the vicinity.

"When will the FBI get here?" Ben asked Jeff.

"They've been in position for nearly an hour." He dropped his voice so it wouldn't carry beyond their little porch circle. "When I described the saltwater pool leading into the gulf, they went a little nuts."

"I hope the activity hasn't signaled NINA." Kelly fretted that it might have, and who knew when another opportunity would come to nab NINA red-handed. "How many agents are out here?"

"Together with my folks," Jeff said, "nineteen."

She hadn't seen the first sign of any of them. The vise gripping her chest loosened. She could actually draw a deep breath.

He rested a hand on the butt of his gun. "Just lay low, don't talk or make any noise, and stay put. No matter what happens, do not leave this porch."

Kelly sat on the bench at the far end of the porch, leaving the two chairs for Ben and Mark.

They sat down and the wait began, minutes creeping by.

At 9:45, two cars drove up the street and stopped near the curb at the beach house. The tension on the porch went dense in an instant and grew thick enough to slice. Kelly stiffened, folded her hands in her lap, gazed heavenward, and prayed.

A man got out of each of the cars. She recognized them both: Chessman and Alexander Denham. Betrayal shot through her, sharp and swift. Denham had taken her into his house but never into his heart. She'd regretted that, wondered a million times what was wrong with her, why she was so unlovable. She'd put herself through years of anguish in all the ways only a confused child and teen could. *So self-destructive but oh, so human.*

She'd regretted, but not until this very moment did she realize just how much she'd also resented.

Yet he'd never treated her as Samuel had. He'd never put her in a closet or cursed her or called her a stupid girl. He'd controlled and manipulated her, but he'd also spent countless hours teaching her how to manage money, to delegate authority, to make sound decisions. She owed him for that, and it made doing what she was doing here hard.

And real.

The secret hope that he had known Chessman

but hadn't been involved in his criminal activities died. Her former guardian was here, and that alone conclusively proved his guilt.

The back of her nose burned and her eyes stung. She blinked fast, swallowed hard—and the truth she'd been too preoccupied to notice slammed into her.

He was involved.

And he'd known where she'd been most of the past three years they'd been looking for her.

NINA.

Of course, NINA. Frequent trips to Europe—he was up to his Russian neck in NINA. So why hadn't he told Chessman or that NINA guy on the terrace where to find her?

Money.

He made a fortune monitoring her assets when she was on the run. *He's manipulated you all your life, but even more so the past three years. Power. Control. Points with his cohorts. Money from you.*

He'd used her—and them.

Now he stood on the sidewalk, talking with Chessman. In the silent darkness, their muffled voices carried across the street, though she couldn't make out what they were saying.

As the minutes ticked by, Gregory grew more and more agitated, pacing the walkway, checking his watch. He had to be waiting for someone else to arrive. Paul Johnson, perhaps?

Plausible, considering he had caused the photos

and note to be delivered and they were responsible for the authorities being here.

For the next fifteen minutes, Gregory tried a half-dozen times to reach someone by phone, and each time he failed his voice elevated more and his tone sharpened.

By ten o'clock, the man was outraged. Denham was saying something to him, using soothing hand gestures. But they seemed futile.

Something rustled off the end of the porch. Kelly's heart skipped a beat, then thudded. She clasped her mouth to stay silent.

An officer dressed all in black—head to toe—slid onto the porch. Getting close, he whispered in Kelly's ear. "I need to get you civilians out of here. We've had a change of plans."

Why? She mouthed the word but didn't utter a sound.

Again, the officer bent close. "Stay close." He signaled Ben and Mark to follow, then slid off the porch.

Kelly, Ben, and Mark followed, cut straight away from the street, and moved quickly between two beach houses to the backyard.

The officer stopped and everyone gathered close.

"What's up?" Ben asked.

He pulled off his mask. Jeff Meyers. "Bad news. Mayor Green had a massive heart attack last night in New Orleans. He's dead."

"I'm sorry," Kelly said, adding her regrets to those of Ben and Mark.

"The FBI says we're covered, but I need Kelly here, and yet I can't risk anything happening to any of you, so I want you to stay back here until I come after you."

Meyers stilled, held up a staying fingertip, then clearly listened to some earpiece transmission. He swung his lip mike down, then whispered, "Roger."

"Did someone else arrive?" Kelly whispered.

Meyers shook his head. "They've gone inside. I've got to get back. Stay here, and lay low."

Kelly waited until he left, then started back to the porch, reversing the path they'd just taken.

Ben circled her in his arms from behind, tugged her back, close to him, and whispered close to her ear, "What are you doing?"

"We need to see. They don't know what to expect any more than we do. What if a small army comes through there? Someone's got to get word out that more help is needed."

"No." Ben frowned at her. "They're professionals and know what they're doing. Jeff said—"

She broke loose and kept moving, hugging the slatted house at her back, slid back up onto the porch, but stayed on the floor rather than the bench.

Ben and Mark flanked her and simultaneously chewed her out.

She ignored them and kept watch on the porch

across the street. That bad feeling had come back, and it was blaring warning alarms like the ones used to signal five-alarm fires. She had no idea why or what she could do, but she felt strongly compelled to get back on the porch. And believing it was God nudging her, she listened.

Ben's phone must have vibrated; he pulled it from his hip, cupping his hand to block the light, and read a text message. "It's Peggy," Ben whispered close to her ear. "Says to call her."

Whatever it was, for Peggy to text him here, it had to be more bad news. Inside Kelly staggered. She just couldn't take any more. She was already under attack on all sides.

Gunfire erupted.

Shouts filled the night, and flashes of fire broke through the fog and darkness going both into and out of the beach house. Who had moved first, she had no idea, but both sides were now fully engaged.

The front door to the beach house burst open.

Armed men hurled themselves through windows, pouring out. They hit the ground running, taking off in all directions with guns firing fast and steady, providing cover.

Full pandemonium erupted.

Chaos reigned.

Kelly had a difficult time telling who was who.

Then Denham ran out and jumped off the beach

house porch. A beefy man opened the path for him. He crossed the street and ran in a zigzag pattern down the block, the beefy man knocking out anything that threatened his path. The farther away he got, the more anxious Kelly became. She couldn't stand it anymore. "Denham's getting away!"

Mark and Ben took off down the street, hugging the lawns, and quickly closed the gap. Mark took down the beefy man, hitting him hard from behind, and Ben lunged, tackling Denham.

On three sides of Kelly, men battled. A flash of movement on the beach house porch snagged her eye. She'd thought it was empty now, and so apparently had everyone else.

Chessman.

He'd waited until everyone was engaged to surface.

He rushed down the steps and cut straight across the street, coming right toward her.

Kelly eased off the porch, hid behind a row of bushes, and bumped into the water spigot. Pain shot through her thigh. The hose was attached. She strained to see its snaky path across the lawn. There was no way she could win in hand-to-hand combat against Chessman, but maybe, with divine intervention, she could slow him down.

She dropped to a squat, grabbed the hose attached to the spigot, and watched his progress. He was going to cut through this beach house's yard. He got closer . . . closer. Sweat chilled her body. Her palms were slick. She swiped them one at a time against her pants, then tested her grip. Closer. And closer. Then judging the timing right, she jerked hard.

The hose came up.

Chessman went down with a loud grunt and swoosh of breath.

"Help! Chessman's loose! Chessman's loose!" There was no weapon, nothing she could use to restrain him.

And then Ben and Jeff were there, fighting Chessman. Ben took a series of hard blows that had him staggering backward, and finally Jeff knocked out Gregory's knee with a hard kick.

He dropped like a stone onto the ground, and Jeff cuffed him.

Kelly crawled out of the bushes and ran toward them.

"I should have killed you myself." Chessman spat on the grass.

Ben pressed his foot over Chessman's throat.

"Don't do it, Ben," Jeff said. "Let him live and suffer. Dying is too easy."

Ben shook, clearly fighting the urge to crush Chessman's throat. He clenched his teeth, stiffened while the battle inside him raged, but he didn't seem able to stop.

"Ben. Ben, don't." Kelly stopped beside him, adrenaline rushing through her, fear squeezing her chest. "Please."

He stared at her.

"Please, Ben." She couldn't be responsible for him too. Not Susan and him too.

Finally, he withdrew his foot and backed away. "Live, Chessman. Live a long, long time."

Relief swamped Kelly, turning her knees to rubber.

"Weak." Chessman grunted again as Jeff pulled him to his feet. "Pathetic."

Battling her own temptation to slap him, Kelly took his criticism for what it was worth: nothing. "I'll try to forgive you, Mr. Chessman, but I'll be honest. I'm going to have to really, really work at it."

He pulled his shoulders back, puffed his chest, and glared down at her. "I don't want your forgiveness."

She smiled right up into his outraged face. "I'm not doing it for you. I'm doing it for me."

His eyes narrowed, squinted. "You're a brainless idiot."

"I'm a woman of faith," she corrected him, "and forgiving you frees me." The wind whipped at her hair. She smoothed it back from her face. "Every day for the rest of your life, you'll be in prison, thinking of me. But after tonight, Mr. Chessman, I will rarely think of you. I'll be living my life. Going to church, building my safe centers, and being content."

Chessman spit at her and missed.

Kelly held her smile.

He swiveled his glare to Jeff. "Get me out of here."

"In due time. You gave up your right to choose much of anything." Jeff nodded to Kelly. "If you want to preach to him a little, I'll see to it that he stays put."

Kelly considered it but knew his ears were closed. He wouldn't hear her, or see the truth. "Maybe after a couple years alone with his thoughts, he'll make better choices." She turned away and looked at Ben.

Stiff, pale, and shaken, he stared at her with intense longing.

"Ben." She stepped closer, clasped his arm. "Are you hurt?"

He pulled her to him, tugged her closer, then circled his arms around her and buried his face at the crook of her neck. "Kelly."

It was all he could manage.

It was more than enough.

Kelly hugged him hard and pressed a light kiss to his forehead. "It's okay, Ben." He'd heard her scream, and somehow she knew he feared he would lose her too. "I'm fine and so are you." She rubbed little comforting circles on his back, feeling his tremble in her fingertips. "We're going to be okay now. Everything is going to be fine." She said and meant it and whispered a quiet prayer of gratitude.

• • •

Kelly sat beside Ben on the porch steps while the FBI loaded the twelve men into separate vehicles and took them and then Denham away. He avoided looking at her, and she didn't stop looking at Alexander until he was out of sight.

Chessman was the last to leave.

After two agents departed with him, Jeff and Mark locked down the scene. Then Jeff left to begin the paperwork, and Mark joined Kelly and Ben at the porch.

"That's the last of them," he said. "Jeff says we can do our paperwork in the morning—your statements and such. They're leaving two men on site, so we can leave whenever you're ready."

"Do you know who any of them were?" Kelly asked.

"One of the agents told me they were from all over, but every one of them was on the watch list. They're all NINA operatives with heavy biological-warfare expertise."

Kelly's heart seemed to stop. She pressed a hand to her chest, willing it to keep beating. "Chessman was smuggling in terrorists, helping them to harm us. How could he do that?"

"He and Denham," Mark said with disgust. "Not too bright, is it? No germ I've heard of is biased about the nationality of the people it kills."

"What were they thinking?" Ben asked.

Kelly frowned. "Obviously they weren't, but

I'm sure it had to do with lots and lots of money." She stood and brushed a hand over the seat of her slacks to get off the sandy grit. "And it makes sense as the reason for Denham's trips to Europe."

"Trips?" Mark asked. "As in more than one?"

"Oh yes." She nodded. "He's gone every year for as long as I can remember to meet with a business associate. Karl Masson is his name, but I've never seen him."

Ben cocked his head. "But Denham was here when he was supposed to be in Europe."

"Yes, he was—for the dinner party at Chessman's, anyway. But was Denham here for months, or just for sprints on his way to or from Europe?" Kelly thought a second. "Masson is real. I've answered the phone when he's called. He has to be Denham's NINA connection. There just isn't anyone else. Not that I recall, anyway."

Ben frowned. "Masson could have been the third man on the terrace, Kelly."

"Maybe. Like I said, I've never seen him."

"I'll pass that on to the FBI. Denham could have been a courier for NINA." Mark blew out a breath. "We'll know more after they check his passport."

"What about Chessman?" Ben asked.

"From his phone, he's talked to Paul Johnson often, and he's been texting another number regularly. Meyers ran a trace on it."

"Who owns it?" Ben shook the sand from his shoe.

"The phone's in John Green's name, but it can't be his unless he's mastered texting Johnson and Chessman from the Other Side." Mark looked from Ben to Kelly. "John was definitely dead before the last one came in to Chessman's phone."

"Then it has to be Darla."

Kelly struggled to wrap her mind around this new development. "What's the mayor's wife got to do with any of this?"

"No idea—yet," Mark said. "But that's a very good question."

Kelly stared down at the ground. Denham was different than he appeared to be, but it seemed that fit other people involved in this conspiracy too. "Chessman was nothing like he appeared to be."

"No, he wasn't." Mark tucked his phone back into its case. "I don't know who he really is, but he's as dirty as they come. None of these foreign NINA operatives could have gotten into the States without a lot of help, and we know for fact he helped them."

"They almost succeeded too."

Ben sighed. "We believe they have before too—the Mobile mall bombing."

"It's scary." Kelly shuddered, crossed her arms, and stroked warmth into them. "If Paul Johnson hadn't led us to them, they would have succeeded this time too."

"And, no doubt," Ben added, "they would have launched a major biological attack on U.S. soil."

Mark popped a mint into his mouth. "Yeah, the Feds will remember that when it comes time to sentence him." He answered Kelly's questioning look with an angry one of his own. "Johnson is neck-deep in all of this, Kelly, including the attacks on you. He's not a victim."

Ben nodded. "He informed us to shift blame and cover himself. That's the bottom line, and what he did doesn't make him guiltless." Ben stared off into the night. "That's a lesson I learned once from Peggy."

"Peggy." Kelly tapped Ben's knee. "You haven't yet called her."

"All the crush . . . I forgot about it." Grimacing, he called her, then stepped away to talk.

In short order, he came back, and the look on his face signaled there was yet another challenge brewing. "Paul Johnson just returned from New Orleans with Darla Green. The mayor is confirmed dead. Darla's a wreck. Hotel housekeeping found her sitting like a stone beside the bed. John died in it sometime during the night. The coroner hasn't released his body yet, but the house doctor felt Darla would be better off here, with people she knows. She's at the center talking with Harvey Talbot now."

"Where's Johnson?" Mark asked.

"At the center talking to Lisa." Ben frowned.

"Darla being 'catatonic' freaked him out. Lisa is trying to calm him down."

"She'd better give him a sedative and stay out of striking distance," Kelly said. "Of both of them."

"I did what I could to warn Peggy about them. But I had to be careful, not knowing who could be listening."

"We'd better get over there."

"Call Jeff," Kelly said. "Get him over there now. He's closer."

"On it." Mark whipped out his phone. Hit speed dial. "No way do I believe that woman's really catatonic."

"Why?" Kelly asked.

Mark slid her a flat look. "She was in New Orleans when Massey was shot."

"Better have his assistant . . ."

"Emily," Mark reminded Ben.

"Get Emily to check security tapes." Ben shook his head. "I can't believe I'm saying it, but I'm betting Darla Green is on them."

Mark made the call, requested a still photo of any women be forwarded to Crossroads. Then he called the New Orleans coroner and warned him John's death might well include foul play.

When Mark stuffed his phone back into his pocket, Kelly voiced her confusion. "Why can't you believe you were saying that about Darla Green?"

Mark answered. "It's common knowledge that

she's John's trophy wife. Everyone considers her an airhead, but she's nice, so no one says anything about that. She seems harmless, easy to ignore, but . . ."

"She's not what she appears to be." Dread dragged at Kelly's stomach. "She's a lot smarter than anyone thinks."

"So it appears." Ben hustled them down the street toward his SUV. "She or Johnson. I'm not sure Peggy picked up on my warning."

Mark ran alongside them, talking to someone on his phone. "I've got Meyers. Ben, try warning Peggy again."

"Ask for Doris," Kelly said.

"We can't trust her. She worked for Denham."

"I trust her," Kelly said. "And I'm careful who I trust."

"Something's bothering me," Mark said while they got in the SUV. "Why would Darla and Johnson go to Crossroads?"

"I've wondered that too."

"They're waiting for me." Kelly looked from Ben in the driver's seat to Mark next to him, then back to Ben. "I'm a loose end that can tie Johnson to NINA. I heard it that night on the terrace."

"So they went there to find you?"

"No. Johnson knew I'd be at the beach house."

Mark chimed in. "He figured you'd go to the center afterward."

Kelly saw it differently. "I figure he followed

Darla there. He could have killed me—he had the chance. Several of them, actually. But he didn't do it." She stared out the window. "No, he followed Darla there."

"Why did she go there?" Ben asked.

Kelly sent him a level look. "To kill me."

"Johnson wouldn't do it," Ben said. "But she couldn't leave you alive because you could lead authorities to him, and he could lead them to her."

"Exactly."

"Why not wait until later, when you're alone?" Mark asked.

"My guess," Kelly said, "is Johnson was focused on getting out of town, not on hanging around until I made it convenient for him to kill me. But Darla doesn't yet realize she needs to run, so waiting suited her purposes just fine."

"Their priorities clashed," Ben said, tracking Kelly's thinking.

She nodded. "And Darla won. Johnson had to follow her. He had to leave town with her, or when she was caught—and he'd know she would be—she'd turn on him. He couldn't leave her here to do that."

Mark grunted. "You figure Chessman wouldn't turn on Johnson."

"No, he wouldn't," she said. "Who would run his empire while he's in jail?"

"Good point." Ben called someone. "No answer from Peggy."

He tried again. And then again. "Still no answer."

Kelly curled her hands into fists and clenched until her nails dug into her palms. "I hope that doesn't mean none of them are able to answer . . ."

27

When they drove up to the center, Meyers hadn't yet arrived.

"Stay here," Ben said.

"No," Kelly told him. "I'm going in. I'm a crisis counselor, Ben. I know how to deal with these things; I do it all the time in my own work."

"We have no idea what's going on in there. You're not going in."

"She is the better choice," Mark said, cutting in. "But no one is going in until Jeff and backup get here. They're going to try to kill you, Kelly."

"That's why I have to go." She looked at Ben. "You should understand. If anything happens to anyone in there, it's my fault. It's Susan and Christopher all over again. I can't wait, Ben. Seconds could make a difference."

"Okay, okay. I understand. Seconds could make a difference," Ben said.

Mark heaved a sigh. "Ben, you and I will go. Kelly, you stay here, and I mean it."

"Why? Because you're big, strong men and I'm a fragile woman?"

"No," Ben said. "Because we're armed, you're not, and we're trying to keep you alive."

"I've done a decent job of keeping myself alive for a couple years now. I don't need a white knight. I do need allies that don't underestimate me."

"No one is underestimating you. Believe me, I know your capabilities." Ben stopped the SUV, then shifted into Park. "But there's no way I'm agreeing to you walking in there when we know something's going on and we don't know what it is. I don't like it."

"You don't have to like it, Ben—or you either, Mark." She flipped open the glove box and snatched out Ben's weapon. "Now I'm armed."

Ben and Mark exchanged frowns, and before they could stop her, she shot out of the vehicle and through the Crossroads door. Some things a person just had to do herself.

Melanie sat at her desk looking as grim as Ben and trying to cover it. "Hi, Mel," Kelly said lightly, scanning the entryway and seeing nothing amiss. "I'll be right back. Needed a rest room for hours." Kelly made her way through reception to the hallway. Senses hyperalert, she called back, "Everything okay?"

"Fine, Ms. Walker," Mel called back, her voice uneven.

Kelly had to make her feet keep moving. Not

once had Mel ever called her Ms. Walker. Susan, Karen, Kelly, yes. But never Ms. Walker.

Something was definitely wrong.

She entered the rest room and looked for another weapon. Empty, except for mouthwash, tissues, a can of air freshener, and a fire extinguisher. It was her best choice. Scared half to death, she lifted the extinguisher off the wall.

Oh, God, be with me. Give me strength and wisdom and the courage to do what I have to do. Please, don't let me make a mistake and get anyone hurt. Please . . .

She cracked open the door. Darla Green strode past.

"Paul?" Darla shouted, her mascara smudging the skin beneath her eyes and trickling in tear streaks down her face. "Paul, take me home. I want to go home." She paused to pound a fist against each door she passed. "Paul, where are you?"

Definitely not catatonic. Kelly waited for Darla to round the corner, checked to make sure no one else was following her, and then stepped into the empty hallway. Where was everyone?

Darla kept yelling for Paul.

At the corner, Kelly paused and listened to the hum of voices. They were all in the reception area, and Darla was creating a stir.

"I'm going home, I tell you! Harvey Talbot, don't you dare come at me with a needle."

"I'm not coming at you with anything, Darla."

Footsteps sounded behind her. Kelly ducked around the far corner.

"Darla?" Paul rushed past, the left side of his face twitching. "I'm coming."

Lisa trailed behind him. Kelly grabbed her sleeve and jerked, pulling her back. "Shh."

Lisa's eyes stretched wide. "What are you doing?" she whispered.

"Trust me." Kelly chanced that warning only because she had no choice.

"Oh, Paul." Darla grabbed him. "They won't let me leave. I want to go home."

Paul wrapped a protective arm around Darla and glared at Peggy. "Explain this."

Peggy tried. "She needs help right now, Mr. Johnson. That's all we're trying to do."

"She doesn't want your help." He moved toward the door. His instincts clearly had alerted him that he was in trouble and this was a delay tactic. "Any further challenges and Mr. Chessman's attorney will be all over you."

Mark Taylor walked into reception from the alcove by the door. "Mr. Denham can't help you right now, Paul. He's being questioned by the FBI, along with Mr. Chessman."

"What are you talking about, Taylor?"

"You know exactly what I'm talking about."

Darla tried to move away. Paul pulled out a knife, grabbed her, and positioned her as a shield, then pushed the tip of the blade against her jugular. "This is not going to happen this way."

Harvey stepped forward. "Paul, don't do anything foolish. We can talk through this."

He laughed hard and deep. "Sure we can, Doc." Paul inched toward the door, baby step by baby step, the left side of his face seemingly frozen by muscles in lockdown. "Everybody just stay calm and still—don't move. Darla is leaving with me. Just don't try to stop us and no one will get hurt."

Darla put up token resistance, but behind it was genuine fear. Kelly sensed it and slid along the wall, dropped down to her belly, and crawled across the floor, hidden from his view by furniture and partitions. She crawled along the last of the partitions, then pulled the pin on the extinguisher.

Paul stood not three steps on the other side, the entire left side of his face twitching. If Darla moved her head, Paul would see Kelly, and then she had no idea what to expect.

Darla heard her; Kelly saw her stiffen. "Right."

Paul spun right.

Kelly aimed and discharged the extinguisher, spraying foam directly into his face.

Mark and Ben rushed in. "Get the knife!" Kelly shouted, catching a glimpse of Jeff Meyers.

Ben tackled Johnson. He went down clutching his jaw, then stilled—and stayed still, as if he couldn't move, and a distant haze clouded his eyes.

Kelly stared down at him. Had he blanked out? What?

Ben noticed it too. "Harvey, Lisa—something's wrong with him."

Darla inched back and then tried to run.

Jeff Meyers intercepted her with little physical effort. She heaped curses on his head, but her verbal abuse seemed to roll right off him. He sent a relieved look at Kelly. "I'm glad you're all right, but if you ever pull a stunt like running in here on your own again, so help me, I'll arrest you for nearly giving us all heart attacks."

"It wasn't one of my finest moments," she admitted. "But there were extenuating circumstances."

"Not enough of them to keep you out of jail."

Kelly smiled. "Yes sir."

Mel let out a heartfelt sigh. "Whoa."

Lisa was stooped near Paul Johnson, checking him out. "He'll be fine."

Mel told Kelly, "He has a history. When he gets acute anxiety, he zones out. It's a self-preservation thing. Dr. Talbot explained it to me one time— using different words, but that's what he meant."

"Ah." Kelly rubbed her forehead.

"You okay, Lisa?" Mark asked from beside her.

How had Kelly missed that tenderness in his eyes when he looked at Lisa?

"I'm glad you're here." She glanced up at him. "Next time, don't wait so long, though, okay?"

"I'll make a note of it."

Kelly looked at Peggy. There was a definite twinkle in her eye.

"I'm seeing Cupid getting a fix on them," Mel whispered to Kelly.

She agreed but didn't say so.

"Mel, can you get an ambulance?" Lisa said. "Mr. Johnson's going to require transport."

Jeff had Darla cornered. "Mark, I need a hand."

"Sure." He walked over. "Ben, run a quick check in the back, will you? Make sure neither of these two left us any *gifts* back there."

Ben double-timed it down the hall.

"Watch that one while I get some backup to escort Mr. Johnson to the hospital."

Ben came running through from the back of the building, took in what was happening, and went straight to Kelly. "Everyone okay?"

"Fine." She smiled. "Glad you avoided that knife."

He dropped a kiss to her temple. "So am I."

"You can't arrest me," Darla spat at Mark.

"I'm not." He nodded toward Jeff. "Meyers is."

She tried to twist free of Mark's hold. "He can't either. I am the mayor's wife. His wife!"

"The mayor is dead, Mrs. Green." Peggy stepped closer, a still photo in her hand. "So is a man named Richard Massey. Maybe you knew him?" She held up a photo of Massey and Darla in Massey's office.

Having Paul secured, Jeff turned to Darla. "Well, well. Interesting photo, Mrs. Mayor." Jeff grunted. "You are coming with me."

"Whatever for?"

The remnants of humor left the detective's face. "You're a person of interest in the death of Richard Massey."

"No. No. I will not stand for this."

"Then sit down, because this is where we are and what we have, and you've got a lot of explaining to do." Meyers motioned to Mark. "I could use a little help getting this one into my car. Ambulance should be here for him any moment," he said, gesturing toward Paul.

Mark and Jeff led Darla out of Crossroads.

Ben watched over Johnson. Minutes later, the EMTs arrived, put Johnson on a stretcher, and took him out. Through the window, Ben saw Jeff Meyers instructing one of his men to escort Johnson to the hospital.

When the ambulance pulled away from the curb, the group inside the center let out a collective sigh, and none was louder or more deeply felt than Kelly's.

"Glad that's over." Lisa frowned. "Reminds me too much of the way things go at my mother's."

A wave of regret that Lisa Harper had to live through that crashed over Kelly.

"You can always do something about it." Peggy looked at Lisa with concern and genuine empathy.

"As soon as I can afford it. Two more months, I'll have my license and she'll be out of there," Lisa added, in a tone that fairly screamed that two months could seem like a lifetime.

That sparked an idea. One for the beach house.

Kelly mulled over the idea on the way back to the cottage and as she went to sleep. It was on her mind the moment she awakened.

Okay, God. I've got the message.

She smiled at the cottage ceiling. There had been no path for Ben and her. But God created one. It was true, what the Bible said. He turns what is meant to harm you to good.

Now, if Peggy and Ben would just cooperate . . .

As Kelly dressed and prepared to go to the center, she dared to hope God was talking to them too.

Wednesday, October 14

"Kelly." Peggy greeted her from Mel's desk as she walked in the door. "I'm surprised to see you here this morning."

"Doris drove me in. She's parking the car. I need to talk to you. If you have a minute."

"Sure."

"I have a plan for the beach house," she told Peggy, then briefly explained.

"Well," Peggy said. "Your enthusiasm is contagious. Just what we need around here after some very demanding days."

"You like the idea?"

"No. No, I don't." Peggy looked down, her expression sober, then flashed her a beaming smile. "I love it."

"Oh, good." Kelly let out a laugh. "You had me worried there."

"Sorry, I couldn't resist."

Doris came in, her handbag swinging at her hip, her coffee cup in hand. "Morning, everyone."

"Hi, Doris," Peggy said. "She's got you up early, huh?"

"Just a little." Doris slid Kelly an indulgent look. "Not that I mind."

"Morning, Doris. Kelly." Ben joined them at the front desk. "What are you doing here at this hour? You're supposed to be sleeping."

"I was too excited."

His smile faded. "I guess you're eager to get back home, huh?"

He sounded desolate but resigned, fueling her hope that this would give them just what they needed: time. "Actually, no."

His eyes brightened. "No? You're not eager to get home?"

She shook her head. "I'm glad you came in. I need to talk to you about something."

"What?"

"I've made some plans that will require me to

stay here for a while, and I was wondering if I could rent your cottage. I'm already settled in there, and the security puts my mind at ease. Who knows how many more NINA operatives are out there."

Ben's smile returned and kicked up several watts. "Of course. Stay as long as you like." Confusion crossed his face and tugged at his expression. "Um, why are you staying?"

"Because you and I need time, and I have some remodeling to do on Aunt Beth's beach house."

"You loved being at that beach house."

"I did," she said, surprised he remembered. "Nora and I have been talking about it, and we think it can be put to good use. Peggy agrees."

He looked from her to Peggy, who nodded, then looked back at Kelly. "Oh?"

Kelly resisted the urge to fidget. "I'm calling it Safe Haven, in Susan's honor. Maybe it can be a safe haven for someone like Lisa and/or her mother." Kelly shrugged. "A place to heal."

"That's terrific, Kelly." Ben glanced at Peggy. "Mark will love it."

"Mark?" Kelly asked.

"He worries about Lisa."

"Ah." So Mark definitely had a thing for Lisa. Kelly had suspected it, and Ben had mentioned it, but apparently it was a serious thing that had been going on for some time. Would they end up together? Did Lisa know it? "It'll be at least a couple of months until the beach house is fit for human habitation. It needs a first-rate security system too." If things went as she hoped, then Annie and Lisa would be living in it and they wouldn't have to worry about Dutch bothering them. "Are you sure you're okay with me being in your cottage for that long?"

"Positive." He let his gaze linger, studying her face a long time. "Stay as long as you like."

Such warmth in that look!

"Um, I hate to be abrupt, but could you excuse me for a second? It won't be long," Ben said, a hand in his slacks pocket. "But there's something I have to do, and it can't wait."

"Of course." Kelly watched him go. Maybe she'd been wrong. Maybe things could work out for them after all.

"Give him time," Peggy whispered to Kelly.

Craning her neck, Kelly glanced at her. "Time for what?"

Peggy dipped her chin and looked at her over the top of her glasses. "Time to realize he's in love with you, and then time to accept that loving you is not betraying Susan."

"Do you think he'll get there, Peggy? Honestly?"

Peggy smiled. "Pray on it."

Faintly disappointed, Kelly promised, "Oh, but I am."

"You know how this works." Doris patted

Kelly's shoulder. "If you're sure something is what you want, then praise God like you've already got it."

Kelly frowned at Doris. "Does that work without infringing on the free will of people involved?"

Peggy and Doris shared a mischievous look. "What do you think?"

"I think I'm not going to get a straight answer from either of you." Kelly let them see her frustration, which was only partly feigned.

"You'd be right about that." Peggy turned to Doris. "How about a refill on your coffee, or a cup of hot chocolate?"

"Love some." They moved together toward the kitchen.

"Some help you two are."

Walking by, Harvey chuckled. "I think there's a point to them not helping you, Kelly." He caught her snarl and lifted a hand. "Don't bite. It was just a friendly thought."

"Harvey," Mel called out to him. "Emergency Management. Line two."

"I'm on it."

Kelly looked around. Everyone had been going full out countless hours, but still sandwiched in life. She loved that about this place.

This was Susan's dream.

A sense of loss swept over her that Susan hadn't lived to see it. She would have been so happy, so proud.

Could Kelly ever earn her own place here, living in Ben and Susan's world? A world that Susan would have survived to experience herself if Kelly hadn't been on Chessman's terrace and been mistakenly identified as Susan.

Would Kelly feel as if she were stealing Susan's future? Always feel like an outsider who shouldn't be here?

God, if this is my place and Ben is the one You've chosen for me, I need a sign. I can't live my whole life feeling guilty. I know I didn't kill her or Christopher, but . . . You know what I mean and how I feel. Show me if this is my path. I believe it is, but my heart is conflicted. I need Your steady hand. I need to know that I won't get lost in preserving her dream. Our life can't be their life with me substituting for her. I need my own life. My own place. And I need to know I'm loved for myself. Can You do that for me, God? Give me a sign?

Your will, Lord. Not mine.

Prepared for whatever the outcome now that she'd put the matter in His hands, she waited for His answer.

It would take time for both Ben and her to find their answers. And for now, she would dare to live with hope and possibility.

Regardless of God's answer, she would honor it. Knowing He would settle for nothing less than her greater good, how could she not?

While her vision of the future was limited and flawed by narrow perception, His was not.

In knowing it, there was enormous confidence and peace.

Ben walked up behind her. "You ready to head back to the cottage?"

"Yes." She gave him a smile. "I'm so exhausted I'm not sure I can walk."

"Swinging extinguishers and making tripwires of hoses will zap your strength."

"Is that an insult?"

"Absolutely not." His eyes twinkled. "Just remind me never to get on the wrong side of you. You're resourceful."

She forced a snooty sarcasm into her tone. "I'll make a note to send you all necessary memos."

"Thanks." He lightly bumped their shoulders. "And if you're too weary to walk, I'll carry you."

She stilled. Looked up at him. "Really?"

"Really." He licked his lower lip. "Would that be okay with you?"

"Definitely." She moved toward the door. When he reached to open it, she added, "Ben?" He paused to look at her and she said, "When you're too weary to walk, I'll carry you too."

He gave her a smile so warm and full that it melted her heart. "I'm counting on that."

28

A week before Thanksgiving, Kelly parked her white Blazer in the lot, then rounded the corner and entered Crossroads Crisis Center.

Mel was at her desk, nose buried in her biology book. "Hi, Kelly."

"How's the studying going for the big exam?" She had been preparing for at least two weeks.

"Dr. Talbot's been helping me," Mel said. "But now that he's heading up the disaster team—hurricane heading toward Texas—"

"I heard. It's late in the season for a Category 3." Kelly shivered. There'd be significant damage.

"They're expecting it to be a Cat 4 before it hits."

"So Harvey had to divert. You need help, then?"

"No, he's passed the torch to Dr. Harper." Mel blew out an exaggerated breath. "I don't know how anyone makes it through college without a team of experts helping her." Mel hadn't gotten the foundation most get in high school, so she needed extra help. "It's not a cakewalk, but it's worth it."

Kelly snatched a mint from the bowl on the corner of Mel's desk. "I'm pretty good in finance, civics, and history if you need help on any of those things."

"I'm counting on you next semester." Mel grimaced. "Statistics. Why I need that to teach, I have no idea, but I have to take it."

"No problem," Kelly said. "Where's Ben?"

"In the back."

Kelly was halfway down the hallway before it hit her that both she and Mel had assumed Kelly would still be here next semester.

Lisa's voice carried out into the hall from her office. From her tone, it was her stepfather again. It seemed to be reserved just for him.

Worrying her lip, Kelly hoped Clyde Parker got that tunnel sealed and the beach house remodeled before the end of the year. It would sure be nice for Lisa and her mom to be in a safe place for Christmas—if they'd do it. There was a place for Annie at The Towers now, but Lisa's mother wouldn't go there because her husband knew where it was and he'd come after her. He'd been there before, for Lisa, which is what convinced the judge to sign that restraining order. Ben had offered relocation, but Annie wouldn't leave the village. Kelly could appreciate that. Seagrove had been Annie's home all her life.

"Kelly!" Peggy called out as Kelly walked past her office.

She stopped and ducked her head in. "Hi there."

"You're a certified crisis counselor, right?"

"Yes, but I've never had a practice."

"Great. A practice isn't important, the credentials are. I need your help."

Kelly walked into the office. "What do you need?"

"Harvey's heading the crisis counseling team for Delia—the hurricane projected to hit Texas. I'm short two counselors. Will you go?"

After all they'd done for her, how could she refuse? "Sure."

"Great." Peggy looked immediately relieved.

"Do you want me to round up another counselor?"

"No," Peggy said softly. "I corralled Ben. He's agreed to do it."

Shock rippled through Kelly. "Our Ben?"

"Our Ben." Peggy's eyes gleamed.

That was pleasant if unexpected news. He'd been getting involved in little things but still tried to keep his distance from the center. "That's great news."

"I thought so." Peggy bit a smile from her lips.

Kelly left the office and ran into Mel, who was quietly laughing. "She's Cupid in a skirt," Mel whispered. "And she thinks she's being so sly."

Peggy Crane was about as sly as a sledgehammer. Kelly loved that about her, and with Ben, she'd take all the help she could get. "Where exactly is Ben?"

"I'm not sure," Mel said. "He was pretty upset when he heard the mayor had been poisoned. Paul

Johnson is blaming everything on Chessman and Darla Green. Apparently, Paul and Darla created a partnership and kept it from Gregory."

"How could he not know it?"

"Chessman thought the mayor was his partner. He had no idea it was Darla. They communicated through text messages, so he couldn't tell."

"What a shocker." Kelly could but imagine. Everyone seemed to be crossing everyone. Guess it worked that way when you dealt with terrorists like NINA, who were involved in all manner of horrific things, and with nefarious types like Chessman and Johnson. Kelly shuddered.

The third man on the terrace, the NINA operative, was Karl Masson, according to the FBI, but so far he'd evaded capture. Though NINA was certainly a large organization with plenty of operatives still working, Kelly would personally sleep better if Masson, too, had been caught. Having him on the loose, even if he'd gone underground and wasn't likely to surface soon, never strayed too far from her mind. Even if on every watch list known to Homeland Security, people like that historically showed up at the most inopportune times—not that there was an opportune time to collide with a terrorist.

"What about Darla and Richard Massey?" Kelly asked Mel.

"You know they've got her on tape leaving his office, but she's still denying it."

" 'Course she is."

"Won't work anymore, though. They've found the gun in her possession."

"That's pretty much it, then."

Overwhelmed, Kelly made a U-turn and went back to the reception area. She stopped at the long table, above which Susan's portrait hung, and looked up into her smiling, still face.

"I'm sorry, Susan. For all of us, but really for you and Christopher. I've said it before, but I feel the need to say it again. Frankly, I'm having a hard time with it because I'm in love with your husband."

Kelly rocked back on her heels, wishing she could hear Susan's voice, see her face animated. "Of course, I feel guilty. Who wouldn't? I want you to know that if I could trade places with you and change things so you and Christopher were still here and I wasn't, I would do it. But I can't do that."

Kelly paused, let her thoughts and emotions settle and opened her heart. "You did well, Susan. What you built here on hopes and dreams in Crossroads is . . . it's wonderful. You should be so proud."

This was the tough part. The part that kept her awake at nights. "I know you were a woman of faith, Susan. You loved Ben, and I'm certain you'd want him happy. Loved. I know you'd want him to love again too. But I'm not sure you'd choose me to be the one to love him or be loved by him. But I promise you, I will love him well. And I'm praying hard he chooses to let me love him.

"There's still his faith issue to be resolved and, of course, that's a major thing to me, but I'm being patient. I've prayed for a sign about all this. It hasn't come yet, but it will in its own time. I wanted to tell you one other thing, Susan. I'll never replace you. Not at Crossroads or in Ben's heart. I know that. But both really are big enough for both of us. I believe that, down to the marrow of my bones and in every chamber of my heart."

Feeling better now that she'd settled that, Kelly turned and went in search of Ben.

Harvey met her in the hall. "Hey, thanks for coming on board the team."

"Glad to do it."

"We're finalizing departure. I'll get with you on that shortly."

"Just call my cell." When he agreed, she asked, "Have you seen Ben?"

"I have, but if I told you where he is, you'd never believe it."

"Why not?"

Harvey's lips spread in a broad smile. "He's in the chapel."

Kelly nearly hit the floor. "You're serious?"

"Definitely."

Elated, she rushed down the corridor and

stopped outside the etched-glass door, next to Peggy. Looking through the glass, she saw Ben inside.

At the altar on his knees.

Her sign.

Tears slid down Kelly's cheeks.

Peggy patted her shoulder. "A praying man is a beautiful thing."

"It certainly is." Kelly sniffed and smiled at Peggy, having difficulty looking away from Ben. "One of the most beautiful things I've ever in my life seen."

Thank You, God. Thank You . . .

The toe of her shoe bumped the door.

Ben looked back, then motioned for her to come in.

She was too choked up to speak.

Still on his knees at the little altar, Ben smiled and raised his hand. "Join me?"

Kelly took his hand, knelt beside him, and together they prayed their first joint prayer.

During this entire crisis, she hadn't known who she was but had never doubted she believed. Faith carried her. And Ben had known exactly who he was and had only doubt and disbelief. He'd felt forgotten.

God, with His extraordinary insight, had brought them together to support each other's weaknesses and strengths.

"Father," Ben said, "it's been a hard road, but

You've proven that while we might not always see or understand, You do, and Yours isn't just convenient memory."

Kelly listened to Ben go on to say the very things she'd sensed deep inside even during her memory lapse.

"God, You never abandon, never give up, never walk away from anyone. And even when we wonder, You remain steadfast and sustain us."

With a full heart, Kelly lifted her gaze upward. God took one position with those who dared to love Him:

Forget me not.

And Kelly continued their prayer with gratitude for that truth.

Readers Guide

1. "Even when we forget who we are, at core level we remember whose we are." That belief prompted author Vicki Hinze to write *Forget Me Not.*[1] What core-level memory do you feel you could never forget? Why? Do you think bad memories are more easily recalled than good ones?

2. Do you believe forgiving means forgetting? The Bible states that repentance washes away our sins and that God no longer remembers them.[2] Are human beings capable of that kind of forgiveness without God's help? Have you struggled with not being able to forget what you thought you had forgiven? Are there times when not forgetting is constructive?

---

1. To see what the Bible says about these things, you can begin by reading the following Scriptures from the New International Version (NIV): "Moses said to the people, 'Do not be afraid. God has come to test you, so that the fear of God will be with you to keep you from sinning'" (Exodus 20:20).

2. "Repent, then, and turn to God, so that your sins may be wiped out, that times of refreshing may come from the Lord" (Acts 3:19).

3. Would it be a blessing to be able to forget parts of your past? Or do you believe it takes all of those parts—good and bad—to be the person you have become? Why? If you could wipe your memory clean and start over, how would you construct your life differently?

4. Do specific names evoke a specific emotion in you? If you could choose your name, what would it be? Why would you choose it?

5. The heroine in *Forget Me Not* is a woman of serene faith. It gives her certainty and calm in horrific circumstances. What has brought you calm and certainty in troubled times?

6. Much has been written about the power of prayer. What, to you, is the greatest benefit of individual prayer? Is a group united in prayer for a specific purpose more or less powerful than individual prayer?[3]

7. Kelly is warned that "some people are the opposite of what they appear to be."[4] Have

---

3. "Again, I tell you that if two of you on earth agree about anything you ask for, it will be done for you by my Father in heaven" (Matthew 18:19).

4. "Watch out for false prophets. They come to you in sheep's clothing, but inwardly they are ferocious wolves" (Matthew 7:15).

you found this to be true? What about people of great wealth, like Gregory, who endowed inspiring works of art, gave prestigious scholarships, and benefited charities? Can people who do these things yet live dissolute personal lives be redeemed? Can enduring humanitarian works help erase the personal harm done by an unbelieving, evil, or corrupt personality? Or must that redemption be made solely through repentance and God's grace through Jesus Christ?

8. We all have challenges and bear burdens. Matthew 11:28 inspired the entire Crossroads Crisis Center series of books.[5] In times of trouble and burdens, has your relationship with God given you rest? Has that aided you in coping with your challenges? resolving your conflicts? easing your burdens?

9. Ben and Kelly are wealthy people. Is it harder, do you think, to be a rich or a poor Christian?[6] What makes it harder or easier?

---

5. "Come to me, all you who are weary and burdened, and I will give you rest" (Matthew 11:28).
6. "Then Jesus said to his disciples, 'I tell you the truth, it is hard for a rich man to enter the kingdom of heaven. Again I tell you, it is easier for a camel to go through the eye of a needle than for a rich man to enter the kingdom of God'" (Matthew 19:23–24).

Do material possessions impact a person's inner life at all?

10. Repeatedly, Kelly hears God's instruction: *Be patient with him.* She listens and tries, but it isn't always easy. Is being patient difficult for you? What experiences have led you to trust in God's perfect timing?[7]

11. Ben had a loving, content marriage. As a widower, he had challenges starting over in a new romance. If you suffered such a loss, what would encourage you to try again? What would discourage you?

12. Kelly was orphaned, abused, and mistreated. Often in abuse cases, those abused become abusers. Yet she did not. Neither did she grow bitter or engage in destructive self-pity. Instead, she made God her escape plan from the abuse and learned to pray. She relied on Him, and as an adult she commits to helping others stay safe. That is this story's tie to Matthew 11:28.[8] Did her reliance on God, her trust in Him,

---

7. "There is a time for everything, and a season for every activity under heaven" (Ecclesiastes 3:1).
8. "Come to me, all you who are weary and burdened, and I will give you rest" (Matthew 11:28).

break the cycle so often present in abuse cases?[9]

13. Have you experienced situations like Kelly's where you felt the hand of God at work in your life?[10] If so, please explain.

---

9. "When Jesus saw this, he was indignant. He said to them, 'Let the little children come to me, and do not hinder them, for the kingdom of God belongs to such as these'" (Mark 10:14).
10. "You saw with your own eyes the great trials, the miraculous signs and wonders, the mighty hand and outstretched arm, with which the LORD your God brought you out. The LORD your God will do the same to all the peoples you now fear" (Deuteronomy 7:19).

Author's Note

Dear Reader,

As I write this, I imagine you sitting at my kitchen table, and we're sharing a cup of coffee. I'm trying to contain my excitement about having written *Forget Me Not*. I'm failing and smiling about it.

I've been writing for a long time, and yet this is fresh and new and in so many ways for me an exciting adventure. You see, this is my first book of Christian fiction, and like so many people of faith who take leaps of faith, my heart is full.

Crossroads Crisis Center came in a flash—where it was, who worked there, the types of cases they dealt with, and the stream of faith that was present in all the work done there. I loved that. The story took a little longer—a lifetime of living and learning and seeking truth.

My journey has had many starts and stops and wrong turns, but always God was there, sustaining me and giving me the strength to endure and persevere and persist. After a particularly dreadful challenge, I realized that He has always been there and that even when I didn't know who I was, I knew whose I was. That realization became the spine of the story in *Forget Me Not*.

Thank you for taking this journey with me. I'd love to hear from you and invite you to visit my Web site at www.vickihinze.com and e-mail me anytime. In His light and love, I wish you and yours many . . .

Blessings,
Vicki

Center Point Publishing
600 Brooks Road • PO Box 1
Thorndike ME 04986-0001 USA

(207) 568-3717

US & Canada:
1 800 929-9108
www.centerpointlargeprint.com

9-13